FALLEN ANGEL

"You are a perfect treasure," Carey said, his voice deep and rich. "Even the cold cannot diminish your loveliness."

"Thank you." She smiled and brushed an errant curl from her shoulder with a nervous movement. "I—I didn't quite expect a compliment. I thought you were going to proposition me, or taunt me—call me a murderess."

His eyebrows lifted a fraction. "Murderess? Heavens no!" He took her hand, caressing the cold fingers.

She gave him a sharp glance. "Surely you have read the newspapers. I am presumed to have killed my husband."

Carey looked at her pale face, so honest and innocent. A quality of goodness shone from within her. He couldn't tell her that she had haunted his thoughts and his dreams since that first moment he'd seen her lying in the sand . . .

Forever Love

MARIA GREENE

AVON BOOKS ◆ NEW YORK

AVON BOOKS
A division of
The Hearst Corporation
105 Madison Avenue
New York, New York 10016

Copyright © 1989 by Maria Greene
Inside cover author photograph by Mark Josephs
Published by arrangement with the author
Library of Congress Catalog Card Number: 89-91344
ISBN: 0-380-75773-7

First Avon Books Printing: December 1989

AVON TRADEMARK REG. U.S. PAT. OFF. AND IN OTHER COUNTRIES, MARCA REGISTRADA, HECHO EN U.S.A.

Printed in the U.S.A.

RA 10 9 8 7 6 5 4 3 2 1

For Patricia Veryan, whose novels brighten my life.

And for another Patricia who gave me a helping hand.
Thanks, Patti.

Prologue

Sussex, England
April, 1747

His heart heavy with sorrow, Carey McLendon rode toward Seaford, where he would board the northbound stagecoach. He had faced tragedy in the battlefield, but nothing had upset him as much as the news described in the letter his cousin Jack Newcomer had read aloud yesterday. Carey remembered every word as if it were engraved on his soul.

Dear Jack,
   I regret to be the bearer of unfortunate news, but since Carey's half-brothers and sisters surely won't attempt to contact him, you must be the one to tell him that his father, Angus McLendon, Lord Dunkeld, died at the end of March. According to the doctor, he had an apoplexy. Personally, I think he died of despair because of his clan's heavy loss during the Stuart rebellion. Not only did they lose many members of the family in the battles, but they lost their estate, their fortune, and their pride . . .

The letter was from Lady Fraser, Jack's aunt, and Carey was grateful that she'd had the decency to inform him of his father's death. The rest of the family would never include him in the McLendon circle, although he bore their name. They would never forget that he was Angus's bastard, despite the fact that the old man had acknowledged him as his own.

Carey heaved a deep sigh and set his jaw. He would visit his father's grave; no one could stop him from paying his last respects to the man who had meant more to him than anyone else. Had it been only six months since he had last seen his father? Angus had been an embittered man then, a shadow of the proud Scottish laird of his younger days—before the Rebellion brought ruin to the family.

The sea glittered nearby as Carey's horse turned west and galloped along the winding Eastbourne road toward Seaford. Rocky cliffs abutted the sea, but occasional sand dunes with tufts of grass softened the landscape.

Carey's mount followed a bend in the road and trotted across an arched stone bridge, coming suddenly upon an overturned carriage on the other side.

"By thunder!" His breath caught in his throat. He shaded his eyes against the harsh sunlight and saw a woman lying beside the road. She lay with one arm flung straight out in the sand, like a limp doll. The Channel tide was rising, and the water lapped at her peacock-blue skirt.

The muffled sound of receding hoofbeats sounded faintly on the wind. Carey tried to see the riders through the blinding glare, but the dusty lane was empty. He reined in his horse, slid off, and knelt by the seemingly lifeless woman.

Every inch of her was dainty loveliness. Entranced, he touched her face, and found that it was still warm. He had seen many dead men on the battlefield, but no death tableau had touched his heart as this one did. Moving an unsteady finger under the lacy shawl across her slim shoulders, he felt for a pulse. Nothing . . .

She had dark arched eyebrows, a narrow patrician nose, and a delicate, oval face. He touched her hair, a glorious tangle of ebony curls covered with a lace-edged cap. Her small ears were as finely molded as shells, her eyelids were pale and smooth as a child's, and her eyelashes were a rich upturned sweep. Her plump bottom lip looked bruised and sad, and her translucent skin was devoid of color.

Carey couldn't help wondering about her eyes. Were they blue? Gray?

"What a waste," he murmured, strangely touched by her broken beauty.

Carey forced himself to his feet, dashing a hand across his eyes. Taking a deep ragged breath, he wrenched his gaze from her face.

From her satin dress, lavishly embroidered with gold thread, he deduced that she was a gentle-woman. The dress was partly hitched up over wide panniers, revealing shapely ankles. A satin slipper with a broken heel lay nearby in the sand.

The scene was strangely ominous, making Carey uneasy. He ran across the road to the overturned carriage and looked inside.

Bile rose in his throat as he viewed the corpse of an expensively attired, middle-aged man who had been shot through the head. Carey averted his gaze. A cold sweat broke out on his forehead as he went around to the other side of the carriage. The coach-man hanging limply from the box had shared the same fate. The team of horses was gone.

It never became any easier to confront death. Filled with dread, Carey studied the ground around the carriage. The sand bore the imprints of many hooves. The marks might be from coaches that had traveled the route earlier, or they might belong to the murderers.

The woman had not been shot. Acting on that knowledge, Carey hastened back to her body, but before he could examine her more closely, the sound of wheels grating through the sand reached his ears.

A coach pulled by four horses was silhouetted against the sun. As the coachman yelled "Whoa," Carey noticed that one of the grays had a perfect star-shaped blaze between his eyes.

An old man dressed in a brown velvet coat and a moleskin waistcoat with pewter buttons stuck his powdered, bewigged head out of the coach window. "What's amiss?" he shouted querulously. "Get on with it, Bertie."

Before Bertie could obey, Carey stepped forward.

"Sir, terrible deeds have transpired here, not many minutes ago. I'm afraid we need to contact the authorities." Carey glanced up at the old man's harsh face, looking into wintry eyes. This old geezer's pity would be hard to arouse.

"What is it?" The old man's words were clipped and edged with anger.

"Murder, sir." Carey stepped aside and helped the old man to alight. Together they walked to the overturned carriage.

"Blast and damn! The highwaymen have been at it again," spat the old man. "Squire Dow, the magistrate, swore he would capture them, but that mealymouth has done nothing about it, as usual. Takes bribes, I'll warrant."

"Highwaymen?" Carey furrowed his brow. "Do they usually shoot to kill?"

Glaring, the old man shrugged and stabbed his cane in the sand. "What does it look like? A tea party? This area has been plagued by vicious highwaymen for half a year."

Heavyhearted, Carey forced himself to look at the woman in the sand. "She wasn't shot."

As the old man viewed the pathetic sight, his

breath hissed slowly between his teeth. "A veritable beauty." His hand trembled on the knob of his cane as he moved closer. A brittle tension cloaked him, and Carey found it hard to breathe. He resolutely steered his steps toward his horse. "I will ride into Seaford and fetch the magistrate."

The man snorted behind him. "That old sod won't lift a finger to help you."

Carey ignored the harsh voice. "Don't touch anything until the magistrate arrives," he warned, and swung into the saddle. Spurring the animal forward, he galloped down the road.

When he returned an hour later, with the lawman and a wagon for the corpses, he stared at the lane in shock. He jumped down and took two uncertain steps toward the spot where the murders had occurred. "What the hell . . . ?" Muttering another oath under his breath, he scanned the ground. "What happened?"

There was no sign of the overturned carriage or the bodies, and the sand showed no trace of what had taken place there. Had the old man in the coach taken the bodies? It was hardly likely. He had looked as frail as a dry leaf, and the coachman could not have managed it all on his own. Where was the carriage now, and who had moved it?

"You must have mistaken the place," said Squire Dow, the magistrate, giving Carey a suspicious glance. "Have you been drinking spirits, or is this a prank?"

"They were right here! I'm sure of it." The place where the woman had lain was also smooth and untouched. Then Carey saw something in the dunes. With a triumphant shout he pulled the broken slipper from the sand. Although the magistrate looked doubtful and shrugged his shoulders, it was the only proof Carey needed. The incident hadn't been a horrifying dream after all. But where were the corpses and the carriage? Unable to forget the sight of the beautiful girl, Carey suddenly felt an urgent need to solve the strange mystery.

Chapter 1

Six weeks later

After visiting his father's grave in Aviemore, close to the Cairngorm Mountains in the Highlands, Carey returned to his lodgings in London. As he stepped into the soft twilight of early summer, he thought about what had happened in Scotland.

The proud McLendon castle had stood among the rugged rocks for centuries, until zealous British soldiers reduced it to rubble after the disastrous Stuart rebellion. Reliving his memories of the Rebellion, Carey snorted in anger at the ruthless treatment of his kin. The British had been determined to capture the "Young Pretender," as they called Charles Edward Stuart, and had burned and looted every village as they searched for the Prince. Thank God, they never captured him, and he was now safely in France. The thought brought some solace to Carey's aching heart. Charles would have made the perfect ruler, but too few Englishmen had seen his potential. Charles was a Stuart, and the Stuarts had reigned for hundreds of years. The crown should have been his. Anger burned within Carey as vivid mental images of Scotland's destruction filled his mind.

The peasants of the McLendon village had

watched Carey approach his father's home with bitter, suspicious expressions. Are ye comin' as friend or foe? they had seemed to be asking him. He wished he could have reassured them that better times would follow. But would they, with a German elector on the British throne? Frustrated, Carey kicked a pebble in his path.

Had only one year passed since the catastrophic battle at Culloden Moor, when the young Prince's fate had been determined? Carey sighed, personally feeling the defeat of the man he had hailed as king. The Scots could not easily forget the massacre at that battle, or other encounters where fathers and brothers had fallen before British musket fire.

Being part of the Rebellion had changed him, Carey thought, remembering the many new granite headstones in the churchyard, and the fresh earth covering his father's grave. So many of the Highlanders Carey had known were dead.

He inhaled deeply to ease the pain in his chest, and waved absently to an acquaintance in Jermyn Street. Giddy, noisy London made his memories of the Rebellion and his father's recent demise seem like long-ago nightmares.

Longing to dispel his sadness, he headed toward Covent Garden, to Tim Sutton's gambling house on Russell Street, for supper and a game of cards. He was bound to meet someone he knew there.

Flicking a speck of dust from the immaculate lace of his shirt cuff, he traversed Haymarket, shaking his head as if to clear the cobwebs from his mind.

A lovely dark-haired woman crossed his path, reminding him suddenly of the dead woman in the sand outside Seaford. What had happened to her and the other bodies? Driven by an almost obsessive need to learn her identity, he had combed the countryside for clues, asking in the Seaford taverns for the name of the old man who had arrived on the scene shortly after the slaughter—all to no avail. No one could identify him.

Carey remembered the lovely woman as if he'd discovered her only yesterday. No one had recalled ever seeing her. He had bribed ostlers for information about the carriage and its whereabouts, but his every effort had been futile.

Carey halted as a man with a wheelbarrow darted across the street. He must forget the puzzling deaths on the Eastbourne road and look to the future. Nevertheless, he found himself pondering the mystery more often than he would have cared to admit.

"Are you deaf?" chided a voice close to his ear.

Carey turned abruptly. "Morty, old fellow!" His smile felt stiff, the skin on his face tight. "As far as I know, I've not yet lost my faculties."

Charles Boynton, the Earl of Mortimer, swirled his cane, showing off a new gold top with a single diamond in the center. "I know that something is seriously wrong when you go about with unpolished boots, McLendon. However, I'm green with envy over your new coat. Superb cut, as usual. Your tailor is a treasure—"

"—who charges a king's ransom," Carey drawled. He sent a cursory glance at his boots, realizing that since his father's death, he had cared less and less about his clothes. To him, dressing had always been an art and a challenge. At the moment it seemed a shallow and unnecessary exercise.

"As the saying goes: When Carey McLendon stops caring for his appearance, the world is coming to its end," Lord Mortimer teased. He nudged his friend's shoulder. "You frighten me."

Carey's lips curled sardonically. "Heaven forbid!" He adjusted the top button on his waistcoat with studied indifference. "Tell me, do you see *me*, or only the cut of my coat?"

Lord Mortimer's eyes widened. "An absurd question! What's the matter with you? You know you're a handsome devil who sets all the ladies' hearts aflutter. I, however, think your nose is too long and sharp, and I find the cut of your coat much more interesting than the imperial tilt of your chin.'' He fell silent as he looked into Carey's slate-gray eyes. ''Sorry, old fellow. We've been friends for a long time, and I know you. Most people see only that other, flippant side of you.''

''Yes, that's what's expected of me—impertinence and rapier wit,'' Carey said somberly.

Lord Mortimer shot him a curious glance. ''If I didn't know you better, I'd say you were in love, or desperately ill. What has brought about this profound sadness?''

Sudden anger flared in Carey's eyes. ''Love's a word I don't use,'' he said with icy softness.

Lord Mortimer raised an eyebrow. ''Biting my head off, old fellow?''

Carey sighed, instantly contrite. ''Forgive me. I'm not myself today.'' He told Lord Mortimer about his father's death.

Lord Mortimer whistled between his teeth. ''The old boy was a rare gem. You must miss him terribly.''

Carey nodded. ''I don't want to inflict my gloomy presence on you.''

''Leave it to me, McLendon. I'll find a way to cheer you up.''

Morty's words warmed Carey's frozen heart, and his steps grew lighter. ''Thank you.''

''You need to rest your weary head against some lovely female's warm bosom.''

The image of the dark-haired woman in the sand floated through Carey's mind. ''Perhaps you're right, Morty.'' Would indulging in a love affair erase the questions about the dead beauty and soothe his grief? He doubted it.

The two men were rapidly approaching Russell Street. The square of Covent Garden spread out before them, packed with carriages and pedestrians. The sounds of grinding wheels, shouting drivers, and drunken laughter filled the air. Outside one of the gin shops two whores in bright tattered satin accosted them, but Carey impatiently waved them aside.

"You're so silent. Other problems as well?" Lord Mortimer probed.

Carey sighed. "I'm lost in thought, that's all. If I think hard enough, without any interruption, I might come up with an answer to a puzzle that's been preoccupying me." He studied his old friend. Mortimer's face was thin, his flaring nostrils like those of a high-bred stallion, his pale-blue eyes narrow and keen. A powdered tiewig covered his brown curls.

"What answer?"

Carey sighed. "You'll think I've lost my mind." Taking a deep breath, he told his friend about the chilling events on the road outside Seaford in Sussex.

"That's strange!" Lord Mortimer exclaimed. "If only I had been in town before today, I could have told you about the murders. As you well know, my estate isn't far from there. I was home when it happened."

Carey gripped his friend's arm. "Blast it, Morty, what do you know?"

Lord Mortimer pulled loose from Carey's hold. "Calm down. My arm will be blue with bruises." He pretended to smooth a crease from his sleeve. "I heard about the 'accident,' as they call it, and that a gentleman from London found the corpses, but then they disappeared. Carey, I had no idea *you* were that gentleman." He dodged a drunkard weaving across his path. "Supposedly one of the dead men was Leonard Kane of London. You didn't read about it in the papers?''

Carey shook his head. ''No, I just got back from Scotland.'' He gave his friend a piercing glance. ''What about the dead woman? Who was she?''

''No female was mentioned.''

Carey narrowed his gaze. ''Extraordinary! How did they discover the dead man's identity?''

''The papers didn't explain. They hinted that the murderer has already been apprehended.''

Carey turned his full attention on Lord Mortimer. ''Did the paper give a name, perchance?''

''Yes, Kane's wife, Francesca.''

''Intriguing. Do you know her?''

''Of course. Don't you remember the Honorable Francesca Childress, the daughter of Lord Childress? A beauty who threw herself away on Kane, a man twice her age. They were married four years ago, an event that set the gossipmongers on their ears. Kane was *trade*—a very wealthy jeweler who had his shop at Ludgate Hill. It's now run by his younger brother.''

''So the marriage created a scandal? I don't recall the incident,'' Carey said thoughtfully.

''You might have been in Scotland at the time. By the way, how are the Cairngorms at this time of the year?'' Lord Mortimer nudged Carey's arm. ''You've been away from London many times since last July. Not involved in Charles Stuart's desperate Rebellion, were you?''

Raucous laughter from a tavern punctuated Morty's question. Carey smiled enigmatically and shrugged. ''My father *was* Scottish, y'know, but that doesn't mean—''

''Say no more of the wretched Cause. Let's enjoy ourselves. I will fleece you of your last groat.''

Carey raised a haughty eyebrow, but his eyes sparkled with humor. ''Who says I would play with

you? I know better than to risk my last money on a
cardsharp."

"Cardsharp?" Lord Mortimer laughed and
pushed his friend through the door of Tim's establishment. "You wound me, sirrah!"

Thick smoke curled toward the ceiling, and the
sweet aroma of punch filled the air. The two tables
covered with green baize were occupied, and the
card players wore tense expressions. Other men
talked and laughed, some raising their cups high in
salute to Carey and Lord Mortimer.

Carey's favorite table was already taken, so they
decided to eat supper. Sitting down on a bench,
Carey leaned back against the wall in a less crowded
corner of the room. They ordered pork chops, pi-
geon pie, and punch from a passing waiter.

Carey gave his friend a rueful smile as he thought
of the money he'd probably spend that evening. For
his work on behalf of Charles Stuart, he still had
funds supplied by London's wealthy Stuart follow-
ers. But the money wouldn't last forever, and now
that his father was dead, he would have to think
seriously about alternative means of support. Gambling always gave temporary relief to an empty
purse, but he needed a nest egg for the future.

"We should have something to drink with dinner," he said. "Order a bottle of claret."

"I'm not sure Tim will give me any more credit
here," Lord Mortimer said with a shrug.

"You're my guest tonight, Morty."

Lord Mortimer had chronically empty pockets
since his family—despite its lofty heritage—had been
poor since Morty's grandfather lost the family fortune in a series of disastrous business enterprises.

"Generous as always, old fellow." He called the
waiter back and ordered the wine.

"What has happened while I've been gone,
Morty?"

Lord Mortimer shrugged. "Balls, routs, and assemblies. The usual. I haven't attended."

"Mingling with gamblers and ruffians, eh?"

"You must admit that card games hold more allure than balls."

The waiter returned with their punch cups.

Carey shrugged. "Yes . . ."

"The ladies have inquired after you." Lord Mortimer downed his punch. "They count on you to enliven their dull gatherings."

"I take it you haven't found a young heiress to become your countess," Carey said with a smile.

Lord Mortimer snorted. "This Season's crop is horse-faced and cross-eyed. Not a single fair maiden."

"Tragic, isn't it?" Carey remarked, and raised his cup. "You'll be old and doddering before you find someone to suit your fastidious tastes." He waved to a waiter and pulled out his purse. "Some more punch?"

"You're never without funds, are you, McLendon? Even if you were sired by a Scotsman."

Carey chuckled. "The lode is drying up, I'm afraid. I might have to go on some lucrative diplomatic errand soon if my luck doesn't turn at the tables."

"I suppose I shouldn't ask the nature of your business."

Carey gave him an inscrutable smile. "No, you should not. Secrets of State." In a way it was true, although his "errands" weren't connected to King George's government. There were Stuart sympathizers in the highest circles of the land. Carey's contact was the Earl of Mountjoy, who had lent his powerful protection to Carey after the failure of the Rebellion. Carey had acted as a link between Charles Stuart and his influential supporters in London. But since Stuart's defeat and exile in France, Carey had grown weary of political intrigue. After aiding Stuart, and acting as a scout for the Scots in the campaigns, it was a miracle he was still alive.

Other than Morty, his cousin Jack, and Jack's wife Bryony, no one had ever suspected Carey of being involved in any higher drama than assembling a perfect suit of clothes every morning.

Lord Mortimer shifted his legs under the table. "Your secrets are making me nervous."

Carey laughed. "Don't worry. I'm seriously thinking of retiring to a country house to raise cattle and chickens."

Lord Mortimer's jaw dropped. "Chickens? Now I *know* you've truly lost your mind!"

The waiter arrived with their meals, and Carey ate hungrily.

"If I want to sup tomorrow," Lord Mortimer said, wiping his mouth with a napkin, "I have to earn some money tonight." He threw a glance around the room. "It seems that everyone has the same idea here."

Carey cut into a juicy pie. "There are other gambling salons."

They finished their meal in silence, then Carey said, "Come along, Morty. I've had too many dark thoughts for one day. I feel reckless tonight, and restless. Perhaps we should visit some vile pit of debauchery. Should we fleece old 'Lucretia Borgia' in her den?"

Lord Mortimer chuckled. "Lucretia Borgia indeed! Letitia Rose's Crimson Rooms is the best—if most dangerous, not to mention decadent—gaming salon in town. If we go there, we might make our fortunes tonight."

"Or find ourselves in dun territory by dawn. There are all sorts of possibilities."

Laughing, they left Tim's and headed toward the south corner of Covent Garden.

* * *

Joss "Cauliflower" Arnold, the doorman and official dunner at the Crimson Rooms, had once been a pugilist. His swarthy, sullen face stopped many a drunk and boisterous gambler from placing one unsteady foot inside the threshold. Arnold's nickname was inspired by his misshapen ears. The man who dared to call him "Cauliflower" Arnold to his face would be at the mercy of a blinding right hook capable of crippling a giant.

Arnold's passion in life was gratuity, and no one entered the dimly lit caverns of the Crimson Rooms without first liberally greasing his palm.

Carey knew the rules. After Arnold had counted the coins, he went so far as to hold the door open for the Scotsman and his friend.

"Ye can't be no bloody Scot," he said, shaking his head. "I usually don't let them bloomin' tight-fists past these doors."

"Easy come, easy go. Arnold, I know I can always count on your protection in a difficult spot," said Carey, patting the doorman's huge shoulder.

Cauliflower Arnold's chuckle was impressive. "Ye don't need me, Mister M. Niver saw a better 'and at swords."

"Swords, indeed. I do hope we won't experience your volatile temper tonight, McLendon," Lord Mortimer said. "Even if you lose your last guinea."

As soon as he entered the main salon, which was primarily dedicated to the faro table, Carey found that a group of society bucks and ladies had invaded the Crimson Rooms. He knew most of the gentlemen, who had far from pure reputations, but the females were concealed behind voluminous dominoes and silk masks. "Looks like we might have a chance to win a great deal tonight, with these wastrels in attendance," he said as Morty waved at an acquaintance.

Lord Mortimer's eyes glittered with anticipation. "You took the words out of my mouth. Young Halden is here. Did you know that Baronet Halden, his father, disowned him for being such an inveterate gambler? He's on the fringe of society now, shunned by all the hostesses. Not a groat will he get from the baronet. The wild Widow Garnsworth is with him, if I don't mistake that hysterical giggle. A domino can't disguise that."

Carey studied Lucas Halden, whose high color contrasted starkly with his powdered wig. His narrow shoulders were heavily padded with buckram, and the white stockings were surely filled with sawdust so as to enhance his spindly legs. Carey's gaze wandered to a young man with curly red hair who stood behind Halden. The face was pale, the eyes glazed from excessive drink. Carey had never seen him before, but he surmised he was some unsuspecting lord fresh from the country, whom Halden had lured onto the path of dissipation.

"As you implied, the evening looks promising," Lord Mortimer concluded.

They sauntered toward the group and Carey ordered a bottle of brandy from one of Letty Rose's girls, who displayed an extremely daring décolletage.

Lord Mortimer watched a game of piquet in progress, but his eyes strayed to the girl's bosom as she returned with the liquor and two glasses on a tray.

"Well! If it isn't Carey McLendon," Lucas Halden said. His voice affected a high-pitched lisp, and one of his cohorts snickered. "Where have you been hiding? Lost your shirt in a card game, mayhap? Or is your tailor dunning you?"

Carey's face froze into a mask of indifference as he let his gaze travel leisurely over the group. Besides Halden and the redhead, there were four young blades, all gamblers and heavy drinkers.

"Fancy that bills should be on your mind, Halden. You owe me one hundred pounds." His lips curved in a faint smile.

Halden looked uncomfortable, his gaze wavering under Carey's stare. "Ah . . . well, only joking, y'know."

"Jests of singularly bad taste," Lord Mortimer said, lifting a brandy snifter to his lips. "A gambling debt is a debt of honor."

"I'd like to win the hundred pounds back from you, McLendon," Halden said, a scornful smirk on his face. "And if you must stake your shirt, it's a handsome article." He took a step closer and flicked aside the lace of Carey's jabot to study the shirt more closely. "Everton is a deuced fine tailor, but very choosy. He doesn't sew for *quality* customers, only—"

Carey pushed away the offending hand. "He's so conscious of *quality* that he only sews for those who appreciate his genius," he said with icy softness.

"Bah! Tailoring is a subject of interest to fops only," Halden scoffed. "A real man leaves such discussions to females, and—"

"I say you wouldn't recognize a great tailor. Taste never was one of your stronger points, Halden." Carey took a step back and shot a disparaging glance at the earl's waistcoat, his face slowly contorting in disdain. "Pink simply doesn't go with bile green." He circled the red-faced earl and gingerly touched the peony-hued satin coat. "Much too gaudy, and the embroidery is distasteful." He clucked his tongue. "The buttons are much too large." With a twist of his hand, he ripped one from the pocket flap and held it against the light. Shaking his head, he tossed it back to the owner.

Crimson with anger and embarrassment, Halden caught it. "I will not have your insults, McLendon. Fops are no friends of mine."

Carey chuckled and folded his arms across his chest. "Do you *have* friends, Halden?"

Silence blanketed the group, and the ladies stirred uneasily. Halden fingered his dress sword, but Carey's lips curled in contempt. "Don't challenge me," he warned.

Perspiration showed on Halden's face. "I don't fight with effeminate fribbles."

"As far as I can tell, Mr. McLendon is endowed with abundant masculinity," interrupted a lady in a pink lustring domino. "And he's a deadly swordsman. *You* ought to know that, Lucas." The other ladies laughed appreciatively.

With an extravagant flourish of his handkerchief, Carey buffed his fingernails. "I don't fight with scoundrels who owe me money," he said.

An ominous silence fell once again. Halden's shoulders dropped. He whispered something to the redheaded man, who instantly pulled a money pouch from his pocket. Halden extracted several notes and gold coins, and shoved them into Carey's hand. "Here! Shall we play a hand of piquet now?" he asked testily. "I'll win back that money and then some."

Carey yawned, ignoring him. A lady standing nearby fanned herself slowly. "I like your diamond pin, McLendon," she said. "Where did you find such a rare gem?"

"It was a gift." He didn't add that Lord Mountjoy had given it to him for his services during the Stuart rebellion. "I know that it came from a foreign jeweler who has set up business beside George Wicke in Haymarket. He's Italian, I believe. Has a great collection of gems. He's evidently going to give old Wicke serious competition."

"Will you play or not?" Halden demanded. "I haven't got all night, y'know."

Although he suspected Halden of habitual cheating, Carey shrugged and sat down to a game of cards. It wasn't the first time he had been the target of insults. Some gentlemen never let him forget his less than illustrious birth. They obviously resented that the ladies held him in high esteem and always included him on their guest lists.

Carey scrutinized Halden, following his every move. Had he even now hidden a few cards up his sleeve? From the corner of his eye, Carey noticed that Widow Garnsworth was standing to his right, peering over his shoulder. When had she moved to his side of the table? As he held his cards close to his chest, he saw her exchange glances with Halden. Ah, so that was her part in the game. He could stop playing right then, but he was curious to see Halden's tricks.

Half an hour later Carey had won two hundred pounds from Lucas Halden. He rose, but Halden challenged him once more. With a sigh, Carey complied, regretting it when, after the next two hands, he lost everything he'd won. Halden had obviously slipped some extra cards into the deck.

"That will be the end of it," Halden said with a smirk. "I told you I would win."

Carey leaned slowly across the table and gripped Halden's jabot. "If you think I'll pay a thief, you're quite mistaken." He gathered the money and put it in his pocket.

Halden sputtered and turned red. "Not pay? But it's a debt of honor." He stabbed the table with his finger. "You must."

Carey snorted and began to move away, but Halden came after him and grabbed his arm. "You shall pay," he hissed.

Carey shrugged and walked on. "I won't."

Halden stopped him by jerking his arm back, but Carey braced his forearm under Halden's chin, threatening to break his neck.

"My seconds will call on yours," Halden wheezed, fingering his dress sword.

"Very well," Carey said in a bored tone and let his arm drop. "It will be a pleasure to pierce your traitorous heart."

Halden's eyes blazed with fury. With a mocking smile Carey flourished a bow and went in search of Lord Mortimer.

Morty was at the faro table, flirting with the owner of the Crimson Rooms, Letitia Rose. She was a woman of many talents, and Lord Mortimer was not the only man drawn to her full-blown beauty. She had more than once tried to seduce Carey, who could never see past the ice in her eyes. He steered clear of scheming ladies as much as possible.

Never again would he lay his heart bare to a woman. They were all devious, some more than others. Lady Daphne Dewthorne's betrayal had shredded his heart.

Lord Mortimer was whispering in Letty Rose's ear now, his hand sliding across her generous bosom. Carey felt a stirring of desire as he watched. It had been too long since he'd touched a woman's silky skin. Sighing, he leaned against a pillar and drank brandy straight from the bottle.

Letty Rose evidently preferred crimson and gold above all other colors. The wall panels were covered with crimson silk damask and the ornate Louis XIV furniture was gold and white. Crystal chandeliers winked, and wall sconces held expensive wax candles.

Although the ceilings and windows were high in the old town house, the rooms seemed small. The gamblers' tense concentration blended with the thick smoke, making for an oppressive atmosphere.

The chandelier sparkled as a couple strolled by. The woman was wearing a half mask and a domino.

Her escort let his hand stray to her derriere, but she didn't seem to mind.

Cauliflower Arnold was admitting a steady stream of patrons, and the tables were filling rapidly. Carey went from room to room watching piquet games, silver-loo, basset, *vingt-et-un*, and quadrille.

Longing overcame him as he watched a man kiss one of Letty Rose's beautiful girls, coaxing her upstairs to the discreet chambers set aside for more intimate games *à deux*.

He would never find a woman to love at the infamous Crimson Rooms, but he might be able to drown his loneliness for the moment, Carey thought. Letty's girls were always more than willing.

"I've been looking for you," said Lord Mortimer, jolting Carey from his reverie. "I noticed you had some words with Halden."

"He cheats." Carey offered Lord Mortimer the bottle. "He promised to send his seconds around."

Mortimer laughed. "He never fights. His cowardice is legendary in the clubs."

Carey sighed. "He'll be a thorn in my side from now on."

"He will, but if he provokes your anger, he might find himself pierced by steel one day," the earl said. After taking a gulp of brandy, he added, "Come along, old fellow. I have a surprise for you."

Carey did not resist as Mortimer hauled him into another salon.

"There," he said, pointing.

Carey followed the direction of his finger and gasped. The whole room tilted as his gaze was captured by a slender beauty in a shimmering white low-cut gown. Her black curls, caught up with glittering combs, formed a gleaming cascade on her shoulders and revealed perfect, shell-shaped ears. Her oval face was porcelain-pale, her expression forlorn. Her eyes were wide and midnight-dark, veiled with fear.

Carey's heartbeat quickened, and he took an eager step forward. ''By God—''

''Francesca Kane, the supposed murderess,'' Lord Mortimer said.

''It's the woman I found lying in the sand of Seaford,'' Carey said in a hoarse whisper.

Chapter 2

S ensing that someone was looking at her, Francesca glanced at the approaching men. Her head ached from her illness and she sneezed. The gathering of gamblers and rakes repulsed her, and she was worried that she would be the target of another indecent proposal—the third one this evening. She wished she didn't have to work in this den of ill-repute. London was humming with the scandal of Leonard Kane's death and his body's bizarre disappearance, and people came to the Crimson Rooms simply to gawk at her—the murderess.

Her nose tickled, and she fished desperately in her pocket for her handkerchief. This ague would be the end of her, she thought glumly, sneezing again. Over the handkerchief's lace edge, she recognized Lord Mortimer, whom she'd known since her society debut four years ago. But it was his companion who captured her attention.

He had the sinfully handsome looks of a fallen angel, his face as hard as if it had been hewn out of rock, and just as cold. His granite jaw showed that he had no patience for weakness; his nose was narrow and sharp, and his cheekbones cast shadows over his lean cheeks. His wide, sensitive mouth seemed curiously out of place in his masterful face. Her gaze wandered to his eyes, which were shadowed by heavy eyelids and dark brows. His wavy dark hair, caught at the nape with a velvet bow, shone in the light of the chandeliers.

Her heart pounded in her ears, and she was doubly aware of her red nose and sore throat. A strange restlessness fluttered through her, and she felt as if his eyes were peeling away the barriers she had carefully erected around the pain in her heart. Were they here to insult her, like all the others who had once called themselves her friends?

The tall man was immaculately dressed in black satin knee breeches, with a matching coat and a white waistcoat embroidered with silver thread. His lace jabot was a study in elegance. He came quite close, and she smelled the faint scent of sandalwood. He looked dazed, as if he had just received a blow to his head, and he was staring at her quite rudely.

She dabbed furtively at her nose.

"Mrs. Kane," Lord Mortimer said, his eyes inscrutable, "I would like to introduce my friend. Mr. Carey McLendon, meet Mrs. Kane."

"If you've come to gloat over my fall from respectability, or to offer me an indecent proposal, I beg you to leave," she responded coolly. She tried to sound haughty, but her sore throat roughened her voice. Blushing, she lowered her gaze.

Lord Mortimer raised his eyebrows. "Gloat? I hope I will never stoop that low. No, Mr. McLendon is quite taken with your beauty, and I can assure you that he won't embarrass you with vulgarities."

A violent sneeze overcame her. Mr. McLendon's strong fingers steadied her elbow, and he pressed a large handkerchief into her hand. She tried to smile, but it turned into another sneeze. Finally she managed to lift her gaze to his. His eyes were a surprisingly warm gray, like the color of a rainy sea.

Without moving a muscle he seemed to reach out

to her. It was as if his very presence was embracing her, and she relaxed, releasing an inaudible sigh.

"You don't look well, if I may say so," he said, his voice deep and rich. "But Mortimer is right, you are a perfect treasure. Even that cold cannot diminish your loveliness."

"Thank you." She smiled and brushed an errant curl from her shoulder with a nervous movement. "I—I didn't quite expect a compliment. I thought you were going to proposition me, or taunt me—call me a murderess."

His eyebrows lifted a fraction. "Murderess? Heavens no!"

He took her hand, caressing her cold fingers. His touch was incredibly soothing, and she found that she could not pull away from him. He smiled, and his face grew soft. His smile was like a warm cloak around her.

Lord Mortimer nudged Carey with his elbow. "See you tomorrow, old fellow," he said and left abruptly.

"May I assist you in any way?" Francesca asked, her voice shaky. "A glass of brandy perhaps?" The full force of Mr. McLendon's attention made her feel weak inside. "My task here is to see to the comfort of the guests."

"You're the one who needs the brandy, and a warm bed." Something roguish glittered momentarily in his eyes. Unable to meet his intent gaze, she let her head drop forward. Her temples had begun to throb viciously, and her legs were unsteady.

"Tell me, why would I—or Morty—call you a murderess?" he asked gently.

She gave him a sharp glance. "Surely you have read the newspapers."

He shook his head.

"I am presumed to have killed my husband."

Carey looked at her pale face, so honest and innocent. A quality of goodness shone from within her. He was overcome with relief that she hadn't died in the sand dunes. "That's ridiculous! I came riding along that road after Mr. Kane and the coachman were killed. The carriage had overturned, and you were lying in the sand, some distance away."

"*You* were the one who found us? The magistrate told me everything you reported to him."

Carey smiled and pulled her arm through his. "We must discuss this matter more fully." He escorted her into the shadow of a tall marble pedestal.

She glanced at him with suspicion. "Your intent is foolish. For your own good—"

"Don't worry about me." He hesitated, smoothing the pocket flap of his coat. "The murders were a gruesome sight, I might add." His dark gaze probed her face. "I was certain that you were dead."

Francesca swallowed hard. "I almost wish I were." Guilt weighed her down. Why was she alive, when both Leonard and the driver were dead? She moved away from the pedestal.

Carey took her hand and held it tightly, as if to give her courage. "My memory of that day is very clear."

They entered an adjoining salon, which was almost empty. One of the tall windows had been left open, and the air was fresher. "I'd like to ask you some questions. I hope you don't mind," he said. When she shook her head, he continued, "What really happened that day?"

"We were traveling to Eastbourne, on our way to the Continent, when a group of masked men surrounded the carriage. They did not ask us to surrender our valuables. After ordering me outside, they hit me on the head." Her voice grew thin. "Just as I blacked out, I heard two shots—perhaps three. I knew no more. When I woke up, I was lying on the square in Seaford, and my clothes were dirty and wet." She caught her breath. "I must have lain there all night, because I was covered with dew."

Carey noticed that her plump bottom lip was trembling, and compassion surged through him. "Why were you blamed for Kane's death?"

"I told the magistrate all I knew, but he didn't seem to believe my innocence since I had survived the attack and I couldn't account for the missing bodies. While he investigated the case, he locked me into the gaol on suspicion of murder. When my husband's body remained missing, he was finally obliged to release me." She paused. "The local newspaper printed that I was a murderess . . . then the London papers seized upon the story."

Carey told her about the old man who had arrived on the scene shortly after him. "Do you have any idea who he was?"

Francesca shook her head. "I'm surprised he left without speaking with the magistrate. Do you think he recognized me or my husband?"

Carey rubbed his chin thoughtfully. "I don't think so. Yet I recall that he was very tense."

Francesca sighed. "Probably frightened. I would be if I came upon such a hideous scene."

"We ought to find him. Perhaps he knows something we don't."

She stared long and hard at him. "Why do you want to become involved? You have nothing to gain from helping me."

He looked utterly serious, his lips set in a thin line. "The mystery troubles me. I'd like to discover the truth. As far as I know, I was the only witness, besides the old man."

"No other passerby has stepped forward."

"You're in a difficult situation, Mrs. Kane."

His kindness made her want to weep. She groped for the handkerchief. Her headache was clouding her mind, making her feel weak.

Carey took a glass of brandy from a passing lackey. "Here," he said, and she accepted it gratefully. The warmth of the liquor soothed her jangled nerves.

"I know that everyone will blame me for the murders. The gossipmongers would love to find me truly guilty," she whispered and took another sip. The cool evening wind from the open window made her shiver. "But honestly, I didn't do it. I did not kill my husband."

Carey's eyes darkened. "I believe you. We'll just have to find out who did." He couldn't tell her that she had haunted his thoughts and his dreams ever since that first moment he'd seen her lying in the sand.

"The case obviously titillates the public. They come here to ogle me—the notorious Mrs. Kane."

"I don't care what people think." Carey caressed her fingers and thought for a moment. "You should not be working here," he murmured, so close that his breath tickled her ear. "It is too vulgar by far, and sometimes dangerous. By the way, why *are* you here? According to gossip, Mr. Kane was a very wealthy man. Didn't you inherit—?"

Francesca stiffened. "I don't wish to discuss him," she said, disentangling her arm.

After returning to London she had visited her old home in Ludgate Hill, only to find it barred against her. Leonard's brother had kept her clothes, her jewelry, her books—everything. They had called her a murderess . . . as had the coachman's family when she informed them of his death.

The accusation had hung upon her like an iron chain, so that when she had applied for work designing jewelry at the workshops of Kane's associates, they had refused to give her employment, although her skills rivaled the best of the master craftsmen.

At her wit's end, she had finally sold her last piece of jewelry, a simple pearl, to Letty Rose and accepted the employment the gambling-salon owner had offered—on one condition. She refused to entertain the guests in bed. Letty Rose had intimated that she might have to provide more services in the future, but for now Francesca's "untouchable" presence added a hint of mystery. The gambling gentlemen, Letty knew, desired what they couldn't have.

"This type of employment is . . . corruptive," Carey said.

Francesca took a step back. "I went to the only place that would give me work," she said in a tight voice. "I have to eat, don't I? Letitia Rose has been kind to me. My father knew her, and I remembered her when I needed to sell my last piece of jewelry. Instead of going to one of the moneylenders, I came here, to the Crimson Rooms. Letty bought my pearl—which didn't fetch much—and offered me employment when no one else would."

Carey recaptured her fingers and ran his thumb along the smooth skin on the back of her wrist. "Letty's already counting the profits. Your lovely and scandalous presence has attracted additional customers to the Crimson Rooms."

Francesca tilted her head proudly. "It's better than walking the streets." An embarrassed flush colored her cheeks, matching her red nose. Why did he make her feel so vulnerable? "I don't have any duties other than to oversee the waiters and chat with the guests—"

Silence fell between them, and she followed the comforting movement of his thumb with her eyes.

"With my help, you shall learn the truth about your husband's death, Mrs. Kane."

Her gaze returned to his face, and she saw compassion and determination there. "Involving your-

self in my problems will only ruin you." Why would
he want to bother with her unless he had an ulterior
motive? she wondered.

He smiled cynically. "I cannot be ruined. In the
eyes of society, I'm a fop, a hanger-on, an eccentric.
They will adore me until they find someone else to
capture their fancy."

His stark honesty surprised her. "I've heard of
you, Mr. McLendon. You have many powerful
friends who speak of you with respect. You're the
darling of elegant hostesses."

His laugh was cold. "I'm no more than a man
who knows how to advise others in elegance, and
there are those in polite circles who would like to
see me gone."

"Gentlemen will continue to look to you for the
latest fashion."

Amusement crinkled his eyes. "Thank God I don't
have to dress them every morning," he joked. He
touched one of her dusky curls gently. "No, you
cannot ruin me, Mrs. Kane. There is nothing to
ruin."

She sensed a deep sadness in him, as well as an
unconquerable strength. She was overcome by a
need to lean her head against his broad chest and
empty every ounce of her pain into his ears, but life
was never that easy. She must keep her anguish to
herself.

Another lackey bustled by, carrying a tray of
glasses. A laughing couple passed the open door.

Leading her to the nearest window, Carey gave
her a sudden heart-stopping smile and patted her
hand. It would be so easy to accept his offer of help,
she thought. Too easy . . . No, however heavy, she
must carry her burden alone. That way she wouldn't
have to rely on a man. A man would only control
her life, just as Leonard Kane had.

"Is anyone else investigating the murder at the

moment?'' Carey asked, gazing at the dark night outside. His fingers played with the golden fringe on the crimson curtains.

''No.''

''I didn't think so. Your family?''

''My father is dead, and my notoriety has ruined my mother's health. She had a seizure when she found out what had happened. Her heart is weak.'' Francesca's voice trailed off, and she buried her nose in her handkerchief to conceal her distress. ''There was always a gulf between us,'' she added in a muffled voice.

''Pardon?'' He touched her shoulder and gently massaged her taut muscles. It never occurred to her to pull away, yet his attention threatened to destroy the dam she had built against her sorrow. She dreaded the thought of dissolving into tears in front of him.

''Mrs. Kane, you shouldn't condemn yourself. You're innocent, and your mother should know better than to believe otherwise.''

''What makes you so sure that I'm without blame?'' she asked, her nose still buried in the white cloth. She glanced at him warily. Was he trustworthy?

He didn't respond at once. He seemed mesmerized by her curls. ''It just isn't logical. Why would you kill your closest kin, and then hit yourself over the head so hard that you were on the brink of death?'' He sighed. ''I was certain you had died.''

Francesca straightened her back and met his gaze squarely. ''For everyone's peace of mind, it might have been better if I had died—''

''That is utter nonsense, my dear. Hardships exist only to be overcome.''

She read pain in his face. ''You sound like one with experience in that area.''

''Some, yes.'' His lips quirked in a wide, sensuous smile. Suddenly she wanted to kiss him. Blushing, she turned away. Gazing into the darkness, she said, "My name is buried in the mud, along with my mother's. She'll never forgive me."

"I'm sure she doesn't approve of your working here." His voice was coming from behind her ear. She could feel the warmth of his body pressing against her back, although he wasn't touching her.

"She doesn't know, but I'm sure she wouldn't care at this point. She has refused to speak to me ever since the day—" What was she doing, letting her tongue rattle on so?

"When?" he coaxed softly.

"Ever since the day my brother, Teddy, died."

"Oh," was all he said, but she could tell that he was waiting for an explanation.

Francesca remained silent. She must escape the spell of this intriguing stranger before she bared her heart completely. A gargantuan sneeze put an end to the conversation.

He chuckled, a sound that would have made her toes curl with pleasure if they weren't so tightly confined in her satin slippers.

"I will escort you home and make sure that you cure this cold."

She gave him a tired smile. "For a stranger, you're very thoughtful, but I must work—"

"I'll talk to Letty Rose. You cannot work when you're so ill."

"Thank you. You're most kind."

"You have brightened my evening considerably. Please don't deny me the pleasure of escorting you home," he continued. "You don't have to be afraid that I'll take advantage of the situation. I might as well put you at ease right now. I'm not looking for a . . . well . . . a romantic relationship."

Francesca flinched at the sudden anger in his eyes.

"Of course not," she said quickly. "There would be no question of an entanglement."

At her words, a shadow flickered through his eyes, but was instantly erased by his smile. "Good!" he said, entwining his arm with hers. "Where do you live?"

Another sneeze prevented her from answering immediately. "Well?" he said.

"I live upstairs in the attic, with free room and board."

"In the attic?" He sounded incredulous. "Letty Rose could have given you something better."

"It isn't as if I can afford to pay for it," she said quietly.

He led her through the boisterous crowd. With Carey, she felt protected, isolated from all danger. The gamblers' leering smiles and suggestive glances could not distress her.

"Pay? Letty Rose should compensate you handsomely for the customers you attract," Carey said.

They had reached the foyer, where Cauliflower Arnold's voice boomed louder than anyone else's.

"I make do. I really don't care to discuss my finances," she said firmly.

Carey bowed. "As you wish. Promise me that you'll be careful with that flu. It might lead to inflammation of the lungs. I will speak to Letty Rose."

Francesca smiled and nodded. He truly looked worried. For the first time since that awful day when her world had disintegrated, she felt a glimmer of hope.

Chapter 3

For the first time in weeks, Francesca slept without nightmares. When she awakened the next day, however, her forehead burned with fever and her throat ached. The morning air was chilly, even though the month of June was well underway. The noise from the market stalls in Covent Garden floated in through her open window where a scrap of yellow lace curtain wafted in the breeze.

Although her aching body protested, she dragged herself up in bed and propped herself against the lumpy pillows. She leaned her head back and looked around the room in disgust, taking in the stained plank floor she had scrubbed until her fingers ached, the cracked washbasin, the mottled mirror she had polished with scant improvement. Wallpaper hung raggedly on the thin walls. She had gone from castle to cave, she thought glumly. She had attempted to make the room into a home, with little success. A vase of pink carnations, a red velvet pillow, and a crocheted doily on the nightstand failed to conceal the room's obvious decay.

Today she wouldn't fall into the dark hole of despair that had swallowed her every morning since the murders, but she was too weak to get up. She would make herself think happy thoughts and plan for the future. The problem was that she could not imagine a better tomorrow. She closed her eyes and burrowed into the mattress, pulling the thin blanket over her head. It would be easier to think ahead if she didn't feel so sick. Her head ached as if it had been clobbered with a mallet. At least she had a bed in which to rest.

"I wish I could find respectable work," she whispered to herself.

A hard knock sounded on the door. At first Francesca refused to answer, but her visitor would not stop his hammering.

"Please enter," she finally called out in a hoarse voice, lowering the blanket. A sneeze tickled her nose, and she sneezed as her visitor flung open the door.

It was the stranger from the previous evening, Mr. McLendon, the man who could testify that her husband had been murdered.

"What are you doing here?" she demanded suspiciously. Why was he so interested in her? What did he have to gain? She clutched the blanket to her chest. Did he want to take advantage of her precarious situation and demand physical favors? She had no strength with which to confront the insistent man who came striding into her room as if he owned it.

"I came to offer you breakfast," he said, stopping at the foot of the bed. He displayed a basket covered with a damask cloth. "Are you going to send me away?"

"I should." She gripped her blanket harder. "You're very daring, Mr. McLendon, visiting a lady in her boudoir without her invitation." Her voice was edged with irony. "But then, I cannot be called a lady any longer, and this is hardly a boudoir—a garret more likely." She waved her fingers over the edge of the blanket. "Very well then, show me the basket. But if you so much as touch me, I'll scream for Cauliflower Arnold."

His lips curved in amusement. "Don't worry. I dare not risk listening to your piercing howls."

His nearness made her feel the same warmth she had experienced last night. A small flame of hope flickered in her heart.

Dignity was the word that came to mind as she looked at him. Tall and distinguished, he seemed out of place in the dingy room—a polished gem in his well-cut chocolate-brown coat edged with velvet braiding. His jabot was snowy-white, and his glossy dark hair was brushed back from his broad forehead. The enigmatic look in his gray eyes made her heart flutter most uncomfortably. The breadth of his shoulders and the sensuous curve of his bottom lip conjured up sinful images.

Francesca settled more comfortably against the headboard, still shielding her body with the blanket. "I must admit that I'm surprised to see you here," she said.

"And I in turn must confess that I'm terribly eager to solve the riddle of the missing bod—ahem, your husband, simply for my own peace of mind." He smiled guiltily. "Forgive my intrusion so early in the morning, and my haste to get on with the investigation. But you see, I couldn't sleep last night for thinking about it."

He closed the door and placed the basket on a wobbly table. From the basket he produced a white linen tablecloth which he spread over the scarred top. "Let's see what we have here." His hard face showed no emotion as he lifted out a bottle of wine and a napkin filled with fresh pastries. "Call it what you will, but fate has thrown us together, and together we'll solve this mystery. But first we must eat."

He sounded so confident that Francesca couldn't help but like him. Yet . . . Leonard's death must mean nothing to him. He lifted two glasses from the basket and poured the wine. Handing her one glass, he said, "To us. Two minds together will be better than one, and if you promise to help me, I swear I'll do my utmost to clear your name."

Her throat grew tight with emotion, making it painful to swallow. She blinked and turned her gaze to his square-toed buckled shoes, polished to a rich gleam.

"Thank you," she whispered, and took a sip of wine. Suddenly she became conscious of her appearance. Her hair must be a wild tangle, her nose red, and her eyes heavy with sleep.

"Are you going to share breakfast with me?" he asked, pulling two rickety chairs to the table. "My cook makes wonderful apple tarts, and she sent boiled eggs and slices of ham as well."

"Wine and apple tarts so early in the morning?" She touched her nose with a handkerchief. "How decadent."

He chuckled and handed her the voluminous wrapping gown she had draped over the back of a chair. "I don't know what you like to eat for breakfast, but I have yet to meet a lady who shuns pastries. The sweeter the better."

Francesca pushed her arms through the wide elbow-length sleeves and wrapped the pale-yellow muslin bodice over her chest, closing it with a brooch. Then she stepped out of bed. Without panniers, the skirt dragged on the floor. Shivering, she tied a woolen shawl over her shoulders.

How many ladies had he served breakfast? she wondered fleetingly, her mouth watering at the sight of the pastries. She had been eating dry bread and cheese for weeks, it seemed. If he expected her to pay for this feast with special favors, she'd find a way to thwart his plans. But first she would eat . . .

When she dared to glance at her companion, she saw a long-stemmed red rose in his hand. There was a faint tinge of color in his lean cheeks as he handed her the flower.

"I saw this at a stall in Covent Garden and thought of you. You are far lovelier than this rose, y'know."

He looked so uncomfortable that she had to smile. "You are too kind. Your compliments quite turn my head."

He snorted. "You must be used to every kind of praise." As he gave his full attention to setting the table, Francesca breathed in the heady fragrance of the rose. She put it in a glass of water, which she placed next to the wine bottle on the snowy table-cloth.

"There." Clasping her hands reverently, she surveyed the delicacies with longing.

He held out her chair. "Please, don't hesitate. You must eat to get rid of that horrible cold."

Francesca sat down and watched as he took the other chair. He reached into the basket and came up with a square brown bottle.

"What's that?" she asked.

"Medicine." He smiled wryly. "I told my cook about your predicament and she insisted that you have this bottle."

Francesca pulled out the cork and sniffed the dark liquid suspiciously. "Ugh! Smells vile."

Carey took the bottle from her and poured the murky syrup into a spoon. "Drink up."

She glanced at him, and saw by the steely glint of his storm-gray eyes that he would not accept any resistance. Grimacing, she let him put the spoon in her mouth. She swallowed quickly, expecting to be overcome with nausea. Then she relaxed. "It doesn't taste as bad as it smells."

He laughed and poured more wine into her glass. "You're a good girl."

Francesca blushed and played with the lace that

edged her sleeves. " 'Tis strange that you should say that. My father always called me his 'good girl.' Mother calls me gullible."

He served her slices of ham and hard-boiled egg. "She must be jealous of your breathtaking beauty." His keen gaze assessed her until she had to lower her eyes. "I have a feeling that a person would have to look very deep to find your flaws."

She laughed and cut a piece of ham, then chewed it hungrily. "If you believe that, you're more gullible than I am!"

A smile crinkled his eyes. "I have a feeling that this is the beginning of a great friendship."

"Why are you so eager to have my companionship? We hardly know each other."

"You're right, but I think you can use my help." He seemed embarrassed. "And to tell you the truth, my helping you would stop me from brooding on other things. Besides, you're very agreeable to look upon."

"You certainly know how to charm a woman." For a moment Francesca forgot her pain, and her heart was light. They laughed together. This stranger had brought unexpected hope to her dark world, where each moment of every day was a struggle.

"To friendship," he said, raising his glass.

The crystal glasses tinkled, and sunshine filtered into the room through the curtain, adding warmth to the good feeling that flowed between them.

"If we're going to be friends, you should perhaps tell me something about yourself," he said. "It might help us to solve the mystery."

Francesca took a deep breath. "How much do you want to know? About my marriage? My childhood?" She paused and looked at him expectantly. "My family?"

He leaned closer and placed his hand lightly on her arm. He seemed entranced by the faint freckles on her skin under his long sun-bronzed fingers. "I'd like to know everything about you, Mrs. Kane."

"I'm afraid there isn't much to know. I had an ordinary childhood." She sneezed and blew her nose. "I was very close to my father, who died three years ago. I don't know why I loved him so much. He was gentle, but also a wastrel, an incorrigible gambler. With him it was a disease—a disease that almost brought ruin to our family. My mother and I never got on well, but I still love her." Her voice trailed off. "After all, she's my mother." As he nodded gravely, she continued, "The greatest upheaval in my life occurred when I decided to marry Leonard Kane."

How could she tell him about that terrible time? She still wasn't ready to face the results of that one mistake, and she certainly couldn't bare her heart to a stranger.

"Go on," he prodded gently. "I admit I heard that those in your circle thought it was odd that you married Mr. Kane, when all the young men worshipped you. Kane was practically the same age as your father."

Agitation churned within her. Pushing away her plate, she rose to her feet and moved restlessly about the room. "I married Kane because I—er—had to."

Carey stood, too. "I'm certain that he loved you. Who would not?"

"You're very kind, Mr. McLendon, but you're wrong. Leonard didn't love me. He wanted distinction. When he found that he wouldn't be accepted in polite society, despite his advantageous marriage to me, he blamed me." She hunted for the handkerchief in her pocket, but it was gone. "He began to hate me, and placed me in a domestic prison. He supervised my every waking moment." She pressed her fingertips to her temples. "Orders, demands . . .

and more orders, from morning 'til night. It was horrible!"

"I'm sorry if I've upset you, Mrs. Kane." Carey found her handkerchief on the floor and handed it to her. "Why did you marry him?"

"I accepted his proposal because he promised to pay all of Papa's gambling debts, and settle a large sum on him. Papa was on the brink of ruin."

"Did Mr. Kane dispense with the debts?"

"Yes." Francesca grimaced. "But whatever settlement Papa gained, he wagered most of it away before he died." She flung the handkerchief onto the bed. "I abhor gambling! It's evil. It brings nothing but sorrow to the people involved."

"You're right. I have watched gentlemen bet their entire estates and lose. And then, without a thought to their families, they put lead balls through their heads."

Francesca gave him a keen glance. "Do you gamble?"

Carey cleared his throat and shifted his weight to the other foot. "Occasionally."

" 'Twill be your ruin, if you're not careful," she said quietly.

Carey did not reply. Then after a few moments he said, "It would help if you could tell me where you were going on the day of the—er—accident."

"We were going to Italy."

"Italy?"

She shrugged. "We were going directly to Florence. Kane had business contacts there."

"I see. Were you against making the trip?"

Her lips trembled so much that she could not speak. She nodded miserably. Because of the row she had had with Leonard, their trip had been delayed by several hours. That delay had indirectly caused his death. She felt she was to blame.

Her fever was making her dizzy, and the objects

in the room were slowly receding. The rose glowed blood-red in the water glass. Francesca wanted to smell it, but she was unable to move. As if from a distance, she heard Mr. McLendon's shoes scrape on the floor. His breath was warm against her ear.

"Are you feeling poorly?" His voice washed over her, mellow and rich, like old brandy.

"Yes . . . my head feels huge and my legs have disappeared." Was that desperate voice hers?

He chuckled. "Too much wine, too little food. Come here and finish your breakfast." His hand was so warm on her arm. She could not refuse his kindness.

Francesca sank into the chair. "I'm sorry," she murmured. "I'm unable to continue right now, but if you come back in a few days—"

"You're doing splendidly. Just concentrate on your breakfast now, and we'll talk some other time." He cut the ham into small pieces and fed them to her. She chewed and swallowed automatically.

"I only want to say one more thing," Carey said. "The murderers might have thought you were dead, but there is a possibility they let you live so you would be blamed for the crime." He gazed into the distance, rubbing his chin. "What I cannot understand is why they didn't leave your husband's body." He snapped his fingers. "For some reason, they didn't want you to be imprisoned."

Francesca shivered. "I can't say that your observations relieve my mind about the situation."

"Well, the point is that if highwaymen didn't kill your husband, there has to be a *reason*, other than random brutality. When we know that reason, we'll be able to find the people who arranged your husband's death."

Francesca sighed, impressed with his cleverness. "There aren't many clues to go on. I didn't know anything until I woke up in Seaford."

He nodded thoughtfully. "I'll have to tell you exactly what I saw," he said. "But some other time." He coaxed her to eat a raspberry-filled pastry.

"What about yourself, Mr. McLendon? If we're going to be friends, I'd like to know you, too."

He looked long and hard at her. "Then you might refuse my friendship."

She impulsively placed a hand on his muscular forearm. "I took the risk of trusting you, so now you must trust me."

He stood up abruptly. "Very well." Pacing the room, he began, "I was born in Scotland, out of wedlock." He paused to gauge her reaction, and his heart sank when he saw her obvious dismay. His voice became cold. "My mother was a traveling actress, my father a Scottish nobleman, Angus McLendon, Lord Dunkeld." He sighed, remembering the moments he had spent beside his father's grave. "I think they loved each other, but Father was married to someone else. He always acknowledged me as his own, and I deeply respected him for it. I have no prospects, and my half-brothers and sisters in Scotland now live in reduced circumstances since the Stuart rebellion."

Carey sat down at the table and poured himself another glass of wine. "The Scots suffered heavily for the Stuart Cause, but give them some time, and they'll prevail. The hardest part is that King George has forbidden the Scots to practice their old traditions. The Highland dress is prohibited, and the clans have been shattered. It is a sad time indeed."

"You took part in the Rebellion?"

He scrutinized her face. How much could he safely confide in her? "I might be a fool to confess this, but yes, I played a small part with my cousin. We retrieved a hidden treasure in gold for the starving Scottish soldiers." He kept the largest part of his secret from her—the fact that he had been working closely with the young Prince.

Francesca's eyes shone with admiration, and something seemed to break open in his chest.

"You were very brave," she said. "But even now, you could be executed for treason."

He sighed. "I'd never tell you any of this under normal circumstances, but I have to convince you that I'm serious about helping you. Knowing my secret, you now have a weapon against me should I fail you—which I won't. I only ask that you trust me in return."

"I can see that you're honest. Your life must have been difficult."

"Yes, but once I grew up, I learned to fight everyone who called me a bastard. I've also learned to survive under very trying circumstances."

"I could not live with the stamp of illegitimacy," she said slowly. "Both of your parents are dead then?"

"Mother died five years ago, and Father died in Scotland at the end of March. He took part in the Rebellion and lost everything, especially his pride. My half-brothers and sisters never accepted me, but I don't miss them. I traveled quite a bit in the past, but those days are over, I hope. I'd like to settle down in the country, on a small estate, and raise cattle."

Francesca laughed, and he glanced at her in surprise. Her face, transformed by her smile, was bright and full of mischief. " 'Tis difficult to picture you in the country, stepping across a meadow in your fine clothes and highly polished boots."

He smiled enigmatically, fluffing up the lace at his throat. "Times can change. To be at the height of fashion in London suits my needs for the moment. Many a gentleman who desires me to teach him to tie his neckcloth with utmost flair also invites me to dine at his table. Fashion is my trade, m'dear. For some reason I was born with a talent for it," he added, his voice edged with derision. "You doubtless despise me for it."

"No! Not at all." Her eyelids lowered slightly, and her cheeks glowed scarlet. "Somehow it enhances your . . . masculinity."

For a moment he couldn't breathe, and he had difficulty tearing his gaze from her face. He clenched and unclenched his hands, gripping the wine bottle as if it were a rock in a stormy sea. "More wine?"

But Francesca looked as if she was about to faint, and he rose abruptly. "Let me assist you back to bed. I've been thoughtless in keeping you up so long."

She could only nod, and he lifted her gently into his arms. Although she was endowed with generous curves, she seemed to weigh no more than a feather. Her skin was burning through the thin layers of her shift and wrapping gown, and he became seized with worry. Surely she hadn't survived the violent attack in Seaford only to succumb to the flu. The thought was more disturbing than he cared to admit. What if she died—?

He lay her down against the pillows and arranged the blanket so that she was nestled in a cocoon of warmth. Taking his cloak, which he had hung on a peg beside the door, he placed it over her still form. Her eyelids fluttered, and she tried to smile.

"Don't talk," he admonished. "Don't worry. I'll take care of you. Just go to sleep, m'dear."

"You'll become ill, too," she whispered.

"I've never been sick a day of my life," he said, tucking a corner of the blanket around her shoulders. He walked to the washbasin and found the pitcher half-full. Discovering a clean towel on top of a rickety chest of drawers, he dipped it in the lukewarm water and dabbed her face with the dampened cloth. Her eyes opened. They were huge and dark, burning with fever.

"I don't know if I have the strength to fight this illness," she breathed. "I don't know if I *want* to fight it. My life is in ruins."

Anger flashed in his eyes. "Nonsense! You have every reason to live, if only to fight the people who set out to harm you."

"They might try again." She moistened her cracked lips with the tip of her tongue.

"Not as long as I'm here to protect you," he said gently. "Besides, Cauliflower Arnold would never let any strangers up here to disturb you."

"Perhaps my enemy is not a stranger," she said, her eyes wide with fear.

Apprehension seeped through him. Her ominous words might be true. But come friend or foe, he would be there to protect her.

Chapter 4

"You're still here, Mr. McLendon," Francesca whispered as she floated up from her feverish sleep. She recognized him instantly, although she had only met him for the first time last night. Or *was* it last night? How many days had she been ill? "I can't recall your first name," she said with great effort. Her lips were dry and rough. How long had he been at her bedside?

His laugh comforted her. "Carey."

"Carey." The name was soothing on her lips. He was little more than a dark outline against the sunlight streaming through the windows. Her neck hurt when she turned her head on the pillow. His hands were cool on her forehead.

"You shouldn't talk, Francesca." Slowly his image faded, and as she sank once more into the redhot grip of fever, she heard him say: "You were calling for Harry."

In a flash of memory, her long-dead son stood before her. The image was so sharp that she cried out and bent as if to gather him into her arms. The soft round face, the pale-pink cheeks, the downy curls around his ears, the button nose, the trusting blue eyes—all were as vivid as real life. "Harry!" Her voice broke. He dissolved as if he was painted in watercolor, and agony gripped her, sucking her into a hole from which she feared she would never emerge.

Something nagged at her, something soft and insistent, but all she wanted was solitude and peace—to forget everything. Still, the image of Carey's worried eyes tugged at her dreams, preventing her from sinking completely into oblivion.

Carey studied the beautiful wan face against the pillow. Several long hours had passed since she had awakened for a few minutes. It had been two days since he put her to bed, and his head was heavy from lack of sleep. Afraid that she might slip away from him, never to return, he could not take his eyes from her pale face. Her will to live seemed to grow weaker every day. Was she going the same way as his father?

He tested her forehead with his fingertips and found it hotter than ever. She moaned and tossed her head from side to side.

He had to do something to lower her temperature. Walking downstairs, he found Cauliflower Arnold sitting by the door. After they discussed Francesca's condition for a few minutes, the doorman promised to carry up a hip bath and pitchers of cold water. "Per'aps I should arsk one o' th' girls to assist ye, Mr. M., but there might be nasty talk if I do. They are envious o' Miss Francie as it is. They claim she's stealin' th' attention that should rightfully be theirs, y'see."

Carey nodded, too tired to discuss Letty Rose's assistants. "I'll take care of Mrs. Kane."

Half an hour later he was gently pulling down Francesca's blanket. He held his breath with guilt as he spread open the bodice of her wrapping gown and pulled it from her slim shoulders. The skirt parted, and he dragged the shift over her head.

He stared in awe as her naked body was revealed

to his gaze. Her skin glowed like a lustrous pearl, her limbs slender and daintily formed. Her full, pink nipples drew his gaze. He yearned to take one into his mouth, and he marveled at the perfect roundness of her breasts, which rode higher as Francesca flung her arms deliriously above her head. Sweet God! The sight could make a saint fall from grace . . . His loins tightened painfully as he slid his arms under her hot body and lifted her. She moaned and clung to him. Her face was flushed with fever, and he quickly lowered her into the cool water of the hip bath.

Francesca writhed momentarily in his arms, and her black hair fell like a mantle around her. He gathered it up into a topknot and tied it with a gauzy scarf that he could just reach in the drawer of her nightstand. She hung like a limp doll over the edge of the bath, moaning.

Goose bumps were rising on her skin, and she made feeble attempts to rise from the cold water, but he restrained her. He wiped her face lovingly with a wet towel, ashamed at the feelings her nudity was stirring within him. He longed to caress every inch of her body, to plant kisses along the slender column of her neck. He wanted to hold her delicate foot and kiss each rosy toe . . . then lick the tender spot right behind the ankle bone . . . trace the rounded calf . . . then he would . . .

With a sudden, involuntary movement, Francesca turned sideways, leaning into him.

He swallowed hard at the sight of her nicely rounded derriere, which cried for his caress. God, was she lovely! Her neck was long and shapely, her back narrow, her waist tiny. Her hips . . .

Her thrashing about in the water brought him back to his senses. Her eyes were wide and confused, and her teeth chattered. "What—?"

"Shhh," he whispered, holding her head. She lay

still for a moment, then great sobs wracked her body.

He didn't know what came over him, but he started to sing a soft lullaby with which his mother had once comforted him. Francesca grew quiet, and he was overcome with relief. Why did he bother with this sad, lovely woman? he asked himself. Something about her stirred his deepest emotions. He held her head tenderly and pressed a kiss upon her temple.

"How is she?" came a voice from the door.

Carey dragged his gaze from Francesca with difficulty and nodded at Letty Rose. He continued sponging Francesca's face and shoulders, fully aware that her employer might not approve of the situation.

"She's dreadfully ill, but I think she might be on the mend," Carey said. He had to say the words aloud to convince himself.

Letty Rose was dressed in a crimson silk gown spread over enormous hoops. Without hesitation, she tilted the hoops and, showing a generous amount of leg, squeezed through the narrow door. "She should be working downstairs, not wallowing in self-pity up here." Letty's voice was as hard as rock, but there was a flicker of worry in her eyes.

"Can't you see how ill she is?"

Letty pouted and plied her fan. "I will have to get rid of her if she doesn't work soon. Can't afford to feed parasites. And now that you have claimed her body, she won't be worth much downstairs. You know how gossip travels—"

"If it's money you're after, I'll pay for her lodgings—if you can call this rat hole such," Carey said testily. "You ought to treat a valuable asset like Mrs. Kane better."

Letty Rose fanned herself disdainfully. "She's

naught but a common villainess, and should be grateful I took her in when no one else would."

"Due to her beauty—and notoriety—she brings in more business than any of your girls, and well you know it." He disliked Letty's snobbish airs, but she was a survivor, having risen from the slums by her shrewdness alone. She always spoke slowly and carefully to hide her gutter accent.

She smiled at him invitingly. "How right you are, McLendon. But then, you always are." She pulled at the edge of the deeply cut bodice, expertly drawing his attention to her neckline. There was an unmistakable allure in the generous display of her ripe breasts, round arms, and full lips. The musky perfume she wore made gentlemen think of naked flesh and tangled sheets. She certainly knew how to use her attributes to best advantage.

"What do you want with a criminal like Mrs. Kane?" she scoffed, glaring at the pitiful woman in the bath.

Carey glanced at Francesca's slim body. It was so delicate, so utterly beautiful. He sighed. "I'll help her clear her name."

"Fool!" Letty spat, her eyes flashing. "Consorting with her, you'll be shunned by your friends within a se'nnight, especially if you've made her your mistress."

"She's not my paramour," he whispered as Francesca opened her eyes once again.

"How do I know if you're telling the truth? I had great plans for her before you arrived." She paused. "You will pay for her anyway, won't you, McLendon?" Her eyebrows shot up. "Because of you I lose a tidy profit."

Carey walked to the door and opened it. "If you put it that way, I suppose I must," he said curtly. "Good night, Letty."

She gave Francesca a scornful glance. "She will

never clear her name. She should be grateful that I took her in. From now on, if she wants to stay here, she'll do as I tell her." With a swish of her skirts, she turned from the bath and swayed across the room.

"All you have is a burning desire for profit." Carey dragged a tired hand through his hair.

"As for men, I know a real man when I see one. Why do you keep yourself aloof?" She sidled up to him and pressed her breasts against his chest. "We could be so good to each other."

He pushed her firmly away. "Your efforts are wasted, Letty. My participation ends at your gaming tables."

She drew herself up and spread her arms wide, a scarlet Valkyrie ready to do battle. "Such lordly airs! You're what you are, McLendon, nothing more than an illegitimate Scot. Not even English."

He smiled mirthlessly. "I got used to that fact a long time ago, so don't waste your scorn on me." He slanted a meaningful glance at the hallway. "Your guests must surely miss their fair Letty."

Her eyes flashed, and her lips worked. He bowed gallantly and she tossed her head, sweeping past him with her skirts held high. "Your smooth tongue doesn't impress me."

Carey's gaze was arctic. "I'm not trying to influence you with words, Letty. Only a sizable heap of coins could do that. You don't want the truth because it touches you too closely and makes you start thinking about your own life."

Her eyes blazed. "Don't you dare talk about my life! Compared to me, you don't have one. When the Quality tires of you, they'll throw you into the gutter. You don't even have a home to call your own, only rented lodgings." She slammed the door so hard that the walls vibrated.

She'll force Francesca to sell herself, Carey

thought, sinking down on the floor next to the bath. Letty Rose would not have offered to shelter Francesca unless she had an ulterior motive. But as long as he was with Francesca, Letty Rose's schemes wouldn't succeed.

Infinitely tired, Carey threw a glance at Francesca's face. She was staring at him, big tears spilling down her cheeks. "Why have you put me through this humiliation?" she whispered. "I thought you said you were my friend."

He took hold of her hand. "I *am*. Don't you see? Your fever will kill you if we don't keep it down."

Her head fell forward, and he stood up and lifted her from the bath. He dried her shivering body with a threadbare towel and tucked the wrapping gown and blanket around her. Now he could only wait and pray.

Harry appeared to her again, but this time on the other side of a wide lake that shimmered and moved like a silver sheet. He was laughing and beckoning with his arms. She took one impulsive step forward into the water. It was freezing cold. In dismay she watched as Harry grew smaller and the lake wider. How would she ever swim that far? she wondered with growing despair. And it was so cold! She looked back, surprised to find a small room and a man leaning over her. His eyes were dark and worried.

Torn, she looked at Harry, whose image was growing smaller and more distant. She had to leave him now, and try to forget.

She peered through a viscous haze, and her eyes flew wide open. She became instantly aware of the man bending over the bed. She flinched, thinking for a moment that it was Leonard, but as he looked down at her, she recognized Carey.

"You're awake at last, Francesca. I was afraid you had given up the battle."

She reached blindly for his hand. "You're still here?"

"Yes. I promised not to abandon you, remember?" He placed something cool on her forehead, and her thoughts cleared.

She moistened her dry lips with the tip of her tongue. "You held me back. I wanted to go to Harry—my son who died three years ago."

Sadness lined his face, and he squeezed her fingers gently. "I'm glad you didn't. Hurry up and get well, so that we can continue our friendship." His smile was forced, and she wondered what made him so sad. He raked a hand through his thick, disheveled hair.

"I was worried about you, and I'm tired now that you've won the battle," he said with deceptive lightness, obviously sensing that she had noticed his sadness. He rose and righted the pillows behind her head so that she rested easier.

"Why do you wear such a sorrowful expression?" she asked.

He avoided her eyes. "I didn't want to lose you like I lost my father."

"You didn't," she whispered. "You know, I had the strangest dream. I thought I took a bath earlier."

"You did. Last night I had to soak you in cold water to keep your fever down."

She lowered her eyelashes. "I was . . . naked?"

He cleared his throat. "Yes, as God made you—a masterpiece, Francesca."

Burning with embarrassment, she said, "You had no right to undress me."

"Don't say that! I undressed you only to save your life!"

Swallowing her mortification, Francesca asked, "And Letty Rose was here, demanding money?"

"Yes—"

"And you paid? Then I'm beholden to you," she said. "I don't like that."

His shoulders dropped. "Please don't argue. You may pay me back later."

Lacking the energy to fight him, she had to let it go at that. His very presence gave her strength, as if his will alone could keep her alive. Holding a glass of water to her lips, he added, "I'll order us a sumptuous breakfast."

"Breakfast?"

"Yes, dawn has just arrived, and another glorious day 'twill be. The gods are casting a benevolent eye upon us. The lovely weather is proof of that." He stretched, and his white shirtsleeves clung to the powerful muscles of his arms. "Am I stiff!"

Francesca rubbed her eyes and massaged her neck, trying to rid herself of the leaden fatigue that pinned her to the mattress. After a few minutes her arm fell to her side. "I thought I heard many voices," she said, watching Carey as he buttoned his waistcoat of light-blue and silver brocade and pulled on his chocolate-brown coat.

"No. Letty Rose was the only one to inquire after your health and give me a tongue-lashing." He smiled grimly. "She's counting her loss every day you're away from work."

Francesca thought with horror of the gambling salon downstairs. Down there she had no life. "Tell her I'll be back tomorrow."

He chuckled. "Then I'll have to carry you. You're too weak to stand on your feet."

She turned away, not wanting him to see the dismay in her eyes. Letty Rose would dismiss her if she didn't work soon. "I'll be better tomorrow."

He threw his gaze heavenward as he headed for the door. "Then you'll have to eat some food today. I'll go downstairs and ask Letty's cook for a tray."

* * *

Nearly a week passed before Francesca could walk about her shabby bedchamber. Every day, Carey brought from the market hampers of food, flowers, bottles of wine, and more medicinal concoctions. Francesca was surprised by his loyalty to her. He treated her like an old friend who deserved all his attention, or a dear relation who needed cosseting. She was too weak, too timid, and too grateful for his care to question his presence.

One afternoon he stood over her as she sat in a chair by the window. His quiet strength and confidence attracted her immensely, and her bones turned to jelly at the brilliant smile that so transformed his hard features.

"You look almost well, m'dear. Would you like to take a ride in the park?"

Francesca glanced down at her wrinkled gown and smoothed her tousled hair. "If you'd consider escorting a scarecrow," she replied.

"A very lovely scarecrow in this case." He took her hand, pulled her up, and spun her around. "A princess."

She snatched her hand away and laughed. "You must be blind." Nevertheless, his compliment delighted her. "A ride in the park would be lovely, but allow me an hour to prepare myself."

He bowed, his eyes glittering silver, as they always did when he was pleased. "Whatever you command. I'll have my carriage brought around from my lodgings in St. James's." With another smile, he left the chamber.

Francesca sat down on the bed for five minutes and mulled over her mixed emotions. She was not ready to fall in love, to be controlled by a man's will, but Carey awakened an undeniable warmth in her heart. It was only because of him that she could live one day, then another, and place some distance between herself and the horrors of the past.

A vortex of grief lurked constantly within her, waiting to pull her down, but she braced herself against it. She had gained strength and confidence, and would not slip back into the blackness. Weary of feeling responsible for Leonard's death, she wanted to forget the past and look ahead.

Francesca sighed and went in search of a hip bath. Cauliflower Arnold carried up four huge ewers with steaming water, and an hour later she had washed and was looking through her meager assortment of dresses when a knock sounded on the door.

"Are you ready?" Carey asked from the hallway.

"No . . ." She tossed the clothes she would wear over the edge of the privacy screen and stepped behind it. "You can come in anyway," she said, then remembered that he'd seen her naked. Blushing, she pulled her wrapping gown more tightly around her.

He came inside, tossing his tricorne onto a peg behind the door. "Females! They're never ready when they say they will be." Watching her topknot over the edge of the screen, he sat down on the bed.

" 'Twill take only ten minutes," she defended herself, glaring at him around the corner of the painted panel.

He laughed and winked. "I'll count the minutes. However, we can use this time to discuss what we really saw that horrible day in Seaford." The bed creaked under his weight. "I've been thinking about it."

Francesca sighed. "A sober idea, but you're right. Will you begin?"

"The sharp sunlight that afternoon made it hard to notice details, but I found the slipper you left behind in the sand and gave it to the magistrate. The old man's carriage had unusual wrought-iron lanterns on either side of the door. One of his horses had a perfect white star on his forehead. The coachman's name was Bertie.'' Carey grew silent and stared absentmindedly at the faded paint on the screen.

''Was the old man traveling alone?'' she asked, slipping into her shift.

''Alone? I think so, but I didn't look into the coach. What did you see, Francesca?''

''The men who assaulted us wore masks. The memory sometimes gives me nightmares.'' Francesca glanced at the wafting curtain speculatively. ''I remember that one man was dark; his hair was sticking out on both sides of his hat. Another man was small, of slender build. There was a third man some distance away who seemed to be standing guard. He was fat and wore a gold earring. Two others had just arrived and were sliding off their horses.''

''Good! Perhaps you can recall something else . . .''

''Wait! The man who arrived had a mustache, and his companion held a pistol in his hand.'' Excitement mixed with dread flowed through her. She wished she could recall more. She relived the moment when the men had pulled her out of the coach. She had fought them and screamed. It was the larger man who had dragged her away from the coach, his hands surprisingly strong.

Francesca fastened panniers over her hips and pushed her arms through the tight sleeves of the bodice. The gown was secondhand, a faded pink muslin she had purchased at a stall in Newport Street. She'd washed the dress thoroughly, and it was neat and sweet-smelling, if very different from the fine apparel she had been accustomed to wearing while married to Leonard Kane. As Francesca laced up the bodice and draped the skirt over the panniers, Carey paced the room. She had difficulty stepping into the tight secondhand slippers she had purchased, and muttered a curse.

"Do you need help dressing?" he asked, teasing her. "Don't be shy. You have nothing to hide. I will long remember your . . . loveliness."

Embarrassment burned in Francesca's cheeks as she stepped forward. "You are a rogue, Mr. McLendon! An incurable, unmitigated rogue."

"So it isn't Carey any longer?" He adjusted the lace at his throat, never taking his warm gaze from her.

"You're laughing at me." Lifting her chin in defiance, she combed her hair and piled the curls into the low crown of a wide straw hat. After tying the brown velvet ribbons under her chin, she arranged a thin cape across her shoulders and pulled on a pair of worn silk gloves. Every garment she owned had seen better days. Since Leonard's relatives had barred her from her old home, all she had left from earlier times was the peacock-blue dress she had worn on the day Leonard died.

"You look lovely, as always," Carey said gallantly, retrieving his hat.

She smiled. "I don't believe your smooth words, but your kindness comforts me. This dress is naught but a modest body covering." With longing, she viewed the sumptuous gowns she wore at night in the gambling salon, costumes which Letty Rose had purchased. Letty had issued strict orders that the gowns were to be used for work only.

Francesca sighed and touched the white-and-silver dress she had worn the evening she'd met Carey. It hung on a hanger on the wall beside five other brightly hued ballgowns. The tiny chamber did not contain a clothespress. It was hard to adapt herself to living without the comforts she had known since childhood. She would have to make the best of it, since poverty might be her future if she couldn't find respectable work. As soon as she found an opportunity, she would leave the Crimson Rooms. She was surprised that Letty had let her stay during her illness, but she suspected that she had Carey to thank for that. He was paying for her food and lodging as if she was already his mistress. The thought made her uncomfortable. Then Carey interrupted her thoughts, saying, "I had hoped you could recall more details."

"The tall man who pulled me out of the carriage wore a hat like yours." She stared at Carey's head, noticing the gold braiding around the rim of the tricorne. "Only gentlemen wear hats with trim like that, don't they?"

Carey shrugged. "I would say they do, but highwaymen—if they were the ones who attacked you—might have stolen their fine hats from hapless victims."

"Our memories are rather vague, aren't they?" Francesca said with a sigh. "I fear that the mystery will be impossible to solve." Going to the window, she held the curtain aside and stared across the square.

"We must solve it in order to clear your name. While suspicion hangs over your head, you will be unable to find decent work."

Francesca nodded. "I know." If only she could find some use for the jewelry-designing skills she had learned while married to Kane. Although Leonard had disliked her presence in the shop, he had recognized her talent and let her learn the craft. As far as she knew, she had no friends left in the goldsmith guild who would be willing to help her. No one had contacted her since the tragedy. She shrugged, deciding that she didn't want to dwell on the fact that Leonard's friends had never really been her friends.

They went downstairs and stepped outside. Francesca waved at Cauliflower Arnold in the doorway.

"I'm glad ye're well again," he said to her.

A cloud of pigeons swept past the pillars of St. Paul's Church in the square. From the market stalls the scents of cut flowers and overripe fruit mingled with those of horse dung and dusty air. The shouts, the curses, the singsong voices of the vendors, the hoofbeats on the cobblestones, all contributed to the pulse-beat of the living, breathing beast called London, her home. She had been born and grown up here, albeit in a more sedate part of town. Her mother still lived in Leicester Fields, in a brick town house with tall narrow windows and intricate wrought-iron balustrades. The house boasted a spacious walled-in garden with flower borders in the summer.

Awnings over the vegetable stalls flapped in a sudden gust of wind, and Francesca had to hold on to her hat. Carey assisted her into an open carriage, and the driver headed toward Southampton Street, which would merge into the Strand.

Off the square, the air became more foul-smelling, as the houses clung together around mean alleys and courtyards. A nightly walk in the streets was fraught with danger, as Francesca well knew. Visitors to such respectable places as the theater at Drury Lane or the Royal Opera House had to watch out for pickpockets and infamous street gangs.

"Still feeling poorly?" Carey inquired.

"I enjoy being outdoors."

"I'm glad to hear it. You're definitely on the mend, although you look pale. The fresh air in the park will be just the thing for you. Tomorrow we might travel into Sussex." His smile melted her heart.

"Yes." A longing to touch his hard, smooth cheek overcame her, but she instantly suppressed it. She realized that she was yearning for intimacy and his attentions. He was already giving her so much, in a friendly, almost taunting sort of way. Still, she hardly knew this man at all . . .

"I'd rather go to Green Park than Hyde Park," she said, frowning slightly.

He glanced at her in surprise. "Why?"

Francesca twisted the thumb of her glove. "If we happen to meet your influential friends, they'll ostracize you for accepting my company."

He touched her hand lightly. "I'm not afraid of what they might say or do," he said, and pressed his lips together.

"You don't know how it feels to be shunned by everyone." She clung impulsively to his arm. "I don't want you to suffer because of me."

"I'm flattered that you worry about me." He released her grip and leaned back against the brown velvet squabs. "But don't. Still, if you like, we might watch the milkmaids in Green Park and visit Hyde Park some other time."

Green Park was almost empty at this early hour. Spreading tree branches formed canopies over the sandy lanes, casting a green light on the carriage. The shadowy, romantic paths were for lovers, Francesca thought, her throat constricting with sorrow. That part of her life had been over as soon as she had married Leonard Kane.

Suddenly the carriage emerged into the sunlight. Cows were grazing in the meadow, and a group of people were admiring artists at their easels.

"The art students from the Vanderbank Academy, I suspect," Carey said. "Do you want to stop? They seem to have attracted admirers aplenty."

"Yes, why not? I almost have a desire to paint this lovely scene myself."

He gave her a keen glance. "You haven't told me that you like to paint."

"Oh, I was only joking. I'm all thumbs when it

comes to oil paints and brushes," she said with a laugh.

He grabbed the thumb of her glove. "So you are," he teased, twisting the silk into a corkscrew. He ordered the driver to stop under the shelter of a huge oak tree. Then he alighted and assisted Francesca from the carriage. "Let's watch some experts."

The wind bore the sounds of laughter and animated discussion to their ears. Francesca hesitated when she saw the ladies in their fashionable silk dresses and the handsomely dressed gentlemen. Among the spectators might be someone she knew, and she had no desire to answer awkward questions.

Carey's grip tightened on her elbow. "Don't be afraid." His face was hard and determined, and she complied with an inaudible sigh. He didn't know what it felt like to be branded a murderess.

"Just remember that you're not guilty of any crime," he added, as if reading her mind.

She studied his inscrutable face. It still puzzled her that he would believe her innocence so readily. Not daring to delve deeper into that mystery, she forced a smile to her lips and walked with her head held high. Nevertheless, she breathed a sigh of relief when she recognized no one of the elegant assembly.

They strolled from one easel to another, admiring the evident talent of the young artists. The motifs were conventional landscapes, Green Park appearing as a lush peaceful meadow somewhere in Kent, where the cows grazed with placid contentment under quiet skies.

Carey's arm suddenly stiffened under her fingertips, and she threw him a quick glance. His features grew even harder, and she followed his smoldering gaze.

Behind one of the painters stood a couple. The

woman's hair was a striking blonde, barely covered with a beribboned cap. She was dressed in a white-and-pink-striped dress with a matching cape. Her face had the softness of youth, but the bright, polite smile hid a sharpness that could be discerned only after long and careful examination. Francesca did just that, sensing that the woman was someone important in Carey's life. He stopped on the path, apparently unable to move or take his eyes from the beauty.

"Anything amiss?" Francesca asked, the words catching in her throat.

He did not answer. The couple had not noticed his rude stare, and Francesca tried to divert his attention. "Look at that newborn calf," she urged, pulling his arm. "How sweet and innocent."

"Far from it," he murmured.

She started at the vicious edge in his voice. A tight fury was coiled almost visibly within him. The young beauty was strolling away, her arm entwined with her escort's, her hips swinging under the wide panniers.

The man was tall and burly, although not quite as tall as Carey, and lacking his refined elegance. However, the man had an air of crude power, of owning the world. There was something about his smile that sent shivers of apprehension down Francesca's back. His face was long and thin, a face which did not fit the heavy shoulders and the barrel chest sporting a blue satin waistcoat encrusted with black embroidery. His widow's peak and silver temples gave him a demonic appearance.

"Do you know them?" Francesca ventured, not certain that she wanted to hear the answer.

"Yes." His response was abrupt. "Lord and Lady Abelard. She was previously Lady Daphne Dewthorne."

"Dewthorne," Francesca repeated thoughtfully,

trying to remember where she had heard that name before. Had there been some sort of scandal attached to it? "Lord Abelard is unknown to me. Is he foreign?"

Carey's laugh was harsh. "Yes, foreign, as in imported from hell."

Francesca tapped his arm, unable to conceal her dismay. "How melodramatic." When he didn't reply, she added, "Shall we continue? You look positively haunted."

He seemed to shake off the spell that gripped him. "The Abelards and I don't see eye to eye."

She noticed that Carey had turned pale, and his eyes were dark with anger.

"I see." Realizing that the business was of a hostile nature, and none of her concern, she began to change the subject. But at that moment, the young woman turned her head slightly, a coquettish movement, and stared straight at Carey.

Once again, he stiffened. The air was charged with anger and some other emotion . . . something dark and dangerous. Lord Abelard looked to see what had caught his wife's attention. His widow's peak was a sinister accent to the wrath reddening his face.

Francesca held her breath as everything except the two men and the young woman faded around her. Color flooded Lady Abelard's cheeks, and she smiled tremulously. As she lifted her hand and waved, it was evident that she knew Carey well. Carey did not respond, and Lord Abelard gripped the woman's slender wrist and jerked her hand down. They hurried away.

Carey was as stiff as marble when Francesca touched his arm. He looked stricken. "Why didn't you greet her? Is it because of my company?"

He shook his head, as if emerging from a nightmare. His skin had lost its pallor, and he looked once again like the Carey she knew. He touched her shoulder absently. "No, this has nothing to do with you, Francesca. It's nothing but old—bad—memories."

Sadness quivered within her. "Is there anything I can do to help?"

His expression was savage. "No!" he said in a low, hoarse voice. A look of pain crossed his features, and then he took her hands in a gesture of contrition. "I'm sorry. I had no right to startle you."

Francesca nodded and forced a smile to her lips. She could not speak. She placed her hand lightly on his arm, and they strolled onward. But something cold had crept into him, and the day wasn't quite as bright as it had been earlier.

Chapter 5

Francesca had tried to befriend Letty Rose's girls at the Crimson Rooms, but they refused to acknowledge her as one of them. She longed to leave the house where she was not welcome. Letty Rose treated everyone in her employ condescendingly, but she was fair, and she concerned herself with the welfare of her girls. Yet Francesca sensed the unspoken pressure that Letty had placed upon her—that she should sell herself to the gentlemen, or leave.

The trip to Sussex and Seaford that she and Carey had planned would offer a reprieve from her work, but it was not a journey she looked forward to. Now the time had come at last.

"I'd like t' accompany ye to th' coast," said Cauliflower Arnold the next morning as Francesca told him about their immediate departure. "Niver seen the sea."

They were standing by the door, watching the bustle in the vegetable market. Arnold was the only friend Francesca had made at the Crimson Rooms, and she abhorred the thought of disappointing him. "Of course you can come with us. Perhaps you should pack something. We don't know how long the investigation will take."

"I can come?" Arnold's heavy features lit up, and

he chuckled. "I'd better keep an eye on that Mr. McLendon. By no means do ye know what goes on in 'is 'ead. With a pretty wench like yerself . . ."

"Better hurry, and you must ask Letty Rose for leave, although she might resent you going with us."

The huge man went in search of his employer and arrived less than ten minutes later, his face bright with anticipation. "She let me travel to see my sick grandmother," he said with a wink.

"What about your packing?" Francesca asked, thinking that he looked like a child who had been offered an unexpected sweet.

"I don't need nuffin', Miss Francie." He clasped a hat under his arm. His lanky brown hair had been newly brushed and tied back. "Where's that Mr. M.? A veritable slowtop, 'e is."

Carey glanced at Cauliflower Arnold dubiously when he arrived in his traveling chaise, with Hitchins, his coachman, driving. "Where are you going, Arnold?" he asked as he took Francesca's bundle, a shawl tied at four corners, and placed it on the seat. She had packed only a change of clothes, soap, a hairbrush, pins, and ribbons to tie up her hair.

The huge doorman thumbed his cocked hat uneasily, and gave Francesca a sideways glance. "I . . . er—"

"He'll accompany us, Carey," Francesca said, adjusting her straw hat. "He has never seen the sea before. Letty Rose gave him permission."

Carey's lips quirked and his eyes twinkled. "I see." He nodded at the awkward giant. "Well, you must see the sea. You can ride with Hitchins on the box."

Arnold's smile displayed an impressive row of white teeth. "Thankee, Mr. M. ! I knew ye would understand." He heaved himself up beside Hitchins and made himself comfortable in the narrow space.

The driver gave him a sour look, as Arnold left him only a small wedge of the seat from which to handle the reins.

"I'd 'preciate it if ye'd plant yer posteriors else-wheres," Hitchins said gruffly, giving Arnold a dark look. But he lowered his gaze hastily as Arnold flexed his fists and smiled wolfishly. With a grumble and a gloomy expression, Hitchins watched as Carey assisted Francesca into the coach. As the door closed, he flicked the reins.

"Where shall we start?" Francesca asked as she arranged her skirts around her. The day was sunny and breezy.

"We should try to locate the old man. Since I searched for him in Seaford, we might as well look farther afield. Lewes is on the way, so we can stop and visit the carriage-makers. 'Tis possible the old man had the lanterns made at some shop there. The craftsmen might know his identity."

"I hope you're right," Francesca said with a heavy sigh.

Carey studied her pale face. She was so lovely. Merely watching her was not enough. He yearned to touch her, to run his fingers through her silky hair, to kiss that plump bottom lip, and caress the delicate column of her neck. "Do the memories plague you?" he asked softly.

"They do sometimes, but I try not to dwell on the past."

"You're brave." His heart constricted with compassion. "The faster we find the solution to your husband's puzzling death, the easier it will be for you to forget. 'Tis unfortunate that you have to live through this humiliation."

Francesca raised her chin, determination sparking in her eyes. "I *must* learn what happened to Leonard's body, not to mention the coachman's, and the horses. Were they killed as well?"

"I don't know," he said, sensing her fear.

She folded and unfolded one neat glove in her hand, and he marveled at the meticulous care she took of herself.

"However unfair and . . . calculating Leonard was, he merits a decent burial," Francesca said. "Everyone has the right—" She halted in mid-sentence, and Carey wondered exactly what had been her relationship with Kane.

They traveled at a brisk pace, stopping only to eat at an inn along the way. As they reached Lewes, Hitchins halted the team in the square and jumped down. He rubbed his sore buttocks and scowled at Cauliflower Arnold. The giant stared wide-eyed at the old town, which was nestled in the very lap of the South Downs. "Hills, begad!" he exclaimed.

"Daft, ye are, Mr. Arnold. Molehills, is more like't," Hitchins said scathingly.

Arnold shook his head. "By all that's sacred, 'tis th' first time I've seen such." His gaze shifted to the shops in the square. "I didn't know a town could be so *small*, and so quiet." After scratching his neck in wonder, he climbed down and walked to the horses' heads. "Prime flesh, these two."

"Don't maul King's nose, or ye'll be sorry." The squat and bowlegged Hitchins ambled closer, staring belligerently up at Arnold. "A fearful set o' teeth 'e 'as, and 'e doesn't like strangers," he said, touching the steed possessively.

The horse looked nervous as it rolled its eyes and stomped the cobblestones. Cauliflower Arnold suddenly let out a gargantuan sneeze and rubbed his eyes. "Blast yer silly nag, Mr. 'Itchins! Th' confounded beast makes me ill." With supreme indifference, he stalked off, wiping his runny eyes. "Nuffin' but a moth-eaten bag o' bones anyhow."

"Bottle-'ead," Hitchins muttered, patting King's shining blaze. "Comin' 'ere insultin' ye, ol' King.

We'll show that great meat-mountain a thing or two, won't we?"

Francesca stepped out of the carriage and stretched her legs. The wind grabbed her skirts and swirled them around her. Clouds dotted the sky's blue dome. "It's lovely here." She gazed at the half-timbered buildings, with their steep thatched roofs and flowerpots on the front steps. The smithy was a large barn, its wide portals open to reveal an anvil and glowing embers in the brazier. The walls were black with soot. An edifice adjoining the barn housed the carriage-maker's establishment.

"We ought to visit the smithy first to find out if he knows who made the wrought-iron lanterns on the old man's carriage," Carey said as he joined Francesca, but her dazzling smile struck him speechless, and he momentarily forgot everything except her presence.

"You're right. It's as good a way to start as any."

"Especially since I had no luck with my previous investigation in Seaford." Escorting Francesca, Carey walked inside. Smoke and the acrid scent of hot metal filled the air. Water in a trough bubbled and hissed as the swarthy blacksmith thrust a red-hot iron rod into it.

"What's yer business?" he asked, peering closely at the iron. The deep wrinkles on his face were filled with soot, giving his visage a demonic cast.

"Do you fashion ornamental lanterns here—to adorn carriages, for instance?" Carey scanned the walls, noticing axes, sledgehammers, mallets, and five lanterns. None of them had a design similar to that of the old man's lamps.

"It depends," said the blacksmith. "These—" He pointed at the lanterns on the wall. "—are the only styles I have."

Francesca glanced inquisitively at Carey. He shook his head. " 'Tis not the kind I'm searching for. Do you know of other smithies in the area who make wrought-iron lanterns?''

The blacksmith shrugged sullenly. ''There are smithies in every village betwixt here and London. I wouldn't know the kind of lantern you're seeking.''

Carey had brought a piece of paper. He flattened it on a workbench and, with a stump of coal, drew a crude picture. The body of the lamp had bands of iron forming a grill, and thin rods were curled into circles around the perimeter of the base. He showed the drawing to the blacksmith.

''Never seen a lamp like that before,'' the man said, wiping his hands on a grimy leather apron. ''You'd better take your questions elsewhere. Can't chatter all day. I have work to do.''

Anger flared in Carey's eyes, and Francesca pulled him outside.

''We should ask next door,'' Francesca said. ''I didn't expect an answer at our first stop.''

Carey sighed. ''You have the patience of an angel.''

Cauliflower Arnold joined them outside the carriage-maker's. ''Me 'ead is reelin' from all th' sights. These hills—I 'aven't seen an'thin' like 'em.''

Francesca laughed. ''They aren't very high, Arnold. But to a Londoner they must seem tall indeed.'' She pulled at Carey's arm. ''Let's go.''

''Whatever they are, I like 'em,'' Arnold said with a scowl following them.

The carriage-maker's shop was dark and was packed with tools and materials. Leather sheets were hanging on the walls, and half-made wooden chariots filled the huge floor space. Francesca watched an apprentice painting a set of doors black.

The din of hammers made speech almost impossible. Carey located the master craftsman and pointed toward the door. The man followed the small group outside. He was corpulent, his features lost in folds of ruddy flesh, his head covered with a horsehair periwig. His blue gaze darted from Carey to Francesca, and it widened as he observed Arnold's huge shoulders.

"You aren't from Lewes, or I would know you," the carriage-maker greeted them. "From London, eh?"

" 'Ow didya know?'' Cauliflower Arnold asked.

The man's face creased with mirth. "Oh, I can always tell. London is writ all over you." He rubbed his hands as if anticipating a lucrative order. "If you need a new coach, you've found the right shop."

"We are looking for an old man who has a set of unusual lanterns on his carriage. We thought you might be able to help us find him," Francesca said.

"Lanterns! We don't make them here." His expression changed to one of disappointment. "If you're only searching for a set of lamps, you're talking to the wrong man." He snorted. "Only Londoners have these outlandish requests."

Frowning, Carey showed him the lantern drawing. "We need to find the man who owns these."

The carriage-maker pushed his wig around until it was completely askew. "You have the wrong town. No man with lanterns like those lives in Lewes. I've been here all my life, and constructed most of the coaches in these parts. My neighbor, the blacksmith, makes the iron parts."

"Where do you get your lanterns then?" Carey asked.

"From the lamp-maker at the end of the street. But he works with brass mostly." The man pushed his wig to the other side of his head. "I could wager my last shilling that your man or one of his servants fashioned the lanterns. If he's a wealthy toff, mayhap he employs a blacksmith."

Francesca and Carey exchanged surprised glances.

"The thought didn't occur to us," Carey murmured. "Thank you for your advice." He gripped Francesca's elbow and hurried her toward the coach where Hitchins was waiting.

"No!" she protested. "Why the haste? We should ask how many 'toffs' there are in this area."

"He said no man with lanterns like these—" Carey flapped the drawing in front of Francesca. "—lives here."

She pulled her arm away. "He could be wrong." She looked down the street. "There's an inn, the Fox and Castle. Perhaps the proprietor would know—"

"We must believe the word of a man like the carriage-maker who has lived here all his life," Carey said with a sigh of exasperation.

"You may believe what you want, but I'm going to ask at the inn. The proprietor would know what carriages pass through." Without another glance at Carey, Francesca headed toward the Fox and Castle.

Carey stared after her in wonder. Just when he thought he knew her, she surprised him with an unexpected response. Although she was reserved and ladylike, she also had a stubborn and independent streak. Intrigued, he followed her. He noticed vaguely that Cauliflower Arnold and Hitchins were standing next to the coach, arguing.

Francesca entered the dark common room, Carey right behind her. The air smelled heavily of old pipe smoke and ale. Most of the tables were empty, and Francesca approached a man who was stocking a long shelf with clean glasses.

"Good afternoon, miss," he greeted her, flinging a white towel over his shoulder as he paused for a moment. "Do you want a room?"

Carey answered in her place. "No, we only want some information."

The landlord nodded and smiled, displaying a row

of yellow teeth. "Local gossip, you mean?" He clasped his hands over his heavy paunch and waited.

"No . . . not exactly." Francesca flashed Carey a challenging glance. "My friend here maintains that no one in these parts has carriage lanterns like these." She thrust the drawing at the fellow. "We're looking for a gentleman—"

"Lanterns? I know naught about such things," the landlord said.

Seeing Francesca's disappointment, Carey described the old man. "Unfortunately there's nothing unusual about his face. He has a coachman named Bertie."

The landlord sucked in his lower lip and creased his jutting eyebrows thoughtfully. "Can't say I've seen anyone like that gent. However, there are many old geezers around here. According to your description, it could be anyone." He stuck his thumbs into the pockets of his brown homespun waistcoat. "You'd better speak with Willie, my ostler. More than likely, he's asleep in the stables."

Francesca thanked him, and they turned toward the door. "No luck here," Carey said with a shrug.

"We haven't spoken with the ostler." Francesca said, heading toward the stables at the back.

"I have a feeling this is a waste of time," Carey grumbled.

"He might know a coachman named Bertie," Francesca said, her chin set stubbornly. "We'd better be thorough now, so we don't have to return later."

"You're right, of course." Carey forgot their mission momentarily as the seductive swing of Francesca's hips captured his attention. A gust of wind blew her skirt up and he got a glimpse of trim delicate ankles. He had to admit it—this woman intrigued him like no other. He couldn't quite identify what

attracted him besides her beauty. He just knew that
she had a sweet allure, that she was an irresistable
mystery. Sighing, he wished their quest was a more
romantic one . . . In her arms, he could easily forget
everything about the murders in Seaford. But her
future was at stake—her dilemma required his un-
divided attention. Warmth and strength surged
through him at the thought that she needed him.
Helping her gave his life new meaning.

"That must be Willie," Francesca said, pointing
at a young man slouching on a bench by the stable
entrance. His jaw was slack and he was snoring. His
scraggly hair was bound in a queue at the back, and
a red stocking cap hung over one ear.

"Excuse me," Francesca called out, her dark eyes
alight with laughter.

"What?" The youth stretched his bony arms
sleepily. "Who are ye?"

Carey braced his hand against the wall and leaned
over the lad. "We have some questions for you."

Willie yawned, and peered at Francesca insolently. "If ye want a 'orse, ye must pay th' landlor'
first."

"Do you know any coachman named Bertie in
these parts? He works for an old man."

Willie's jaw snapped shut and he shook his head.

Carey sighed and fished in his pocket for a coin.
"Think, Willie!" He tossed the coin onto the bench,
studying with disgust the young man who was
scratching himself thoroughly in the armpit. Carey
wished he could protect Francesca from such sights,
but whatever she felt she showed no sign of revulsion. She was a lady to her fingertips. "Well?" he
prodded.

"Naw . . . I don't know anyone by that name. But
then, I don't know all the local coachmen, seein' as
I just moved t' Lewes two weeks ago." After scoop-

ing up the coin, he gave another deep yawn and squinted at Carey. "Is that all?"

Carey thrust the lantern drawing at him. "Have you seen a carriage with lamps like these?"

Willie turned the drawing upside down. "Outright ugly, if ye asks me."

Carey clenched his jaw. "I didn't ask for your opinion. Well?"

"No . . ." He handed back the drawing with a shrug.

Francesca's lips tightened, although she was trying to maintain a cheerful expression. This must be excruciating for her, Carey thought, suppressing an urge to pull her into his arms and comfort her.

Without a word, she turned on her heel and walked back to the street. Carey thanked the ostler and followed her. Francesca stepped into the coach and sank down on the seat.

"Where 'ave yer been, Mr. McLendon?" Hitchins asked testily. His glance at Cauliflower Arnold was murderous. The giant was sneezing into the crook of his elbow.

"What's wrong?" Carey asked impatiently, anxious to catch up with Francesca.

" 'This bloke's a barmy one," Hitchins said with a snort. "A worse liar I 'ave yet t' meet. 'E says 'e trained th' great pugilist Jack Broughton." His eyes smoldered with disgust. "What a whisker!"

Carey chuckled. "Mr. Arnold is right, y'know. He worked at the Amphitheatre in Tottenham Court Road where Broughton trained. Arnold was a pugilist champion—many years back."

Hitchin's expression changed from scorn to awe, and Cauliflower Arnold swaggered toward the box, wearing a triumphant smile although his constant sneezing somewhat ruined the effect.

"What's ailing him?" Carey asked.

Hitchins shrugged. "Says th' 'orses make 'im sick. Imagine, 'im a pugilist who can't stand nags." With an air of conciliation, Hitchins joined the ham-fisted giant on the box. "Ye must tell me—"

"To Seaford, Hitchins." Carey shook his head in wonder at the two men and stepped into the coach.

Francesca was sitting in the corner, staring blindly out the window. Her eyes were bright with unshed tears, and Carey's heart constricted. He sat down beside her. "I'm sorry we didn't find an answer."

She didn't respond. Her shoulders were rigid, and he couldn't stop himself from placing his arm around her and pulling her slowly against him. She didn't resist, but neither did she particularly respond. Could she feel how hard his heart was pounding?

"We have only just started our investigation. There's no need to be discouraged," he continued. She had removed her straw hat, and her hair smelled sweet, like a meadow of wildflowers. He could not resist planting a kiss on the thick, silky tresses.

Francesca stiffened and pulled away. "You're taking liberties with me," she whispered.

The coach bounced over a pothole, and she was thrown against him. Her huge eyes were like a dark velvet night, mysterious and bottomless. He cupped one cheek and let his thumb glide over the delicate skin of her cheekbone. "God help me, but you're lovely! No normal, hot-blooded man could stop himself from touching you."

His mouth moved toward hers, but she lowered her eyelashes and moved suddenly to the opposite seat. She was as elusive as a butterfly, Carey thought, disappointed.

"You promised there wouldn't be a romantic entanglement," she said, her eyes flaming with accusation.

"Would a kiss be so repulsive?" he asked softly.

"A promise is a promise."

"If the promise becomes inappropriate, it can be broken."

"Your reasoning eludes me," she replied haughtily.

An awkward silence fell between them, and Carey wished he'd shown more finesse. A delicious rosy tint spread on her cheeks, so he knew that she wasn't entirely indifferent to his advances. He heaved an inaudible sigh of longing.

"You'll see that together we'll discover the solution to the puzzle," he said.

Her eyes smoldered angrily at the double meaning of his words, and he chuckled. "You just wait and see . . ."

Chapter 6

Seaford was a small town built on terraces at the edge of the Channel. Waves slapped against the shore unceasingly, yet the houses and cottages high on their stone ledges were protected from the ocean's savage force. The breeze was warm, and spiced with salt and the aroma of scythed grass. Gardens flowered, and birds sang in trees behind stone fences. Curtains flapped in open windows, and bees droned from blossom to bloom. Tree branches swayed, and clouds scudded across the sky as if playing tag. Francesca was enchanted.

"I never realized how beautiful Seaford is," she said as the coach rode through the town. "I was too distraught to notice anything on the morning after the . . . accident."

"I'm not surprised," Carey said. "Had I awakened in the middle of the square at dawn without knowing how I had gotten there, I would have been distressed as well."

In the square Hitchins reined in the horses. They could hear him arguing heatedly with Cauliflower Arnold.

"Arnold has found a new friend," Francesca said.

Carey chuckled. "I'm not so sure about that. In Lewes, Hitchins called Arnold a liar and a braggart."

Francesca smiled. "At least they aren't tired of each other."

Carey moved to her side and clasped one of her hands. "Do you feel bored in my company?"

She studied the hard planes of his face and felt herself drowning in his magnetic gray eyes. Did he notice how her hand trembled in his? His strength, and his sensitivity to her every mood, made him more attractive than she could put into words. No man had ever showed pure and simple interest in *her*. To her husband, Leonard Kane, she had only been a pawn. "No, I'm not weary of you, but you seem to forget our true purpose in Seaford."

The air hummed with tension, and Francesca held her breath. Her gaze was riveted to his mouth, and she wished she had let him kiss her earlier.

Hitchins knocked on the door. "Asleep, Mr. McLendon?" he asked insolently, thrusting his head into the carriage. "Where to?"

Carey cuffed him lightly on the ear. "What cheek! I didn't ask you to enter, Hitchins."

The coachman grinned. "I'm standin' outside, by gorm."

Carey groaned and closed the door. Leaning out of the window, he explained the route to the site of the murders.

"By th' way, Mr. McLendon, is it true that that bracket-faced Mr. Arnold was knocked down by a female pugilist called Bruising Moll? Farradiddle, ain't it?"

Carey laughed. "Nay, true it is. I had fifty pounds on Arnold, thinking he was bound to win—but that was before I saw Moll, who had fists that would unnerve a larger man than Arnold. She could have lifted you by the scruff of your neck, Hitchins, and thrown you clear across this square."

Hitchins's eyes widened. "Well, strike me dumb!"

He pulled his hat down over his ears and hurried back to the box.

Hitchins set the team on the right course, and Carey leaned back against the squabs, laughing. Then he noticed that Francesca was sitting utterly still and pale.

"You're afraid of returning to the spot where the murders occurred, aren't you?" he said quietly.

She averted her eyes.

He took her hand and held it tight, well aware of the turmoil within her. "Don't worry, I'm here," he said.

A pleasurable shiver ran down her spine as his other hand caressed her neck. With a sigh, she leaned into his shoulder, drawing from his strength.

The carriage continued along the Eastbourne road, skirting the Channel. The lane wound up and down, from one cliff plateau to the next, until it reached the flat salt marshes. Then it veered off toward the sea again.

It wasn't far now.

Her every nerve tingling, Francesca felt a sudden urge to flee. The strain became almost unbearable when she recognized the road. "The last time I traveled here, I had no idea what was in store for me," she said, her voice hoarse with sadness.

"We should not forget our vow to solve this mystery. We have to go forward, and not look back."

A sigh trembled on her lips. "You're right. Yet for some reason I feel so guilty." She glanced out the window. It was sunny like that other day, the light blinding. "You don't have to protect me from reality, Carey. I will have to come to terms with my feeling of guilt, in case we don't find the answers to Kane's death. Why, oh why, didn't the ruffians kill me as well?"

He gave her a long glance that simmered with unspoken words. "I'm grateful they didn't." He paused. "I think we're slowing down. We must be arriving at our destination."

"Whoa," Hitchins cried, and the coach came to a complete halt. The horses fidgeted as Carey opened the door and stepped down. The roar of the waves reached Francesca's ears, and she was instantly transported back to the terrible day of Leonard's death.

She stepped outside. Her heart pounded thunderously, as if she were about to see the bodies of Leonard and the coachman. However, the lane threading through the rolling sand dunes was empty. It was hard to believe that a massacre had taken place in such a serene setting, she thought. Sea gulls wheeled in the air, and sunlight glittered on the restless sea.

Carey put his arm around her and pulled her close. "Where did you discover me that day?" she asked, finding it hard to breathe.

With Hitchins and Arnold silently watching them, he led her toward the bridge. It was narrow and arching, with low stone balustrades. He pointed at the end closest to them. "The carriage looked as if it had been driven into the wall and overturned. Kane was still inside." He let go of her and kneeled at the balustrade. "You can still see the chipped rock." He pointed to where pieces of stone had broken away. "The wheels must have ground against it. Perhaps the horses were frightened and bolted, capsizing the carriage."

Carey rose, gripping Francesca's shoulders and turning her around. "The coach was here." He measured about ten feet. Then he stared at the dunes beside the road. "And you were lying right there." He measured another fifteen feet and pointed at a spot beside the lane.

She shivered, although the air was warm. The rippled sand lay baking in the hot sun, with no sign that anything had ever marred its surface.

"I thought you were dead," he explained, a slight catch in his voice.

She studied his face, reading compassion there.

"If I were in your position, I would go mad with questions," he continued.

"I have done my best to lock my questions away, just to keep my sanity, but if we search for one answer at a time, it might be bearable."

He caressed her cheeks tenderly. "I truly admire you, sweet Francesca."

She blushed, deeply aware of the silver light that shone within his gray eyes. "You're such a comfort." His expression made her color deepen, and desire rushed through her body. Stepping away from him, she bent to study the ground between the spot where she had lain and the end of the bridge, even sweeping the sand away with her hands.

"The only thing left after the bodies disappeared was your broken slipper. The magistrate took it."

She nodded. "Yes, he gave it back to me the next day. If only it could have told us what happened here."

"As far as I know, shoes don't talk." He winked at her, and her spirits lightened.

Carey scrutinized the length of the bridge, peering into the crevices between the stones. He was ready to tear every stone apart if only he could find some clue.

Francesca gave up first. There was naught but sand as far as she could see. Any object would have been covered a long time ago. "I found nothing," she said as she joined Carey on the bridge. She leaned over the balustrade as she waited for him to finish his search.

The water in the riverbed below had evaporated. Sand mixed with mud had formed hard furrows on the bottom where reeds grew from a few damp spots.

Francesca then noticed something black under the bridge. She slid down the bank and tested the solid surface, then stepped out under the bridge and lifted the black object. A jolt of excitement shot through her.

It was a face mask of black silk, the type ladies wore at the Crimson Rooms when they wanted to remain incognito.

"This might be something." She scrambled up the bank. Back on the bridge she dusted off the mask and studied it closely.

Carey joined her, frowning. "A mask?"

"Yes, the kind one uses at masquerades. The guests at the Crimson Rooms often wear them."

"Yes, you're right." He took it and studied it from all angles. "I would wager my last groat that one of the ruffians who attacked you wore this."

"Perhaps, but there's no way of finding out unless we find someone who recognizes the mask." Hopelessness weighed her down. She walked slowly back across the bridge toward the carriage. "I can't remember anything really significant from the assault." She sighed. "After the men pulled me outside, everything happened so fast, and then they dealt the blow to my head."

Carey caught up with her. "You're bound to remember something more. The fabric of the mask is of fine quality. I will ask my tailor in London if he knows who might have fashioned it."

"There's only a remote chance of that." Francesca shaded her eyes with her hand and looked back toward the bridge. "The men must have come from somewhere up the coast. They didn't pass us on the road."

"They could have ridden out earlier and lay in wait for you. I asked all the way up the road to Eastbourne for clues. There is a gang of highwaymen operating in this area, and they probably wear masks during their forays.''

Francesca's face brightened. ''We ought to contact them!''

Carey looked at her incredulously. ''Contact highwaymen? You must be mad.''

''Not at all. You already asked the villagers about the old man on the day when the murders occurred, and you gained no useful information. We can offer to pay the highwaymen for some facts. I'm sure we'll find out if they were anywhere near Seaford at that fatal hour.''

Carey chortled, his gaze teasing her. ''You have more pluck than sense. The highwaymen would never admit to killing anyone. Besides, if they murdered Kane, they might not hesitate to finish the task by killing you. Are you prepared to take that risk?''

Francesca sighed. ''I only want some answers. If nothing else, they might give us an idea of where to look next. They might not have killed Leonard, and they certainly didn't steal anything. The pearl pendant I wore that day was still around my neck.''

Carey gave her a keen glance. ''Very well. We'll ask at the local tavern if they know how to get in touch with the highwaymen. If this route doesn't provide any answers, we ought to look into Kane's past. He might have had an enemy of whom you weren't aware at the time.''

''Let's get on with it then,'' Francesca said. Fortified with that faint glimmer of hope, she stepped into the coach.

Cauliflower Arnold approached them. '' 'Scuse me, Miss Francie, but I might be able t' advise ye,'' he interjected. He thumbed his cocked hat nervously. ''I wouldn't tell just anyone this, but seein' as ye're me friend.'' He cleared his throat. ''I 'ave a cousin who used t' be a smuggler and a 'ighwayman in these parts, and probably still is. We could leave a message t' 'im in th' nearest tavern, an' I'm sure 'e'd receive it, since 'e provides th' locals wi' French brandy. 'E knows ever'one, 'specially th' likes wot break th' law." Arnold's face reddened, as if he was embarrassed to be connected to such a man. "I know 'e'd 'elp ye."

"That sounds like a good idea," Carey said.

"You're right," Francesca said, and smiled. "I didn't know you had such an illustrious relation, Arnold."

"Aw, well, I don't 'xactly brag 'bout Ollie Arnold. Th' black sheep o' our family."

They decided to follow that plan. When they had passed through the outskirts of Seaford earlier, they had noticed a run-down tavern right beside the road. Carey banged his fist against the roof as the coach drew abreast of the building, and Hitchins turned the horses into the yard.

"This is as good a place as any to leave word," Carey said, glancing at Francesca. "You'd better stay here. This is not a place for ladies."

"I'm not made of porcelain," she retorted as he stepped down, but she didn't pursue the argument. The tavern door banged behind Carey, startling a scruffy hen pecking in the yard.

The wind had abated, making it unbearably hot. The mud on the ground was baked hard, and the dust kicked up by the horses clung to everything. A clump of bluebells wilted by the stone wall of the tavern. The roof needed new thatch, and the walls a whitewash.

Francesca fanned herself while she waited for Carey. Hitchins and Arnold had followed him into the taproom. There was a brooding stillness in the air, and uneasiness seized her. She didn't like this

strange, evil place, and drew a sigh of relief when
Carey returned.

He sat down on the seat beside her. Arnold and
Hitchins jumped up on the box.

"Well? What did they say?"

"Naturally, they denied any knowledge of smug-
glers or highwaymen in the area. But when I showed
the glint of a guinea, the landlord promised he
would do his utmost to find someone who could
contact Ollie Arnold. I'm sure he'll do it himself as
soon as may be. I promised him another guinea if I
could meet Ollie tonight, but then he confessed that
the smuggler was in France with his contraband vessel, and might not return for a fortnight. Seems he
has to deliver brandy further down the coast first,
all the way to Devonshire."

Francesca's hopes crumbled. "Then we must return to London and wait for word. Letty Rose didn't
give us indefinite leave."

"Yes, you're right." Carey rubbed his chin in
thought. "Ollie might be just the contact we need."

"Yes, I suppose so. I'm grateful for your perse-
verance, since I have lost mine for the time being."

Carey smiled, gripping her hand. "They say we
Scots are stubborn."

"So you are."

As they drove back toward Seaford, Carey remained deep in thought. "I remember every detail
of the old man's face, and I wish I could describe
him to you. He's the missing link." Carey sighed
and beat his fist lightly against the squabs. "If only
we could find him!" He thought about the carriage
with the unusual lanterns and distinctly marked
horse. "Since we can't locate Ollie today, we could
investigate the horseflesh in Seaford. Someone
might know the old man's horse, as it sported a star-
shaped mark on his face."

Francesca knew that the chance of finding such a

steed was slight. "Plenty of nags have white blazes," she said.

"Nevertheless, I shall inquire at the inn at the square."

Twenty minutes later Carey entered the inn and returned shortly thereafter, triumphant. After giving Hitchins instructions, he jumped into the carriage. "There's a horse with a star on his forehead in a hamlet slightly north of here. The owner is an old man by the name of James Grey." Carey rubbed his hands together. "According to the proprietor, Grey is a sour old man. He lives at Hodmore Cottage—and he could be the man I met at the murder site."

Francesca smiled, her spirits slowly rising with a sense of elation. She squeezed Carey's hand gratefully. "You're so clever. This time—"

"I'll do anything for you . . . don't you realize that, Francesca?"

Overcome by the heat in his eyes, she lowered her gaze. She searched fruitlessly for something to say. His presence filled her thoughts, and desire flared within her. The smoky expression in his eyes made her quiver with longing. Leonard had never made her feel this way. All his touch had ever inspired in her was revulsion.

Carey seemed to sense her desire as he moved closer. His arms went around her and he pulled her against him. Her breasts pressed into his chest, and she looked up at him breathlessly. His touch seared her. Liquid fire gathered in the center of her being, radiating along her every nerve ending.

She wanted him, desperately wanted to shed all the barriers that held her apart from him. His kiss ignited her, and she melted against him as he probed the soft insides of her mouth. The world grew still, and her worries seemed eons away. She moaned, her need for his loving touch swelling within her.

"My precious heart . . . I knew your lips would be delicious," he whispered against her hair. He looked into her eyes, and she blushed at the desire she saw smoldering within him. What did he read in her soul?

"Care to try it again?" he asked seductively.

She shook her head with difficulty. "You promised—"

"Promises can sometimes be broken. In this case it might be for the best." He held her tightly in his arms and covered her throat with kisses, trailing the tip of his tongue down the cleft between her breasts. As she pushed against him, he held her closer, robbing her of breath. She pounded his shoulders with her fists, but he only chuckled.

Francesca couldn't help but groan. He had a domineering streak that reminded her of Leonard. Was he forcing his attentions on her without really caring about her, as Leonard had? "I'm not so sure it's honorable to break promises. You're a very persistent fellow."

"Persuasion is one of my many skills."

"Are there others, or shouldn't I ask?"

"I shall show you." He laughed triumphantly and loosened his grip. "Your defenses are finally crumbling."

Her anger flared and she scrambled away from him. "You rogue! You *would* think it fair to take liberties with me, even though you made a promise."

Still exultant, he leaned back and studied her from under half-closed eyelids. "You have nothing to be afraid of. I'm as innocent as a newborn babe."

Francesca tossed her head and shot him a scornful glance. "You expect me to believe that?"

They passed the rest of the journey in silence. A smile played over Carey's lips, goading Francesca beyond patience.

North of Seaford, Hitchins pulled into the hamlet of Welksham, a cluster of fenced-in thatched cottages. After inquiring about Hodmore Cottage from a farmer in the lane, Hitchins drove the carriage to the last building in the village. It was slightly larger than the others, with an ample garden and a marble birdbath in the front yard. A cat was sunning itself on the stone step by the door.

They alighted and Carey opened the iron gate and strode up the flagstone path, Francesca right behind him. The cat slunk off around the corner of the house as Carey knocked on the green-painted door.

"Anyone home?" he called out. "Mr. Grey?"

Heavy steps sounded within. "Who's there?"

"I want to ask you about your horse," Carey said.

The door opened a crack, and Francesca looked eagerly at the gentleman's face, then at Carey. Was this the old man whom Carey had met at the scene of murder?

"Who're you? Want to buy one of my horses?" Mr. Grey asked suspiciously.

Carey's face didn't show any recognition. It wasn't the man they were looking for. "Does it have a star-shaped blaze?"

Francesca was deeply aware of the disappointment in his voice.

"Aye, it has a star." The door opened fully to reveal a portly old man with wispy white hair. "Who says my horse's for sale?" he asked and clamped a clay pipe between his teeth.

"No one." Carey sighed. "In fact, I was looking for a man, not a horse."

The bushy eyebrows pulled together in a frown. "What's that, young man?" He sucked on the pipe. "Here to see my horse or not?"

"Yes, please," Francesca asked, to soothe Mr. Grey's rising temper. "We're searching for a man who owns a horse with a star-shaped blaze, and the proprietor at the inn in the Seaford square said—'' She broke off in frustration when Mr. Grey didn't seem to be listening. He stamped outside and closed the door behind him. ''Since I've had him for a long time, I don't know if old Rider's for sale. Depends on the price you're offering,'' he muttered, leading them down a path behind the cottage. Bees flew from a cluster of phlox to a patch of peonies with large pink blossoms.

Behind a forsythia hedge were the stables. Mr. Grey opened the creaking half-door and leaned over it.

''Rider's right here. Have to take him down to the smithy for a new shoe.''

Carey glanced into the dim box, and a black horse with a star-shaped blaze looked back at him. ''I don't believe it! That mark is perfect, but it's the wrong horse.''

Francesca looked at the animal, hopelessness tasting bitter in her throat.

''You force me outside to show you the horse, and all you can do is ogle the star on his face,'' Mr. Grey said belligerently. ''Well, take yourself off if you don't want to buy my nag! I've better things to do than to wait on goggle-eyed Londoners.'' He stomped back up the path, and Carey followed with Francesca in tow.

''Your horse is splendid, but we're looking for a particular gray. Do you know of another steed with such a mark on his forehead?'' Carey called after the old man.

''No, and I don't want to know another. A more worse-tempered nag than Rider would be hard to find. Comes from that star on his forehead, I'll warrant.''

Carey and Francesca exchanged exasperated

glances, but they didn't argue with Mr. Grey. "Thank you for your patience," Carey said as he helped Francesca into the carriage. "By the way, does Rider have any offspring with the same type of mark?"

"No. And if you're not going to purchase Rider, I'd rather you leave."

"You took the words out of my mouth," Carey replied, his temper rising.

"Idiots! Londoners, of course," Mr. Grey muttered and slammed the cottage door.

"So much for that," Carey said with a frown of disappointment. "But we won't give up. Who would have thought there were two horses with identical stars? It's most uncanny."

They drove into Seaford and strolled among the stalls at the market, listening to the fishwives haggling with customers over the price of fresh fish. Carey bought two oranges and peeled one for Francesca.

"There's not much else we can do here now. We must return to London and wait for Ollie Arnold's reply," Carey said. His voice was harsh with frustration.

"At least there's some hope that we will learn the truth." Francesca made her voice bright, even though frustration gnawed at her. Would her name ever be cleared, or would she be labeled a murderess forever?

"I wish you wouldn't work in that infamous gambling salon," Carey said as they turned back to the main road. "I would worry less if you were staying with your mother."

"Out of the question."

Carey sent her a wary glance. "I don't know how to say this, but I have a premonition of . . . evil, and if you stay at your mother's house, you'll be safer."

''Evil?'' Francesca shivered as his face turned grave.

''Yes, I sense that something sinister is afoot,'' he said, drawing her close as he gazed off into the distance.

Chapter 7

They returned to London the next day, after spending the night at an inn in Lewes. As Hitchins halted the team outside the Crimson Rooms, Cauliflower Arnold jumped down and headed inside. Francesca was about to follow him when Carey said, "As I suggested yesterday, I wish you would try to make peace with your mother, my sweet. She cannot reject you forever."

Francesca sighed. "She might. We never shared confidences."

Carey scanned the gambling salon's facade and crimson door. "Your presence here worries me, and your mother does have a responsibility toward you."

Francesca's heart grew tight. "I cannot force her to take me in."

Carey's eyes were full of compassion. "Mayhap she has changed her mind. You must go and visit her."

Francesca promised to see her mother, although she suspected it was a futile mission. Carey lifted her down and kissed her lightly on the lips. "I abhor the idea of leaving you here, but I promised to meet Lord Mortimer."

"I'll be safe here. Cauliflower Arnold will protect me."

Carey smiled wryly and saw her safely inside the

door. "Better protection you couldn't find," he agreed.

After Carey left, Francesca felt lonely and bereft. She decided to fulfill her promise to visit her mother. Later that afternoon, she went to the Childress's house in Leicester Fields.

"Lady Childress is not well enough to see you," said Perkins, the maid, as the door to her mother's sitting room opened. Perkins gazed at Francesca's worn cape and wrinkled her nose. Her very bearing indicated her hostility.

Francesca steeled herself. "I don't care. Tell Lady Childress I'm here," she ordered. "I have to see her." The butler had let her into the house, but there was no guarantee she would succeed in gaining entrance to her mother's bedroom.

"You'll have to wait outside until she's ready to see you, Mrs. Kane. The doctor is with her now." Perkins shut the door right in her face, and Francesca fought a desire to bang on it until it burst open. She walked to the window at the end of the first-floor corridor and waited. A regal stillness reigned, which only fine furniture, soft carpets, and precious art could create. Yet an air of dilapidation permeated the house. Dust covered every surface, and the flowers wilted in their vases.

A wave of unhappiness engulfed Francesca, but she quickly reminded herself that she wasn't carrying her burden alone. Carey had brought new hope and energy into her life. But how long would it last? She lifted her shoulders, feeling the aching tension in her neck. She could not rely indefinitely on him as a source of strength. No one could live her life for her. She would have to come to terms with her predicament and go on. She closed her eyes and sighed. Somehow she would solve her problems, and be free to carve out a new life.

A door closed carefully behind her and steps

whispered along the Persian rug. Francesca turned to see Dr. Pierson, her mother's physician. He was extremely tall and narrow-shouldered. His spectacles were perched on his beaky nose, and his powdered wig looked as if it could use a good brushing and curling. His dark coat and knee breeches were wrinkled, as if he'd slept in them, and his shoes were dusty.

He extended a long spindly arm and bent over Francesca's hand. At least he did not shun her presence, she thought gratefully.

"I'm sorry about your plight, m'dear Mrs. Kane," he said in his nasal voice. "I assure you that I don't believe in rumors. I'm certain you're innocent of such a heinous crime as—er—murder."

Francesca smiled. "Thank you. Your confidence is reassuring."

His pale lips stretched into a thin smile. "However, until you can prove your innocence, I would strongly advise against visiting your mother. She's very weak." He cleared his throat, and righted his spectacles. "To see you might set her recovery back, alas."

"She unjustly believes I'm guilty," Francesca said, choking. "For shame! My own mother—" She could not withhold her bitter outburst.

Dr. Pierson looked uncomfortable, and lifted his long chin a fraction. "She has not confided her innermost thoughts to me, Mrs. Kane."

"How . . . bad is she?" Francesca asked, struggling to conceal the tremor in her voice.

"The apoplexy was severe, but she has regained movement in her arms and legs. She speaks with some difficulty." He paused momentarily and stabbed the heel of his shoe into the carpet. "If she sees you, she might suffer another attack." His voice was placating. "Let some water flow under the bridge. There's no hurry . . . surely?"

Francesca blinked away a tear. "I suppose not."

A heavy silence ensued. "You're distressed and pale. Are you ill, Mrs. Kane?"

Francesca sensed that he meant well, and she mentioned her recent illness. "I get stronger every day." The need to describe the depth of her despair and claim her innocence seized her, but none of the words clamoring in her mind came out.

"If 'twill ease your conscience, Mrs. Kane, I believe that some other worry might have contributed to your mother's illness. Has she mentioned any recent upheavals to you?"

Francesca shook her head. "She keeps her problems to herself—she always has. However, I'm convinced that the scandal of my husband's demise was the sole cause of this attack." Guilt weighed her down at the thought that she was indirectly responsible for the apoplexy.

"Don't blame yourself, m'dear. Something else seems to be heavy on her mind, but she won't tell me what it is."

"I'm sure she won't confide in me, Dr. Pierson." Her mother had never shared any secrets, but Francesca was tied to her by an invisible bond, and she would not shun her responsibility now. Someone had always looked after Mother, and since Father was gone, she was the only one left to perform the duty, even though her mother had despised her since the death of her brother Teddy.

Francesca had come regularly to the house in Leicester Fields until Teddy's accident had turned her mother completely against her. Francesca shuddered when she recalled the loathing in her mother's eyes the last time they had met.

The doctor creased his brow. "Perhaps in time she will confide in you. It's a pity she has no close friends, but at this point she needs to rest in solitude."

Without anyone saying it out loud, Francesca knew that she had no more chance of being admitted to her mother's bedroom than would a gin-soaked tramp at the back door. With her breeding and her elegant house and her servants as a powerful barrier, Lady Childress was protected from her scandalous daughter—if not from the effects of the scandal itself.

Even though Lady Childress was punishing her by not acknowledging her presence, her mother was powerless against the disgrace. Had she been fit to go out in society, she would no doubt have been snubbed by her erstwhile friends, and no one would have invited her to society gatherings.

"Thank you for looking after Lady Childress so carefully," Francesca said, hardening her voice to hide her hurt feelings. She inclined her head toward the doctor and swept past him, down the curving staircase to the quiet hallway below. A hushed stillness prevailed. The silver platter usually bearing a thick stack of invitations was empty on the porphyry table by the door. The vases which usually held arrangements of fresh flowers in the summer were empty, and the furniture in the drawing room was shrouded in holland covers.

Perhaps the apoplexy was a blessing in disguise, Francesca mused as she slipped out the door and closed it gently behind her. Mother would not have to suffer the humiliation of being ignored in the shops and the streets.

"May she conquer her disappointment in me," Francesca prayed.

The day was warm. She decided to walk along the Strand to Southampton Street, and go from there to her temporary home in Covent Garden. Although the goldsmiths of London rejected her now, she was convinced that someday she would find decent employment, which would allow her to leave the Crimson Rooms and find respectable lodgings. "One day soon," she whispered. " 'Til then I have to be strong."

It was difficult to walk everywhere when she had always traveled by carriage or sedan chair. The running footmen and the street dwellers, men and women in tattered clothes, and children so dirty she could barely make out their faces, shouted lewd comments at her as she hurried along. The seething, teeming mass of humanity seemed to close in on her, making it almost impossible to move. Carriages and horses heedlessly pushed pedestrians closer to the walls, and rude comments from street vendors and drivers sliced the air.

"A penn'orth for a warm bun," cried one hawker.

"Sod off, Moll," bellowed a rough individual in Francesca's ear as he shoved her up against the wall. He reeked of gin and sweat. Francesca pulled away and blushed, lowering her gaze. Moll—a woman of ill repute . . . She drew her cape closer around her as she turned up Southampton Street. She would have to become accustomed to taking care of herself, to protecting herself against the crowds where polite behavior simply did not exist.

Twilight filled the city. It would be dark within half an hour. Before reaching the Crimson Rooms, she would have to pass dark, stinking alleyways and courtyards that had sprung up as the building of the square developed. Into those areas crowded hangers-on, pickpockets and prostitutes, tricksters and ruffians. Stiffening, Francesca threw fearful glances at the dark recesses.

Flickering candlelight shone in the open gin shops, where barrels of liquor were stacked on top of each other, and the customers were served across a counter made of rough planks. There was nowhere to sit, except on the dirt floors or filthy straw bales. Francesca quickened her pace. She had almost reached the square. She could already see the dark bulk of St. Paul's Church.

Two maids hurried past her, arm in arm, and a footman dressed in fine livery almost ran into her. From behind her came the clacking of hobnailed boots against the cobblestones. The steps appeared to keep pace with hers. By now she was almost running. She could already see light pouring from the open door of the Crimson Rooms at the opposite end of the square. Fear rushed through her. Was someone really following her? She threw a cautious glance over her shoulder and saw the dark outline of a man. Other shadows joined him, and Francesca ran faster.

A big hand gripped her arm. Francesca screamed, but no one paid any attention to her. A dirty, sweaty palm closed over her mouth, and she gagged against it. Her lungs ached with the attempt to breathe, and she struggled as another hand grabbed her waist and lifted her into an alley. The door of the Crimson Rooms was only a few feet away.

"Arnold!" came her muffled cry. "Help me!" Anger and unspeakable terror filled her. Was she going to die?

"Now listen 'ere, slut, shut yer gob an' fork over th' dibs."

Francesca stared in shock at the three men surrounding her. Dibs? They must be talking about money. She had no money at all, or she'd happily give them her last penny to save her life. Yet she nodded, just to have the hand removed from her mouth. But the grip did not lessen. One of the men started groping the length of her body and tore off her cape, which he bundled into a burlap sack. Francesca cringed and tried to kick out, but the men only laughed. It was too dark to see their faces, but she could discern their ratty layers of clothing. One man wore a gaudily embroidered coat over another of drab frieze. His head was covered with a fur hat even though it was summer. She noticed every detail, as if this would be the last view her eyes would see before they closed in death.

"Where's it hidden?" The man with the palm across her lips snarled and jerked her head back. "Search 'er dairy," he said to the other man scornfully. Callused hands groped inside her bodice and pinched her breasts. At last fury exploded within her, giving her the strength to shove the man in the chest and bite down on the flesh pressed against her mouth. The man swore, and the hand fell from her face. Dragging air into her lungs, Francesca screamed, "Help! Help me!"

The lighter opening of the alley filled with the dark silhouette of a man. In an instant, he was upon the first ruffian, his cane raised to whip the burly back. As Francesca watched, the two other villains melted away from the scene, hurrying deeper into the alley. Her toes hit a rock on the ground, and she reached down and hurled it after them. "Thieves!" she yelled, but they managed to slither away unhurt. The third man was flat on his face in the gutter, her rescuer still whipping his inert form.

Francesca moistened her dry lips. "Who are you?" she called out, filled with gratitude. "Shall I fetch the Watch?"

Silence filled the passage. Francesca slowly became aware of the stench of urine and rotting meat. She needed light and sounds. Without another glance at her rescuer, she ran into the square, releasing a great sob of relief.

"Wait!" he called after her. In the light from the Crimson Rooms, she saw that he had followed her. He wore what she recognized as the clothes of a wealthy tradesman—an elegant coat of brown silk with matching knee breeches and a yellow camlet vest. His stock was immaculate, the fall of lace modest but graceful.

"You should not be out alone at night," he admonished. "You placed yourself in grave danger."

"I didn't think it would take me this long to reach my destination," she defended herself, studying him covertly. He was darkly handsome, with flashing black eyes, dark hair that had begun to thin at the temples, a strong nose, and a fine sensual mouth. She judged him to be in his thirties, perhaps slightly older than Carey McLendon. His broad shoulders bespoke strength, and she remembered the merciless whipping he had given the ruffian in the gutter. Fear ran through her, but was instantly dispelled as he grinned. His smile charmed her.

"Giorgio D'Angelo at your service," he said, and bowed. "I'm most delighted I could be of help." He had a foreign accent that she identified as Italian. His name was as romantic as his smile, and Francesca could not help but beam in return.

"Thank you, Mr. D'Angelo. Without your help I might have been killed." She smoothed her hair with a self-conscious gesture, noticing that his gaze was straying to her untidy bodice. Since her cape was gone, she crossed her arms over her chest. "I'll be late for work," she added.

"Work? A beautiful lady like you works?" He spread his arms as if shocked, and his eyes glittered with surprise. "You should not work!" He pressed his fingertips to his lips and sent the kiss toward her. "You should grace some lord's table, should arrange flowers in crystal vases, dance all night long wearing lovely gowns."

She shook her head and averted her gaze.

His eyebrows shot up. "Where are you employed?"

Francesca pointed to the door of the Crimson

Rooms. "At that gambling salon," she said uneasily.

Evidently shocked into speechlessness, he bowed and looked away.

"I'm late. Thank you again." To spare him further embarrassment, she steered her steps toward the door.

But he was immediately at her side, offering his arm. "Let me escort you."

" 'Tis not necessary. I shall not detain you."

He would not hear of it, and tucked her hand possessively into the crook of his arm. Slightly uncomfortable with his familiarity, Francesca stiffened.

"I'm certain that you weren't heading for the gambling salons," she said. "People lose fortunes at the tables."

"If it means that I can spend some time in your lovely company, I'll be more than happy to visit the Crimson Rooms. I've heard of them, of course. However, I've been too busy establishing my new business to have time for an evening of gambling." He leaned very close. "You're the most beautiful lady I have seen in London."

She glanced at him to see if he was serious. "Pure exaggeration, I'm sure."

"No, truly! I wish I could ask your name, but that might be too rude."

Since he accompanied his words with that devastating smile, she could not be offended. "Francesca Kane," she said.

"I'm exceedingly glad that I happened along here tonight. You see, I was walking from Russell Street to Haymarket, where my business is located. I seem to have misplaced my sedan chair."

"I see. May I inquire as to the nature of your business?"

He nodded vigorously, his gaze beaming into hers. "Of course! My work is my pride. I've just registered my mark at the Goldsmith Company. I also deal in fine gemstones. My mother was British, so I decided to spend some years in her home country to learn more about my heritage."

Francesca started in surprise and gave him a keen look. "Goldsmith? An interesting coincidence: my husband was a goldsmith as well. I know quite a bit about the business, especially designing jewelry."

"Kane?" He pondered the name. "Leonard Kane, the famous jeweler in Ludgate Hill?"

Evidently he had not heard of Leonard's death. "Yes. Unfortunately, he's no longer alive." She could not bring herself to say the word *dead*. Or *murdered*. Dark memories seized her, and she dreaded the moment when Mr. D'Angelo would find out the truth and his eyes would turn cold and full of scorn. Would he also blame her for Leonard's murder? It didn't really matter; she was accustomed to being rebuffed, even if it still hurt savagely every time.

Mr. D'Angelo's deep voice startled her out of her reverie. "I wouldn't like a wife of mine to work at a gambling salon. Mr. Kane—if he was as successful as his reputation implies—should have provided for you. He would be upset if he knew that you have to work at an infamous gambling salon."

"His death was very sudden." Her voice choked at the mention of Leonard. She balked at even speaking his name, since that only brought back the vile memories of that fateful day in Seaford.

"A gentleman *provides!*" He sounded outraged. "There are no excuses. I have arranged an ample sum for my sister, in case I should lose my life in some accident."

They had arrived at the door, and light streamed over his features. He was remarkably handsome, with such vitality that he gave her the impression he would live to be at least a hundred years old. His eyes danced and his lips parted in a smile. "I would be honored if we could meet again someday. Perhaps I could escort you on a ride in the park?" He must have noticed her hesitation. "I would bring my sister, of course. She would be happy to meet you. She has not many friends as yet, though she speaks English very well."

"Your mother taught you properly."

He shrugged nonchalantly, but he looked pleased. "My mother was a stern woman who longed to go back to her home country. Perhaps she wished that my father . . . ah, well, you don't want to hear my life story."

Francesca smiled graciously. "It sounds most interesting."

"How about that drive then? The day after tomorrow?"

She hesitated. If he discovered the truth about her, he might regret his kind offer. "Perhaps that's not such a good idea, after all."

"Nonsense! I insist."

She smiled. "Very well. I would enjoy a drive."

He held her hand to his lips. "How about at five in the afternoon?"

She nodded, hesitating only for a moment. She knew next to nothing about this man, but she could not ignore an offer of friendship when all her former acquaintances had turned their backs on her. "That will be lovely."

Rapid steps echoed along the cobblestones next to the wall. She shivered with fear. Had the ruffians returned to finish what they had started? D'Angelo must have sensed her discomfort, because he squeezed her hand.

"Don't worry. I'll allow no danger to come to you while you're in my company—not as long as I'm alive to protect you."

It was strange, but Carey McLendon had offered to shield her with exactly the same words. God knew she needed such help until she could get back on her feet financially and emotionally. But the word *protection* had an ominous ring to it. It must be her overly vivid imagination playing her false, she decided.

The footsteps, belonging to two male figures, came much closer. The men stopped right below the stairs leading to the Crimson Rooms. In the light from the door, Francesca saw Carey McLendon and Lord Mortimer.

Sweet excitement fluttered like butterflies in her chest as she looked into Carey's gray eyes. Although only a few hours had passed since their earlier parting, she had missed him. Something flickered in his eyes, and she knew that he had sensed her feelings. The realization frightened her. He meant more to her than she dared to admit.

Chapter 8

C arey was furious with himself for the hot jealousy shooting through him. What did he care
if Francesca Kane stood close to a stranger in the
dark?

But he did care.

He wanted to knock down the stranger, then drag
her into a private chamber and ravish her. He
burned to claim her lips and slide his palms along
her curves, to familiarize himself with that tiny waist
and the rounded hips that he had so often admired.

He was ready to explore the obvious magic that
existed between them—yet a flutter of doubt curbed
his desire. Would she soon become as cold and cruel
as so many of the society ladies were? After all she
was descended from that class. But she had shown
only a kind and gentle disposition.

"Carey, I didn't expect you," she said. Her voice
was soft and warm. Every time she spoke, he became more deeply enchanted.

He cleared his throat. "I'm surprised to see you
out in the dark," he reproached her, staring point-
edly at the stranger, who was now holding Francesca's elbow possessively.

Her smile faded at Carey's hard tone, and he
cursed himself for his churlishness. So as not to
make matters worse, he bowed politely to Francesca

and walked with Lord Mortimer up to the door, where Cauliflower Arnold greeted him enthusiastically. "Bloody good gamblin' t'night, Mr. M.," he said.

"I'm glad you came," Francesca called after Carey, her words softening him inside. Her voice made him think of slow-moving streams and a light summer wind in the leaves. He hesitated on the topmost step, inclined to wait for her to join him, then he pressed his lips in determination. He would fight the spell her presence wove around him, or he'd say something cutting and reveal his jealousy. He was not ready to admit how strong his love for her had grown.

"Which game are you planning to play tonight?" Carey asked his friend once they had tipped Cauliflower Arnold and entered the large foyer.

"The game that will give me the largest return in the shortest time," Morty replied, throwing a speculative glance into one of the salons. "I take it you only accompanied me to get a glimpse at the lovely Mrs. Kane."

"Am I that transparent?" Carey asked. "Perhaps it was a mistake to come here."

Morty laughed. "Not at all. You bring me luck."

Carey watched Francesca run up the stairs after speaking with Cauliflower Arnold. The doorman showed the stranger to a chair in the vestibule. He was obviously waiting for her to return.

Carey followed Morty across the room. Glass-domed sconces hung on the walls, and the crystal chandeliers cast a seductive glow. One of Letty Rose's assistants preened herself before a tall gilt-framed mirror and waved at Carey invitingly. If only she were Francesca . . .

Morty noticed the wave. "She's pining for you, but are you yearning only for the fair Mrs. Kane, old fellow?"

"Enough, Morty! I know how you like to tease me, but if you don't take care, I might cut out your tongue."

Laughing in mock terror, the earl encompassed the room with a sweep of his arm. "You can have your pick of these beauties."

"They are all yours," Carey said indifferently, and immediately regretted his flippant response. "Sorry, old fellow. I'm terrible company tonight."

Lord Mortimer slapped his shoulder. "I'll pick someone for you, and we'll meet later this evening." He slid through the throng and Carey wished he had his friend's uncomplicated view of life. The man didn't seem to have any problems, even though he was practically destitute. The ladies liked him, but as far as Carey knew, his friend had never been in love.

Carey spent an hour watching the gamblers at the hazard table. The ivory dice clacking in the leather cup held little interest for him tonight, nor did the slightly fanatic expressions on the gamblers' faces. What had he hoped to gain from an evening at the Crimson Rooms, since he had no desire to play cards? Francesca's undying love? He snorted silently and wanted to kick himself.

A movement at the corner of his eye caught his attention. Turning slowly, he watched Francesca descend the main staircase to the foyer, a graceful swan in a white-and-silver dress. The impact of her loveliness melted everything inside him.

There was something about her that drew people to her: perhaps it was her kind voice, or her lovely fine-boned oval face, her ivory skin flushed with pink. Most of all he was drawn to her eyes, mysterious dark pools that sometimes sparkled and glittered with mischief. She was a silver princess in that lustrous gown. Jeweled combs flashed in her midnight-dark hair, which was swept away from her forehead and slender neck, forming a crown of curls atop her head. He longed to touch the wayward ringlet at the nape, to blow it aside as he planted a kiss on that tender spot right below her ear. He could almost hear her sigh of pleasure . . .

His breath rasped painfully in his lungs. There was no doubt about it. He was in love with Francesca Kane. The knowledge jolted him. He had never anticipated that his bitterness against women would dissolve. Not after Lady Daphne's betrayal. Yet here he stood, humble as a greenhorn under the spell of his second shattering love.

Not that he would let his feelings sweep him away, as they had with Daphne. This time he would temper his adoration, let it mature slowly before he was burned by the fire of his own fierce passion.

Francesca waved to Cauliflower Arnold at the door, then entered the room on the stranger's arm, a brave smile on her lips. After nursing her through her illness, Carey knew the depth of her despair, and recognized her effort to conceal it as she offered her escort a glass of brandy.

Her companion seemed interested in the betting at the faro table, and said something to Francesca. She nodded and left him there, then swept through the salon, making sure the gamblers had drinks in their hands and chairs at the tables. The proud tilt of her head never faltered.

Carey noticed that Letty Rose followed Francesca's progress pensively. The gamblers loved Francesca, the beautiful new attendant with the mysterious air. A calculating smile lurked on Letty's rouged lips. Francesca brought in new gamblers every night. Carey knew it wouldn't be long before Letty demanded more from her. How could he prevent the owner of the Crimson Rooms from pushing Francesca into the ruinous world of prostitution?

"Deep in thought tonight?" Francesca's voice floated to his ears. "Care to share them with me?"

Could she read his turmoil? He smiled. Her lips looked vulnerable, eagerly parted, so close that he could just bend his head and touch that plump bottom lip with his own if he cared to.

"Yes, I was thinking how lovely you looked as you came down the stairs," he said honestly. That was something they would always have in their friendship—honesty. He knew he could safely reveal his admiration. She would not use it to manipulate his feelings. Still, he could not admit his love. It was too raw, too savage to express.

She blushed, and her eyes sparkled as she swayed toward him. "I missed you," she whispered.

He offered his arm, delighted with her confession. He couldn't explain that he'd been struggling against his passion, which was threatening to overcome his reason. "Shall we walk about the salons?"

She threw a glance at Letty Rose. "I have my duties to perform. I cannot single out one of the guests."

"Let her complain to me," Carey said. "How did the meeting with your mother go?"

"The family physician advised me not to see her." Tears rose in Francesca's eyes, but she blinked them away. "If only she understood me better, my guilt would be easier to bear. Imagine your own mother suspecting you of murder."

He took her fingers, long and sensitive, and placed a light kiss on the knuckles. "I understand. In time, your mother will see the truth."

"There has always been an invisible barrier between us. It grew worse three years ago when my younger brother died. He borrowed my carriage, and it overturned, killing him." She sighed. "Mother worshipped him, and she blames me for his death—because he died in my coach."

"She sounds irrational."

Francesca shrugged. "I'm accustomed to her moods. As I grew up, I sometimes caught her staring at me with such longing, such pain in her eyes. Then she would push me away, as if she couldn't bear to look at me. She never confided what brought on those bouts of rejection. Teddy, my brother, was the apple of her eye."

There was an intense sadness in her words, yet she smiled bravely. Although he held her cool fingers lightly, he wanted to cradle her in his arms and kiss her passionately.

A sharp laugh from a lady in a half-mask and a powdered wig jarred the fragile intimacy that had sprung up between them. Carey could find no more consoling words to say. Instead, he brought up the matter that was on his mind night and day. "We should travel back to Seaford as soon as we receive word from Ollie Arnold. And any details you might have forgotten could be invaluable in our investigation."

Her cheeks paled, but she held her despair at bay. "I have told you everything I know," she said, her animation gone. "Don't you realize I'm as eager as you are to learn the truth?"

"I'll be there to help you, don't forget that."

She caressed his sleeve briefly, and a wistful expression fleetingly crossed her face. "Yes, I trust you will, and I can't find words to express the depth of my gratitude."

They had returned to the main salon and the hazard table. Quite a crowd had gathered, watching the caster. Carey glanced briefly at the stakes on the table. A large stack of coins had accumulated at the caster's elbow. The man's face was flushed with triumph as he threw the dice for the chance point. Carey sighed as he recognized the gambler. It was Lucas Halden, who'd become his antagonist since he'd accused him of cheating. As Morty had predicted, Halden's seconds had not appeared to schedule a duel after that last disastrous card game. He's not only a cardsharp, but a coward, too, Carey thought.

"What's the main point?" he asked the closest onlooker.

"Six."

The dice rolled. Six and six—a nick. The caster had duplicated the main point and won the bet. The man next to Carey swore under his breath. "The fellow has the devil's own luck," he said.

He'd most likely cheated, Carey thought. He watched Halden through the haze of smoke. It was difficult to judge whether his eyes gleamed more than his smile at the pleasure of winning the bet. Intense dislike surged through Carey. He pulled Francesca toward the faro table before Halden would recognize him and make a scene.

"Who's the fellow you met outside?" he asked Francesca.

"An Italian goldsmith and gem merchant, Giorgio D'Angelo."

"I've heard of him. How did you meet him?"

She hesitated and averted her eyes. "I was . . . attacked by three ruffians in the street tonight, and he saved me." Her explanation was rushed.

"Attacked? Francesca! You walked alone in the dark?"

"Yes." She placed her hand over his. "Please don't be angry. I had no idea it would grow dark before I arrived at Covent Garden. Mr. D'Angelo appeared most conveniently, and chased away the thieves."

Carey sighed in exasperation. "Well, I hope you've learned your lesson. You're not accustomed to fending for yourself in the streets, and you are easy prey for a seasoned thief." He found himself

trembling at the thought of what might have be-
fallen her. "Perhaps I ought to thank D'Angelo."

He had an urge to show the man that Francesca
was—his? What a preposterous idea. She was attached to no one, least of all himself. Any gentleman
could try to win her love. The thought made him go
cold inside, then he grew hot with indignation. His
emotions were reducing him to a blithering fool!
He'd better save himself before it was too late.

"Why would *you* thank him? I'm not your responsibility."

He gently released his grip on her arm. "You're
right, of course. Now I must see that old Morty
doesn't lose everything at the faro table," he said,
and bowed, disgusted with himself for hiding behind such a bland excuse.

Her dark eyes were lowered, so that he couldn't
read her thoughts, but she seemed to hesitate, as if
she wanted to detain him but could not think of a
reason to do so.

"Perhaps tomorrow we can discuss our next trip
to Seaford," he said, leaving abruptly.

She merely nodded, her brow creased . . . with
anger? He wasn't sure. Clenching his jaw, he sought
out Morty. His friend was winning steadily, and triumph glowed on his face.

"I'll buy you a bottle of champagne later," Lord
Mortimer said conspiratorially. "At dawn."

Carey wasn't listening. He was watching Francesca's every move, yearning to be at her side. When
she disappeared into another salon, he waited impatiently for her to return. An hour later she left the
piquet tables on D'Angelo's arm. Something he said
made her laugh, and Carey's jealousy flared. The
Italian deserved to get knocked out cold for making
her laugh out loud, when that was a feat he himself
had yet to accomplish.

Her gaze met his across the room, and something

ignited between them, a sensation so strong it
chased his breath from his lungs.

Francesca thought the floor moved under her as
she stared into the crystal glitter of Carey's savage,
haunted eyes. A sweet weakness spread through her
body, and she forgot to breathe. The only thing that
saved her from falling was the Italian's strong forearm. She clutched it so hard she could feel his taut
muscles.

She was aware only of Carey's wide shoulders,
the steel-molded chin with its slight indentation, that
subtly softened the harsh features. The vulnerable
lips held an intimate promise, and she yearned to
taste them once again. His smoky, desolate eyes with
their arched brows made her long to kiss his eyelids
gently until the hurt look went away. Why was he
angry?

"That gentleman is staring at you most rudely,"
D'Angelo said.

With utmost difficulty Francesca pulled her gaze
away.

"You're tense, Mrs. Kane. Has that man somehow offended you?" Mr. D'Angelo's voice was
suave and consoling.

She shook her head, unable to trust her voice.
"I'm glad I joined you here tonight," she said.

Giorgio D'Angelo straightened with pride. He
looked deeply into her eyes. "You bring me good
fortune, I can feel it."

"You flatter me, but surely I don't bring you luck.
You seem to know the world of gambling." She enjoyed his company, although his speech was too
flamboyant for her taste. Every sentence was accompanied by a dramatic gesture.

"I enjoy a game sometimes." He changed the
subject. "I'm certain that Estrella—my sister—will be
pleased to meet you."

Francesca let go of his arm. "I look forward to making her acquaintance."

Admiration shimmered in his eyes. "You're so gracious and polite, so ladylike." He assumed a thoughtful pose, tapping one fingertip against his bottom lip. "Tell me, what twist of fate placed a well-bred lady in a gambling salon?"

If she told him the truth, accusation would replace the light in his eyes. " 'Tis a mystery," she said, unfolding her fan. Flapping it gently before her face, she realized that it was the truth. Only when the mystery was solved would her reputation be salvaged.

His eyes twinkled. "You intrigue me more than I can say," he murmured, moving closer. Feeling slightly trapped, Francesca took a step back and bumped into an obstacle. A familiar hand closed around her wrist, steadying her.

"Carey!" she breathed.

"I want to say good night before I leave," he said with a smile. His dark eyes probed hers, and she blushed, her heart racing. The intensity of his gaze made her lose every coherent thought.

"You haven't introduced us," Carey reminded her, his voice wary.

Fanning herself vigorously, Francesca made the introduction, and the men bowed with restrained courtesy. They were almost the same height. Carey was lean and lithe, with long limbs, while D'Angelo was broader, of more massive stock.

"Good evening," D'Angelo said and Carey nodded. Tension hummed in the air.

"Did you find Lord Mortimer?" Francesca asked.

"Yes, and he won enough to live like a king for another month," Carey said with a chuckle.

"Unless he stakes it all tomorrow," she said ruefully. She leaned closer, whispering, "What's wrong?"

The tension visibly went out of him. "Nothing, m'dear. I merely wondered if I could have a word with you."

She nodded and turned to the Italian with a gracious smile. "I haven't forgotten our drive."

His teeth flashed and he bowed with a flourish. "I will be here at the stroke of five," he said, and turned on his heel after inclining his head politely to Carey.

"I hope I didn't interrupt your tête a tête," Carey said coolly, tense again, a muscle working in his jaw.

Francesca snapped her fan shut. "And if you did? Would it have stopped you? You looked as if you were ready to fight with him." She walked away so that he had to follow her if he wanted to talk. "What did you want to tell me?" she asked suspiciously.

"You shouldn't consort with strangers. What do you know about D'Angelo? It might be foolish to promise him your company in the park."

Her anger burned bright, and she pinned him with stormy eyes. He had paled under his tan, but she didn't heed the strained look in his eyes. "Was I foolish to go with *you* to the park, pray tell? I know you little more than I know him. Please point out the difference."

"At least you know that I never took advantage of you during your illness." His voice was so cold that she shivered, and his smile mocked her. "I could have, y'know. You told me when you were ill that your mother used to accuse you of gullibility, and perhaps she's right."

He knew well how to hurt her. Mentioning her mother brought back the heavy burden of guilt that she carried every waking hour of her day, a burden which the Italian's flattering words had charmed away for a few minutes.

"I didn't ask for your help when I was sick. You pushed your way into my life, whether I wanted it or not." Anger and desolation swept through her. Why were they arguing? "Besides, you don't own me, and you cannot tell me what to do."

His face was carved of stone. "By Jove! I'm merely concerned about your well-being."

"Your words are like a knife." Hot tears rushed to her eyes, and she whirled and hurried into the foyer. Blindly, she rushed up the first set of stairs, then the next, until she reached the dark narrow flight leading to the attic. He caught up with her before she reached the top.

Panting, Carey yanked her into his arms. She was powerless to stop him. With a groan, he crushed her to him. Their hearts pounded from the mad race up the stairs—and from something else . . . She yearned for his kiss, but he held her so hard that it was impossible to move. As she melted helplessly against his solid form, she was aware of a longing to touch him intimately, a desire so intense that she shivered uncontrollably.

Carey's warm breath tickled her bare shoulder, and he whispered into her hair. She could not make out the words, but she knew that he was as overcome by desire as she was. His hands moved over her back and circled her tiny waist.

His hair was silky to her touch, the skin of his neck soft and inviting. Without realizing what she was doing, she pressed her lips to his throat. He smelled faintly of sandalwood, a tantalizing, virile scent.

"My darling," he murmured as his hand strayed to her breast. Her breath caught as he squeezed gently, then untied the knot that laced together her bodice. His fingertips moved under the stays and skimmed the smooth roundness of her breasts. As her arms went around his neck, he caressed one throbbing peak and planted a row of feverish kisses along her neck.

"We shouldn't . . ." she whispered, but she could not make him stop. She clung shamelessly to him, and his kisses grew bolder. His tongue dipped into the cleft between her breasts.

"You smell so sweet, so intoxicating," he said softly, his forceful caresses stirring delight in her every nerve.

She squirmed against him. "This is—" He stopped her protest with a kiss, and she forgot what she'd been about to say. His embrace felt so wonderfully right. She wanted to yield to his urgency, and she found his coat and waistcoat—not to mention her panniers—great obstacles between them. He was about to lift her into his arms when Letty Rose's voice reached them.

"I thought I saw you slink up here. Francesca, I need you downstairs immediately. Have you already forgotten your duties?"

Francesca tore herself guiltily from Carey's arms. Her cheeks flaming, she righted her bodice and hair. "Not at all," she said. Was that breathless voice really hers? She turned to Carey and whispered, "Please go. Don't embarrass me further."

Remorse flashed across his face, but he winked as he headed downstairs. "Don't berate Mrs. Kane, Letty. Remember she's your most valuable treasure."

Francesca faced Letty Rose, wishing desperately that her employer hadn't witnessed Carey's embrace.

"I thought you held yourself aloof from lovemaking outside your bedchamber. But then, McLendon has paid amply for you, and should be expected to take all sorts of liberties," Letty Rose said, her chest heaving in anger. "Well, what I just saw is ample proof that you're ready to take on more paying customers." Flapping her crimson silk fan, Letty circled Francesca slowly. "I will set aside a chamber for you next to those of my other girls. I will only offer your services to my most valued guests."

Francesca shook with fury. "No! I can't agree to your demand. You promised—"

Letty Rose laughed. "What choice do you have? I make all the decisions here. If you want a roof over your head—"

"Give me a few days to think about it," Francesca begged, knowing that she would have to leave the Crimson Rooms if Letty refused to change her mind.

Letty glared and snapped her fan shut. "Very well, but the moment I want you to start, you'd better be ready—or McLendon will have to pay double fee."

Boiling with anger, Francesca lowered her lashes. "I will." Clenching her fists, she hurried back downstairs in search of Carey. "I'd rather be dead than comply with her order," she added under her breath.

She found Carey watching a card game, and she gripped his elbow forcefully. "You have utterly humiliated me."

"What—" he began, as she pulled him to the privacy of a bay window.

"How dare you pretend to Letty Rose that I am your *mistress*?"

"You must understand that it was the only way she would let you stay on here. You know that I only paid for your room and board, and a little . . . extra, for Letty's lost profit when you were ill." His eyes darkened. "I did it out of concern for you."

Francesca seethed. "You did it to gain control over me, to make me beholden to you."

Carey spread his hands in surprise. "Is that what you think?"

She nodded, unable to find her voice.

He sighed. "You're sorely mistaken, Francesca.

Where would you have gone when you were ill if I hadn't paid your rent?"

"I should have made the decision whether to pay Letty Rose or not, not you!"

His lips twisted cynically. "If I recall correctly, you were unconscious," he drawled.

"Oh, you!" she said between clenched teeth. She turned away. "I will find a way to repay you. And from now on, do not meddle in my affairs."

Chapter 9

$\sim \! \! \curvearrowright \! \! \circlearrowright \! \! \! \curvearrowleft \! \! \sim$

His evening ruined by Francesca's outburst, Carey went in search of Lord Mortimer, and together they left the Crimson Rooms. He wondered whether he should have gone after Francesca, but he realized it was better to give her a chance to consider what had happened between them. In time she would understand that his motives to support her were sincere. And, if he wasn't mistaken, she was as drawn to him as he was to her. Every time he remembered the sweet softness of her breasts, his heartbeat quickened. His loins tightened at the thought of her plump bottom lip, so eminently kissable. He sighed deeply.

"Lost in thought, are you, McLendon?" Lord Mortimer asked, cradling a bottle of wine under his arm. He was rather unsteady on his feet after celebrating his winnings with champagne. "We were to find two of Letty's girls and—"

"What you need is your own bed, Morty. You'll have the devil of a headache tomorrow."

Lord Mortimer laughed, rocking back and forth. They had barely descended the steps of the gambling salon when he said, "Look! There's Lucas Halden and his friend. What are they doing?"

Carey threw a cursory glance at the two men, barely recognizable in the weak light coming from the open door. A woman appeared to be struggling between them.

"Let go o' me, ye great block," she squealed. "I'll tell Letty Rose that ye're maulin' me."

"I paid her fair and square for your services," Halden replied, sounding angry.

"She doesn't know ye forced me outside. Ooow, ye're 'urtin' me." The woman started sobbing, and Carey let go of Mortimer's arm. He glanced at the door, but Cauliflower Arnold wasn't at his post.

"I want t' go back inside," the woman cried. "Letty Rose would niver allow this—"

"Shut up, you trollop," Halden snapped.

Carey stepped up to them. "What's amiss here? Are you bothering the lady, Halden?"

Lucas Halden shoved the doxy at his companion, the red-haired man. "What's it to you, McLendon? Besides, she's no lady. You're dipping your long nose into matters that don't concern you." Halden's face grew red with hostility, and he bunched his fists in Carey's face. Like Lord Mortimer, he had been drinking heavily, and his movements were sluggish and unsteady. Hatred contorted his features.

"Let her go." Carey's voice was icy. He wrenched the red-haired man's grip from the woman's arm and pushed her toward the lighted entrance. With a shriek, she ran inside.

The red-haired man clutched his arm. "You'll regret hurting me."

Carey shrugged and headed toward Lord Mortimer, who was leaning against the wall, watching. Halden blocked his path. "I paid for that whore."

"You weren't following the rules. Letty Rose keeps her girls in the house. And if I'm not mistaken, you were mistreating her."

Halden thrust out his chest, but he still had to look up to confront Carey's steely gaze. "She's naught but a tart."

"Nevertheless, she's a human being." He pushed Halden aside. "Get out of my way."

Halden tottered, then regained his balance. "You bastard! I haven't forgotten that you called me a cheat, and you will not go scot-free." He flew at Carey from behind, jumping up on his back as agilely as a monkey. "I've longed to give you a fight you won't forget."

Carey laughed. "You fight? You're a coward. I looked forward to fencing with you, but naught came of that. You're a disgrace, and a cheat as well." They both tumbled to the ground, and Carey swore. In an instant he had rolled over and leapt to his feet. Halden was still struggling to stand. Carey bunched his fists, and when Halden had risen, he delivered a right hook that sent him sprawling. Halden groaned in pain and fury.

"We'll meet in the dueling field for this." Halden rubbed his aching jaw, and his eyes burned with anger.

"What's stopping you?" Carey taunted. "I'd like any excuse to pierce you with a blade."

The red-haired man, who was even more inebriated than Halden, took a faltering step toward Carey. He stumbled on Halden's leg and fell to the ground.

With an oath, Carey brushed off his satin breeches and righted his shirt cuffs. Without another glance at the men on the cobblestones, he took Lord Mortimer's arm and led him along the street.

"Just send your seconds to my lodgings," Carey threw over his shoulder.

"A lot o' force in that fist of yours," the earl commented. "Halden will have a black eye come morning."

"You shall pay dearly for this, McLendon," Halden shouted after them.

"Listen to the little man," Mortimer chided. "He always had a sore spot for you. I wonder why."

"I was a fool to play cards with him," Carey said. "I won't repeat that mistake."

"I would watch my back if I were you. Halden is a nasty, swaggering weakling. It wouldn't be beyond him to ambush you in some dark alley."

"I'm not afraid of Halden," Carey snorted as they continued into the darkness.

"Are you ready to go, Mrs. Kane?" Giorgio D'Angelo asked when he came to escort Francesca to the park two days later. He looked handsome in a full-skirted coat of gray plush with matching knee breeches. The front of the yellow waistcoat was stiffened with buckram and adorned with an impressive row of brass buttons. The frilled shirt was impeccable, and his buckled shoes were polished to perfection.

Francesca nodded and let him assist her into the landau waiting outside the Crimson Rooms. A woman smiled at her from the opposite seat.

"Let me introduce my sister, Estrella D'Angelo. She's been anxious to meet you," Giorgio said, as he stepped inside and closed the door. He ordered the coachman to drive to Hyde Park, and the wheels rolled over the cobblestones.

Francesca smiled and murmured a greeting.

"I'm delighted to meet you," Estrella said, her Italian accent more pronounced than Giorgio's. Her smile made her beautiful and animated. She extended her hand. A fringed black shawl hung from her elbows.

"Yes, your brother has told me many nice things about you," Francesca replied, trying to remember exactly what he had said. "How do you find England?" She studied the other woman. Estrella reminded Francesca of a younger version of Giorgio, with coarse black hair, dark eyes, arched eyebrows, and a sallow complexion. Her features were regular except for a slightly hooked nose.

Estrella D'Angelo said the inevitable. "Damp and cold." She sighed. "I'll have to get used to it. My brother wants to make a life for us here, so I have no choice. You see, I look after Giorgio's home." She darted a veiled glance at her brother, and Francesca tried to decipher the woman's expression which fluctuated between fondness and exasperation. "I'm afraid I spoil him terribly."

Francesca was surprised that Estrella wasn't married. She appeared to be in her mid-twenties, and it seemed as if the family was wealthy, so there wouldn't be the problem of a dowry. "You must be devoted to him to deny yourself a family of your own," she said pensively.

Estrella patted her hand suddenly, and her voice became thick with emotion. "My family always comes first." A slight pause ensued. "Now tell me about yourself."

Francesca recoiled at the thought of sharing her past. "I work at the Crimson Rooms. I don't have a family." At least that was true. Everyone was dead except her mother. "You're fortunate to have a brother." She thought of her own brother, who had died so tragically.

"Brothers can be both a blessing and a curse," Estrella said with a laugh.

Francesca instinctively liked the Italian woman. "I admire your hat, Miss D'Angelo," she said. "Is it the Italian style?"

"Yes," she replied, touching her wide bergère hat trimmed with long red satin ribbons. Estrella wore an extravagant rose-colored gown which was stretched over enormous hoops. It was adorned with a multitude of red bows and layers upon layers of exquisite lace. She looked very elegant and worldly, and evidently took great interest in her attire.

Beside Estrella's grandeur, Francesca's mint-green gown of Indian muslin with its tight bodice and simple closed skirt looked shabby. She drew her lace shawl closer around her and settled herself more comfortably on the seat.

"Please call me Estrella, everyone does." The Italian woman leaned forward with a sincere smile, closing the space between their seats.

"I told Mrs. Kane how lonely you are, m'dear," Giorgio said. His words almost commanded that the ladies become friends.

Francesca was flattered that he desired her companionship. She hoped they wouldn't find out about her past too soon, not until trust had grown between them, or she had cleared her name. They would help to relieve her loneliness. Smiling warmly, she said, "If we're going to be friends, you both had better call me Francesca."

They laughed, and that cemented the pact.

The day was perfect. Light clouds floated across the sky, and the sun warmed the city. It wasn't too hot, and as the carriage reached Hyde Park, the air was filled with the scent of flowers and newly cut grass. The sandy lanes were crowded, and Francesca hid behind her widespread fan, lest someone recognize her. She had covered her head with a lace-edged cap with lappets at the back that hid most of her hair. Fortunately for her, the D'Angelos had few acquaintances, and her old friends of the nobility would never deign to look twice at the wealthy tradesmen "aping after their betters."

The tragedy in Seaford and the scandal of Leonard's death had buried Francesca's last hope of taking her place among her peers. Her recent difficulties had humbled her attitude toward the lower classes, and she enjoyed the boisterous and friendly London tradesmen more than she thought she would.

"Giorgio tells me your late husband was a jeweler," said Estrella.

"Yes, he had a shop in Ludgate Hill. Due to some excellent journeymen in his goldsmith's shop, Mr. Kane's reputation was growing stronger each day. He catered to most of the aristocracy. His younger brother is now managing the business."

"Then you have one less worry," Estrella said lightly. " 'Tis difficult to carve out a market in a city which has so many excellent gold- and silversmiths."

"I hear that your shop is quite popular. If your designs have a foreign flair, you'll soon catch the interest of the most influential Londoners." Francesca temporarily forgot her fear of being recognized and lowered her fan. "I used to accompany my husband to his shop almost every day, where the journeymen taught me the skills of jewelry design. Five of my creations now adorn the necks of duchesses and countesses."

Giorgio looked thoughtful. "You would be a great asset to my business, Francesca."

Estrella turned to her brother and wound her arm through his. "Perhaps we could offer our new friend a position with us. I would love to have female company."

Francesca was overwhelmed with surprise. This would be a perfect way to leave the Crimson Rooms, where Letty Rose was demanding that she offer more "comfort" to the gentlemen.

Yet Carey had warned her not to be too trusting of strangers . . .

"What part do you have in the business, Estrella?" she asked.

"I keep the accounts. I sometimes wait on customers, and I also order supplies. We just had a shipment of gems that demand elegant designs. Fresh ideas would be welcome." She tugged at Giorgio's sleeve. "Isn't this a splendid opportunity to add expertise to our business?" He was silently watching Francesca. "Say something, Giorgio!"

He shrugged, and his lips parted in a brilliant smile. "How can I say no? But we must not impose on Francesca. This is all so sudden. She might feel that we're forcing her to accept our offer."

Francesca glanced away. His gaze was too direct and disconcerting. She feared he might read more into their friendship than there was. She was not ready to give herself to any man, and if she did, it would be to Carey.

"What do you say?" Estrella was pulling eagerly at Francesca's sleeve. "You'll have freedom and your choice of work in the shop. There are empty rooms above ours which you could rent. You see, we live above the shop. Even though my brother likes to dress as if he's at the pinnacle of success, we are still struggling." She glanced guiltily at Giorgio. Her throat worked convulsively, and her fingers pleated the lace at the edge of her cuff.

Giorgio frowned. "You should not reveal my weakness for well-tailored clothes, Estrella. You're embarrassing our friend." He looked searchingly at Francesca. "My understanding is that a careful choice of costume inspires confidence in the customers. Success breeds more success."

Estrella's cheeks flamed red. "I'm sorry." She trembled visibly.

"I like elegance in a gentleman," Francesca said, trying to dissolve the tension. Elegant clothing was something she had always taken for granted—until she could no longer afford it. Now she didn't care one way or the other. Survival was more important than clothes. "You are wise to understand the ways of the nobility."

Giorgio seemed to swell with admiration. "You're a gracious lady, Francesca." As his bout of temper fizzled out, the two women breathed easier.

"I'd like to consider your offer," Francesca said slowly.

"Take all the time you like," Giorgio said. "I'll wait for your decision."

Estrella beamed. "You must come for a visit soon. I'll show you around the goldsmith's shop and the empty rooms upstairs. You'd be ever so comfortable there. Our maid could do your cleaning, and you could have your meals with us."

Her enthusiasm was contagious, and Francesca's heart expanded with gratitude. "Give me a week to think about it."

During the rest of the drive they enjoyed the fair weather and the warm breeze which sent skirts and hat ribbons fluttering. Couples strolled on the lawns, the ladies like bright flowers in their pastel summer gowns. The gentlemen were distinguished in their silk broadcloths, with cocked hats and frills at their necks. On these lanes the squalor pervading the darker side of London had no foothold, at least not at this hour of the day. Like the vermin in the sewers, the poor and starving came out to forage at night. Although she had lived a sheltered life, Francesca had seen every aspect of poverty in the streets. She was so thankful that she wasn't one of the creatures of the dark. She might well have been if it hadn't been for Letty Rose . . . and now she had Carey McLendon's compassion to be grateful for.

"Francesca, you never told me—how did you find employment in a gambling salon?" Giorgio asked suddenly, as if he had read her thoughts. He placed both his hands on the top of his thin ebony cane, obviously interested in her reply.

They had a right to know something of her life. "There was an . . . accident on the road, an accident in which my husband was killed," she began. " 'Tis awful when someone close to you dies. Three years ago I lost my only child to illness."

"How terrible!" cried Estrella, fanning herself breathlessly. "I couldn't bear such a tragedy."

"Yes, it was hard. Harry was only one year old." Francesca blinked away a tear and pushed aside the sad memory. "My husband's family blamed me for the accident that killed Leonard Kane. They literally barred me from my former home."

"Surely there must be legal means . . ." Giorgio interrupted.

Francesca lowered her gaze. "No. I can't talk about it, and my own family rejects me. My mother has lived on the brink of bankruptcy since my father died. You see, my father lived rather extravagantly."

An uncomfortable silence followed, and she wondered if she'd been careless to divulge so much about her background. "Father used to know Letty Rose at the Crimson Rooms, and I recalled her name when I wanted to sell my last jewel. I had heard that the proprietor was a woman, and thought she might take pity on me and pay well for the gem. She did, and offered me employment as well. She's as hard as rock, but rather fair-minded. I have been fortunate."

Estrella sighed deeply. "I would die of despair if anything like that happened to me. You are so brave."

"When you're faced with problems, you either solve them or go under." The horrifying vortex of grief she had held at bay for several days was now threatening to pull her into its black depths again.

"Tell me, what kind of . . . accident happened?" Giorgio asked.

"Really, Giorgio, we shouldn't pry," Estrella said

quietly. "It isn't easy for Francesca to talk about. And we've only just met."

Giorgio's temper flashed in his eyes once more, and Estrella patted his hand nervously. "Please, don't be angry," she begged, and the storm in his eyes died. "I know you don't like it when I make demands, but Francesca's past is her own."

"Don't worry about my problems. I understand that you want to know my background if you're going to employ me," Francesca said, wondering why she felt the need to smooth the waves between brother and sister. To divert their attention, she pointed and exclaimed, "Look at the swans!"

A pond glittered between the elms and weeping willows. Clusters of people stood on the shores, and children were feeding the ducks and swans bread crumbs.

Giorgio ordered the driver to stop, then jumped down. After assisting the ladies to alight, he led them across the lawn to the pond. Giorgio had one lady on each arm, and although Francesca tried to pull away, he squeezed her hand harder against his side. Her strength was no match against his steely muscles.

"Don't deny me this pleasure," he murmured. "You're quite the loveliest creature I've ever met, and I'm proud to be escorting you."

Francesca blushed. How could she fail to appreciate such ardent admiration? "I wish I had brought some bread to feed the birds." She laughed. "I have a weakness for animals. They make me feel needed."

He chuckled. "Any animal in your care would be impossibly spoiled."

"I'm afraid so."

"An endearing quality in you," he whispered.

Feeling uncomfortable, Francesca lowered her lashes.

The pond was muddy. Lily pads grew in the middle, and two white lilies rose on slender stalks from the water. Weeping willows trailed along the shore, and a family of mallards squawked at Francesca's feet. The sun glittered in the water like so many diamonds.

"The next time we come here, we'll make sure to bring a basket of old bread," Estrella said, evidently enchanted by the swans. They swam so close to shore that she could have reached out and patted one on the head.

Francesca shaded her eyes with her hand and glanced at a man and a woman on the other side of the pond. There was something familiar about them, but she could not see them clearly in the glaring sunlight.

Giorgio brought her around the side of the kidney-shaped pond, pointing out newborn ducklings paddling in a vee behind their mother. They imitated every move she made, ever cautious to stay close to her.

"Adorable," was all Francesca could say, thinking of Harry. Did the mother duck feel the fierce protectiveness she had felt for Harry? More than likely.

They walked slowly around the pond, and suddenly she found herself face to face with the couple she had glimpsed earlier. Eyes the color of a rainy sea, proud shoulders, glossy dark hair—Carey! Her heart pounded faster. The frail blonde beauty at his side was already etched on her memory. It was Carey's mysterious friend, Lady Abelard.

Francesca suddenly felt chilled. She didn't want to see Carey here with *her*. It was as if the friendship she had shared with him was sullied. Then she grew angry with herself. Was her confidence so weak that she required his entire attention, or did the reason for her jealousy go deeper?

"Good afternoon," Carey greeted her. He smiled briefly and nodded at Giorgio and Estrella.

The Italian gave Lady Abelard his close scrutiny, obviously liking what he saw. There was no emotion on Carey's face. He never took his eyes from Francesca and his presence took her breath away.

Francesca tore her gaze from Carey's face and looked at the woman standing so close to him. She sensed that Carey had loved this woman, perhaps still loved her. The heart-shaped face, the delicate features, the pink-and-cream complexion, the deep-blue eyes with their heavy lashes, and the artful crown of golden curls would stir any man's heart. Giorgio looked enchanted. But Francesca also noticed Daphne's slightly puffy eyes, as if she had just been crying. Had Carey said something to make her weep?

Francesca resented the way the other woman clung possessively to Carey. She was a married woman—and what business did Carey have with Lady Abelard? Her heart sank as suspicion stung her, and she forgot her attentive company and the glorious weather.

She started when Carey touched her arm. "I need to talk to you," he said.

She glanced hesitantly at Lady Abelard, who was already involved in a discussion with Giorgio and Estrella. She nodded, and Carey led her several yards from the others. Pretending to admire the birds, they stood silent for a moment at the pond's edge.

"I am still angry with you for paying Letty Rose," she said, but her voice was soft.

He smiled enigmatically. "Anger is a wasted emotion."

"What is so urgent that you have to leave your lovely companion and speak with me?" Francesca asked at last, unable to contain herself.

"I was rude the other night when I saw you with D'Angelo at the Crimson Rooms. I apologize for my churlish behavior, and for what happened later."

She shot him a probing glance. "What do you mean?"

"I didn't behave in a friendly manner; instead I was rather like a jealous lover." His handsome face twisted in a wry smile. "I don't know what came over me."

Francesca wanted to touch him, yearned to feel once again the length of his hard body pressed against hers. A longing so strong that she couldn't speak came over her, and she averted her gaze to the rippling water. Silence stretched between them, filled with unbearable tension.

"You're not going to say anything?" he asked, his voice hard.

"What is there to say?"

"You could accept my apology."

She turned slowly and looked at him. His face was expressionless, but pain darkened his eyes. She had a fleeting impression that desperation simmered under his cool surface.

"Please don't feel guilty. There is nothing to forgive. Nothing came of your rash behavior." She forced a smile to her lips. "In fact, I admire your control." Oh, how she yearned to touch that lean cheek and dark hair. He was so irresistible it felt like an ache in her limbs, but where would an affair with Carey lead? Yet she was sure that she read longing in his eyes. "However," she continued, "I have yet to forgive you for going behind my back to settle my account with Letty Rose."

He held out his hand, palm up. "You can start paying me back."

She glanced at him suspiciously, and saw that his face had softened in a smile. Fuming, she reached into her pocket and pulled out a money pouch. She placed a shilling in his hand. "Do I get a receipt?"

"Yes . . . but don't you trust me?" His eyes glinted wickedly.

"No!" she retorted, and glanced toward the other three. The nerve of him!

"You have made friends with the Italians." His voice was thoughtful.

Francesca picked up a pebble and threw it into the pond. "Yes, they have been kind to me. They offered me employment in their shop today."

The tension between them rose again, and Francesca struggled for breath.

"Did you accept it?" he asked sharply.

"I don't understand why you don't like Giorgio," she snapped.

"He undresses you with every glance," Carey replied harshly.

Her eyes grew wide, and anger welled up within her. "That was uncalled for."

"Are you shocked?" he continued. " 'Tis true, even if you refuse to see it."

" 'Tis a lie! He's been nothing but polite."

"Merely toying with his prey."

Francesca could not take her eyes from his. What was happening to him? Restrained savagery seethed under his words, and his jaw was clenched in anger. But why?

"Nonsense, Carey. You choose to see what you want to see. Giorgio has no dark designs on me. He has offered me friendship, just as you did."

Carey sighed, but the tension did not leave him. He changed the subject. "Has Cauliflower Arnold heard from his cousin yet?"

Francesca wanted to shake him, to make him understand that he didn't have to worry about her, but she didn't move. "No, but he expects word soon."

"We might have to stay overnight in Seaford. It

depends on what we find.'' Carey's brow was furrowed in thought, and his gaze scanned the water.

''I'm prepared to spend the time it takes to solve
the puzzle. What do you expect to find?'' She was
worried about his reply. The thought of seeing the
highwaymen filled her with dread.

He shrugged. ''I don't know. Hopefully something that might lead us to the murderer.'' He
searched her face. ''Don't be afraid.''

She swallowed hard and nodded. ''We'll have to
confront the . . . murderer sooner or later.''

His face softened once again, and he took a step
closer to her. For one desperate moment, she felt
that if he would only touch her, the dreadful memory of Leonard's death would go away. ''You have
courage, Francesca.''

''I have nothing,'' she said quietly. ''The murderers took everything away from me.''

Then he touched her. The warmth of his fingers
sent currents of excitement racing through her blood.
''You have me, for whatever 'tis worth.''

She choked momentarily. ''I cherish our friendship.''

He stood over her, his lips inviting her. They
looked so vulnerable, even though they formed a
taut line. Then he said, ''You're so breathtakingly
lovely, I quite forget myself sometimes. One day I'll
ignore our pact of friendship and make a fool out of
myself.''

Please do, cried her senses.

''You seem perfectly in control of yourself, Carey.
I know you won't do anything you'll regret later.''
Where Leonard's presence had revolted her, this
man excited and confused her beyond anything she
thought possible. Under the honed elegance there
was savagery, a virile intensity that made her every
nerve tingle. Did her nearness do the same to him?
Without saying a word, he beckoned her closer. She

took an instinctive step forward and slipped on the muddy bank. She would have slid into the water if it were not for his steadying hand on her elbow.

"Why did you take that step?" he murmured. A light danced in his eyes.

Embarrassment reddened her cheeks. "I don't know." But she did know—she had only heeded the call of her senses.

"Perhaps we should join the others." He kept his hand on her elbow, and she made no effort to pull away.

"Where is Lord Abelard?" she asked.

"I don't know. Perhaps Lady Abelard locked him in his wardrobe and threw the key in the Thames," he said wryly.

She glowered at him. "She's so very lovely."

"Do I detect a trace of jealousy?"

Francesca blushed angrily. "Not at all! Anyone would notice her beauty."

"I think your friend Giorgio would agree with you on that point."

Francesca glanced at the Italian. He was talking to Lady Abelard with great animation, and had clearly forgotten Estrella's presence. The Italian woman, looking sad and lonely, was watching two children feeding birds.

Francesca reluctantly broke away from Carey. "I'll ask Letty Rose's permission to leave my work and travel to Seaford as soon as we hear from Ollie Arnold."

Carey nodded. " 'Tis very important."

He joined Lady Abelard. Francesca went to Estrella, but her gaze kept straying to Carey's tall form. His face was once again set in a mask of taut indifference, and she sensed the animosity that flowed between the two men. Could it really be that Carey was jealous of Giorgio D'Angelo? A shiver of doubt traveled through her.

Carey watched as D'Angelo led the two ladies around the pond toward the carriage. His heart ached as he followed Francesca's slim, graceful body. Her hips swayed invitingly, and her back was straight, her slender neck vulnerable, made for a trail of passionate kisses.

"You're lost in an illusion, my love," Daphne said. Her tinny voice dispelled his mood, and he glanced at her with irritation.

"I still don't understand why you begged to see me, Daphne."

She pouted. "You sound so hard, and—well, cold. I haven't seen you since we separated. Have you already forgotten what we had?"

" 'Tis over, Daphne. Our affair ended the moment you turned your back on me. I thought you were a fine, trustworthy woman, but you showed your true nature. I'll never return to you, and now I'm glad that you left me before it was too late." He gripped her shoulders hard. "You're fickle and thoughtless. Don't try to tell me you'll change, because you won't, not ever. When I thought that the love we shared was rich and sacred and untouchable," he continued, "you left me for Abelard. You will never understand true commitment. I adored you once, but you ruined our love. Thank God the war helped me overcome my feelings for you. There's nothing left."

She leaned into him. "I still want you," she whispered. Her eyes were molten, but all Carey could feel was disgust. He had been foolish, but he had learned from his mistake. His love for Daphne had almost killed him. He was free now, and the knowledge filled him with elation.

Daphne's eyes were the most vulnerable, the most beseeching he'd ever seen them. But no one knew better than she how to use them to her own advantage.

"I don't love you, Daphne. And don't run to me again the next time you have marital problems. You chose Abelard, and now you must learn to live with him, even if he mistreats you." He moved away from her, indicating her carriage. "You'd better leave now."

She clutched his arm. "You were a wonderful lover, Carey. I need you."

He clenched his jaw so hard that he thought it was going to snap. "I don't want to see you again." She was using all her tricks, but this time he'd be strong enough to withstand her. It was the mistake of his life to have become involved with her. God only knows how she'd convinced Abelard that she was a virgin when he came to her on their wedding night . . . Carey shuddered. He had escaped by a tight margin. And he was never going to fall for any woman as witlessly as he'd fallen for Daphne.

He made sure that she entered the carriage, then he slammed the door. "Good-bye, Daphne."

He heard her sharp gasp as he swung around and stalked away. He walked fast, until his pulse pounded. A good pace always cleared his mind. The shadows were lengthening, and darkness would soon fall. The lanes grew empty as a few carriages rumbled past him toward the gates. The park was lovely in the blue summer dusk, and birds sent out intermittent trills. He thought that he really should have brought his horse, however. The park was not safe at night.

He glimpsed the tall gates at the south corner of the park just as a shot exploded in his ears.

Chapter 10

❦❦

"W hat—?" Carey instinctively threw himself to the ground as another shot followed. Something seared his skin above his left ear
and excruciating pain spread across his face and
down his neck. Footsteps pounded past him, and a
dark shadow flickered among the trees.

"Blast!" Carey hoisted himself to his knees. Pushing his fingers against the hard soil, he tried to stand.
The pain made him dizzy, but he ran through the
trees after the figure. He touched his head, and his
fingers came away sticky and wet. The scoundrel
had nicked him! A hairbreadth deeper and he would
have been dead.

Carey peered through the trees where the would-
be assassin had disappeared, but nothing stirred.
Was someone even now waiting for him behind a
tree? He proceeded with more caution. Who wants
to take my life? he wondered desperately. Thieves
hungry for his purse? He doubted it. Robbers usually resorted to clubs and cudgels, not pistols, to incapacitate their victims. "Who?" he groaned aloud,
and pressed his handkerchief against the wound that
was slowly draining his strength. He could not go
on pursuing the villain, who would surely be long
gone by now. Stumbling forward, Carey saw
through the trees orange-yellow torches on either

side of a tavern door. The sounds of conversation
and laughter came from within. Perhaps he could
rent a horse to take him home.

Just as he was about to enter, he saw a farmer
with a wagon who was setting out toward the
Strand. "Where are you going?" Carey called out.
His wound ached more every passing moment.

"Down th' Strand, then 'Aymarket and Long
Acre," came the cheerful reply. "Ye look like ye 'ad
one too many. Want an escort 'ome?"

Carey nodded and climbed into the cart with difficulty. His eyesight was blurring. He thought about
Francesca and yearned to see her. "I would be grateful if you'd take me to Covent Garden."

"Aye, that I will." The farmer smacked his lips at
the horses. "Saw th' 'anging at Tyburn Fields. A
sight 'twas; fifteen prisoners from Newgate kicked
at the end of the rope . . . Were ye there? Seems
that all o' Lunnon was there."

Carey shook his head. Who had delivered the
shot? Was someone afraid of him because of what
he had witnessed at Seaford? As far as Carey knew,
he had no enemies—at least no one who hated him
enough to seek his death. Perhaps Lucas Halden . . .
The pain intensified, shattering his concentration.
He needed to see Francesca. If this attack was connected to the crime in Seaford, she might be in
danger too.

"I'm delighted that you accepted my dinner invitation, Francesca," Estrella exclaimed. "That's the
least we can do to repay you for your delightful
company today."

"I hadn't made other plans. Later tonight I have
to work." Francesca climbed down from the carriage
and studied the D'Angelo residence in Haymarket.
The last rays of evening sunlight bathed the roofs
and the half-timbered walls in a rosy glow. The

premises were built around a courtyard. At the back
was the goldsmith workshop, and at the front was
the shop, with its wooden sign suspended from a
black iron rod in the wall above the door.

"D'Angelo, Goldsmith," Francesca read aloud.
The words *Fine Gemstones* were etched underneath,
next to a painted picture of a brilliant-cut diamond.

"Yes, I'm proud of that sign," Giorgio said. He
stood beside her. "As I would be proud to add you
to my staff."

"Perhaps." Thoughtful, Francesca moved toward
the stairs leading to the living quarters above the
shop. Had it been a mistake to accept Estrella's dinner invitation so impulsively? She barely knew these
people. Estrella had pleaded until Francesca had
given in. Still, a fine dinner was a treat to someone
who had to count every penny, Francesca mused.
The Italian woman was ahead of her on the stairs,
her step light and excited.

As Francesca followed, she had a view of the
street. It was tolerably clear of refuse, and the cob-
bled yard was swept scrupulously clean. A guard sat
in the guardhouse outside the shop entrance with
his pole leaning against the wall. Due to rampant
crime, store-owners hired guards to screen all visitors.

"What a lovely fireplace," Francesca remarked as
she entered the parlor. It had an old wooden mantelpiece with clusters of fruit and a garland of leaves
carved into the front. A small fire crackled in the
grate to ward off the dampness. The windows had
tiny diamond-shaped panes. The walls were white-
washed, and the furniture looked new and somehow impersonal. Perhaps it was the lack of
knickknacks that gave the room a barren look. An
embroidery frame was set up by the window, displaying a half-finished motif of flowers in a basket.

"I see you've found my sewing. I'm making a fire

screen," Estrella explained, touching the canvas. "At night, when I sit and wait for Giorgio to return home, I embroider." She went to take Francesca's cape, but Giorgio was there first. His hands lingered longer than was necessary on Francesca's shoulders.

"Do you like to embroider?" Estrella continued, leading the way through an arched doorway to the dining room. She pulled a bell cord.

"Yes, as a matter of fact I do. I sewed cushions and chair covers at my former home," Francesca said, stepping away from Giorgio. He gave her a long, veiled glance and went to a tray hidden behind a glass-fronted cabinet door.

"A glass of wine?" he asked. Without waiting for her answer, he poured three glasses of burgundy. He beckoned Francesca toward the table, as Estrella spoke to a servant standing just inside the doorway.

"I have ordered an extra plate. Dinner will be ready in twenty minutes," she said, brushing crumbs off the tablecloth. She flashed a smile to her brother and accepted the glass he gave her. "Shall we show Francesca the empty rooms before dinner?"

"Very well, if she's interested in seeing them." Giorgio crossed the room and held out another glass to Francesca. "We promised this morning not to pressure our guest. 'Tis a great pleasure that she will dine with us this evening. You should be content with that, Estrella."

"I don't mind at all," Francesca interrupted. "If you would like to show me the chambers, by all means . . ."

Estrella's smile was almost as brilliant as her brother's. "They are waiting for you, dear Francesca. Once you see them, you won't be able to refuse our offer."

Holding her wineglass, Francesca followed the pair. Her heartbeat quickened with anticipation.

Perhaps this really was the opportunity she had been looking for, her chance to escape from Letty Rose's establishment.

Narrow steps wound to a dark landing above. The humble door under the eaves creaked alarmingly. It was almost dark outside, the windows black rectangles against the sky. Estrella lit candles on an old table. The third-floor lodgings consisted of two small rooms, unfurnished except for a table and a four-poster bed. At least it was clean and the paint was almost fresh, Francesca noticed. The floor planks were scrubbed and smooth. A fireplace with a mantelpiece of simple design took up most of one wall. It had an iron grate and a hob.

"This is the parlor, and you could use the other room as a bedroom," Estrella explained. "I'll help you with the curtains, and we could hang draperies in this arched doorway."

Francesca did not reply. She went to the inner room and inspected the cupboards built into the wall. The drawers were clean and lined with new paper.

"I did that myself," Estrella said proudly. "There's space aplenty for all your things."

Francesca nodded thoughtfully and walked to the window. It had the same type of diamond-shaped panes that distorted the view of the street below. However, she could see the dark sky and the tall narrow building across the street that housed a tavern. She remembered Carey's warning about Giorgio. Would he increase his advances if she moved in?

"Well?" Estrella prodded.

"I don't know . . . this has all been so sudden. This is very comfortable, but I will have to think about it."

Francesca could have sworn that both Estrella and Giorgio let out their breaths slowly, as if each had been holding it. Why were they so intent on her having the rooms? Were they in such dire need for help in their shop? Or was Estrella simply lonely and in need of female company? She was kind, but she seemed rather spoiled, eager to have her own way. "I'm very grateful for your offer."

Estrella wound her arm through Francesca's and pulled her toward the door. "I'm glad I could show it to you tonight. We would consider the rent as part of your wages. You don't have to pay us a penny, and we would give you slightly lower wages—since we're struggling to establish our business."

"Yes, that would suit me well," Francesca mused aloud. Rent free. She didn't need much—a bed to sleep in at night, two meals, work. Freedom.

"And you would take your breakfast and dinner with us, of course. You can make tea in a kettle on the hob up here, but hardly much more."

Francesca smiled at Estrella. "Your offer is irresistible, but please give me a few more days to consider it."

Estrella's smile flashed in the candlelight. "Of course. But I know you'll accept."

Francesca smiled wryly. "You may be right."

Dinner consisted of three courses: fish soup, boiled chicken and beans, and roasted rump of beef with green peas. Francesca tasted everything, delighting in the crisp flavor of the vegetables and creamy gravy. The dessert waiting on the sideboard was strawberry cream and assorted cakes. "You have an excellent cook," she said between bites.

"English-bred. We could offer you Italian fare, but in England we live and eat like the English, except that we use more spices," Giorgio explained.

"Don't you miss the Italian air, the sunshine?"

Giorgio and Estrella exchanged glances. "When it rains for several days in a row, I do long to return to Rome," Giorgio said and patted his lips with his napkin. "But I'm rapidly growing accustomed to life in London. A business has every opportunity to succeed here."

"I'm surprised you would offer me a position of such importance when you could hire a full-fledged goldsmith to design your jewelry." Francesca glanced from Estrella to Giorgio. "Your offer is rather unusual."

"We have two apprentices besides Mr. Preston, the journeyman," Giorgio said. "Estrella needs a female companion more than anything, but since you have experience in the jewelry business, we thought—"

"We thought you might be bored acting solely as my companion," Estrella broke in. "I know I would be. But I look forward to visiting the dressmakers and milliners with you."

"You don't have to employ me for that. I'd accompany you anyway." Francesca tasted the green beans. They were crisp and full of flavor. "Tell me, what is Italy like? I have never been there."

Estrella started talking as she speared peas on her fork. " 'Tis hot and dry in the summer. The air is sharp, full of the spicy scent of flowers and animals. The roads are always dusty, and the grass dry and rough, not green and carpet-soft as here in England. Umbrella pines, cypresses, and olive trees grow in abundance. Not to mention almond—"

"Don't bore our guest," Giorgio admonished his sister with poorly concealed anger. He smiled at Francesca. "You see, Estrella longs for Italy more than I do. She often speaks of the old days."

"Does the rest of your family live there?"

An uneasy silence fell, and Francesca wondered if she'd been rude. Foreigners had a different code of etiquette than the English.

"We came here because our father died a year ago.

We have two older brothers who live off the land that belonged to our father," Giorgio said.

"I'm sorry, I had no right—" Francesca began.

" 'Tis all in the past. I'm the youngest," Estrella said. "Giorgio and I are close. Our brothers are much older. They have their own families, and there isn't enough land to feed us all."

"That's how I got interested in the jewelry business," Giorgio added. "A man has to make his own way in this world. I have never shunned hard work. In fact, I like a challenge."

Francesca could not help but admire her two new friends. "Your courage is great. It must have been difficult to pull up roots and begin a new life."

Giorgio reached across the table and touched Francesca's hand lightly. "You're facing the same problem yourself."

"I'm not starting anew in a foreign country." Somehow her words sounded so serious that they all laughed.

Giorgio's eyes caressed her as he refilled her wineglass. "Perhaps I'll have the chance to show you Italy one day. I hope so."

The memory of Leonard's terrible death flashed in Francesca's mind. They would have been in Italy now if it hadn't been for the murders. Francesca shivered and closed her eyes momentarily. Yet she did not miss Leonard. Her relief to be rid of him only added to her guilt. Perhaps she would never be quite free from guilt, but she would not repeat her mistake and become the chattel of a man. She would be in control of her life. She would create a world in which she could be happy.

Carey's face suddenly appeared before her. When she had planned her life, a life without romantic entanglement, she had not counted on meeting Carey.

She finished her wine and dessert. The wine was going to her head, and she saw a rosy glow around the man at the head of the table, the sister at the other end. They were both looking at her intently.

" 'Tis late. I think I should return to the Crimson Rooms."

"We should have a cup of tea first," Estrella said.

Francesca glanced at the clock on the mantelpiece. It chimed nine times. "No, I'm sorry, but I'll be late if I don't leave now." Suddenly she longed to be alone to think about everything that had happened that day. Would Carey come to the gambling salon? She longed to see him. There were so many unspoken words between them, and so many unexplored feelings.

Giorgio tossed his napkin on the table. "I will escort you."

Francesca wanted to protest, but she recalled the time she had first met Giorgio, the night the villains had threatened her life. "You're very kind to protect me."

" 'Twould be a shame if I didn't." He smiled and fetched her cape. The D'Angelo household had only one servant beside the cook, a quiet, sullen young girl who came in and began stacking the plates.

Giorgio placed the cape over Francesca's shoulders as carefully as if she were made of Dresden china. "There." He handed her her gloves.

"I hope that the next time I see you, you'll tell me you've accepted our offer," Estrella said, gripping Francesca's hands.

As soon as Giorgio's carriage reached the Crimson Rooms, Francesca jumped down. "I'm going to be late, and Letty Rose will be angry." She was supposed to start working in fifteen minutes. Smiling, she said, "Thank you for a wonderful dinner."

He alighted and took her hand. After planting a kiss on her fingers, he said, "I will eagerly await your decision. Estrella and I are convinced you'd be happier working for us."

"I'm sure you're right." He watched as she climbed the steps, and she turned and waved.

Cauliflower Arnold was in the doorway, scowling. "Is 'e molestin' ye, Miss Francie?" he asked, and flexed his hands.

"Not at all. Mr. D'Angelo kindly escorted me home."

Cauliflower Arnold rumbled something ominous. Then in a louder voice, he said, "I must warn ye, sum'un is 'ere—"

But Francesca had already sped up the stairs. At the bottom of the steps leading to her chamber she halted in surprise.

Carey was leaning against the balustrade, his face pale. "Francesca . . . ?" His voice was deep with worry and pain. He was holding a bloody handkerchief against his head.

Francesca's heart almost stopped with shock. Her mouth went dry as she rushed up to him. "Oh, my Lord—what happened?"

Carey glared at her. "What was the Italian doing here, and where have you been?" he spat out, his jaw clenched in anger. "I saw you from the window."

"Is this the Inquisition?" Faint with alarm, Francesca looked at the blood-soaked cloth and gingerly touched his hand. "Let me take care of that wound."

Carey's knuckles were white on the rail. "I thought something had happened to you. I was so worried . . ."

His tension made Francesca knot up inside, and she fretted about his wound. He looked so weary and out of temper.

He slanted her a quicksilver glance, and she lowered her gaze. "What did D'Angelo want?"

She was too weary to cope with his jealousy. "If

you don't want to treat your injury, I'm going to change," she said angrily, and darted upstairs.

Carey caught up with her outside the door to her room. The landing was dark and the boards creaked under his rapid steps. She hurried inside and whirled around when he followed her.

"I have to talk to you," he snapped.

"You are in a terrible mood, and I have done nothing to deserve your anger."

"I was shot this evening," he muttered.

"Shot?" Her legs seemed to lose their strength, and she sank down on the edge of the bed. A candle glowed in the holder on the nightstand. The blanket and sheets were rumpled, as if someone had slept in her bed. Her room had been tidy when she went for the drive in the park with the D'Angelos.

"I waited for you all evening," Carey said, sitting down beside her.

"Here? You should have asked Letty Rose for help." She touched his hair, which was matted at the edge of the wound. "What happened?" Her hands trembled as she brushed aside his hair and tied it back at his neck with a ribbon she found on the nightstand. She fetched the candle and held it near his wound. The shot had grazed his skin right above the ear. Blood still oozed from the cut. She touched his taut shoulder. "This needs to be cleaned and bandaged."

He did not resist when she pushed him back against the pillows and heaved his legs onto the mattress. She sensed that his tension stemmed as much from mental strain as from the wound. "I got a ride from the park with a farmer since I left my horse at my lodgings—at number four St. James's Street."

She dipped a clean towel in a washbasin filled with fresh water. As she returned to the bed, she could feel his gaze following her, but when she reached him, he had thrown his arm over his eyes. She gently lifted it aside and began bathing his wound. He was still, as if deep in thought.

"Go on," she urged.

"As I reached the gates, someone fired two shots at me. I was dazed, and the villain got away before I got my bearing." He sighed. "All I could think of was you—of the need to protect you." His eyes were dark and restless, his skin tight over his cheekbones. "I feared you might be in danger. We don't know who shot your husband, or why. Perhaps they aim to kill you, and me for witnessing the murders." He groaned in frustration. "We know absolutely nothing about their plans. We have to solve this mystery as soon as possible, or we might go the same way as your husband."

Dread stiffened her movements, and she struggled to suppress the horror that threatened to suck her into its black vortex. "We must return to Seaford immediately. I'll ask Letty Rose—"

"No! You must not work here any longer," he protested. " 'Tis too public a place. Anyone could assault you here—" He gripped her hand to silence the protest on her lips. "I know you think I meddle too much in your life, but remember that I promised to help and protect you until the mystery is solved." He pressed a kiss on her knuckles and ran his thumb across them. "Don't reject my help."

Francesca set the towel on the nightstand and placed a folded handkerchief against his wound. "Hold this," she ordered, and tore a strip of dry towel to wrap around his head. "What shall we do?"

"While you were gone, Cauliflower Arnold received word from his cousin. We're to meet Ollie Arnold and his men the day after tomorrow at the tavern outside Seaford. I sent word to Hitchins. My carriage will be here at dawn. You'd better be ready by then. My valet will pack my valise and put it in the carriage."

"So we're returning to Seaford at daybreak?" she asked. Foreboding gripped her at the thought of meeting the gang of highwaymen.

"Yes, if you agree."

"Of course." Francesca adjusted the white strip around his head.

His dark gaze searched her face. "What about the Italians you've befriended? Are they trustworthy?"

She hesitated. "They are kind. I haven't told them the whole sordid story, of course."

Carey moved restlessly on the bed. "I don't trust the man."

"Are you saying my judgment is poor?" Anger flared in her. "Beyond dealing with our shared problem, you have no right to control my life."

He scowled. "I'm learning fast that, besides being kind and beautiful, you're also stubborn."

"I don't want to discuss Giorgio D'Angelo with you, and that's final. I abhor your jealous outbursts." She folded her few garments, a shift, a petticoat, an overdress of peacock-blue satin—the one she had worn on that horrifying day in Seaford—and heaped them on a chair. Tying a towel around the bundle, she had soon finished her packing. "I'm ready to travel."

Carey's eyes glowed with sudden warmth. "I'm grateful. You don't lack for courage."

Francesca felt her insides melt. "Neither do you."

"Come here and lean your head on my shoulder. I'll behave, I promise. We need all the rest we can get. Who knows when we'll sleep next."

"Your wound must be painful," she said.

"Yes . . ." he said sleepily.

She eased gingerly onto the mattress next to him. "I'll stay here for a while, then I must work." Fully dressed, they lay in silence under the blanket. Francesca curled up close to Carey, her head fitting perfectly in the hollow of his shoulder. He smelled of sandalwood and, due to the wound, of gunpowder. An irresistible urge to touch him came over her, to run her fingertips along his lean cheek, his hard jawline, then farther down . . . over his chest, down to his flat stomach.

She drew in her breath sharply. If they made love, their friendship would be over. He would change, might even turn into a tyrant, like Leonard. His feelings toward her would evaporate. He would tell her what to do, how to dress, how to talk, even how to sleep. He would think that if she gave herself intimately, she would be his possession. And she *would* be.

Dismayed, Francesca eased away from his shoulder, her head landing on the hard bicep of his left arm. He didn't deter her, and she hesitated. No matter how far away she moved, she was still under his spell.

Of its own volition, her hand traced the hard outline of his jaw, explored the cleft in his chin, and touched his strong neck. Her heart raced as she moved lower, her fingertips sliding over the battered jabot and finding his shirt open at the neck. She swallowed convulsively as she skimmed over the honed muscles of his chest.

A sweet yearning stole through her, and in its wake came a pounding desire. She wanted him with such intensity that it frightened her. She hated the thought of becoming dependent on any man, but with Carey . . . she felt shameless . . .

Her roving hand encountered his rapid heartbeat, but it wasn't nearly as rapid as her own. What did he feel? She peered at him through the gloom, but all she could discern was his dark profile. He lay so still.

She stifled an urge to explore further and lay quiet,

listening to his breathing. Then his arms stole around her and he held her close. "Go to work, Francesca, or I might ravish you right now," he said thickly.

She blushed. After a few minutes his grip slackened, and she realized he had fallen asleep.

Carey dreamed about Francesca. He felt a vague pulsing ache in his body that seemed to concentrate in his loins. He imagined what it would be like to touch her silky, naked flesh . . . to kiss her . . . to explore her secrets . . . He clenched his jaw, swallowing a groan.

For a moment, he stirred and opened his eyes, realizing that the tightness in his groin was real. Sweet curves were pressing against his body, but he couldn't quite reach out and touch the round, soft limbs. A millstone weighed down his head, and pain thundered above his ear. Defeated, he gave a great sigh, wishing he had the strength to caress the beauty beside him. *Francesca* . . .

Chapter 11

Although it was barely light outside the follow-ing morning, heavy wagons and drays were pulling into Covent Garden from the countryside. The vegetable and fruit trade was the best during the early morning hours.

Standing outside the Crimson Rooms, Francesca rubbed her tired eyes and viewed the procession of early traders. On the other side of the square, torches shone on the walls of gin shops, and two men lurched outside, singing at the top of their lungs.

"There's the carriage," Carey said and waved at Hitchins. "Cauliflower Arnold is late."

The doorman would accompany them to intro-duce them to his cousin.

The steel-banded wheels rattled over the cobble-stones, and the horses snorted as the driver pulled in the reins. Carey waved a greeting, his cocked hat pressed low over his head to conceal his bandage from curious eyes. He looked handsome in a dark-gray silk cloak, his hair brushed back over the stand-fall collar.

Francesca noticed that the carriage was different from the one Carey had driven to the park. This one was a covered chaise with leather curtains at the windows.

The coachman jumped down from the driver's seat. "Who are you?" Carey asked suspiciously.

"Caleb 'Itchins took sick last night," the man replied sullenly. "I'm 'is brother. I'll drive ye wherever ye need t' go."

"I didn't know Hitchins had a brother." Carey walked around the two horses and the coach. The lanterns on either side of the door gleamed dully. "What experience do you have? Are you employed elsewhere?" Carey caressed the noble head of one of the two black steeds.

"Worked for Lord Rowhill, I did, 'ntil I took sick. Now I'm lookin' for employment. Caleb said ye might 'ave use fer me. I'm a bruiser with 'orses."

Francesca glanced at the driver, a squat, bow-legged man with a full-length cloak and a three-cornered hat in his hand. His appearance was shabby in the cool, gray light, his face ruddy and plump, his brown hair tied back with a wilted velvet bow.

"What's your name?" Carey asked.

"Abel 'Itchins."

"Well, Hitchins, I suppose I have no choice but to trust you with my horses this time." Carey sighed. "This is a dashed nuisance. What happened to Caleb?"

"Got the ague, 'e did." Abel Hitchins shifted his hat from one hand to the other. "I'll serve ye well until Caleb is fit, Mr. McLendon."

Carey nodded curtly and held out his hand toward Francesca. "Come. We have no time to lose."

He helped her climb in, then waited while the coachman lifted her bundle inside. Arnold came running down the steps, a valise in his hand. "Sorry, guv, but Letty Rose complained sumthin' arful at me leavin'."

Carey smiled. "But that didn't stop you."

"Naw. 'Avta 'elp Miss Francie outta 'er problems. More important than Letty's conniptions."

Francesca beckoned to him, and the coach shuddered as he entered. "Thank you," she said, and kissed him on his unshaven cheek.

The giant man blushed and cleared his throat. He threw a guilty glance at Carey, who only shrugged and chuckled. "Where's Hitchins?" Arnold asked as he laid eyes on the driver.

"He has taken sick. Do you miss him?" Carey asked with a teasing grin.

"O' course not! Thinks 'e knows summat 'bout 'orses. A true braggart—"

"Where to?" Abel Hitchins asked before closing the door.

"Seaford in East Sussex." Carey jumped up and sank down on the seat next to Francesca. He leaned back and closed his hand over hers. "Are you tired?"

She nodded. "But I'm glad we're making this sad journey. We'll be one step closer to the solution."

He lifted her hand to his lips and blew lightly on her tense fingers. "I'll be there to support you, as will Arnold."

"I know." She watched Carey's sharp profile until he turned his head. His gray eyes were dark slate in the hazy dawn light. He looked different this morning. Perhaps the pain had changed him. His hard face had softened, and his eyes were shadowy, somber . . . searching.

"I slept poorly last night," he said, his voice gruff.

"So did I," She sighed, wishing she could fully understand this enigmatic man who was hard as rock, yet vulnerable underneath.

"Were you uncomfortable beside me?" His breath swept over her knuckles again before he enclosed her much smaller hand in both his own.

"No . . . I thought about us," she whispered.

He whipped his head around and searched her face. "What was the nature of those thoughts?" He spoke so softly she could barely hear the words.

Francesca blushed. How could she explain what his closeness did to her? How could she describe the exhilaration, the danger she felt, and the . . . fear? "Your question is very intimate."

"My thoughts about you were intimate."

"I suppose that was inevitable," Francesca said. "I find you very desirable. I'm not ashamed to confess that fact."

His face lit up with a grin. "Such a compliment from your lips is pure sweetness." Swinging an arm around her shoulders, he pulled her closer. "I admit, all I could think about last night was kissing you."

"That would ruin our pact." Francesca trembled with longing for his kiss. His bold glance invited her, and she yearned to touch the slight indentation on his square chin. Yet with Cauliflower Arnold in attendance . . .

Carey's sigh was audible. "It wouldn't be the first time. At any rate, I brought this pact upon us, and I can undo it."

Francesca lowered her gaze. "We'd better keep it. I don't want to lose your friendship. Still, as my ally, there's no need for you to make my decisions for me—as you did when paying Letty Rose."

He sucked in his breath sharply. "Yes, you're right. Of course." His grip on her hand loosened and his face took on a closed look. "Suspicious of my motives to the end."

"Only honest," she retorted.

As the carriage left the clutter of buildings forming the city center, the sun rose over the horizon. A light fog hovered along the streets, and the sunlight shone ghostlike through the haze.

"How's your wound?" she asked.

"A bit sore, I suppose, but I'll live."

"You should rest."

He nodded, pulled his hat deeper over his face, and leaned back into the corner. "Wake me at dinnertime."

For the next hour Francesca thought about her future and the work the Italians had offered her. When she returned from Seaford, she would accept their offer. Employment in their shop would make her free—allow her to live her own life. Carey would argue against her decision, but he would have to learn that she was capable of sound judgment. She wanted Carey's love, but not if it entailed giving up her freedom. Carey wasn't a tyrant like Kane, and he never would be. Still, she needed time to discover herself, her real feelings, her own thoughts, before she committed herself to Carey . . . and to allow lovemaking would be to commit . . .

Leaning her head against the corner, Francesca slept. She didn't awaken until Cauliflower Arnold opened the carriage door and stuck his head inside. The coach had stopped.

"It be time for a meal," Arnold said. "The sun is 'igh in th' sky."

The carriage had stopped at the Blue Hen Inn at Burgess Hill. It was comfortable, if somewhat rustic with its rough plank floors and stout ceiling beams.

Carey stretched and yawned. He glanced at the sky. "Since we won't see Ollie Arnold until tomorrow night, we might as well break the journey here," he said. "That way we'll be rested when we arrive in Seaford. What do you think?"

Francesca had nothing against the scheme, although they could easily reach the coast before dark. She suspected that Carey was exhausted with pain. To fully appreciate the fresh country air and open fields, they had traveled slowly through Sussex—so different from the crowded London streets.

In the late afternoon, after enjoying a leisurely tea, they took a walk along the dusty lane. Cauliflower Arnold was sleeping heavily under a tree in the yard. The sky was overcast, and thunderclouds loomed on the horizon.

"Sussex is beautiful," Francesca said with a sigh. "The hills are like a sea of rolling green waves."

Carey chuckled. "The Downs are lovely—but a rolling sea? I don't know."

Francesca frowned. "You have no poetry in your soul."

"The gods passed me by in that regard," Carey said matter-of-factly. "But I have a wealth of other talents." His eyes gleamed with amusement. "I haven't shown you anything yet."

"I'm sure of it," Francesca said drily. "Even though I've seen a great deal of you lately, you're still a stranger."

He stepped closer to her and placed his arms firmly around her shoulders. "Regretting our friendship?"

She shook her head. "I wish I knew more about you. You keep everything to yourself."

He shrugged. "That way no one can take my secrets and use them against me."

She regarded him earnestly, eager to penetrate his defenses. "Why would anyone want to hurt you? I can't imagine why you have enemies who would shoot at you."

He pondered her words at length. " 'Tis difficult to say. Besides the murderer at Seaford, someone else might have taken a shot at me."

"Who?"

"Lucas Halden holds a grudge against me because I accused him of cheating, and there is always a chance someone has found out that I participated in the Stuart rebellion."

The lane turned sharply to the east and the thick

hedge bordering it gave way to a long shadowed drive. At the end of the drive, surrounded with tall elms, stood a two-story brick house. The double oak door was framed by two white Dorian pillars, and on every stone step bloomed red flowers in marble urns.

Carey whistled between his teeth. "Isn't it lovely? A small country manor surrounded with peace and birdsong. I would like to live here someday."

"Perhaps it's dark and gloomy inside and riddled with dry rot."

He smiled wryly. "Are you trying to ruin my dream?"

Francesca laughed. "No, I'm merely teasing you."

His gaze was drawn once more to the idyllic place. "It must be lovely inside. The outside is immaculate—the drive is raked, and the flower borders weeded."

"Yes. 'Tis lovely." Francesca peered at the closed windows. Curtains were drawn across the panes, barring any snooping. "Shall we step inside the gate?"

He looked incredulous. "Have you lost your mind? They'll set a pack of vicious dogs on us before we can blink."

Francesca felt reckless, and she wanted to see the garden. "I don't think anyone is home. On a warm day like this, the windows would be open, and we would hear voices."

"A caretaker is bound to be here."

Francesca pushed him lightly. "Where's your sense of adventure?"

"Are you challenging me?" He was fighting a smile.

She nodded vigorously and tried the handle on the gate. It opened. "We're fortunate." Slipping inside, she added, "I wonder who lives here."

"A young family with five children," Carey suggested.

"No, an elderly woman with a deaf companion and a bully for a housekeeper." She skirted a box hedge and turned away from the drive, Carey close behind her. He chuckled softly.

A narrow path led through the trees. A luxurious green lawn spread beyond the trees, and a white-painted folly stood surrounded with blooming honeysuckle. Formal borders and fountains created a haven of peace behind the house.

"An old curmudgeon with a clubfoot and a blind and mute servant live here. He also has a pet monkey," Carey improvised.

Francesca held her hand to her mouth to suppress a giggle. "The old curmudgeon has killed his hump-backed wife and buried her in the cellar. The servant knows the truth and is using it to blackmail the old man."

"How would the servant divulge the secret to the world if he's mute?" Carey said very close to her ear.

She whirled around, and he collided with her. "He could write it down."

Thunder rumbled above their heads, and the foliage concealing them from curious eyes rustled softly. He caught her in his arms and pressed her against his chest.

"Most likely some young lovesick fool lives here," he whispered into her hair.

She looked up into his eyes. They glowed dark with desire, and there was a faint sheen of perspiration on his brow. His skin seemed to be on fire, and his heart pounded heavily against her chest. His hair was unruly and she pushed it back, an involuntary gesture filled with tenderness. "A fool?" she whispered.

Before she could protest, he had possessed her

mouth. A sweet intoxication swept through her, clearing away any protest, robbing all coherent thought from her mind. His tongue was rough and passionate in her mouth, and strangely fulfilling. It was as if by their kiss an invisible cord had been tied between their hearts and a deep longing had been assuaged.

Breathless, Carey trailed rapid kisses across her cheek to the tender spot beneath her ear. She shivered with pleasure, and a molten sensation flowed under her skin. His breath was harsh as he branded her on the collarbone and down her neck. His fingers were hard around her shoulders, and she could not move. When she opened her eyes, the leafy dome above them swirled madly. His tongue probed the cleft between her breasts, and a tickling sensation filled her abdomen, spreading into a glow of warmth and deep yearning. How easily she forgot her determination to abide by their pact of friendship . . .

He pulled away slowly, easing his tense grip. ''You're so beautiful, Francesca. I could not help myself. God knows I wanted to kiss you. Every time I look at you, I long to sweep you into my arms.'' A guilty smile crept over his face and a tinge of red colored his cheeks. ''I'm too weak to resist your allure,'' he murmured. ''When I'm alone with you I forget myself, and all I want to do is relax against your bosom and smell your sweet scent.''

She sighed in wonder. ''I didn't resist, did I?''

He groaned and lay his face against her breasts. Her nipples grew taut with desire, pressing against him through her simple gown. She blushed and closed her eyes, waiting for his forceful caress, but he didn't move. He nuzzled her neck, still holding her close, so close that she could barely breathe. His arms encircled her as if he would never let her go, and his breath was hot and tantalizing on her skin.

Slowly she wound her arms around his neck and played with the curls at the nape. He had removed the bandage at the inn; the dark shiny hair hung in a thick wave across his eye, and the glossy strands flowed through her fingers. His shoulder muscles then tightened under her arms as he lifted her high and twirled her around and around until she was quite dizzy.

"I don't ever want to hurt you, my darling," he said, his voice hoarse with emotion. "Again and again, I forget our pact."

Francesca's blush deepened. "I've noticed," she said wryly. "But half of the blame is mine."

He set her down and captured her hands. Silent, he led her along the path until they reached the edge of the trees. A small pond lay at their feet, surrounded by half-grown cattails. The pond was hidden from the house by an ancient yew tree with a wide gnarled trunk. He pulled her down to sit beside him on the soft, cool grass. A green frog leaped from a reed into the water.

"Before I met you, I dallied with the ladies, but no one captured my heart—except Daphne." He thoughtfully traced a vein on the back of her hand. "I think it's time I told you about her." He face was somber.

"Lady Abelard?" Francesca felt a twinge of apprehension. She wasn't sure she wanted to hear about Daphne.

"Two years ago I met Lady Daphne, the daughter of the Earl of Dewthorne, a celebrated beauty, and destined to marry a duke, or at least a marquess." He took a deep breath. "One day I saved her from two bullies in an alley when she'd visited the milliners. When she smiled in gratitude, I thought I'd met an angel."

"Yes, she's very lovely."

"She's beautiful. I fell instantly in love with her,

and she claimed that she loved me. We invented ways to meet late in the night. Yes, she even came to my lodgings. Had her father known of her escapades, he would have killed me and locked her in her room.'' He sighed and tore out a blade of grass at the roots. ''We were deeply in love—in every sense. She was very young and innocent, but she never hesitated to give herself to me. Not only did her body enchant me, I truly cared about her.''

He gripped Francesca's hand convulsively and looked at her intently. His brow was furrowed. ''I had never loved a woman before I met her.''

''You wanted to marry her, didn't you?'' she queried softly.

He nodded. ''I asked her to become my wife, and she said yes.'' He threw his head back as if suffering a stab of pain. ''You should have seen her face; it was radiant. I was quite dissolved with happiness.''

Francesca stiffened at his revelations, hating his every word. She envied Daphne for ever pleasuring the man whom she herself desired. ''Why are you telling me this—each painful detail?'' she demanded, pulling away her hand.

''Because I want you to know that I don't take love lightly. I want to give my all, or—nothing.''

''What happened with Daphne?''

''Since she was not of age, I wanted to do the honorable thing and ask her father for her hand. He rejected my offer outright. He was incensed at my—gall he called it. An adventurer and a bastard he called me, and he was right, since I had nothing but my love to offer Daphne.'' He laughed harshly. ''She agreed to elope with me to Scotland. The following night, I came to the back door in the wall that surrounds her parents' house and waited as we had planned. That's when I got this scar.'' He pulled away his waistcoat and shirt and exposed an old white scar on his shoulder. ''Daphne had a new admirer—Lord Abelard. We dueled with swords, and I got this wound on my shoulder, and a shattered heart." His voice lowered so that she could barely hear him. "Daphne came out and told me to leave. She claimed that my love stifled her. She begged my forgiveness, but I couldn't pardon her actions. I was—more than disappointed. It took my involvement with the Stuart rebellion to show me that my sorrow was nothing compared to the despair the Scots suffered. In any event, the morning after the sword fight, I read in the paper that Daphne was betrothed to Lord Abelard."

"He's so much older."

Carey nodded. "Yes, it was a match set up by Daphne's father. When I later approached Daphne and asked her why she had left me for Abelard, she said she'd been too young to settle down with me. She cried and said she regretted her rash decision." He paused, an expression of disgust on his face. "She never really loved me, and I'm glad I found out before it was too late."

Francesca could scarcely breathe for the tension in the air. The storm was building. Thunder crashed above, closer with every passing minute, but she was unable to move. Her gaze was riveted to Carey, each fiber of her being soaking up every nuance of emotion on his face. At that moment, she realized that she loved him wildly, overwhelmingly.

She stood up abruptly. "Perhaps we should return to the inn. The storm will be upon us soon."

Carey rose too, his gaze searching hers. "I only told you this because you're so different from Daphne. Since I met you, I can trust once again."

"That's a lovely compliment," Francesca said quietly.

The sky had darkened, and lightning sliced the air.

"My emotions run so deep they sometimes

frighten me. I don't want another blow like the one Daphne dealt me. If we became lovers, Francesca, and you then decided to leave me—"

"Don't think about the future." She wound her arms around him. "I can't give you any promises. Not yet. But I am not like Daphne."

"No, you're not," he murmured. He would have kissed her again if the rain had held back, but it started pouring. "And I hope you'll never become like her," he added as they rushed toward the inn.

She smiled, water dripping from her hair. "I won't do anything to risk losing your friendship."

Warmth curled around his heart.

Chapter 12

The rain had stopped when Francesca came down for breakfast the next morning. "Good morning," she greeted Carey, who looked as if he hadn't slept any more than she had. Fatigue darkened the skin around his eyes and he was tense. She had spent a turbulent night, her burning emotions ignited by his confession of the previous day.

He mumbled a greeting and smiled.

They were the only guests, and Carey was not yet wearing his waistcoat and coat. With his shirtsleeves rolled up over the elbows, he was polishing his boots in front of the fireplace. It was strange, yet oddly soothing, to see him engaged in such an intimate task.

Francesca sat down and watched him. "I'm grateful for your confidence yesterday. However, I have one question. Why did you escort Daphne in the park if you dislike her as much as you say?"

For a moment, Carey stopped what he was doing. "Daphne asked to see me. It seems she has problems in her marriage to Abelard. She regrets her hasty marriage, and wants me back."

He studied the sheen on his boots and went over them with the rag once more. "I told her I couldn't help her," he added. "Especially since I have met the woman of my dreams . . .'' He gave Francesca a keen glance.

A warm current coursed through her, all the way to the soles of her feet.

"You know, Carey, you're a rare man."

He smiled and winked. "And you're a jewel."

A new shyness stretched between them. Carey broke the spell, saying, "I have to polish my boots myself since I left my valet in London." He paused, then added as if to himself, "During the Rebellion we didn't need valets. But I met a slightly mad fellow in Scotland, Bigelow, who tried to polish the mud and blood off my boots. I sent him to London after the battle at Culloden. He's still with me, but the revolt scarred him terribly. He has awful nightmares."

Francesca shivered. "I can't imagine what the battles were like."

"A slaughterhouse." He set down one boot and began to work on the other. "My involvement in the Rebellion helped me realize what a fool I had been to fall so hopelessly in love with Daphne. That particular torture was nothing compared to the tortures on the battlefield. What we think are problems aren't really—not compared to the evils of war or other disasters."

Francesca sensed the depth of the horrors he remembered, but she could find nothing to say that would soothe him.

"The war made me cautious," he said with a hollow smile. " 'Tis foolish to wear one's heart upon one's sleeve." His gaze burned into her. "Yet with you, I'm willing to make another try at love."

Francesca was silent, unsure of how to respond. On the one hand, she loved him with all her heart, but how could she be sure he wouldn't rearrange her entire life once she gave in to him?

"Complete honesty is the best thing you and I have, Francesca."

She smiled then. "Yes, and we have time to let our feelings grow." Her legs felt curiously weak, and her heart raced.

The delicious smells of breakfast came from the kitchen, and the cook was singing loudly. A scraggly kitten wound around Francesca's legs and she bent to rub its ears.

Carey sat down on the bench before the fireplace and pulled on his boots, then stood and carefully wiped off his hands. He rolled down his sleeves and adjusted the lace cuffs. "Well, I'm ready to face the 'demons' in Seaford. Are you?"

"Yes." She sighed. "I pray we find some answers this time." She lifted the feather-light kitten and stroked its knobby back. "I won't have any peace of mind until we do."

"I know exactly how you feel."

The kitten clung to her bodice, nuzzling her neck in search of comfort. The proprietor of the Blue Hen entered the common room, smiling. "A good mornin' t' ye, and a good un' it is." He placed two plates filled with ham and eggs on the table closest to the fireplace. "A bit nippy, but ever so bonny sunshine. Yer up early for gentlefolk," he added, beaming.

" 'Tis a lovely day. Bring me a glass of ale as well," Carey said.

"Right away, sir." The host returned a minute later with a glass of frothing dark liquid. "I keep it in th' cellar 'cause 'tis freezin' down there."

Still carrying the kitten, Francesca walked to the table. She cut tiny pieces of the ham and fed them to the hungry animal. Smiling, she realized that she found comfort in the small, warm creature who needed her and showed her simple love. The kitten's trust was a rock in a sea of complicated human emotions.

"I see ye've found our orphan."

"Orphan?" Francesca held the kitten possessively.

"Yes, 'e comes 'ere every mornin' t' get fed, but no one claims t' own 'im. Can't say I can afford t' feed stray cats, if ye know what I mean, missus."

Francesca caressed the orange tiger-striped fur. "Can I have him?"

Their host beamed. "That'd be a problem off me hands, missus."

While chewing his breakfast, Carey listened to their conversation. It was difficult to keep a rein on his desires when Francesca looked straight at him, her face glowing with a soft smile. The rosiness of her plump bottom lip transfixed him.

"I should call him something, don't you think?" She sighed. "Isn't he lovely? His eyes are green, and his tail is just like a plume."

" 'Tis rather uncomfortable for a cat to travel in a coach," Carey said, and drank the rest of the ale. "Yet if I know you right, you will bring him."

"He'll keep me company," she said.

"I had hoped that I would be the one to occupy you," Carey whispered with a seductive smile as the proprietor returned to the kitchen.

"Rogue!" she said, holding the kitten up like a shield in front of her.

"I do like cuddling *kittens*," he said suggestively, and finished his breakfast. Laughing, he rose and shrugged into his coat. "As soon as you're ready to go, we should continue on to Seaford. I will see to the horses and speak with Hitchins."

Cauliflower Arnold entered the common room, having had his breakfast in the kitchen. "Th' confounded 'Itchins pulled out th' team. Time t' go."

"You don't seem to like any of the Hitchins brothers, Arnold," Carey commented.

"I like Caleb well enough, even though 'e is a braggart. But 'is brother's a sour ol' puss."

Scowling, he left the room with Carey.

The driver was in the stables, putting the harnesses on the two blacks. He swept aside the mane and fastened the buckle of one bridle as Carey stepped inside the low, dark building. "Ready?" Carey asked.

Hitchins led the horse outside to the waiting carriage. "In a minute, guv."

Carey caressed the silky flank of the other horse thoughtfully studying the sullen coachman. He didn't have his brother Caleb's chatty disposition, but he was a good driver. Arnold jumped up on the box and waited. Francesca came outside, her cloak hanging loosely over her shoulders, the kitten curled in her arms. With a smile at Hitchins, she stepped into the coach.

Carey let out his withheld breath as he watched her from the shadows of the stables. There was no use denying the violent pounding of his heart. One day soon, Francesca would be his.

The kitten curled up in her lap and fell asleep as soon as the coach moved out of the yard. She stroked its soft fur. She could barely look at Carey when he spoke to her, such was the force of the longing between them. As thick as syrup, it had simmered and seethed ever since their talk yesterday.

"What are you going to call the cat?" he asked.

Francesca gently touched one tiny ear. "I don't know."

Carey watched Francesca's bent head, fighting an intense desire to touch her crown of raven-dark curls. "How about Pumpkin? He's orange, and if you feed him the way you did this morning, he'll be as fat as a pumpkin before long."

"Oh, hush! He won't be." She gazed at Carey thoughtfully, taking in his taut expression and his shimmering eyes.

"I'll call him Copper. 'Tis more dignified than Pumpkin. And this fellow has dignity."

The kitten awakened with a huge yawn and settled more comfortably in her lap.

"He acts as if he owns you," Carey said.

"Nobody owns me. Cats understand that." Francesca laughed, and sudden happiness brought a blush to her cheeks. "I need never be lonely again," she whispered.

Carey's breath caught in his throat, and he couldn't trust himself to speak.

Hitchins brought the coach to a halt in the Seaford square. Arnold stepped down and opened the carriage door. "What are we goin' t' do now?" he asked. "Me cousin won't be at the tavern 'til nightfall."

"We'll have to wait then."

"I'll go down t' th' 'arbor, if ye don't mind," Arnold said.

"By all means." Carey gave him a few coins. "Buy yourself some ale and a hearty dinner. We'll meet here later."

As Arnold strode away, Carey and Francesca left the kitten in the coach with Hitchins and strolled among the stalls at the market. The fishwives were haggling with customers over the price of fresh fish.

"Are you hungry?" he asked.

"No, but I think poor Copper could do with another meal. Perhaps a pilchard or two."

They bought two silvery fish wrapped in newspaper, and Carey carried the wet package to the hungry kitten in the coach. The chariot stood under an elm, and Hitchins was slouching on the box.

"Copper's a greedy little fellow," Carey commented as they watched the kitten eat.

"A saucer of milk would be just the thing." Francesca glanced around the square. "I'll buy some at the inn."

"I'll keep an eye on Copper so he won't run away."

Francesca walked into the dark, low-beamed inn. The air smelled of fried fish, and a stout barmaid was filling a tankard from the spout of a wooden keg. "M'lady." She bobbed a curtsy. "Can I be o' service?"

"Yes, I have a kitten that would like milk with his pilchards," Francesca said.

The maid wiped her hands on her apron. "Just a minute then. I 'ave to fetch it from th' kitchen." She walked away, and while Francesca waited she admired an embroidered sampler on the wall. The barmaid returned and gave Francesca a cup of milk and an empty saucer.

"I'll return shortly with the china." Francesca stepped outside and blinked in the sharp sunlight.

Eager to see the kitten's reaction to fresh milk, she crossed the cobblestone square in a hurry. Then she stopped short and looked from one end of the square to the other. There stood the elm, but there was no carriage waiting beneath it. Had she been mistaken about the exact spot? Confused, Francesca glanced at the other trees, but there was no coach in sight.

She crossed the square, heedlessly dropping the cup and saucer. Her breath catching in her throat, she leaned against the elm. Where was the carriage? Had Carey been called away on some urgent errand? Had something happened to him?

She made her way to the street leading down toward the harbor where the fish stalls were erected. She scanned the harbor from one end to the other, but the coach was not there.

"Have you seen a carriage go by?" she asked at the first stall. Her heart thundered, and tears burned her eyes. Had Carey abandoned her?

"No, nuffin', ma'am." The fishwife stared at her curiously. "I 'aven't seen no fancy coach all day."

Francesca ran up the slope again, and hurried toward the opposite side of the square and the road to Eastbourne. She ran until she reached the outskirts of town. A dog barked at her from an open doorway, and children played in the dusty lane. There was the tavern, but there was no evidence of Carey's carriage or horses.

She caught her breath, fear squeezing her chest with a persistent ache. She didn't want to believe what seemed to have happened.

Carey had abandoned her. Or something so urgent had occurred that he hadn't had time to warn her of his departure.

Panic-stricken, Francesca sprinted back to town. She fought against the stinging tears and the desolation in her heart. Let him be back in the square, she prayed silently. If he wasn't, how was she going to return to London? She had hardly any money, not nearly enough to pay for the coach fare.

Was the terror she had experienced once before in Seaford beginning all over again? Why had he left her? She ran the last part of the cottage-lined street leading to the square. Oh, God, let him be there!

She rounded the corner of the last house. With a racing heart, she stopped, her gaze going immediately to the elm on the opposite side.

The square was still empty.

Chapter 13

Frozen with shock, Francesca stared at the dusty, sunbaked stretch of cobblestones. Why had Carey left her so suddenly? Reeling across the square, she finally leaned against the tall wide elm which had shaded the carriage only twenty minutes earlier.

Digging her fingers into the bark, she tried to collect her scattered wits. Fear, mingling with suspicion, coursed through her. Thoughts tumbled around and around in her mind, preventing her from forming a constructive plan. Tears scalded her eyes. Had she been wrong to trust Carey?

Her throat constricted at the thought. Carey was an honorable and kind man . . .

When her pounding heart had slowed, she stared out over the square as if some answer would rise from the cobblestones. She had to do something. Her luggage was in the carriage. Copper! Why had Carey taken the kitten? It didn't make sense. Something awful must have happened. She looked at the cup and saucer lying shattered on the ground. She would have to pay the barmaid for them. Who would look after the kitten now?

Her fingers trembling, she fumbled in the pocket of her cloak and pulled out her purse. She carefully counted her savings, already knowing there wouldn't be enough to buy a stagecoach ticket. How would she get back to London?

Then anger shot through her, stiffening her resolve. This was a repetition of that morning more than six weeks ago when she had found herself abandoned in this exact same square, alone and without knowing what had happened to her.

"Damn you, McLendon!" she whispered between pale lips. The mystery of the massacre in the road remained. She had returned here to solve that mystery, or at least to try to find a clue. The only thing she had to go on was the fact that Cauliflower Arnold and Carey had arranged to meet the highwayman at the tavern this evening. Where was Arnold? Had he left with Carey? She looked toward the harbor but didn't see the giant. Perhaps they would still visit the tavern this evening. She would wait, and if they kept the appointment, she would find out why Carey had abandoned her. He had a lot to explain.

Feeling lost and desolate, she sank down on a rough bench fashioned from a tree trunk. The wait would be long, but there was nothing else to do.

The clear skies slowly clouded over as the afternoon dragged on. The sounds from the fish market died down, and Francesca pulled her cloak more tightly around her. The wind from the sea was cold and fierce. Hunger gnawed at her stomach, but she decided she'd better hoard her meager savings until her hunger was almost unbearable.

"Where's Mr. M.?" came a voice from behind her.

Francesca jumped and looked over her shoulder. "Arnold! Am I relieved to see you! Where have you been?" She sprang from her seat, eagerly looking for the carriage, as if it had miraculously appeared when she turned her back. But Arnold was alone.

"You haven't seen him then." Disappointed, she sat back down.

"Took a walk along the beach toward Eastbourne. Where's th' coach?" Arnold eased his bulk down beside her.

Francesca told him what had happened, and he groaned.

"Carey has left us without telling us why. I never thought he would be that irresponsible," she added. "Perhaps he had an accident, but where? He was here one moment and gone the next."

Arnold swept off his hat and raked a hand through his thin brown hair. "Sumthin' must 'ave 'appened to 'im. I'd trust Mr. M. wi' me life. A real gent 'e is."

Arnold's forehead was creased in concern, and Francesca's worries eased slightly. "You're right, but his disappearance is odd nevertheless."

"What are we goin' t' do?" he asked.

"See your cousin Ollie, as planned."

He stared at her as if she'd lost her mind. "Th' tavern bain't no place fer ladies, Miss Francie. 'Twould be dangerous—"

"Stuff and nonsense! You'll accompany me, won't you?"

He nodded hesitantly. "That I will, but I don't know if I can pertect ye from an entire gang o' 'igh-waymen. They take what they want."

"Perhaps you can ask Ollie to come outside. Then the men don't have to see me." She sighed. "I won't give up, and that's final."

"Ye're nuffin' if not persistent, Miss Francie." He shoved his three-cornered hat on his head. "So be it, then."

Carey McLendon felt as if his head had exploded, and pain radiated from the area of his right ear. He tried to raise himself from the hard surface on which he lay, but his efforts were in vain. Groaning, he dragged a hand through his hair and flinched as he touched a protrusion above his right ear. He probed the injury gingerly and decided that he must look like a one-horned devil. He explored his surroundings with the same hand and instantly recognized the squabs of his carriage.

A cold sweat broke out all over his body as he forced himself upright. Compressing his lips, he withheld a moan and eased along the seat to look outside. It was almost dark. The coach was surrounded by trees, and the horses were grazing some distance away. He started as something rubbed against his leg. A faint, plaintive meow penetrated the darkness.

"Copper!" He picked up the kitten and held it close to his face. It pushed against his nose and began purring. "You little devil. What happened to us? And where's Francesca?" Dread burst through him. Someone was out to hurt him—perhaps even kill him—and perhaps Francesca as well. But he was still alive, and he planned to remain that way. The thought gave him renewed strength.

He set the protesting kitten on the floor and gently released the latch. The door swung open on well-oiled hinges. Peering cautiously in all directions before slipping outside, he slowly swung his legs to the ground.

The breeze was brisk and cool. He breathed deeply in an effort to ease his aching head and clear his thoughts.

There was no sign of Hitchins. His memory returned to him instantly at the thought of the sullen coachman. He recalled waiting for Francesca at the Seaford square as she went to buy milk for the kitten. Then Hitchins had come around the carriage with an eager look on his face. "Ye must see th' 'orseflesh that just entered th' lane, Mr. McLendon.''

As Carey had prepared to alight and look at the spectacular horse, the coachman had said: ''Naw, be'ind ye. Look through th' other window, sir.''

Carey remembered turning toward the opposite side of the coach, and then he'd been overcome by a blinding pain. Hitchins must have crowned him from behind. But why? He shot a cautious glance around the corner of the carriage. There was no sign of Hitchins—if that was really his name. The regular coachman, Caleb Hitchins, was nothing if not honest and hardworking. This man was obviously an impostor.

Carey circled the coach, but there was no sign of the coachman. The kitten jumped down and scratched at the mossy ground. It kept meowing, and Carey hoped it wouldn't alert Hitchins if he was close by.

The horses nickered as they recognized him. He caressed their muzzles and studied the thicket beyond. It was plain to see that they were alone. Hitchins had abandoned the carriage, obviously reluctant to face Carey when he awakened. At least his life had been spared, Carey thought grimly. How long had he been unconscious? Most of the afternoon, it seemed. It had been around twelve o'clock when they had arrived in Seaford.

Carey swore as he led the horses back to the carriage. Keeping an eye on the darkening shadows, he harnessed the stallions to the carriage.

Worry grew within him as questions hurtled through his mind. Where was Francesca now? Had Hitchins bludgeoned her as well?

He forgot his aching head momentarily and called to the kitten. It came, clearly hoping he had some food to offer. He put it in the coach, climbed onto the box, and gripped the reins. Finding that the lane lay just beyond the thicket, he glanced at the emerging stairs and turned south. Hopefully he wasn't far from Seaford. He debated whether to keep the appointment with the highwaymen, or to return to the square. Would he be too late? If she was still alive, Francesca must be wondering and worrying what had happened to him.

Grimacing, he cracked the whip above the horses' heads. They strained against the chains with renewed speed. The tavern was on the way to Seaford, so he might as well stop there for a moment. His talk with Ollie Arnold wouldn't take more than five minutes.

Francesca observed the dark and dilapidated tavern with trepidation. Two smoking torches bracketed the door, and weak light shone through the small open rectangles that acted as windows. Sounds of laughter came from within. Were the highwaymen even now waiting inside? Francesca took another tentative step toward the rough-hewn door. The night echoed with rapid hoofbeats, and, pulling Cauliflower Arnold with her, she hid behind a wide tree trunk beside the tavern.

The horses slowed as they drew abreast of a nearby barn. Francesca stared wide-eyed at the riders entering the muddy yard. They resembled ordinary farm laborers and grooms to her. She didn't know what she had expected the highwaymen to look like—if these men were indeed the feared robbers.

She swallowed hard. "Do you see your cousin?" she asked Arnold. Where would she find the courage to confront him? One of the men burped loudly and they all slid off their horses and entered the low building.

"Better be worth it in gold, this mysterious meetin' t'night," a short heavyset man said as he closed the door.

"That's Ollie," Arnold said. "By gorm, 'e's turned fat as a barrel." He moved from the shadows as the highwaymen filed inside. "Ye'd better wait 'ere."

Francesca nodded, and Arnold slipped into the taproom. Minutes passed and Francesca wondered at the delay. When Arnold did not return, she decided to look through the window.

Before she could lose her courage, she stepped from her cover and sneaked up to the nearest window. She saw Arnold instantly. He was gesticulating and talking with the fat man, who repeatedly shook his head. Evidently, he wasn't going to come out.

"Well, I will just have to go in and talk to him," she said to herself, and clenched her teeth in determination.

Smoke closed around her and her nose quivered at the odor of sour ale and sweat. Steeling herself against the fear weakening her legs, she moved closer to the circle of men seated around a table which was lit by a branch of candles.

The talk and laughter quieted, and the ruffians all turned toward her. Their lips parted in leers, revealing rotting teeth, and their eyes gleamed in anticipation at the sight of her lithe figure.

She didn't recognize any of them.

"Miss Francie! Ye shouldn't 'ave come in 'ere," Cauliflower Arnold said, aghast.

"Come closer, wench!" the fat man called out, waving at her. "Ye be a sight fer sore eyes. Give 'er a chair, or per'aps ye'd like t' sit in m' lap?" The man patted his fleshy thighs covered with coarse filthy frieze, and roared with laughter.

"Mind yer manners, cousin," Cauliflower Arnold said, raising his fists.

Francesca made an effort to keep her voice clear and firm. "I have come for information."

"Ye didn't tell me it was a mort who wanted t' speak wi' me," the fat man said to the proprietor, who was standing slightly outside the circle of light, rubbing his hands in agitation.

"I didn't say't," he protested. " 'Twas a man who arsked fer yer presence, Ollie Arnold."

Ollie must be the leader of the gang, Francesca thought, and cringed as his dark eyes took on a cold, predatory gleam. "Ar, 'tis much nicer talkin' t' a skirt than some toff from Lunnon." He raised his tankard and took a deep swallow. The other men imitated him, without taking their eyes from Francesca. Uncertain, she remained rooted to the spot, ready to flee out the door if anyone moved.

Cauliflower Arnold spoke. "If ye as much as lay—"

"Don't ye worry, coz."

The ruffians wore striped jerseys, patched breeches, leather jerkins, dirty smocks, and caps. Some sported frayed and dusty tricornes on their lank hair, which hung unbrushed beside unshaved and dirty cheeks.

"Well, mort, wot's yer business wi' us?"

"I would like to know if you remember the overturned carriage along the Eastbourne road where it dips down toward the sea," Francesca said. "The accident happened in April. There were two dead bodies in the carriage. Everything disappeared mysteriously, including the bodies and the horses."

A heavy silence gripped the room.

"She speaks like a lady, but wot would a lady want wi' dead bodies, I arsks?" Ollie said. He rubbed his bearded jaw thoughtfully. "Outright morbid, 'tis."

"The gentleman in the coach was my husband," Francesca explained, swallowing nervously.

Chuckles of disbelief came from the group and

tankards rasped against the rough wooden surface of the table. "*Ye're* th' murderess, then," another man said. "We 'eard about ye. Th' rumor 'round 'ere is ye killed yer whole family of five, includin' yer grandmother."

" 'Tis an outrageous lie!" Francesca cried. "I'm trying to clear my name and find the murderer."

"What d' ye want?" Ollie asked, his voice threatening.

"Did you see anything unusual that day?" Francesca's legs ached with tension, and she suspected that she had come in vain. She sensed violence lurking like an acrid odor in the air. "Another rumor is that highwaymen murdered the people, and took off with the carriage and horses," she said with forced bravado.

Two of the men rose, throwing back their chairs. "Are ye callin' us murderers, wench?" one growled. "Is that why ye wanted t' see us, to accuse us?"

Francesca spread her arms in a pleading gesture. "No! I only want to find a clue to the real murderers, don't you see?" Her voice was about to break, and she fought back tears of terror.

Cauliflower Arnold had bunched his fists and was ready to defend Francesca at any moment.

The men mumbled among themselves and threw ominous glances at her. "What's in it fer us?" Ollie Arnold inquired. He pointed at the proprietor. " 'Ubert 'ere mentioned gold. D'ye 'ave gold t' pay fer th' infermation?"

Francesca thought of her meager savings. "I cannot give you what the gentleman promised earlier. He abandoned me to face you alone," she added, hoping to rouse the ruffian's sympathy. But Ollie opened his mouth and laughed, his great stomach heaving.

"Didya 'ear, gen'lemen? She thinks she can get somethin' fer naught."

"If you know something about those brutal murders, you could have the decency to tell me," Francesca said sharply.

Ollie Arnold rose, and Francesca feared he would give the signal for his men to attack her. His eyes gleamed under the floppy brim of his old-fashioned hat. He opened his mouth to speak, then raised his hand to quiet his men as the sound of horses approached the old tavern.

"Who's out t'night? Th' magistrate's men?" He glanced suspiciously at the landlord, who cringed, holding up his arms in protest.

"I swear no 'un knows yer 'ere, Ollie. I told nobody." He backed toward an open door at the rear of the filthy taproom.

Voices echoed outside and the door flew wide before the ruffians had a chance to move. " 'Tis th' bloomin' highwaymen from Saltborough!" one of them shouted and headed for the back door, shoving the proprietor aside.

Numb with fear, Francesca slipped into the shadows. She watched as the newcomers entered, brandishing lethal-looking daggers and cudgels in their grimy hands. Ollie had not moved, and some of his men sidled up to him, forming a tight knot around him.

Cauliflower Arnold was looking for her, but she remained hidden. He must have thought she had left, because he sided with his cousin for the upcoming fight.

"What d'ya want 'ere, One-Eyed Jemmy?" Just as Ollie spoke, Francesca began to move toward the back door, since the front door was barred by a sturdy villain wielding a gnarled club. She crept so slowly that nobody noticed her in the murky light. As she drew level with the table, the leader of the other gang, wearing a black patch over his eye, spoke.

"Ye raped m' sister, Ollie, an' ye'll pay fer it. Ye'll die afore this night's over." He advanced slowly, his dagger raised.

Ollie thrust his head forward and spat on the floor. "Ye're wrong, One-Eyed Jemmy. She gave 'erself t' me just like she 'as t' so many others." He flexed his heavy hands and deftly pulled a dagger from a sheath on his belt.

Francesca watched in horror as the two men circled each other, blades flashing. The other men called out encouragement, the gangs divided on each side of the dim room. Candles in crude tin candleholders flickered in the draft from the open door, and the mounting tension grew suffocating.

"I'll cut yer gullet orf," said One-Eyed Jemmy, making a lunge at Ollie. "From ear t' ear."

The blade flashed in a glittering circle and sliced into Ollie's leather vest. One-Eyed Jemmy was tall and painfully thin. He didn't look strong enough to lift his arms in the air, let alone kill an ox-like man like Ollie. Nevertheless, a clumsy, slow thrust slashed fat Ollie's thigh.

"Those'll be yer last words," Ollie growled, jabbing his opponent in the stomach with a lightning-fast lunge. For a man of his bulk, Ollie had great speed.

The thin adversary swore and staggered forward, holding a hand over his wound, his knife raised. Ollie sidestepped and managed to get in another thrust, this time in the side of One-Eyed Jemmy's neck.

Francesca shivered as One-Eyed Jemmy crumpled to the floor with an awful gurgling sound. When the highwaymen from Saltborough realized that their leader was dying, they let out a great roar of outrage and threw themselves upon the other gang.

Francesca stood frozen at the edge of the room as chairs, tables, and glasses began to shatter wildly around her. Her thoughts were strangely sluggish, making her unable to act.

Ollie Arnold stood with his back toward her, preparing to defend himself against yet another attack. A tankard flew across the room, and Francesca flinched with fear. Sobbing, she eyed the door. How was she going to find the answers she had come for now? It was futile, and she might as well leave before someone impaled her with a dagger. But she trembled so much she could hardly move.

Just as she was gathering her wits to flee, she noticed that a Saltborough ruffian had sidled up behind Ollie. As the room reverberated with grunts, curses, and the sound of breaking glass, he raised his knife to plunge it into Ollie's back. The fat man was unaware of the danger as he desperately fought another attacker. Cauliflower Arnold was fighting at the opposite side of the room and could not assist his cousin.

Francesca reacted automatically, gripping a full pewter tankard from a table and bringing it down on the ruffian's back. His blade went wide, only slicing through a fold of Ollie's sleeve. The man went down with a cry of rage.

Ollie whipped around, his eyes narrow with suspicion. Francesca froze with fear as his bloody dagger pointed straight at her. He threw a quick glance around the room, then grabbed her roughly by the arm and pushed her outside into the cold, wet wind.

"Ye saved m' life, mort," he growled, shoving her brutally up against the wall in the shadows. "But ye were stupid t' come 'ere t'night."

Francesca found her voice. "I had no choice. Please, if you know anything about the murders, tell me now."

He peered at her in the darkness, and she dared not breathe, fearing what villainous thoughts were running through his mind.

"I suppose I owe ye som'thin'," he muttered, "seein' as ye saved me life."

"Do you know what happened that day? Please tell me."

He pressed close to her, so close that she could smell the rancid grease in his hair and the sour odor of his breath. He groped for her face, and she averted it in disgust.

"Ye're a pretty li'l thing, missy. An' quick on yer feet." Suddenly he let her go and rubbed his chin. She sagged with relief. "Ver' well. We were 'ired by an old man t' surround yer carriage. Mind ye, part o' th' arrangement was t' 'ave two masked strangers with us that day. They killed th' man inside th' coach and th' driver. I suppose they wanted it t' look like us, th' 'ighwaymen, killed ye. They were 'bout t' finish ye orf in th' sand when th' sounds o' a 'orse sounded around th' bend in th' lane."

Francesca drew a jagged breath. "That must have been Mr. McLendon—the gentleman who wanted to see you this evening."

"Where's 'e now?" Ollie shot a fretful glance into the gloom, but nothing stirred. The fight was dying down inside.

"I don't know. Who's the old man who hired you? Could you direct me to him?" She prayed that he would.

" 'E didn't tell me 'is name. Niver seen 'im 'round these parts afore. A leery ol' fox, 'e was, an' 'e didn't explain 'is business wi' yer family. Paid 'andsomely all th' same. 'E said we'd done well. A right strange toff, 'e was. But—" Ollie peered at her closely. "—I know o' Bertie, 'is coachman."

Excitement coursed through Francesca. Finally a clue. But who had wanted her and Leonard dead?

" 'E lives not far from Beachy 'Ead. Ye might find

'im there, at the Dog an' Whistle tavern. 'E'll lead ye t' th' old man.''

Francesca smiled in gratitude. ''Your help has been invaluable,'' she said, moving toward the door. ''I must find your cousin, Joss Arnold.''

The fat man laughed. ''Ye call 'im Joss? Ever'one calls 'im Cauliflower.''

''He doesn't like it.'' Francesca drew a sigh of relief as she saw the giant man leave the tavern.

''Ye could stay 'ere t'night, wi' me, missy,'' Ollie suggested, but she shook her head and ran before he would force her to stay. She heard him cursing behind her, but he did not pursue her. She called to Cauliflower Arnold and he joined her, wiping his face with a handkerchief.

''What a fight,'' he said happily. ''It's been too long since I 'ad th' chance t' pound a few ugly faces.''

''You're a disgrace,'' Francesca scolded, but she soon forgot her disgust as she told him about Bertie.

Ollie joined them a while later. ''Ye can use two o' our 'orses to reach Beachy 'Ead,'' he offered. ''Just leave 'em 'ere when ye return.''

After shaking hands with Cauliflower Arnold, the fat man returned to the tavern.

''We must leave right now,'' Francesca said. ''I cannot wait any longer.'' They chose two of the steeds and headed west on the Eastbourne road.

Carey drove into the yard of the run-down alehouse. The door stood ajar and two men were reeling outside as if hopelessly drunk. When two stablehands carried out a corpse, Carey knew he had come too late to speak with the highwaymen. Since the magistrate would be expected to arrive after a violent fight, no ruffian would remain and volunteer information about what had happened inside.

Carey tied the reins to the carriage brake handle

and approached the doorway, where the proprietor stood wringing his hands. The taproom was ruined. Shards of glass crunched under Carey's boots, and broken chairs and benches were strewn everywhere.

"Who fought here?"

The landlord glared at him. "Ye didn't come like ye said ye would, Mr. McLendon."

Carey indicated the aching lump on his head. "I was unavoidably detained."

"Th' wench ye sent could 'ave been killed. 'Owever, she 'ad 'er wits about 'er. Knocked over one ruffian with a tankard."

Worry flooded every inch of Carey's body. "Where is she now?"

"Disappeared wi' fat Ollie Arnold durin' th' fight. 'Aven't seen 'er since."

Carey gripped the other man's collar and pulled tight. "And where's Ollie and his cousin Cauliflower Arnold?" Anxiety made his voice deadly soft.

Cold sweat beaded the proprietor's brow. "Don't know, sir. Th' gangs took orf just as soon as they 'ad broken ever'thin' in 'ere. Ollie's cousin left right before the rest o' th' men."

"Gangs?"

" 'Twas two gangs, fightin' each other over some mort."

Francesca! Carey released his stranglehold on the proprietor's collar.

"Not yer wench who came 'ere t'night. Some'un else."

Carey expelled a breath of relief. Francesca might have escaped unscathed, but how would he know for sure, and where had she gone?

"When was the last stagecoach to London?" he asked, glancing at his turnip watch.

" 'Alf 'our ago, sir. If yer lady friend 'ad some sense, she was on it."

Carey hoped Francesca was safe. All he could do now was return to London as fast as possible and explain why he had disappeared so suddenly. Would she speak to him ever again? "By the way, I need to buy some meat and milk for my kitten." Carey smiled in embarrassment. "I think the fellow is starving. And while you're at it, could you find some food for me as well?" He glanced toward the dark sky. "While you do that, I'll find out if Mrs. Kane left with the stagecoach."

On the square in Seaford, Carey knocked on the locked door of the inn where the stagecoach office was located. It was the establishment where Francesca had fetched the milk earlier in the day. Wearing a tasseled nightcap, the landlord stuck his irate face outside the window right above the door. "What d'ye want at this ungodly 'our?" he demanded.

"I have to know if a Mrs. Kane traveled on the London stagecoach this evening," Carey said briskly. "'Tis a matter of some urgency."

The man glared at him. "I don't know the names of everyone who travels on the London Machine. There are 'undreds o' people every week." He was about to close the window, adding, "Besides, the ticket master doesn't live 'ere, and I wouldn't awaken 'im in th' middle o' th' night. A terrible temper 'e 'as. 'As been known to threaten people with a blunderbuss if they disturb 'is sleep."

Carey was undaunted by that threat. He described Francesca, knowing the man would recall her loveliness.

"Naw, didn't see any lady like 'er," the proprietor said. "Good night." The window closed with a slam.

Defeated, Carey turned the coach in the square and headed back to the tavern on the Eastbourne road, where he'd get food for Copper and himself. Where were Francesca and Cauliflower Arnold? He would not rest until she was back at his side. He had to find her.

Chapter 14

Half an hour later, Francesca and Arnold arrived
at the Dog and Whistle Inn, outside Beachy
Head. The patrons in the taproom knew of Bertie,
the old man's coachman.

"Bertie? Bertie Biggs? Aye, 'e's th' driver wot
works fer old Clarence Ingram. Sour ol' sod, Ingram
is. 'Ermit-like," said one man in a dirty stocking cap.

Francesca's heartbeat quickened. "Yes, that must
be the man we're seeking."

"Ol' Ingram niver shows 'is gob in 'ere, but Bertie, 'e likes 'is ale. Every Saturday 'e comes in 'ere,
as steady as clockwork."

Francesca and Cauliflower Arnold exchanged
glances. "Where does he live?" she asked.

"Why, Bertie lives with Ingram in th' ol' 'ouse up
toward Farmview. Secluded place, 'tis." The man in
the stocking cap inclined his head toward the road
outside. "Ye take that road as far as the road sign,
then turn right."

Francesca pressed a coin in the man's hand and
followed Arnold outside. "This time we won't fail.
Old man Ingram will tell us everything we want to
know about the murders."

"I wish Mr. M. were 'ere. We don't know an'thin'
'bout Mr. Ingram. 'E might be dangerous."

Francesca raised her chin a fraction. "We've come

this far, and I won't go back to Seaford without some answers."

Cauliflower Arnold grumbled under his breath, but he did not argue.

The winding road led inland. The sound of pounding waves faded, and the sea gulls' cries died off into the distance. The lane was riddled with holes.

"A 'orse needs good balance to travel these roads in th' dark. Outright treacherous they are." Arnold scratched his chin. "We should wait 'til th' mornin'."

"We don't have funds to pay for lodging. Besides, why wait? The best time to find Mr. Ingram at home must be during the night. He might be gone during the day, and that would only mean more tiresome waiting for us."

The moon came out from behind a bank of clouds and bathed the landscape with an eerie light.

"This old nag is no more than a bag o' bones," Arnold said, sniffling. He'd been sneezing intermittently all the way from Seaford, and Francesca couldn't help but smile.

"Why blame the horse when you have a cold?"

"Cold? Bah! 'Tis th' nag's fault. 'Orses always make me sick." As if to prove his point, Arnold sneezed again. When his face emerged from a huge handkerchief he'd whipped from his pocket, he wheezed, "Th' steeds 'ave a bloomin' conspiracy against me."

Francesca laughed, but grew abruptly serious as the lane made a turn. The patrons at the inn had said the house was behind that curve. A rush of foreboding came over her as she stared at the road ahead. As it reached the crest of the hills, she could discern a building among the trees. The mansion was there, brooding and ominous—or was it only in her

imagination that it appeared sinister? It was secluded indeed.

The main house was two-storied, built from mellow red brick. The latticed windows looked bare, as
if lacking draperies. The white eaves needed new
paint, as did the peeling black front door. The
grounds were overgrown, and the surrounding
stone wall was crumbling and covered with moss.

"This estate has seen better days," Francesca
whispered. She pointed at the light in a downstairs
window. "Someone is home."

"Aye, an' it might be Mr. Ingram. Mayhap a bloke
of unpredictable temper." He gave her a dark
glance. "I regret listenin' t' you, an' participatin' in
yer wild schemes."

Francesca didn't answer. She stared intently at the
house.

Sneezing, Arnold jumped to the ground and fastened the reins to a low-hanging tree branch. He
lifted Francesca down, and together they ascended
the crumbling stone steps to the front door. The
knocker fell against the brass with a heavy clang.

Nothing happened at first, but after Francesca
knocked once more, steps could be heard approaching from the recesses of the house. The door creaked
open, and an old prune-like woman in a huge mobcap peered at them.

"Wot'yer want?" she asked suspiciously, her
beaky nose quivering.

"Tell Mr. Ingram that Francesca Kane is here to
see him."

"Kane? He knows no 'un by that name. Besides,
he's gone to bed. 'Tis nigh midnight."

" 'Tis urgent that I see him—a matter of life and
death."

The old woman muttered something and opened
the door wider. "Ye wait in the hallway, d'ye hear,"
she said as she walked upstairs.

Francesca trembled with fatigue and fear. Who knew what the old man would do once he recognized her? She threw a grateful glance at Cauliflower Arnold. At least she had a giant to protect her.

The woman was gone for a long time.

"Where is she?" Francesca said to herself and sighed.

Then there were steps on the stairs and the servant returned.

"I'm afraid Mr. Ingram isn't in his room. He must be in th' cellar, in his carpenter shop." She gestured toward a door off the hallway, opened it, and called down the stairs. A male voice responded. "He's there." She beckoned toward Francesca and Arnold. "Come."

Hesitantly, they followed her. A candle glowed dimly behind the grimy glass panel of a wall lantern. Francesca held up her skirts so as not to trip on the steps. The cellar smelled of earth and mold, and two wall sconces lit the narrow corridor. The walls were fashioned from big boulders of Kentish ragstone. There were sounds of shuffling steps at the end of the passage, but Francesca could see no one in the darkness.

"In here," the servant said and opened a door. A faint light illuminated the room. She literally pushed Cauliflower Arnold inside. Francesca followed, curious to see the old man after all the time they'd spent searching for him. To her surprise no one was in the room except Arnold.

The portal slammed shut behind her, and a stout key turned in the keyhole. Francesca flew at the door and pounded her fists on it. "What are you doing?"

Cauliflower Arnold flung his massive weight against the sturdy oak, but the door didn't shift. "Bloody 'ell," the giant swore, massaging his shoulder. "We're prisoners."

Francesca could not accept that verdict, and pressed her ear to the keyhole. In addition to the servant's shuffling gait, hurried footsteps echoed in the corridor. "Let us out! We only want to talk with you," Francesca cried.

The door at the top of the stairs slammed distantly.

Francesca sagged against the door. "How could I be so stupid!"

Arnold grunted something while tossing barrels about in the dim chamber. He overturned a stack of bulging burlap sacks. "Seems they closed us in some sort o' storage room. Stacks o' empty ale casks, and this is wheat if I'm not mistaken." He prodded the sacks with his finger. "We won't starve t' death, even though th' thought o' eatin' flour doesn't 'xactly appeal t' me."

Francesca sat down on the nearest sack, studying the room. "We must break out somehow. There's that window."

" 'Tis too small." Cauliflower Arnold examined the narrow opening near the ceiling. "That's why they closed us in th' cellar, so that we wouldn't 'scape through a window."

"I'll try to get through," Francesca said with determination as she saw something move in a dark corner of the room. "I'm not sharing a room with rats."

Arnold scratched his head. "I don't know 'ow ye—"

"I'll discard my panniers. Without them, I'm quite slender. Perhaps 'tis not too late to catch up with Mr. Ingram." She hurried behind some sacks and lifted her skirts. "While I'm busy here, perhaps you can break the window with something."

Arnold nodded and went in search of a tool. He found a brick, and with two well-aimed blows, he shattered the panes. Gingerly, he pulled out the jag-

ged shards and swept them away after winding a
sack around his hand.

"Blimey, ye must be shaped like a midget t' git
past that openin'." Cauliflower Arnold looked from
Francesca to the window. "And then ye 'ave t' crawl
through th' bushes wot grow outside."

"I'll do it," Francesca said, and clenched her teeth
resolutely before she could change her mind.
Throwing a wary glance toward the corner where
she'd seen the rat, she said, "Please lift me up."
Her skirts dragged on the floor now that she had
removed the hoops. "You'll have to shove me
through."

Arnold chuckled. "Where shall I push?"

Francesca gave him a stern look as he folded his
arms around her thighs and hoisted her toward the
open window. "On my derriere," she said ada-
mantly. "And don't you dare give me any unnecessary shoves."

Arnold heaved from behind, and she struggled to
wiggle through the opening, which was smaller than
it had appeared from the floor. She got halfway outside, her nails digging into the moist earth at the
base of the bushes. "Oh . . . blast," she whispered,
gritting her teeth. The branches caught in her hair,
and she fought to keep free of the wild vegetation.

The window frame caught her hips on both sides
and she twisted desperately to get through.

"Lift me higher," she demanded. Perspiration
covered her forehead as she used the last of her
strength to push herself past the sashes. Once her
hips had emerged, the rest was easy. She crawled
through the hedge unscathed.

"You wait here. I'll go around and unlock the
door."

"I ain't plannin' on goin' nowhere," Arnold
chided, his head sticking out of the opening.
" 'Urry, will ye, Miss Francie."

Francesca crept up the front steps and tried the door. Strangely enough, it stood open a crack. The atmosphere in the house was heavy and threatening, but the hallway was empty. No sounds came from inside the huge building. Where was the old man and his servant?

Before she tried to locate them, she'd better let Arnold out. She needed him to protect her. Thank God the door leading to the cellar was unlocked. It creaked terribly as it swung open, and Francesca held her breath, listening for hurrying footsteps. The house remained as silent as a tomb.

The candles were still burning in the passage, and she got down the stairs without mishap. Then she heard a loud rattling sound outside. Pressing herself against the wall, she feared they had discovered her escape, but a few seconds later, the sound stopped. It was *a carriage!* The sound had been wheels grating over the graveled drive.

Francesca rushed along the corridor and unlocked the prison door. Arnold shot outside and ran to the stairs.

"Didya 'ear that, Miss Francie? A bloomin' coach went by. They're leavin' us."

"Let's ride after them," she said. "They might not have discovered our horses in the dark."

The mounts were still where they had tied them, and Arnold boosted Francesca into the saddle. "Wot are we goin' t' do if we catch up wi' th' chariot?"

"I don't know." Francesca frowned. "Perhaps convince Mr. Ingram we want a chat."

"A chat? Bah!"

They rode over the lawns to the rutted lane beyond. The faint sound of hoofbeats and carriage wheels reached their ears.

"We'll ride faster than that coach," she said, digging her heels into her horse's flanks.

The moon sent a weak light to guide them, and

the lane wound like a silver ribbon among the trees. A startled night bird shrieked, and bushes rustled with movement. The carriage sounded closer.

"We're gainin' on them." Cauliflower Arnold rode faster than Francesca, and as she followed his broad back, the coach suddenly became visible on the crest of a low hill.

It slowed momentarily, the horses neighing in protest as they were reined in. Francesca wondered why the coachman had slackened the pace. The explanation came with blinding speed as a shot cracked in the night.

A lead ball whistled past Francesca's head before she had time to form another thought. Her horse reared, but she clamped her arms as hard as she could around his neck, jamming her knees into his side to remain in the saddle.

Arnold led his mount behind a clump of trees as another flash lit up the darkness and a ball flew toward them. "Get behind cover!" he shouted.

Francesca obeyed as soon as her steed stopped dancing around. She reached the protection of the trees as another shot blasted the night. Then the carriage disappeared behind the hill.

Francesca and Cauliflower Arnold stared at each other in the moonlight. "Bloody 'ell!" Arnold swore, pushing a shaking hand through his hair. "That was close."

Francesca trembled so much she could barely speak. "I suppose we must give up the plan to see Mr. Ingram."

" 'Tis obvious 'e doesn't want to speak wi' us." The giant patted Francesca's arm. "We must find Mr. M. 'E's th' one t' deal wi' blokes like Mr. Ingram. We'd better find 'im soon."

Francesca nodded, her face grim. "He had the gall to abandon us. I wonder where he is."

* * *

Carey spent the entire night scouting the area around Seaford for Francesca and Arnold. They were nowhere to be found, and the proprietor at the dilapidated tavern on the Eastbourne road assured him he had no idea where Francesca had gone, or where the highwaymen were hiding. Carey had left his carriage behind the barn at the inn, and was riding one of the horses.

Carey realized that without Ollie Arnold's help, his efforts were doomed. Had Francesca and Cauliflower Arnold returned to London? It certainly looked that way, since they were nowhere to be found in Seaford.

"Going back to London would be the only sensible thing to do," he muttered, turning his horse around after riding almost all the way to Beachy Head. Worry gnawed at him, and he felt utterly helpless. "At least she has Arnold to protect her . . . or does she?"

His horse was so exhausted that it stumbled several times. Carey knew he'd better sleep a few hours before heading to London. Both he and the horse needed a rest. He'd sleep in the carriage, and at first light he would turn north.

Francesca was so tired when they entered the yard of the old tavern outside Seaford that she saw double. The lengthening shadows wavered before her eyes and she thought she saw villains waiting to ambush her from behind every tree.

"We were t' leave th' nags 'ere for Ollie," Cauliflower Arnold said and slid out of the saddle. " 'Owever, I believe we could use some rest." He scanned the dark building. "I don't think ye should stop 'ere, though, not after th' terrible fight last night. 'Tisn't safe." He fastened the reins to a tree, and took Francesca's horse's bridle, leading her mount back onto the lane before she had time to protest.

"Ye'd better sleep at th' inn at th' Seaford square, Miss Francie. I 'ave just enough money t' pay for one night. Tomorrow morn' we'll find a way t' git back t' Lunnon. I'll return this nag when I've found ye shelter."

Francesca only nodded, wishing that Carey had turned back to the square. But the moonlit rectangle was empty.

Sick at heart, she fell into an exhausted sleep in the bed the landlord provided.

The next morning Francesca and Arnold were fortunate to encounter a young couple who offered them seats in their coach as they set out toward London.

As they rode through Sussex, Arnold said, "I wish I knew what 'appened to Mr. M. Per'aps 'e's back in Lunnon by now." He sent Francesca a cautious glance. "I 'ope 'e's still alive."

Chapter 15

I n the afternoon, Francesca thanked her escorts on the steps of the Crimson Rooms. Tired and drained, she entered the hallway. Her worried thoughts revolved around Carey as she glanced at the empty foyer. The rooms were shrouded in shadow, and the air was stagnant with old smoke and the stale smell of last night's supper. What had happened to him?

"I'll be goin' t' my chamber, Miss Francie. Don't worry about Mr. M. 'E'll be stormin' in 'ere before ye can blink yer winkers."

Francesca smiled. "You have great confidence in him."

Arnold shrugged and tossed his hat up in the air. "I'd trust 'im wi' me life if need be." He crossed the hallway. "See ye later, Miss Francie."

Just as Francesca was about to step upstairs to her room, she heard voices from one of the small salons at the back.

"Haven't you heard a word from her?"

Francesca recognized Giorgio D'Angelo's voice, sounding harsh and worried. He was speaking with Letty Rose, whose voice was softer, yet angry as she replied, "Not a word, but I expect her to work the minute she returns."

Francesca parted the crimson velvet curtains that

206

separated two parlors. Giorgio was squeezing Letty Rose's shoulders. Their closeness was an unexpected sight, yet Francesca suddenly realized that Letty Rose might very well have offered her "services" to the virile Italian.

"Are you talking about me?" she asked.

Giorgio whirled around and his face broke into the wide smile that gave his face such charm. "Francesca, you're back! You don't know how worried I was about you."

Letty Rose coughed behind him and righted her bodice. "You should have been back here yesterday, working, Mrs. Kane," she told Francesca with a venomous glance.

"You gave us leave—"

"Pish! I didn't expect you to be gone this long."

Giorgio placed a comforting arm around Francesca's waist. "Don't scold her, Miss Rose. She's returned, safe and sound." He scrutinized Francesca's face. "What became of you? I was concerned since you left no word."

"I told you she went off with her lover," Letty Rose said with a snort, staring coldly at Francesca. "By the way, I think 'tis about time you start giving the customers what they want, Mrs. Kane."

Francesca stiffened in anger. "I'm tired of your tirades, Letty. I am resigning."

Letty Rose bristled. "I take it you have found a *better* way to earn your living."

"As a matter of fact, I have." She watched as Letty's face grew red. "And I won't change my mind."

"Very well, you must leave these premises just as soon as you have packed your belongings. And I don't want to see you again." Letty Rose stalked off, muttering an oath under her breath.

Francesca dragged a hand across her eyes. They burned from lack of sleep. This sudden development was more than she could manage.

"You look very tired," Giorgio said.

She braced her hand against the wall. "I'm exhausted."

"Where were you, anyway?"

"I had business to take care of, on the coast." Francesca stopped before she told him too much. Still, she felt cowardly for withholding the truth. He might have heard the rumors . . . Couldn't she trust him to understand? Surely he wouldn't believe she had killed Leonard Kane. Or would he?

"I'm delighted that you're back. London is dull without you." He paused. "Does your resignation here mean that you accept my offer of employment?"

"Yes." Francesca studied his face. He was so eager, and his eyes shone with admiration.

He squeezed her hand. "I am delighted! You can start as soon as you wish."

Listening with only half an ear, Francesca thought about Carey, wondering where he was.

"Your eyes darken, reflecting sad thoughts." Giorgio stood very close, almost overpowering her with his presence. "I hope that in Estrella's and my care you'll be happy again."

Francesca swayed lightly, as if his eyes were hypnotizing her. She felt sleepy and confused. His arm tightened around her waist, his fingers rubbing her back. "No . . ." She struggled against him. "Stop! Please take your hands off of me," she snapped.

He let her go immediately, horror on his face. "Please forgive me! I was beside myself with worry. I can't describe the joy I felt at seeing you unharmed." He touched her hand gently. "Say you'll pardon me."

Francesca smoothed her hair, which had loosened from its chignon as she tore herself free. She tried to steady her breath. He looked so stricken that she relented. "Very well, but if I work for you, I won't tolerate any more embraces on your part. Is that understood? I accept your offer on one condition."

He brightened visibly. "I'll agree to any prerequisites." She had his entire attention.

"I want to come and go as I please from my lodgings, and lead a separate life from you and your sister. I will be a companion to Estrella, but only during specified hours each day."

"And you'll assist in the jewelry designing?"

"Yes, that will be my priority. I'll work very hard, and I accept your offer of room and board."

He gripped her hands and impulsively leaned forward to place a chaste kiss on her cheek, squeezing her fingers in gratitude.

"Francesca?" came an icy voice from the door.

Giorgio released her, and Francesca whirled around. Carey stood on the threshold, his face unshaven and his clothes rumpled. His gaze burned into her, and her heart beat wildly in her chest. Her stomach filled with butterflies. "Carey," she whispered, noticing the lump on the side of his head.

Giorgio gripped her shoulders as if to say he would protect her against Carey. "What do you want, McLendon?"

Francesca pulled away from his grasp. "Carey, where were you? I waited all day on the square." He looked as if he was ready to do battle, his body taut with anger and his face dark with fury.

"*You* worried about me? I cannot describe the torture I went through because of you. Why did you disappear from the square without leaving so much as a message at the inn?"

Francesca placed her hands on her hips. "The gall! Why didn't *you* drop a word before vanishing?"

Giorgio muttered an oath and bowed to Francesca. "We'd better speak later," he said, and left, giving Carey an exasperated glance.

For a long moment, Carey glared at Francesca. She

was so angry that her breath came in short, harsh gasps.

"Come," he ordered tersely.

Francesca crossed her arms over her chest. "I'm not going anywhere with you."

Carey took two rapid steps toward her, then seized her waist and lifted her off her feet. "I need to talk with you."

Raining blows on his chest, Francesca fought to get down. "I have nothing to say to you. You left me without a word."

"Would I search every inn, every road, every *ditch* if I had abandoned you?" He held her so hard she could not move, then carried her out of the room. "I won't leave until we have discussed this—in private." His words brooked no argument.

Francesca was both furious and strangely exhilarated. There was an iron strength in Carey that he had never revealed to her before. He had always been gentle and considerate with her. The power behind his anger awed her, just as it filled her with apprehension.

He strode into the hallway and climbed the steps to the first floor two at a time.

"Where are you taking me?" she demanded, fighting futilely to make him put her down. "Not to my room!"

"Yes, to your chamber, where we'll talk."

"Nothing will change," she protested.

His face was set and grim. "You haven't heard what happened." He kicked open the door to her attic room and stepped inside. When he set her down, he slammed the door shut and locked it. He struck a flint and lit the candle on the table.

Francesca fumed helplessly, her gaze darting to the door.

Dangling the key in front of her furious face, he slipped it into his pocket. "There. And don't ask me to give it to you, because I won't. Not until we've talked."

She saw that he meant it, and she seethed in silence. Then she said, "You have no right to order me about."

He strode to her and seized her about the neck so roughly that her hairpins scattered. "Have you any idea how afraid I was?" His voice was hoarse with tension, and his eyes were blazing.

"*You* should talk about worry! Of all the nerve!" Her face grew red, and she braced her arms against him to prevent him from coming any closer. He was breathing hard after his run up the stairs. His hair fell in a heavy wave over his face.

She realized how very attractive he was, and how dangerous was his anger. She stifled another scathing comment. He must have sensed her hesitation, because he gripped her wrists and dragged her stiff body toward his own. They exchanged searing glances, fighting a silent battle.

Then suddenly he let her go. "This will accomplish nothing." He sat down on the edge of the bed and massaged his neck. Shooting a glance at her from under hooded eyelids, he patted the mattress. "Sit here beside me."

Francesca obeyed warily, sitting far enough away so that they did not touch. "Who starts explaining?"

"You do, if you don't mind." He sounded so tired that Francesca leaned over and examined the lump on his head. It looked painful. She dipped a towel in the water pitcher and held it gently against the protrusion. He recoiled and swore under his breath.

"I waited in the square all day, and then Arnold and I went to the tavern at the appointed time to speak with the highwaymen."

"I'm glad you had Arnold with you, since I wasn't there to protect you." Carey braced his elbows against his thighs and hung his head. "I would never have been able to forgive myself if anything had happened to you."

"Where did you go?" she asked him.

He told her how he'd awakened in the coach, his head aching as if a horse had kicked him. "Abel Hitchins, if that was his real name, wasn't a reliable man," he said grimly. "Someone must have hired him to incapacitate me—or even kill me. A blow like that might have brought death to a someone with a thinner skull than mine." His lips curved upward, but Francesca didn't laugh.

"Who would have wanted you out of the way?"

He shook his head. "I don't know." He placed one of his hands over hers. "You do believe me, don't you? I didn't abandon you."

"Yes, I see that now," she said softly. "That lump looks nasty."

"Now tell me the rest," he urged, stiffening in pain as she pressed the towel against his head.

"I found the old man."

He jerked up from the bed, dashing away her hand. *"What?"*

"Yes. His name is Mr. Ingram." As she related everything that had transpired outside Beachy Head, he grew pale. A muscle worked in his jaw when she told him about the pistol shots.

"He wants us dead for some reason," Carey said. "But why?" He began pacing the room. "It looks as if Kane had a deadly enemy, after all."

"And now I have one," Francesca said. "Ingram was shooting to kill."

He gripped her shoulders and pulled her against him. " 'Tis obvious he's involved in some way, since he refused to see you."

His breath fanned the hair at her temple, and she felt safe with his arms around her. He held her tightly, as if loath to release her.

A sweet tension had sprung between them.

"I'm grateful that you're safe, Francesca." His voice was husky with emotion, and she sensed that he was about to kiss her. She wanted it . . . and suddenly she knew she could not suppress her yearning any longer. This time, she would give herself to him.

"Tell me, does your head ache terribly?" she asked.

His eyes were smoky with desire. "Not unbearably. I can still show you just how much I love you." He pulled her toward the bed. "You drive me to distraction."

He bent his face to hers, ravaging her lips with his own.

"Do you want more?" he murmured. His tender assault shattered any doubts she might have harbored, and she melted against him, sliding her arms around his neck.

"Oh, yes," she groaned as his tongue found hers, a sweet touch that sent her senses spinning. His tongue was both rough and soft, exploring her mouth relentlessly, until she thought she had completely dissolved and become one with him. She was part of him—his sandalwood scent, roving hands, warm skin that seemed as pliant and rich as velvet under her fevered fingertips. She knew she wanted to give this man her love, no matter what tomorrow might bring. The moment was too precious, too full to waste on doubt and fear. For the first time she truly knew what it was to be in love and sense a man's tender response, his respect. It was a novel feeling, since Leonard Kane had never cared for her.

"Come, my darling," he said. He pushed her slowly down against the pillows, then sank to his knees and lifted the hem of her skirts.

His fingers massaged her ankles and worked toward her knees, then higher until they encountered her garters. With the greatest care he rolled down her stockings and, after removing them, kissed the instep of each foot. "Every inch of you is beautifully formed," he said, his voice hoarse with emotion. He laved the tender area behind the ankle bone, then moved to the hollow behind her knee. She moaned with pleasure. As he kissed the soft insides of her thighs, he inhaled her sweet scent. Then he lay down in the bed beside her.

She made no resistance as he unlaced the bodice from her breasts, which were aching for his touch. She realized how desperately she wanted him. He slid the shift down over her shoulders so that he could bend his head to the round full treasures revealed below. The bodice fell to the floor as she leaned back so that he could touch each rose-tipped breast with his warm tongue.

Carey sighed deeply, and he buried his hands in her hair. The glossy curls could drive a man to distraction, as could the sweet curves of her body, so tantalizingly revealed to his gaze.

A wild need came over him, a need to take her right then and there, but he tempered his raw desire. His longing for Francesca had become so keen he thought he was going to burst from the craving within him.

Francesca dragged her hand through his hair and cradled his head to her stomach as he leaned over to undo the lacing at her waistband. His breath was hot on her bare belly as the material fell away. He moved his tongue slowly in the hollow of her navel, and a fire of passion curled sweetly in her abdomen. He released the underskirt and tossed it aside. Then he slid up her body. Holding her face cupped in both hands, he looked at her hard.

His eyes seared her with a fever that came from some deep hidden source within him, and swept her away like a helpless leaf with its torrent of hot sexuality. A throbbing sensation started at the soles of her feet and traveled upward with racing speed to fill her with the same wild fever.

She moaned as his shirt snagged on his breeches, laughing as he tore it loose and dragged it over his head. With the same haste he pulled off his breeches, and finally he stood before her, urgent with desire. In his passion, she recognized her own.

"I can't wait any longer," he whispered. The mattress groaned under their weight as he entwined his legs with hers. "I will make you mine." He took her hand and led it to the core of his throbbing desire. As he leaned back in sheer pleasure, his face suffused with ecstasy, Francesca realized what power she had over him.

She loved the feel of his hard shaft. When he opened his eyes, and with naked, possessive scrutiny assessed every inch of her body, she blushed.

"You're so lovely, my sweet," he said between gasps of pleasure. "Look at me."

He seemed to take enormous delight in her caresses—just as much joy as she felt touching his sculpted body. Her hand traveled over his flat abdomen, his narrow hips, his wide chest and hard arms. She could barely breathe for the excitement bursting within her.

Suddenly he raised himself up and eased her down on her back. Gently he parted her legs and began to massage her tender flesh slowly and rhythmically. Rapture swelled within her and, spreading her legs wider, she proudly offered her secrets to his ardent gaze. He moaned and bit down hard on his bottom lip as if in deep agony.

Sliding over her quickly, he drove into her with a swift thrust that robbed her of breath. His hard, wild pounding within her brought her swiftly to a place where every ounce of her awareness was gathered in the fevered spot between her thighs. Agony that

was a fierce glorious thing turned to ecstasy, as he
brought her over the quivering, spiraling edge of
release. Then she was with him as his climax catapulted him into an explosion of rapture.

Francesca was floating on a cloud, safe and ful-
filled, happy at last. Carey's arm lay heavily over
her waist, and he was nibbling on her earlobe. "This
was more than I ever dreamed of," he whispered.
"To stay in heaven, I'll keep you by my side forever."

His voice was velvet with satiation, and Francesca
touched the smooth muscles of his shoulder. He held
her so tight, as if afraid she would slide out of bed
and leave. She moved against him and he sucked in
his breath. "My Venus of delight," he whispered.
He slid his hand slowly over her. "Your body is soft
and silky, generously curved in the most enticing
places." He kneaded her derriere and Francesca
blushed. The intensity of his passion was intoxicating. She had never felt her heart and soul as naked
as she did with this man.

"And yours is hard in all the right places," she
said with a chuckle.

"You minx!" Murmuring endearments, he cradled her head on his shoulder.

Francesca drifted into sleep, only to wake up an
hour later, remembering that she had to leave the
Crimson Rooms. She had to pack this evening, and
the thought elated her. She would be free of Letty
Rose's orders forever.

She raised herself on her elbow and shook Carey's shoulder.

He opened his sleepy eyes, his face softer than
she had ever seen it. He trailed his fingers through
her long hair, hanging like a gleaming jet mantle
down her back. "You bring pure enchantment to
my life, my darling."

He caught her arm and pulled her down until her

cheek rested on his chest. "Don't worry about anything. I'll protect you from now on. We shall not part again." His heart hammered steadily against hers, and she sighed, thinking that Letty Rose had no power over her any longer. The future looked promising. If only she could find Leonard's killer . . .

"So much for our pact of friendship," Carey said wryly.

Francesca smiled. "I hope we can remain friends after what just happened. Love can be so complicated." She turned her head to look at him. "I died a little in Seaford when I discovered that you were gone. But I should have trusted you. It's so difficult to have faith in another man after Leonard's coldness. After his death, I swore I would create my own destiny, not succumb to some man's demands. And I intend to follow it."

He caressed her head gently. "Kane left you a damnable legacy—mistrust."

"He wasn't violent, but his iron control over my life robbed me of my personality. He made me believe that I was worthless. In the end, I didn't know what was right or wrong. When he died, I was thrust into a life where everyone rejected me, but my strength is now returning little by little. I met you, and I felt a need for your protection, but also a need to find my own way in life. When you disappeared in Seaford, I realized that I can't count on anyone but myself."

"I'm sorry you feel like that. I wouldn't have left you in Seaford—if I'd had any choice in the matter." He sounded sad.

She shook her head. " 'Tis beside the point now." Her voice trembled. "The cold fact is that Leonard Kane *bought* me. I stayed with him because I couldn't bear to see Father suffer. But ultimately Father brought on his own ruin by gambling most of the money away."

"Kane was a ruthless man." Carey rocked her gently.

"I thought I'd never love another man, but then *you*—" She touched the tip of his nose. "—can be so very persuasive. 'Tis a blessing to forget the past in your arms."

"I'll make you forget him completely," Carey whispered, stroking one breast until the nipple tightened.

"Only time will erase his memory, but you will be a great help." She curled her arms around his middle as he explored her delicate face with his lips.

Every memory of Leonard Kane was soon forgotten, as he whipped up a new frenzy of desire in her body. His force swept her into a maelstrom of unparalled rapture.

Chapter 16

"I intend to move away from here," Francesca said an hour later, as Carey cradled her in his arms. "Giorgio D'Angelo and his sister have offered me employment in their goldsmith shop. It's work I know."

He stiffened, and she knew he didn't approve of her decision. "I have already accepted. They've put rooms above their own living quarters at my disposal. I'll be comfortable there, and . . . respectable."

Carey lifted her aside and slid out of bed. "Respectability isn't everything. If you haven't realized it yet, D'Angelo's in love with you," he said flatly, his eyes smoldering with resentment. He paced back and forth, his slim hard-muscled body splendid in its nakedness.

"Nonsense," she said with a twinge of doubt.

"I'm sure of it. Haven't you noticed how he stares at you? How can you go to work for him, knowing that I don't trust him?"

"I don't understand what you have against him. It's your jealousy speaking. Our relationship has nothing to do with Giorgio and his sister." She feared Carey's reply to her next question. "What would you have me do? Work in the Crimson Rooms forever, and be at your beck and call whenever you desire an hour of lovemaking?''

"Of course not! I want to take care of you, protect you. We'll find lodgings for you in a respectable part of town."

"No. I must learn to take care of myself,'' she said quietly. "Only I can salvage my self-respect. What if we don't discover who killed Leonard? Suspicion is still attached to me, and it will be until I find out why Leonard was murdered." She looked at him sharply. "I don't want to spend the rest of my life as your mistress or working in a notorious gambling salon."

He stopped abruptly, tossing back his unruly hair. "As far as I can tell, you just became my mistress—figuratively."

"Don't label, my love. Next you'll tell me what to wear and what to eat. I've made up my mind; I'll work for Giorgio D'Angelo, and you cannot stop me." She rose, pulling the sheet closely around her as if to shut him out. After lighting another candle in the candlestick on the nightstand, she crossed the room and looked out the window. Torches and small rubbish fires burned in the square below, sending wavering orange light through the darkness.

"Don't turn away from me, Francesca. I need you." She glanced at him, moved by the choked sound of pain in his voice.

"You'll have to trust me," she said earnestly. "My life with the D'Angelos will mean only work and companionship."

His face darkened, and a muscle tightened in his jaw. She wasn't sure if it was from anger or sadness.

"What about us? I'm sure D'Angelo won't allow me to visit you at Haymarket. He'll find a way to keep us apart." He paused and spoke the next words with great effort. "Are you telling me to forget this night, and not to love you? Believe me, I fought my love for you until I thought I would burst. Perhaps you'll become another Daphne who'll only betray me in the end, but right now I'm taking that risk, even though I swore I would never put myself in this position again.''

''If you think I'm only another Daphne, then what we did tonight was wrong. Carey, we cannot take another step until you know me enough to understand that I would never betray you as she did.''

His laugh was mirthless. ''That remains to be seen.''

Francesca dared not look at him. She knew he was fighting his objection at her new employment, and his groundless suspicion of the Italians. ''You cannot make my decisions for me, Carey. Your doubts shall not rule our lives.''

He was silent for a long moment, standing quite still in the middle of the room. ''Then what we shared tonight meant nothing to you other than temporary pleasure,'' he said hollowly.

''I don't know what it means for the future.'' Sadness welled up within her. ''Your embrace enchanted me. It felt right, and—'' She blushed. ''—I don't believe anything, save an earthquake, could have stopped us. You showed me what passion can be like—something strong, and earth-shattering, and wonderful.''

He strode to her and gripped her shoulders hard, pulling her into his arms. ''It could be like that for us—always.'' He tilted up her face and moved his lips gently across one delicate cheek.

She slid out of his embrace. ''Passion and jealousy don't make a foundation on which to build a relationship. I need freedom to find myself—not another man to give me orders.''

He flung out his arms in a gesture of frustration. ''Why work for the Italians? There are so many other jewelers in London.''

She nodded slowly, the chamber's golden light softening her features. "Yes, but no one wants to employ a murderess."

He held her close and caressed her hair. "I take it you won't change your mind?"

"I won't alter my decision." She moved away from him and started piling her belongings on the table. "I must leave tonight. I told Letty Rose I won't obey her any longer, and she ordered me out of the house at once."

He sank down on the bed, watching her. "So you're moving this evening?" He sighed heavily. "I cannot stop you. As you say, 'tis your life. However, I hope we continue our friendship and investigation into your husband's death."

She dropped the sheet she'd been wearing and pulled on her shift, bodice, and underskirt. She smiled at him, making him weak with longing for her sweet embrace. "Yes, and I'm grateful to you." She tied the waistband of her skirt and brushed her hair.

"Before you start working for the D'Angelos, we must return to Beachy Head and confront Mr. Ingram." Carey pulled on his clothes, momentarily concentrating on the mystery. He pulled on his waistcoat and laced up his breeches. "I had hoped we could spend the rest of the night together."

She set down the hairbrush and coiled her dark tresses on top of her head. "I agree 'tis urgent that we travel into Sussex. Perhaps it's for the best to depart tonight, even though I'm exceedingly tired."

He put on his neckband, the spidery lace enhancing the dark masculinity of his face. "Yes, I could sleep another ten hours." He paused, then added thoughtfully, "Although I don't like the idea of you working for D'Angelo, I'm glad you're leaving the Crimson Rooms. By the way, have you told D'An-

gelo about how you lost your husband?'' Carey's
voice held a hint of irony.

Guilt washed over her. "No . . . I haven't. If I do,
he will turn away from me with loathing, and I will
end up back at the Crimson Rooms. This is my opportunity for respectable employment and living
quarters." She turned to him, her eyes dark with
anguish. "You must promise not to tell him, Carey."

He smiled ruefully. "He has probably heard the
gossip." Brushing back his hair, he added, "It hurts
to realize that his opinion matters more to you than
mine."

Anger flared in her eyes. "That's not true! You
knew my secret from the beginning, and you didn't
shun me. I will always appreciate that." She moved
toward the door, but he reached it first.

"But I'm not *respectable*, am I?" His gaze was un-
readable.

She paled. "Respectability is important when you
don't have any."

"There are other ways to gain your precious respectability—none of them involving D'Angelo."
Leaning against the old wood panels, Carey was reluctant to let her go. His face was taut with doubt.
"My opinion about D'Angelo is worth nothing, is
it? What have I to offer compared to him? I don't
have noble ancestry, only a noble bastardy. Right
now, all I have to offer is my love."

Silence hovered between them. Francesca took one
step toward him and cradled his face between her
hands. Tears glistened in her eyes. "Your love is the
most precious thing you can offer." She paused.
"Remember this: you will always be valuable to me.
No matter what."

Carey sighed. He yearned to take her in his arms
and crush her against him, as if that would remove

all her doubts about him and their future together. "With me, you would not lack for anything."

Wild attraction surged between them, but he could see her determination to fight it. "Don't accept D'Angelo's offer," he pleaded. "He will keep you a prisoner from the moment you move into his house."

Francesca tossed her head. "Balderdash! He's been a good friend. You're so jealous you cannot see the truth."

He took a step away from her, leaving the way to the door open. "Where are you going now?" he asked.

"Cauliflower Arnold has promised to help me move my things to Haymarket." She placed a hand on his arm. "Then we'll travel to Sussex if you like."

"I still think you're making a mistake in trusting the Italian."

She placed her hand on his arm, but he moved away. "Your accusation is groundless."

He shrugged, avoiding her gaze. " 'Tis only a strong feeling I have."

She laughed. "That's preposterous!"

"Call it what you will," he said and stalked out. "I will fetch the carriage."

Dawn had arrived when they set out toward East-bourne and Beachy Head. Since Caleb Hitchins, the coachman, was still missing, Cauliflower Arnold had promised to drive the team. "I ain't goin' t' miss an opportunity t' give that ol' sod, Mr. Ingram, 'is just desserts fer shootin' at us," he said, and jumped up on the box. There wasn't much Carey or Francesca could do to stop him.

Francesca was so tired she slept most of the way, as did Carey. He awakened her at noon for a meal at a roadside inn. Lines of weariness were etched on his face, and his eyes were somber. She caressed his cheek. "You're still brooding about the Italian?" she asked.

He turned away from her and alighted from the halted carriage. "It makes no difference, does it? You won't change your mind."

"No . . ."

"Then there's nothing more to say." He marched toward the inn.

Francesca followed, wishing they would discuss the problem further. Carey had cut her off, and desolation swept through her. "Stubborn man!" she whispered. Why wouldn't he understand?

Cauliflower Arnold remembered the road to the decrepit old mansion that was Mr. Ingram's home. The sun had begun to slant sharply toward the horizon when he reined the horses to a halt in front of the entrance.

The silence in the yard was broken only by bird chatter and the drone of bees. Carey jumped down while Francesca waited in the coach. The thought of perhaps facing more gunshots made her blood run cold.

The house was shrouded in stillness. Carey knocked, but no one came to open the door. He banged harder, pacing the uneven stone step. There was no sign of life, and the curtains were tightly drawn.

"Try the door," Francesca suggested, and Carey complied. It was locked.

"Wait here. I'll go to the back to see if there are any open windows," he said.

Before she could warn him to be careful, he'd disappeared around the corner. Francesca wrung her hands with worry. Cauliflower Arnold stood at the horses' heads, his shoulders tense and his eyebrows meeting in a fierce scowl.

The minutes dragged, and the silence was ominous. Francesca let out a sigh of relief when Carey finally returned.

"No one is home. The house must have been deserted since you were here. Nobody has replaced the window that you broke."

"Why would Ingram flee like that?" she commented.

"He has something to hide, and I wish I had been here to confront him." Carey glared at her, as if he blamed her for Ingram's disappearance.

Anger shot through her. "Remember, I had no idea where you had gone," she shouted. "Should I have waited all night on the square, praying you would return?" She jumped into the carriage and slammed the door. "You have a lot of gall blaming me for Ingram's departure."

"Naw, listen 'ere. Ye can't blame each other," Arnold said lamely. "What 'appened, 'appened. 'Tis no one's fault."

Carey said nothing. His face set in grim lines, he climbed onto the box. "I'll travel with you, Arnold. We must visit the inn outside Beachy Head and ask if the people there know anything."

Cauliflower Arnold gave Francesca a sheepish smile and gripped the reins. "We'll find that bloomin' sod yet, Miss Francie. Don't worry 'bout it."

They reached the Dog and Whistle half an hour later. Francesca was eager to hear what the proprietor had to say, so she followed Carey inside. She refused to look at him, and the tension was thick between them.

After greeting the landlord, Carey said, "Do you know where Mr. Ingram has gone?"

"Ingram? Naw, I don't, but 'is coachman, Bertie, came in 'ere a few days ago for a pint. In a bloomin' 'urry 'e was. He said they would be gone for a month or longer."

"A month!" Francesca said with a gasp. "How will we ever learn what happened?"

Carey threw her a veiled glance. "If you hadn't been in such haste to solve the mystery—" he said sotto voce.

Francesca wanted to hit him with the first available heavy object. "If you say one more thing, I will—"

"I see ye're eager to meet Mr. Ingram, but as I said, ye must wait until 'e returns." The proprietor lifted his shoulders in an apologetic gesture. "Ingram's very much a recluse, so I don't know 'is comin' and goin's except what Bertie tells me. I do know that Ingram 'eads some sort o' foreign business in Lunnon." He chuckled. "Can't be a lucrative enterprise, since 'is 'ouse is 'bout t' fall down over 'is 'ead."

"You're sure you don't know where he works?" Carey asked.

The landlord shook his head. "Naw, I 'ave no idea."

Francesca walked outside, regret laying heavily in her chest. "We'll never find him now," she told Arnold, who was watching the horses.

"Ingram 'as to return one day. 'E can't be gone forever. We can come back 'ere later." He cleared his throat in embarrassment. "An' don't take Mr. M. seriously. 'E doesn't really blame ye for this. Somethin' else's botherin' 'im."

"That much is obvious." Francesca thought about Giorgio D'Angelo. She knew what was weighing down Carey's mind—her decision to move in with the Italians.

Carey stepped into the carriage. "What now?" he asked, giving her a challenging stare.

"This is such a disappointment. There's nothing we can do but turn back the way we came," she said. "I must begin my new employment, and then visit Mr. Ingram in a month. There's no other choice.''

Carey clenched his jaw and slammed the door. "I suppose you're right,'' he muttered. Leaning back against the squabs, he pushed his hat over his face. "Don't wake me before we've arrived in London.''

Francesca seethed in silence, longing to rain arguments on his head. Darkness was falling as they headed toward the City. The sun's last rays painted the sky reddish-gold, and pewter clouds towered in the distance. Before long, rain would drench the fields. A cool breeze blew through the open window, and Francesca hastened to close it.

Arnold must have noticed the advancing rainclouds, for he had increased the pace. The horses' hooves thundered along the road. Francesca wondered how Carey could sleep through the bumps that jarred the coach, but perhaps he was only pretending to be asleep—while he was actually brooding under his hat. Oh, she could tear that hat right from his head . . . and then . . .

Carey was wide awake, recounting every minute he'd spent in Francesca's company since that first time they had met at the Crimson Rooms. Why had he let his anger grip him, when the last thing he wanted was to push her away? She had a right to a better life. *Any* life would be better than the one she'd lived at the Crimson Rooms. But he had one question he had not dared to ask her earlier—he was still afraid of the thought of proposing marriage to her. An offer would be so final, and he wanted to be sure he desired to spend the rest of his life with her.

He knew now that the answer was yes. He had no doubts; he loved her, and he hoped she would happily accept his offer. The thought of her reply sent a flurry of excitement through him. Her eyes would sparkle, her lips would part eagerly, her cheeks would glow a delicate pink . . . They would get married, and then he could truly protect her.

Suddenly Cauliflower Arnold gave a shout and the carriage lurched to one side. It bounced over rough ground, then tilted over on the other side. Carey flew helplessly across the seat and knocked his temple against the wall. Then the coach lay still. The horses neighed, and Arnold swore.

Groaning in pain, Carey heard Francesca scream. Frantic, he moved toward her, but the seats seemed to be upside down. Confused, he tried to guess where she was. After finding his bearings, he moved over to her. Then, panic gripping his heart, he saw that she was crumpled into a heap, her head leaning against the edge of the seat.

He was vaguely aware of rain pelting down, and a vicious wind gusting through the door.

"Are you hurt?" he asked, his temple pounding. He touched her shoulder gently. Her hair had tumbled loose, hiding her face from his worried gaze.

Arnold stuck his head inside, and raindrops spattered the leather upholstery. "Are ye still alive?"

Francesca moaned and moved. "What happened?" she asked, clutching her arm.

"Somethin' is wrong wi' th' wheels," Arnold explained. "We careened off th' lane."

"What about the horses?" Carey asked, pulling Francesca into his arms.

"Th' shackles broke, lettin' 'em loose. I've tied 'em to a tree. Mighty nervous they are."

Carey lifted Francesca up to Arnold, who dragged her from the overturned carriage. The darkness outside was complete. Carey stumbled from the vehicle, pulling the cloaks with him. "This is terrible. I had hoped to return to London tonight."

"It bain't possible. Th' wheel came right orf th' axle." Arnold placed Francesca on the ground, and she braced herself with one arm against the fallen carriage. Carey placed his arm around her shoulders and pulled her close. He rocked her gently until she sighed and slid from his grip. "Don't worry about me," she said.

Arnold brought one of the lanterns to throw light on the broken axle. In grim silence, Carey and Arnold studied the shattered wood.

"Of all th' rotten luck!" Arnold exclaimed. "Begad, we would all be dead if I 'ad driven faster." He pointed at a place right beside the wheel where the wood had splintered. "A weak spot 'ere, Mr. M."

Carey rubbed his aching temple. "Looks like you're right." He straightened and swore. "Why tonight? Why didn't it happen earlier?"

"Took some time to sheer orf, I believe," Arnold said. "What shall we do now, Mr. M.?"

"Walk to the nearest inn. There's no other choice unless we want to sleep in the woods and be soaked by rain."

"I'm already drenched," Francesca said forlornly.

Carey wound a cloak around her, tying it securely at the neck. "Are you in pain?"

She shook her head. "No. Just dazed."

"Then we must walk." Carey led her onto the lane.

"How far is it to the nearest inn?"

"A mile perhaps, or longer. I don't know exactly where we are."

Cauliflower Arnold brought the horses. "She can ride. Th' wheeler 'as calmed down sufficiently."

Carey nodded and lifted her onto the wet horse. "I'm sorry," he said, patting her thigh once, "that I lost my temper earlier. That was unforgivable."

Francesca was too tired to respond. She nodded, grateful that their quarrel was over. The rain ran in rivulets down her face, and her hands were ice-cold.

She was shaking from the shock, and was grateful to feel the horse's broad back beneath her. It was oddly comforting.

For an hour they walked in silence along the lane. Drops rustled in the hedges on both sides of the road. As they turned a bend, a light shimmered at last through the rain and fog. "Look! A 'ouse of some sort, a farm maybe," said Arnold.

When they drew abreast with the building, Francesca saw that it was a small inn.

"Thank God for this," Carey said. "Fortune hasn't completely abandoned us." He led the horse carrying Francesca into the tiny yard and banged on the door. A few minutes later it opened, revealing a corpulent man wearing a nightshirt and a white tasseled nightcap.

"Mercy be!" he called out. "Ye must be soppin' wet. Come in, come in!" He beckoned them with a wave of his hand. Eager to show his hospitality, he pulled out a chair for Francesca, and Carey carried her inside.

"I'm not crippled," she said with a wry smile, "only cold and wet."

Carey set her down as carefully as if she were made of precious china. "This is nothing to joke about. I'm grateful to still be alive, and you should be too." He spoke quietly with the proprietor, then turned back to Francesca. "He's giving you the best room for the night. I'll help Arnold see to the horses."

When she didn't reply, he carried her upstairs, following the landlord. She was so weary that her head fell weakly against his shoulder.

The chamber was small, but sweet-smelling and clean. The sheets felt crisp, and the mattress was firm beneath her as he lay her down on the bed. She was still wearing her cloak and damp dress.

"Just wait here for a few minutes, and I'll return

to help you undress,'' Carey said and left the room. The landlord had put the candlestick on the nightstand, and Francesca could make out white walls adorned with a single crude painting of a ship in a storm. She struggled to sit up, but dizziness overtook her.

A few minutes later, Carey's steps echoed on the stairs. He stepped into the room and closed the door softly. ''The landlord promised to bring some tea, but I said no.'' Carey held out a bottle of brandy and two glasses. ''We'll have a nip of this and then we'll sleep.''

She nodded and held out her cold hand for one of the glasses that he'd filled. ''Thank you.''

He sank down on his knees and undid the clasp of her cloak. Then he pulled off her wet slippers, stockings, and her damp skirts. She made no resistance when he unlaced her bodice and dragged it off. Before long she was sitting in her shift, shivering. He gently eased her back against the pillows and tucked the blanket around her. Without wasting time, he divested himself of his own clothes and slid into bed beside her. Cradling her close, he kissed her pale forehead.

''I never wanted this to happen,'' he said. '' 'Tis like a bad omen. Everywhere we turn it's a road going nowhere.''

''Yes . . . but our misfortune cannot last forever,'' she said.

He brushed back her hair. Her eyes were huge and dark. ''I hope you're right. It's late and we're both tired.''

She nodded and shut her eyes in exhaustion. '' 'Tis a miracle we're still alive.''

''Yes.'' He curled up close to her, and they lay like two spoons fitting snugly together. He blew at the tiny curls on the nape of her neck. ''While we're waiting for Mr. Ingram to return to Sussex, we might as well solidify our relationship, Francesca."

In surprise, she turned her head and moved so that she could look at him. "What do you mean?"

He held her chin in a tender grip and looked deeply into her eyes. "Will you make me the happiest man in London and marry me?"

Her eyes widened in shock, and she stiffened in his arms. "Marry you?" she whispered, as a look of dismay crossed her features. "No!"

Chapter 17

S tunned, he stared at her. *"No?* Nothing else?"

"No," she said, moving away from his side. "Where did you get the idea I was ready to marry you?"

"Well, I thought for a long time in the coach. After what we've shared—"

"—you took for granted that I would say yes," Francesca filled in. "I'm flattered," she added, softening. She traced his jaw with her fingertip. "But I've explained why I don't want my life to be ruled by a man."

"I wouldn't force you into anything," he argued.

"At this very moment you're trying to coerce me into matrimony." She sighed, pulling the blanket closer around her. "Admit it—you only want to keep me away from the Italians. That's why you're offering me marriage. It galls you to see that I want a life of my own."

He flung himself from the bed. "Balderdash! That was the farthest thought from my mind. Are you so preoccupied with yourself and your future that you can deny our love?" He raked a hand through his damp hair.

"That's not true! Carey, who could stop *you* if you desired to try a different course of life? Why, you say you want to live in the country and raise cattle, and you're searching for a way to finance the venture. When you find the means, you'll realize your dream." She paused. "Like you, I listen to my inner voice, and I won't let anyone dictate my life again." She pounded the mattress with her fist. "For the first time in my life, I have a chance to discover what it is to live by myself, to make my own decisions, and no one is going to hinder me."

Carey stared at her, then he shrugged. His eyes were dark with misery, but he forced a smile to his lips. "Well, I guess that said it all. No more words need to be exchanged on the matter." He dragged on his clothes with jerky movements and walked toward the door. "But I still don't think your choice of employer is sound!"

"Stop this!" Francesca begged, turning away as he left the room. She bit down on a corner of the sheet to stop herself from crying. His proposal had been infinitely tender and tempting, but she couldn't give up her dreams just to adopt his. Not yet. She recalled the shock in his eyes when she'd refused his proposal, and guilt weighed her down. How would she ever find a way to reconcile her longing for freedom with the love she felt for him? She feared she would have to give up one to fulfill the other. Besides worrying about the attempts on their lives, she had to bear the burden of indecision. What was right? Was she too selfish? Or was Carey too demanding?

Her head pounding from the blow she'd received in the accident, she tossed and turned all night. Dawn arrived and her eyes were dry from lack of sleep. The rain had not lessened during the night. Like a gray curtain it hung from the leaden skies. Her spirits low, Francesca dressed and went downstairs.

Carey was already eating a breakfast of eggs, toast, and ham. "Arnold is estimating the damage to the coach. Perhaps we'll hire one here, or ride back to London.''

She wanted to talk to Carey about their argument, but no words came out. He didn't invite her confidence as he finished his breakfast and left the room. She sensed that his words about the coach were the only ones he would speak until they parted ways in London. Feeling bereft and confused, she went in search of food. She wished she were back in the City.

"You'll be comfortable, I'm sure," Estrella D'Angelo said excitedly. "I took the liberty of having some pieces of furniture moved up here." She gestured at a table with a marble top and a plump sofa upholstered in light-blue and gold brocade. Another table held a potted plant and an empty vase decorated with a painted pastoral scene.

Francesca viewed her new abode with mixed feelings. She wished she could have decorated the rooms herself, but where would she have found the funds to purchase furniture and curtains? After she'd parted from Carey an hour ago, a dark mood had seized her. They had hired a horse for Cauliflower Arnold and then ridden back to London. The carriage axle would take two days to repair in the hamlet of Barnham, where they had spent the night at the inn.

Absentmindedly she touched the smooth surface of the marble. "It's very lovely. You've been kind to assist me." Her gaze wandered from the light-blue curtains to the nut-brown armoire in the bedroom beyond the arched opening. The four-poster bed had no hangings, and Francesca was glad she would be choosing her own material for that—later, when she could afford it.

She set down the basket, from which emanated a plaintive meow. Copper leaped out as she lifted the lid. Francesca smiled and darted a glance at Estrella. She noticed the small frown on the Italian woman's brow.

"I hope you don't mind . . ." Francesca said. "Copper's an orphan, you see. I 'adopted' him when I went to Sussex, and I cannot very well abandon him now."

"I suppose not. I don't know how my brother will feel about it. He's no animal lover." A short pause ensued. "But you're kind to care for homeless felines."

"Copper gives me company. He charmed everyone at the Crimson Rooms."

After parting from Carey, Francesca had said good-bye to Cauliflower Arnold. "I'll miss ye and Copper," Arnold had said with an earnest expression. "If ye ever need me, jest let me know, Miss Francie." Cauliflower Arnold had become a good friend during her time at the Crimson Rooms, and his concern warmed her heart.

"I used to have a dog when I was a girl," Estrella remarked as she straightened a doily embroidered with daisies and bluebells. "He died, and I was too distraught ever to risk that disappointment again."

Francesca sensed an almost brittle sadness in the other woman.

Estrella moved toward the door. "I look forward to our visits to the cloth merchants and the milliners." In a sudden shift of mood, she giggled happily. "I never could refuse a new hat or gown." She smiled. "I will see to supper now. I hope everything is to your satisfaction."

"Thank you. I couldn't be happier," Francesca replied. That wasn't quite true, though. She wished she had parted on a friendly note with Carey. His resentment toward the D'Angelos worried her, and she couldn't bear the thought of his jealousy over Giorgio. The Italians had been nothing but kind to

her, and she still seethed at the memory of Carey's
warnings. What right did he have to caution her?

Carey's lodgings on St. James's Street were desolate and dark when he arrived home after one in
the morning, after sharing a bottle of brandy with
two cronies at the Cocoa Tree Club. He was so exhausted he could barely move. He hoped he'd find
peace in sleep tonight. Francesca had made her
choice, and he should ignore the nagging concern
that ate at his insides and kept him from slumber.

His desk, which was stacked with books, looked
dusty and uninviting. The candles had gutted, spilling wax onto the cherry-wood desktop.

His limbs were heavy, and his head throbbed
dully. He walked into the bedroom beyond the sitting room. The chambers were small but adequate
for himself, Bigelow, and the cook. Hitchins lived
above the stables in the mews, and to Carey's relief,
the coachman had returned. He'd been working in
the stables that evening, and when Carey had inquired about his disappearance before their awful
trip to Seaford, he'd said:

"Truly, guv, I don't know what 'it me. I went to
see my sister, an' some bloke came up behind me
an' dealt me a blow on th' 'ead." Hitchins had
rubbed the sore spot under his dusty cocked hat. "I
managed to get t' me sister's 'ouse in Maiden Lane,
an' there I spent a long time in bed." Distress
creased his square face. "Sorry, guv, but I don't recall an'thin' that 'appened durin' th' time I was
gone."

Carey had then told Hitchins about the impostor,
and berated him for not revealing that he had family
in London. "I searched for you, Hitchins, and your
friends in the alehouse vowed you must be dead
since you had disappeared so suddenly."

"Ye don't git rid o' me that easily," Hitchins had

said with a chuckle, and continued his work as if nothing untoward had happened. Casting a fond eye on the carriage horse, King, he'd added, " 'Sides, yer nags need me."

Bigelow was snoozing in a chair by the bedroom door, and Carey didn't bother to awaken the old man. Slowly he began to take off his coat and waistcoat. He glanced at himself in the mirror. The lump above his ear was still faintly visible, but the gash above the other ear had begun to heal.

He untied his velvet bow and shook his hair loose. Then he yawned and gazed longingly at the bed. Massaging his neck, he headed toward the fourposter.

A sharp knock sounded on the door. Carey stiffened, wondering who had business with him at this late hour. Mortimer? No, Charles was in the country. Francesca? Had she changed her mind?

Nevertheless, he unsheathed the rapier which he had unbuckled earlier and went through his study-cum-sitting room to the front door. Putting his ear to the panel, he listened for a sound, a voice, but heard nothing.

"Who's there?" he demanded.

Only silence answered, then a weak voice called out, "An accident outside. A man's bleedin' t' death. *Help!*"

Carey returned quickly to the bedroom and pulled on his coat. He still wore his boots, and his cloak lay where he'd slung it over a chair beside the front door. He buckled the rapier to his side and wielded a loaded pistol in his hand as he opened the door.

He went down the wooden stairs to the street below and sent swift glances in both directions. St James's was dimly lit by a few torches and lanterns.

"Where are you?" he called out. "What happened?"

"Here! Come quickly," the same faint voice called from the side of the building.

Light spilled on the cobblestones from windowsill candles three houses away, but as soon as Carey turned the corner to Bennet Street, darkness engulfed him.

" 'Tis too dark. I cannot—"

The pounding of hobnailed boots reached his ears, and suddenly the shadows came alive. Something struck him violently on the chest, and he momentarily lost his breath. Another blow hit his head. Carey parried with his arm, but hands closed quickly around his throat.

He dragged in air with difficulty. White-hot pain seared his chest as he slammed the butt of his pistol against the head of the man who was trying to strangle him. The blow was angled, but it stunned the villain enough to loosen his grip.

Gasping painfully, Carey pried himself away from the steely fingers and whipped out his rapier. His blood pounded in his ears as he crouched to lunge anew at his attacker, but the man turned and charged off around the corner. As Carey ran in pursuit of the fleeing man, a large rock whistled through the air from the darkness by the wall and hit him squarely on the shoulder.

"Blast!" Carey swore, gritting his teeth. His whole arm becoming instantly numb, he dropped the pistol. He barely had time to whirl around before a black figure in a heavy cloak pounced upon him. Under the weight of this new attacker, Carey went down on the cobblestones. His head ached from the blow, and his right arm was useless.

From the faint light of a distant lantern, Carey saw a glittering blade. He jerked aside instinctively as the knife went for his throat. The steel missed him by an inch and hit the cobblestones, making a deadly ringing sound. Carey twisted desperately to get out from under the weight of the other man as the weapon rose once more.

"Damn you," Carey shouted, bucking under the heavy man. The blade sliced through the velvet stand-fall collar of his cloak, and he saw a flash of the intricately carved handle.

The street brightened with torches, and feet pounded along the street. "Guv? I 'eard th' fight—" At the sound of Bigelow's voice, Carey's attacker jumped up. In the light from the flambeaux, Carey recognized Lucas Halden. With a lightning-fast twist, Carey grabbed Halden's leg.

"I should have known it was you, you coward. You would try to ambush me."

"You know as well as I do that we have a score to settle," Halden spat. "You had no right to involve yourself in my business."

"On the dueling field," Carey returned, his voice icily soft. "But you're too much of a coward to fight fairly." Struggling to regain his breath, Carey held his enemy fast until Bigelow cocked a pistol and pointed it at Halden's chest. "But why waste a good opportunity? We can have that duel right now." He stood and brushed off his knees. "Only an idiot would seek revenge for something as petty as a quarrel over a whore."

"Petty or not, I'm tired of your meddling, McLendon." Halden sent a furtive glance at Hitchins and the stable lad, both holding torches and heavy cudgels in their hands. "Besides, I cannot forgive you for accusing me of cheating at cards. But a duel is out of the question tonight. I have no seconds to protect me—"

Carey laughed derisively and pushed aside the pistol. "Run for your life, Halden, or Bigelow might put a lead ball in your heart. Run!"

Halden's eyes smoldered with hatred. "You'll regret this!"

"Shall I send a bullet into 'im, Mr. McLendon?" Bigelow asked. " 'Twould give me great pleasure."

Carey shook his head wearily. "Not yet. I have a question for the scoundrel." He took Halden's collar and tightened his grip until the other man gasped for air. "Did you ambush me in the park and shoot at me?" He squeezed tighter until Halden's eyes bulged, and his lips turned bluish. "Well? I want the truth!"

He let go of his grip abruptly, and Halden staggered forward, almost losing his balance. "No! I have no idea what you're talking about!"

Carey stared at him with narrowed eyes. "If you're lying, I will most certainly kill you."

Halden rubbed his neck. "Is that a threat?"

"A promise." He shook his fist in Halden's face. "Tell me the truth."

Halden swallowed convulsively. "I didn't shoot at you in the park. 'Tis God's truth, I swear."

Carey cursed and aimed a kick at the conniver's backside as Halden took off running.

"There! Good riddance, but I don't think I've heard the last of him. One day soon, I'll see him in the dueling field, even if it means dragging him there by the scruff of his neck."

"Th' man 'as no pride. A true gentleman 'onors a challenge," Bigelow grumbled.

"Halden never was a gentleman, and he never will be." Carey moved painfully, cautiously rotating his arm. "No broken bones, thank God."

Once inside he poured himself a stiff measure of brandy. Bigelow clucked around him like a mother hen. "Ye should let me take a look at yer shoulder. Per'aps ye need a 'ot fomentation on it."

Carey waved him away. "Nonsense."

Bigelow wrung his hands. "Ye look bone-tired, an' white 'bout th' mouth, Mr. McLendon. Ye need yer rest, or ye'll collapse, mark me words."

Carey headed toward his bed. "Yes, I'll sleep now—for the next twenty-four hours."

Yet as he lay in bed, his thoughts whirled endlessly. If Halden hadn't made the attempt on his life, who had?

Chapter 18

Carey sighed deeply, glancing without interest at the new coat that his tailor, Mr. Everton, had just finished. It was made of white satin with silver trim and intricate loops of braid along the hem and front edges.

"But, Mr. McLendon, how can you be so indifferent to the most beautiful coat I've ever made for you?" Mr. Everton rolled his eyes. "I have always been eager to please you, although your payments are sometimes late—"

" 'Tis excellent," Carey broke in. "I'll try it on later." He reached into the pocket of his cloak and pulled out the silk mask Francesca had found in the dry riverbed at Seaford.

"But Mr. McLendon, you used to be so admiring, so interested in my latest designs," Mr. Everton complained, hanging up the coat with an audible sniff. "You have changed." In dismay he gazed at his treasured customer from head to toe. "You look *untidy*, sir, if you don't mind me saying so."

"That's neither here nor there. I no longer have the inclination to waste my time creating new fashions." He stepped closer, holding out the mask. "Now, can you tell me who made this? 'Tis undoubtedly of good quality."

The rotund, bewigged tailor took the mask between his deft fingers and rubbed the satin. "Ecod, but 'tis filthy!" he exclaimed. "You cannot wear this." He gave Carey a despairing glance and fluttered his plump hands. "I worry about you, Mr. McLendon! You must be ill."

Carey sighed in exasperation. "Calm yourself, Mr. Everton, I don't intend to wear it. I'd just like to know who fashioned it." He wandered around Everton's cramped Bond Street shop quarters while the short man studied the mask. Bolts of elegant damask, silk, and brocade shimmered on the tables. He impatiently fingered a powder-blue velvet.

"Well?"

" 'Tis foreign, Mr. McLendon. Made in France, most likely. The Frogs make this type of heavier silk. Furthermore, 'tis rather old."

Carey creased his brow in thought. "Old?"

"Yes, the mask is made in a winged style that was fashionable twenty years ago."

Mr. Ingram's face flashed into his mind. Had it been his? "French, do you say?"

The small man nodded vigorously. "Or perhaps Spanish or Italian."

"Italian? That means I cannot trace its maker unless I go to France or even farther south?"

The tailor scratched his ear. "You cannot, but I don't see what difference it makes. The milliner who made these types of masks might be dead, her business naught but a memory."

Carey took the mask from the tailor's hand and stuffed it back into his pocket. "Thank you," he said absentmindedly, and headed for the door.

"But—but Mr. McLendon! Your coat! What about your coat?" Mr. Everton sputtered. "You haven't even tried it on."

"Send it to my lodgings." Carey closed the door without another glance at his elegant new coat.

Sauntering along Bond Street, swinging his cane,

he thought about that day in Seaford when he had first set eyes on Francesca. Someone wearing that satin mask had been involved in Leonard Kane's murder. Had that same person hit Francesca over the head? Ah, Francesca . . . His thoughts always returned to her. At first glance her loveliness had been like a blow to his stomach, and when he'd learned more about her sweet character, he had lost his heart. He feared he would not easily recover from his overwhelming feelings. By choosing her work over his love, Francesca had hurt him. Misery had dragged him down ever since their last meeting, but he wouldn't give up easily. He would make her see reason, convince her that he never planned to forbid her to work if it gave her such satisfaction.

He fingered the mask in his pocket. *Italian?* Could it be a clue, or was it mere coincidence that D'Angelo was Italian . . . Carey sighed. How could he voice such a suspicion to Francesca without alienating her completely?

"Dreaming, are you?"

Carey started and eyed the young man at his side. Delight swept through him. "Morty! Thank God you're back. London is boring without you. How was Mortimer's Meadow?" Slapping his friend's shoulder, he glanced at Lord Mortimer's trim form, as elegant as ever in a brown suit, flowered waistcoat, cocked hat, and gold-tipped cane.

"The old heap is getting older, and it needs constant attention." His sharp eyes took in Carey's rumpled appearance and sad face. "You look worse than when I left. Life's been hard?"

Carey smiled wryly. "Life's always hard. I've been lucky at cards while you were gone. Won five hundred pounds the other night at the Crimson Rooms."

Lord Mortimer was silent, prodding his cane into the cobblestones as they walked toward Piccadilly.

Carey could sense the direction of his thoughts, his questions. "And Mrs. Kane, how is she faring?"

Carey stared into the distance. "Francesca's fortune has changed. The Italian jeweler in Haymarket offered her employment, and she moved into their house." His heart hammered painfully against his ribs as he said the name of the woman he loved so much that he could barely speak of her without choking.

Lord Mortimer gave him a swift glance. "You sound unhappy."

Carey could not answer. He gave his friend a hard stare which warned him not to probe further, but Lord Mortimer paid no heed. "You truly love her, don't you?"

Carey nodded.

"From your glum face, I take it you two had a lovers' tiff," Mortimer went on. "You must not let that separate you."

Carey told him about Francesca's rejection of his offer of marriage. To his chagrin, Lord Mortimer laughed. "You cannot stop at that. Ask her again, but wait until she has settled down at her work. After a while, a future with you will truly appear rosy to her—that is, if she really loves you."

His heavy mind much eased, Carey shook Mortimer's arm. "Are you related to Cupid, Morty? The way you go on, one might think you've been married three times and lived a long life filled with love."

Lord Mortimer laughed. "Of course not. But I like to observe others in the wild throes of love."

"You cynical old goat," Carey said affectionately.

Mortimer tweaked the lace at his throat and pulled down the sleeves of his coat. "Whatever happens, life goes on. Shall we have dinner at Tom's Coffee House?"

Carey stared unseeingly at a matron scolding a

ragamuffin boy in the middle of the street. The sound of her voice grated on his nerves. He wished he was going to see Francesca. "Yes . . . yes, I expect we should."

"And then we'll attend the ball at Burlington House." Mortimer sighed audibly at Carey's thoughtful face. "You need distraction, old boy. A ball will be just the thing. This business with Francesca Kane is befuddling your mind."

"Morty, I don't trust the Italian. He's not what he seems. Why, the other night he was at the Crimson Rooms, winning steadily at hazard."

"You mean he's an inveterate gambler while putting up a respectable facade? Well, a lot of gentlemen—"

"It's more than that." Carey paused. It wouldn't help his cause to throw accusations at D'Angelo before he had proof. Morty was a discreet fellow, but his tongue might slip.

"More?" Mortimer commented in surprise. "What murky roads is your mind traveling now?"

Carey decided not to say anything about the mask. "I think he cheats. I've noticed that he always fleeces his opponent heavily."

Mortimer nudged his arm. "Been keeping watch over him, eh? As for D'Angelo liking a card game, you're right. I've seen him at various gambling salons."

"I couldn't help but notice his prowess at the tables." Carey slapped Lord Mortimer's shoulder. "But you said something about a ball at Burlington House?"

"Yes, I think a bit of flirting with some lovely damsel would do you a world of good."

"Nonsense!" Carey snorted, but he agreed to attend the ball.

* * *

The massive gateway designed by Colen Campbell for Burlington House on Piccadilly swung open to admit a stream of carriages. The colonnades were ablaze with lanterns, and the Palladian stone facade of the main complex gleamed like a jewel.

The steps were filled with people in full evening attire. Precious stones gleamed, and satins and silks shimmered. The guests' smiles sparkled as much as the costly jewels. Carey adjusted the sleeves of his new white coat, which had been delivered to him that afternoon. Francesca should have been here, he thought wistfully. She belonged here, although she didn't seem to miss the social whirl.

Carey and Lord Mortimer stepped down from the carriage and joined the other guests waiting to be admitted.

"There was a time when you would have enjoyed this type of entertainment, Carey," Lord Mortimer said, looking handsome in his burgundy velvet coat and white waistcoat encrusted with gold embroidery.

Carey nodded pensively. "Then I spent naught but empty days and nights. Life passes too quickly; I want to settle down. I have decided to leave London as soon as possible."

Lord Mortimer glanced at him curiously. "You have changed beyond recognition, old fellow. Ever since the Rebellion, you've been different."

"War makes one realize one's limitations," Carey said with a faint smile. He sighed and braced his hands on the knob of his cane. "Don't laugh at me, Morty, but I actually long for a house in the country and children of my own."

Mortimer looked thoughtful; his face held no hint of mockery. "And the mother? Who would be their mother? Mrs. Kane?"

Carey compressed his lips grimly. " 'Tis time to greet our hosts," he replied tonelessly, and climbed the three shallow steps to the entrance. After greeting Lord and Lady Burlington at the stairs in the vast hallway, he mingled with the guests. Lord Mortimer sought the chamber set aside for card games.

The staircase behind the hosts wound upward in an elegant sweep, and Carey's gaze lingered on the lovely painting of Grecian gods and goddesses framed by a trompe l'oeil open dome. This house was a treasure trove.

Someone touched his arm. "McLendon, there you are at last! I've been wanting to speak with you, but you've been out of London more often than not. You're as slippery as a deuced eel."

"Mountjoy." Carey greeted his powerful Jacobite ally cheerfully. "Have you heard from our . . . friend in France?" he whispered.

Lord Mountjoy, a tall, slender man with a distinguished nose, shook his head. He was dressed in black velvet edged with gold embroidery and wore a powdered bagwig. "Shall we step into the gardens and talk?"

Carey nodded, and they left the house through a set of open French doors at the back. They walked the length of the stone terrace and stopped at the farthest end. Lord Mountjoy took out a black cheroot from a gold case and lit it, all the while regarding Carey.

"The London 'friends' are grateful for the work you did after the Prince's successful escape, McLendon," he murmured, so softly that Carey could barely hear him. Lord Mountjoy always referred to the Jacobite sympathizers as *friends*. "You should have had part of that gold you found in Scotland, but since it all went toward a higher cause, the 'friends' here have decided to reward you handsomely. Without you—"

Carey gripped his arm. "I've been amply rewarded already." He decided to come right to the point. "I'm not sure I want to act as contact with the Prince any longer." He took a deep breath. "I've decided to leave my life in politics. Not that my allegiance has changed, but ever since I returned to London, I've had a strong yearning for something—permanent. I can't go on like before. I simply cannot."

Lord Mountjoy stared at him for a long time without speaking. "You're really serious, aren't you? But how will you manage? You won't have a reliable income."

Carey sighed. "I'll find a way to buy a house and some land. I suppose 'tis not too late to learn farming. At any rate, I have some knowledge of horse-breeding."

Lord Mountjoy chuckled. "Farming? You, McLendon? If you didn't look so serious, I might think you were joking." He placed an arm around Carey's shoulders. "I believe your decision is good. Besides, you wouldn't be effective working for the Prince if your heart isn't involved in the Cause."

"I'm exhausted, that's all." Carey looked toward the garden, where colored lanterns lighted the paths. "I will always be available if Charles Edward personally requests my aid." He gazed at his friend and protector. "Will he try another rebellion?"

Lord Mountjoy sighed heavily. "He hasn't found the support he needs in Europe. No country is willing to supply the weapons or the wherewithal to launch another battle. The 'friends' here in England can offer only a fraction of the necessary support. Yet we'll be ready when he comes—if ever. However, I know he would like to see you well-rewarded for your crucial assistance at his time of greatest need. You got word to the French so that they sent the ship that carried Charles Edward to safety."

Carey smiled, embarrassed. "I did what I had to do. It's as simple as that."

Lord Mountjoy led him back toward the doors.

"You shall have your farm, McLendon. What else do you intend to breed besides horses? Children?"

Carey laughed cynically. "Chickens."

Francesca settled into her new routine at the goldsmith shop more easily than she had anticipated. On her first evening at Haymarket, Giorgio had immediately sought her out and welcomed her into his home. He was attentive, but he behaved like an older, concerned brother in her company. So much for Carey's suspicions that Giorgio was amorously inclined toward her, she thought.

Estrella was obviously pleased to have a companion. They spent many an hour at the milliners and dressmakers, since Estrella had decided that she needed an entirely new wardrobe. The more time Francesca spent with the Italian woman, the more she learned about Estrella's volatile nature. She was like a colorful, chatty bird that flitted from one pleasure to another, and she spent a minor fortune on fripperies—fans, ostrich feathers, silky scarves, slippers. Estrella was a charming egotist, Francesca thought wryly. She wasn't mean or calculating, yet she was as shallow and self-serving as a spoiled princess.

Giorgio D'Angelo viewed his sister with restrained anger, but he kept a tight rein on his temper since, first and foremost, he wanted to appear the perfect gentleman. Since Francesca had moved to Haymarket she had noticed only one flaw in his upstanding character. He liked to gamble. Although he was careful to conceal his vice, Francesca knew the signs, since she'd spent time at the Crimson Rooms watching the gamblers. His passion was harmless enough as long as he only staked a few pounds now and then. But did he limit it to that amount?

Francesca had heard brother and sister argue

about it in the parlor when she walked up the stairs to her living quarters.

The only clouds in her life were the fact that Carey stayed away from her, and that she had been unable to continue her investigation into Leonard's death. She was eager to return to Sussex and seek out Mr. Ingram. He would soon be back at his house outside Eastbourne.

One golden warm August morning, three weeks after she'd moved into her rooms on Haymarket, Francesca was sitting at a workbench in the back of the workshop. Besides Mr. Preston, the only journeyman goldsmith that Giorgio could afford at this time, there were two apprentices, young boys whose contracts Giorgio had just acquired. They had signed the paper that would make them belong heart, body, and soul to Giorgio until the completion of seven years of apprenticeship.

Mr. Preston was a gentle old man, tall and thin, with sparse brown hair and a stooped back. He supervised Francesca's designs, showing respect for her talent. He had already become a trusted friend, and Francesca got along well with the apprentices. The youngest boy was working at the charcoal hearths at the darkest end of the workshop, annealing a handle that would be soldered to a sugar bowl. The other apprentice was at the wire-drawing bench turning the large wheel that forces the gold through smaller and smaller holes to form the thinnest of wire. Justus Preston was hammering a gold bowl into a doming-block. The walls of the workshop were covered with hammers and mallets, and leather aprons hung on hooks behind the door.

"You seem to like your work here," Mr. Preston said in his soft voice.

Francesca nodded. " 'Tis most gratifying." She felt that her marriage to Leonard Kane had not been entirely wasted, since she had learned the fundamentals of jewelry design during her four years under his roof.

"You have an eye for the simple lines, and your designs have a rare delicacy. I foresee great things for you, Mrs. Kane."

"Thank you," she said with a smile, and brushed perspiration from her forehead. The fires made the room very hot, even though the doors stood open toward the cobblestone courtyard. A faint wind stirred the leaves of the old elm outside. Francesca concentrated on the design in front of her, a filigree brooch in the shape of a flower bouquet with a flowing ribbon that would be set with a cluster of octagonal step-cut diamonds.

She was so intent on her work that she didn't notice the newcomer's entrance until a hand touched her shoulder. She glanced up, looking into Giorgio's dark eyes. He was dressed elegantly in a long black waistcoat adorned with brass buttons, pale-gray breeches and silk stockings, with Mechlin lace at his throat.

Lips pouting, he studied her design critically. "Exquisite, m'dear." He flashed his brilliant smile which reminded her of the diamonds she sometimes spread on black velvet cloth before rich customers in the shop. "Everyone agrees that it was a stroke of luck employing you in my shop. I have come to tell you that Lady Spencerfield visited this morning and commissioned one of your designs."

Delight filled Francesca. "Which one?"

"The willow-tree brooch."

"That's my best effort," she said with a swift smile. She recalled the delicate design of thin gold wires extending from the tree trunk of square-cut diamonds. Pearls dangling at the tips of the fronds created the *tremblant* effect.

Giorgio nodded, his gaze lingering on her face. "I'm going to a meeting at the Goldsmiths' Company this morning. Could you wait on the customers? Estrella isn't feeling well."

Francesca nodded. "I can continue my work in the shop." She smiled at Mr. Preston as she left the workshop in Giorgio's wake.

The old man winked at her. "Well done," he said behind her. "I knew that willow-tree design would be popular, Mrs. Kane."

Francesca's steps were light. Wind played on the curls at the nape of her neck. She was wearing a serviceable brown serge dress with a white kerchief at the throat and an apron over the front. A lacy cap with lappets modestly covered her raven curls. For the first time in her life, she felt really useful. Leonard had always tried to constrain her activities in the shop, even though she had shown talent for the work, but he'd resigned himself when he saw her rapid progress. Her life now would be perfect if only there wasn't the question of his death . . .

"You're so very lovely when you're happy; you're positively glowing," Giorgio complimented her, and held open the door to the shop on the opposite side of the courtyard. "I hope I'll have the fortune to put that smile on your face more often."

"The work keeps me from brooding."

He gave her a penetrating stare. "What would you have to brood about?"

Francesca flinched. "Nothing . . ." She would have to tell him the truth about Leonard's death one day. Leonard brought thoughts of Carey, who had not visited her once in her new surroundings. A vision of Carey's face clouded her happiness.

She busied herself with a tray of rings, arranging them in dignified order on the midnight velvet. Sapphires competed with emeralds and rubies, while diamonds sparked fire, and opals glowed with inner mystery.

Giorgio placed his hand on her shoulder, caressing the nape of her neck with one finger. "Very well, I will leave you here. You need only to send the guard upstairs if you want Estrella's assistance. She's well enough to come down for a few minutes."

Francesca moved away from his intimate touch and sat down behind the Queen Anne desk in the corner of the shop. "I'll spend some extra time with her tonight."

When Giorgio had left, she stared out the window. Why had he touched her when he'd promised to keep their relationship strictly businesslike? A shiver of apprehension coursed through her.

Shaking off her misgivings about Giorgio, she tried to work, but she was unable to concentrate now that he had disrupted her creative mood. She missed Carey terribly and had almost sought him out at his lodgings on St. James's Street. But pride, and the realization that she would probably only argue with him if they met again, had stopped her.

Struggling for half an hour, Francesca finally managed to capture the spirit that inspired her jewelry designs. Bent over the papers strewn in front of her, she barely heard the click of the latch as the door opened and the jingle of the bell. The rustle of a cloak, and the hard decisive step of a boot, brought her back to the present.

She glanced up, her breath catching in her throat as she came eye to eye with her dream—with Carey McLendon. She half-rose from her chair, but he waved her back.

"Let me look at you," he said, his voice warm and inviting. It sent a flurry of emotion through her—love mixed with apprehension. He looked excruciatingly attractive in a royal-blue coat adorned with black braiding, a pristine fold of lace-edged neckcloth, a blue brocaded waistcoat. His smile was wistful, and it made her ache with longing. Color flared in her cheeks.

"The Italians have certainly hidden away your beauty in that drab dress," he commented. "Is D'Angelo afraid he might lose you to some wealthy customer if he dresses you as befits your station?"

"I'm here of my own choice. If you've come to goad me, you can turn around and leave the same way you came."

He leaned a hand on the top of the desk. "Such harsh tones! I'm not here to quarrel, my darling." His voice caressed her senses, his presence threatened her equanimity.

"Why are you here then?"

"Because this shop is rapidly gaining the reputation of being the fashionable spot to purchase your trinkets." He touched her chin, studying her face closely.

Disappointed, Francesca looked away. He had only come to taunt her. His sudden sigh forced her to look at him, noticing anew his fine deep eyes, the refinement of his stern face, the long sensitive lips. Desire flared to life between them as they lost themselves in each other's eyes.

"To tell you the truth, I missed you. It's been much too long since I saw you," he whispered, gliding his fingers along the contours of her face. "The time away from you has been pure torture."

"You always knew where to find me." Francesca struggled to break the enchantment. Her legs trembled, and her heartbeat thundered in her ears. "Are you here to torment me?"

"Have you already forgotten the ecstasy we shared?"

She wrenched herself away from his magical touch. "No, but I haven't changed my mind about your proposal."

His smile was bitter. "I didn't expect you had."

He stretched to his full height, shaking off the tension in his shoulders. With a change of tone, he added, "I've come to buy a bauble. Perhaps you can advise me."

For whom? Francesca wanted to know, but aloud she said, "What do you like, gold or silver? Rings or pendants?"

He hesitated for a moment. "A ring perhaps. May I take a look at those?" He pointed at the tray which she had arranged earlier.

She nodded curtly and placed the tray on a display table close to the window. Bright sunshine spilled onto the gems, making them glow with unearthly fire.

"Lovely," he said, picking aimlessly among the rings.

Francesca glanced at his face, and saw that he was looking at her instead of at the rings. "Your hair shines like the deepest obsidian," he murmured. He had clearly forgotten his errand. "And your lips are red like rubies."

Francesca lowered her gaze, emotion constricting her throat. Silence stretched taut between them. "You're supposed to look at these rings, not at my hair."

He continued his examination of the jewelry, finally picking a ring of six diamonds that formed a star pattern. "This is lovely."

"And very expensive." Francesca glanced at him apprehensively, wondering how he'd be able to pay for it.

Obviously sensing her suspicion, he said with a mocking smile, "Don't worry, I had a windfall yesterday—at the Crimson Rooms." He didn't mention that Lord Mountjoy and the 'friends' had awarded him a large sum of money. He lifted her hand. "Perhaps you could try it on for me. The lady's hands in question are about the same size as yours."

Deeply disturbed that he would buy a ring for another woman, Francesca tried to pull away. "It makes no difference. We can easily change the size after she tries it on."

He forced the ring onto her third finger. It fit perfectly. The diamonds glittered against her pale skin. "There—how beautiful you look. But it fails to turn you into the lady that you really are. Your dress is wrong. Brown's not your color," he added speculatively.

She tore off the ring. "I don't like your little games, Carey. Whoever you bought this for will be happy. Shall I wrap it for you?"

An enigmatic smile hovered on his lips, and he nodded.

Francesca found a box for the ring. Misery overcame her. Carey had already found someone to replace her in his affections! She should have known better than to trust him. But he'd been so kind, as if he'd really cared about her. Now she didn't know what to think. Had she changed so much, or had he?

"Here it is. 'Tis a lovely gift," she said in a low voice.

"Yes, but I'd have liked it even better if you had designed it. You didn't, did you?"

She shook her head. "I only just started here. Anyway, my designs are not made up until someone orders a piece."

"You know where to send the bill."

That concluded their transaction, but, lingering in the doorway, Carey seemed to be searching for something more to say. "I haven't found any more clues to the mystery in Seaford. We ought to travel there someday soon and find out if Mr. Ingram has returned."

Francesca could not hide her eagerness. "Yes, next week 'twill be a month since we were there."

"As a matter of fact, I sent Bigelow down to discover if there's any sign of Ingram, but he hasn't sent word. I thought he might blend in better with the locals, and thereby get information more easily."

"I'm grateful."

Carey took a rapid step toward her, as if struggling to contain himself. "I know we broke our friendship, but that doesn't mean we shouldn't treat each other in a civilized fashion." His gaze seared her. "I only wish we could take up where we ended our last meeting, and explore where a . . . more intimate relationship would lead us."

She wanted to shout "Yes!" but something held her back. "No . . ." she whispered. "Not yet."

His voice was low and hard. "What I see before me is a coward who dares to deny true love." One long stride brought him to her, and he swept her into his arms. Before she could protest, his mouth came down on hers, dissolving any protest.

Something burst within her, a pent-up well of longing that flooded her with delicious warmth. She was aware only of his punishing lips, which softened when she didn't resist. He swept off her cap and brought her hair tumbling down her back. "Ah, how lovely you are, Francesca, so soft and pliant. I cannot stop dreaming about you. That is, when I get any sleep at all."

"Oh . . ." was all she could murmur between love-bruised lips. His arms were tight around her back, and she reveled in his powerful embrace.

"Had you already forgotten what it felt like?" he murmured, weaving his hands in and out of her hair.

"No. How could I forget?"

A puzzled look came over his face. "Really, Francesca, how could you walk away from our love?'" He dipped lower to kiss the hollow of her throat, and that melting feeling she associated with him came over her. It was love; she would be a fool to deny it.

"I do love you," she whispered into his hair.

He stopped kissing her. His charcoal eyes were dark with emotion. "Come with me," he pleaded.

Francesca pulled away, shaking her head. "No, there's no hurry, is there?" She took a deep breath. " 'Tis better not to rush into this. I don't want to hurt you, since you've been betrayed before."

Carey smiled. "*You* cannot wound me. You're gentle and kind. I believe that you won't flit away to some other man as Daphne did—or will you?"

She sighed. "No, I've always been honest with you. Give me a few weeks to think about our relationship. Give me until we've solved the mystery of Leonard's death. We can still be together as friends."

She sensed a calmness settling over him. "Yes. You can have as much time as you like." He lifted her hand to his lips with a gallant gesture. "For you, I would wait 'til eternity, if need be."

The door opened, the bell tinkling. Carey let go of her hand, and Francesca smoothed back her hair with a guilty smile. Her smiled faded as she saw Giorgio.

"Ah! McLendon. Are you pestering Mrs. Kane?"

Carey went rigid. Fearing his tumultuous temper, Francesca went to stand between the two men. Tension hummed in the small shop. "Mr. McLendon came to buy a ring."

Giorgio flicked one of her loose curls. "He obviously got more than he bargained for." A thin smile of displeasure creased his lips. "I had hoped you would understand—without my having to say so—that we try to maintain certain standards in this establishment. This is not the Crimson Rooms. This is a respectable shop where the employees do honest work.''

Francesca lowered her lashes, two bright spots glowing on her cheeks. "I'm sorry."

Carey's hand rested on her shoulder. "Don't speak in that tone of voice to Mrs. Kane," he said threateningly.

Giorgio shrugged with supreme indifference. "Or else?" Silence ensued. "Mrs. Kane is my employee; she lives under my roof, and she'll have to comply with my standards."

'' 'Twill not happen again," Francesca said, hiding her trembling hands under her apron. "You have been kind to offer me honest work."

Carey snorted behind her, and Giorgio's face grew red with anger. If she didn't manage to divert his attention, they would fight. She gave Carey a beseeching glance. He squeezed her shoulder gently and took a deep breath. With a contemptuous glance at Giorgio, he strode to the door.

"A ride in the park tomorrow afternoon?" he asked, his eyes entreating her to accept.

She nodded, all the while noticing Giorgio pressing his lips together in fury.

When the door had closed behind Carey, he said, his voice like a whiplash, "Follow me upstairs."

Chapter 19

⁓~⁓ ⚬⚬ ⁓~⁓

Filled with misgiving, Francesca summoned one of the apprentices to mind the shop and followed Giorgio upstairs. Estrella was still in her bedroom, and the parlor was silent, the air hot and stuffy. Stopping in the middle of the floor, Giorgio turned to her. Francesca expected him to reprimand her, but instead he smiled.

"You look lovely with your hair down. I can't blame McLendon for losing his head."

Francesca pushed her curls back self-consciously. "I—well . . . I didn't intend . . ."

His smile faded. "But I expect you not to do it again." He held a cane in his hand, and he stabbed it into the carpet for emphasis. "What if a customer had entered just then?"

"You're back already?" came Estrella's sleepy voice from the hallway which connected the parlor with the bedrooms.

"Francesca was molested in the shop." Giorgio gave his bright smile, and Francesca flinched at his brutal description of her meeting with Carey. His anger shocked her. "I'm sure it won't happen again," he added.

Estrella smiled at Francesca. "Don't be such a bully, Giorgio. You must trust Francesca. She has done nothing but bring light into our home." She entwined her arm with Francesca's. "You must not listen to him when he's angry," she said. "Giorgio's fits of temper die down rapidly."

"I must go upstairs and tidy my hair," Francesca said, and hurried from the room.

She heard Estrella's voice behind her, saying, "I don't think you were fair, brother. The worst thing you can do now is to frighten Francesca. She'll leave us."

He snorted. "Where would she go? She has no one—nothing, but us. That McLendon fellow is a ne'er-do-well. He'll not have her."

"Nevertheless, you're threatened by his love for Francesca."

Unwilling to hear his reply, Francesca ran up the stairs. She closed the door to her rooms, and drew a breath of relief. She wished she knew how to act with Giorgio. She realized that she held him in respect, but she also feared him. Estrella's footsteps pounded on the steps, and she entered Francesca's rooms after a cursory knock.

"My brother's a fool. You must not take him seriously. He has such a foul temper." She took the hairbrush from Francesca's stiff fingers and began brushing her hair. "Your hair is as dark as mine. 'Tis quite lovely," she added with a giggle. Preening in front of the mirror, she asked, "Do you think I'm lovely?"

Francesca nodded. "Very," she replied automatically. Estrella's constant concern about her clothes and face was tiring.

"Why did Giorgio react so strongly, do you think?" Francesca continued as Estrella tried on one of her lacy caps.

"He might be enamored of you." Estrella whirled around and faced Francesca. "Does that shock you?"

Francesca placed a hand to her throat. "Yes . . .
He promised he would not—"

Estrella laughed. "My brother is a forceful man.
He takes what he wants, and I'm sure he thought
that you would understand his amorous inclina-
tions—in time." She sank down beside Francesca on
the sofa and patted her friend's hand. "But don't
worry, I won't let him harass you, even though I
think you'd make a handsome couple." She held
out the hairbrush. "Now, will you brush my hair?
I'd like to experiment with a new style."

"I cannot accept anything more than friendship
from Giorgio," Francesca said, dragging the bristles
through the Italian woman's thick tresses.

"In time you might see things differently."

No, never, Francesca thought, but she kept it to
herself.

Twenty minutes later Estrella left after saying,
"You'll eat with us like you always do, won't you?"

Francesca said yes as Copper jumped down from
the windowsill where he'd been curled up, and
rubbed against her skirt. She scooped up the kitten
and buried her face in its fluffy fur. "I wish my life
could be as simple as yours," she said to Copper,
who purred loudly in response.

After rearranging her hair under a cap, Francesca
returned to the shop across the courtyard and spent
the rest of the afternoon sketching. But she had difficulty concentrating, as her thoughts returned repeatedly to Carey's kiss. She missed him already. A
shiver of delight ran up her spine at the thought of
seeing him tomorrow.

That night at dinner, Giorgio seemed unable to
take his eyes from her. The flickering candlelight
made his face look diabolical, his eyes like glittering
coals. She wished Estrella was present, but she had
sent word that she was suffering from a severe
headache.

"How fared today's designs?" Giorgio asked. "Preston has nothing but praise for you."

Francesca twirled the stem of her wineglass. "I'm well-pleased with my work." She let her gaze drift toward the windows, noticing that Estrella had put up new golden damask curtains in the dining room. They were a shade too elegant for these bourgeois surroundings, but were lovely nonetheless. Giorgio's eyes were still on her, and she avoided them by cutting the slices of roast duck and boiled carrots on her plate into tiny pieces.

"You don't have to be shy with me," he said, his voice low and intimate.

Francesca refused to look at him. "This goldsmith shop is becoming more popular every week," was all she could think to say. "Many wealthy customers came in today."

"I charge less in order to attract customers." He chuckled. "And one day your designs will be famous. All we need is a little time. We'll be the most fashionable jewelry shop in London."

She threw him a quick glance. "You sound so very sure of yourself."

His smile was superior, and his chin tilted slightly upward. "Mark my word, next year George Wickes—next door—will no longer be court jeweler. D'Angelo will, and you'll share in my success." He reached across the table and held the wine bottle toward her. "More claret?"

Francesca shook her head, but he insisted. "You must not be shy. We have much to celebrate."

"I wish Estrella could rejoice with us. Isn't she feeling better?"

His face darkened in a frown. "No." He gave her a long glance. "I wish you wouldn't encourage her in her lavish spending. As her companion, you should caution her. But let us not speak of that now."

Francesca was silent. She could not refuse a toast as he lifted his glass toward her, but she barely touched the wine. "To our success," Giorgio exclaimed, his eyes smoldering with barely restrained desire.

Francesca was saved from replying as the young servant girl, Elsie Sykes, entered with dessert—strawberry cream and bread pudding. Francesca ate in silence, hardly tasting the sweets.

"Shall we take tea in the parlor?" Giorgio asked at last, forcing her to look at him.

She nodded. "Unless you want to linger over your port."

Giorgio was careful to maintain the manners of gentility, but she suspected that he came from a rather obscure Italian family. The D'Angelos had not offered any more description of their family other than the one they had given her on her first visit to Haymarket. The brothers were landowners, and the parents were dead.

"No, I want to speak with you tonight."

Quivers of uneasiness rolled up Francesca's spine as she led the way into the parlor. The room was lit by a candelabra and an oil lamp on the mantelpiece. The candles spread a cozy light, and Francesca sat on the edge of the sofa, hoping that tea would be served soon so that she could escape to her rooms.

Giorgio stood by the fireplace, his hands clasped behind his back.

"What did you want to speak to me about? Work?"

He shook his head. "No, this is a private matter."

Francesca waited in silence, sensing what was about to come. She threw a desperate glance toward the door. Where was Elsie with the tray?

Suddenly Giorgio fell to his knees beside her and grasped both her hands. She tried to pull away, but his grip hardened. "Don't be afraid." He caressed her hand briefly. "Your fingers are so cold. Are you nervous?"

"Yes. I don't think you should—"

"Shhh. You must know how much I admire you. Ever since that first night when I met you in the street in May, I've been thinking about you constantly." He took a deep breath. "I've fallen deeply in love with you, Francesca. Will you marry me?"

Francesca gasped, jerking her hand from his. She thought about the kindness he had shown her, and the shelter he had offered her. And now he wanted to give her more. "No . . . I'm honored, but no." She pulled away.

His face was blank, then something predatory glittered in his eyes. "If you're hesitating because of the foul rumors about you, I can assure you that I don't believe for one moment that you killed your husband."

"So you know then. I'm grateful for your trust, but that's not the reason—" Francesca wrung her hands. "If you decide that I should work here no more, I understand. It was unfair not to tell you the truth at the outset."

"What's wrong with my offer?" he asked angrily. "Who are you to turn down an honorable proposal?"

"I must be honest; I don't love you." She rose slowly and started toward the door.

"Wait! Tell me the whole story about your husband's death."

Francesca faced him reluctantly. "Carey McLendon has been helping me to solve the mystery. He was the one who found the . . . bodies. I lay unconscious in the sand." She told him every detail she knew, expecting his face to fill with horror, but he maintained a bland expression.

"Hmmm," he said when she had finished her tale. "I don't see how you've managed to endure this ordeal.'' He crossed the room, taking her hand and kissing it.

Francesca pulled back from his touch, but she was relieved by his calm reaction. ''Mr. McLendon was enormously supportive during my most difficult hours.''

''Hmm . . . yes. He must have quite turned your head.'' Giorgio smiled. ''However, I have so much more to offer than McLendon.''

''I'm sorry, but that doesn't change my feelings. And now if you don't mind, I will retire. I appreciate your belief in my innocence, and I can only beg you to keep silent about my past. I'm not sure the others in the workshop would be happy to hear about it.'' Blushing, she walked toward the door.

Giorgio bowed curtly. ''The offer still stands, but I believe you might need some time to think about it.''

She gave him a long glance, wondering if he really meant it. However, she knew in her heart that she could never love this man, no matter how much security and comfort he offered. If she married anyone, it would be Carey.

''You promised that our relationship would be strictly business,'' she reminded him.

''Yes, I know, but I can't help my feelings. I've tried to suppress them . . .'' He lifted his shoulders in an expression of helplessness. ''I'm sorry.''

Francesca could find nothing else to say. Her uneasiness was not soothed by his words. With a brusque nod, she left the room.

The evening continued hot. Since the sun had gone down, some cooler air could be expected, but the heat seemed to intensify, and Francesca's room became hot and airless. A heavy blanket of rainclouds hung over the city. Unlacing her bodice and pulling off her skirt, she sat by the open window in the dark, fanning herself. Her simple shift clung to her skin, and tendrils of hair were glued to her neck. She went over every detail of Giorgio's conversation, wishing now that she had listened to Carey when he had cautioned her about D'Angelo. Giorgio had a streak of mystery in him, and he shielded his thoughts cleverly behind a mask of politeness. It was his right, of course. She couldn't read his expressions as easily as she read Carey's face.

Longing, so intense it almost felt like pain, surged through her. She wanted desperately to see Carey. If it weren't so dark and ominous outside, she would run to his lodgings in St James's.

She caressed Copper, who lay in her embroidery basket below the window. "I'd like a large family someday, and many cats and dogs. Even a chicken or two," she said to herself with a wry smile.

Thunder rolled across the sky like a steel-shod wagon across cobblestones. Lightning flashed over the city. Francesca flinched at a particularly sharp bolt and went to her bed. The open shutters had begun to slap against the wall in the rising wind, but she didn't want to close them. She leaned out and fastened them on the rusty hasps as best she could. Setting the candle on her nightstand, she lifted her heavy sweep of hair away from her neck. The wind whipped through the windows, finally bringing some relief from the oppressive heat.

A new noise came from the outer room, the sound of creaking steps. But no one was in her room except Copper. Francesca looked around the arched opening to see if the shutters had slipped their moorings. As the opening filled with a dark shape, she gasped in fear.

"Francesca?" came Carey's concerned voice.

She ran forward. "Carey? What on earth! Why are you coming through the window?"

He chuckled, pulling her into his arms. Lightning slashed the sky behind him. "I didn't want to meet

D'Angelo downstairs, or I might disgrace myself by planting him a facer.''

''How did you get in?''

''Cauliflower Arnold found a ladder in the courtyard. At this very moment he's treating the guard to ale in the tavern across the street.'' He kissed her on the lips and drew her closer to the light to gaze into her face.

''Cauliflower Arnold?''

He nodded. ''Arnold brought you a present, but first we have other business. He'll be waiting for me in the tavern.''

As she opened her mouth to ask more questions, he silenced her with a hard kiss. As his tongue tasted the sweetness of her mouth, his arms tightened around her. After several moments of paradise, he slowly lifted his head. ''I've dreamt about this every night,'' he said. His voice was soft with emotion. ''Oh, Francesca, you . . .''

She stood on her toes and silenced him, this time with a kiss of her own. A fierce tremble went through him, and it was as if his body grew hotter to her touch. He pulled off his coat and waistcoat even as she clung to his neck, covering his face with kisses. To discard his shirt, he had to release her grip. ''Easy now, my darling. We must savor every second to its fullest.'' His eyes simmered with passion, and his lips curved in a sensual smile. ''By God, I've missed you, my love.''

When he finally stood before her, bare-chested and with heaving breath, she swayed as if in a trance. As her fingertips weaved through the hair on his chest, she felt his heart pound against her hands. Without waiting for his invitation, she dragged her fingernails lightly along his back to the firm curve of his buttocks. His breath grew ragged.

''Dashed ungentlemanly of D'Angelo to berate you this afternoon when he knows you and I are friends—more than friends." Carey snorted. " 'Tis obvious he's jealous, and is trying to drive a wedge between us."

"Yes, he might be. In fact, he offered me marriage this evening." Her lips traced the honed muscles on his left arm. His skin against hers was ambrosia to her senses.

Carey stared at her, aghast. He jerked her chin up so that he could see her face. "He *what?*"

"Matrimony." She clung closer to Carey, whose body was now wholly unresponsive.

"I will find that cur—"

She silenced him with a kiss. "Tomorrow," she said against his lips.

With a groan, he crushed her to him and held her so close that not even air could pass between them. She loved the rigidity of his body against hers, his hot breath on her neck. He slid his hands the length of her back, bunching up the shift so that he could cup her bare derriere. His sinuous hands were warm and demanding on her skin. They made her breasts ache and the place between her legs burn with passion.

She curled her leg around his thigh, and his hand, gliding from the sole of her foot to the top of her leg, ignited a sensation like bubbling champagne under her skin. A molten glow filled her stomach, and a dizzying sweetness swooped in her groin as his fingers skimmed the moist folds of her femininity.

She kissed his chest, inhaling the spicy scent of sandalwood and tasting the salt of sweat on his skin. As she flicked the tip of her tongue over one of his nipples, he groaned against her hair. "Oh, torment . . ." he whispered.

Emboldened by his ecstatic response, she teased his other nipple with her tongue until it grew hard, and massaged his exquisitely taut buttocks under the tight material of his breeches. By then she could barely stand upright because of the havoc he brought to her senses with his intimate caresses.

Thunder reverberated overhead, the pressure in the air building with the pressure of their need for each other.

"We weren't supposed to meet until tomorrow," she said, relentlessly exploring the tight ridge of his manhood straining against the front of his breeches.

"Why wait for this?" he murmured, and pulled off her shift with one twist of his hand. Then he fumbled with the lacing of his breeches.

"Let me," she pleaded, easily untying the knots that held his breeches up. They slid to the floor. Intoxicated by the scent of him, and the smooth velvet hardness of his body, Francesca slowly caressed his slim hips and taut abdomen, moving lower still, to the thick throbbing proof of his desire. He was so hot. With a sigh of pleasure, she sank to her knees and kissed him lightly on the velvety length, then took him into her mouth. He moaned and swayed against her, his fingers digging into her scalp.

"Where did you learn . . . ?" he whispered hoarsely.

Rain spattered wildly against the windows, sweeping a cooler wind in its wake, but Francesca was aware only of the soft-hard feel of him. He seemed to want to burst out of his skin as he tensed and threw back his head. Suddenly he gripped her shoulders and pulled her swiftly to her feet.

"My God, you're killing me, woman." Like a man too long underwater, he inhaled a deep, rasping breath. With a forceful twist of his arms, he lifted her and carried her to the bed. She sank onto the soft feather mattress. Lightning illuminated the room intermittently, and Francesca thought she would be consumed by the fire filling her body, a fire that was as powerful as the flares in the sky.

Carey reveled in the sweet fragrance of her body, and delighted in touching the firm breasts with their taut peaks, which seemed to beg him for attention. His lips could not get enough of her. She moaned in his arms as he charted the slopes and valleys of her slim body with his tongue. Her skin was as soft as rose petals, and just as sweetly alluring. The more he learned about this woman, the more he wanted her. Her innocent-looking, almost virginal body was fast becoming an obsession. Under that cool skin lived a passionate fire that made her glow and tremble in his arms.

His lips slowly worked toward the secret center of her being. He thought he would dissolve with desire at the sweet contact with her most vulnerable, throbbing part. Just being near her whipped up such a frenzy of need in him. He kissed and laved her warm softness, and let his tongue slowly bring the smoldering fires simmering under her skin to a raging inferno. Her thighs quivered under his hands.

"Carey, you mustn't . . ." She moaned and arched her hips. He lifted her legs over his shoulders, exploring her with his tongue until she started to shudder uncontrollably.

Francesca wanted to tell him how much she loved his touch, but only garbled sounds formed in her throat as her pleasure mounted to unbearable heights. Just as she thought she would die with need, he reared up, pushing her legs farther apart and plunging himself into her. He filled her over and over and over, until the intensity of his embrace brought her to shuddering fulfillment. Tears of ecstasy spilled down her cheeks. He almost crushed her as he slowly erupted in searing, shivering bliss, shooting his life's force into her soft flesh. "Oh . . . my love.".

Shortly afterward, he caressed her hair almost clumsily, as if too filled with emotion to coordinate his movements. "My fiery woman," he sighed, utterly satisfied. How he loved her.

The thunder had moved off into the distance, and the pelting rain had softened to a quiet whisper against the windows. A hushed calm lay over the room, over the city, and in their souls.

Francesca sighed in contentment. As perfectly as her body fit against this man's hard muscles, so perfectly was she in tune with his thoughts.

He rolled aside and sagged against the pillows. Then he pulled her close, cradling her head on his shoulder. "So after this, what are you going to tell D'Angelo? Yes or no?" There was laughter in his voice.

She punched him lightly in the chest. "Imbecile! You're humiliating me."

Carey sighed. "D'Angelo certainly doesn't lack an ego, that much is clear." He slid out of bed and went to the other room, fumbling in his coat pocket. Then he returned, holding something in his hand.

"I don't want you to fight him," Francesca said.

Carey leaned over and kissed her lips. "My love for you, and your love for me, is the strongest weapon against D'Angelo. If I have your love, it doesn't matter what he thinks." He sat beside her, and she watched in wonder as he held out the ring he had purchased earlier that morning. He lifted her hand and slid the ring onto her finger.

Unbridled joy surged through her. Entranced by the diamonds' fascinating sparkle, she said, "Why did you tell me the ring was for another woman?"

He shrugged, a guilty look creeping into his face. "I wanted to make you jealous."

Francesca laughed. "Scoundrel! I *was* jealous!"

"Then this ring will seal our love."

"Are you angling for a confession of my undying devotion?"

In the weak candlelight, she noticed a flush creeping over his cheekbones. "Perhaps. I need you to say it. I need to hear it."

She smiled tenderly and threw her arms around his neck. "How could I not love you? You continue to sweep me off my feet."

"Why refuse my proposal then?" he asked suddenly, his body growing tense against her. He leaned over her, his gaze boring into her. "You've given your body generously. Will you join your life to mine as freely?"

Wonder seized her, followed by humility at the fact that he was pursuing her so ardently, but Francesca wrinkled her brow, wishing he hadn't brought up the subject of marriage.

She slid out of bed and lifted her wrapping gown from a hook on the wall behind her privacy screen. "I don't know. How will I know you won't turn into a tyrant in our home?"

"You won't know. No one can look into the future," he said. "You would have to trust that I'm an honorable man who respects you. I haven't much to offer at the moment, but I will take care of you properly. For previous political services rendered, I've come into funds." He sat up, every inch of him tense. "I want to give you a house in the country, like the one we saw outside Burgess Hill. We'll have orchards, flowers, vegetables. The stables will be filled with horses and the farm will have cows, sheep, and chickens. Our children will breathe country air and grow strong in our love."

"Yes, it sounds like a dream come true." Francesca bent her head, hating herself for doubting him. But could she endure another failed marriage? Although she yearned to say yes, she couldn't.

"You think the house is naught but my empty dream? I promise you wouldn't lack for the things you like." He was dressing hurriedly now, his face creased in pain. "But I can already read the rejection on your face, Francesca. So what is our love to you? What if my seed is already growing in your belly?" His voice was rising, and his expression was furious. "Do you want to bring another bastard into this world?"

"Shhh, someone will hear you," she admonished.

"I'm not afraid," he said scornfully. "I'll defend my actions. And unlike you, I'm proud to love you. It gives my life the dignity it never had."

The hard hand of misery gripped Francesca's heart. She twisted the ring on her finger. He was right, but she didn't know what she wanted. "You promised to give me time. You're too impatient."

His voice was low and harsh. "Look at that ring and remember our love. I only hope it won't be too late by the time you make up your mind." With those parting words, he swung his legs over the windowsill and climbed down the ladder leaning against the wall. He stopped then, only his head visible in the window. Above him twinkled stars in the newly washed night sky. "Please put me out of my misery, Francesca. You must give me an answer." Then he was gone.

Chapter 20

"No, don't go!" Francesca rushed to the window, but Carey had already reached the ground. The darkness was complete below her. Voices floated up to her as the tavern door across the street opened. Light spilled from the common room, and Francesca recognized Cauliflower Arnold's massive form on the threshold.

Carey's figure was lit for a moment as he spoke with Arnold. Then he disappeared into the night. Francesca wanted to run after him. There was so much more to say, so much to explain.

A knock sounded on the door. "Please open up, Francesca," came Giorgio's hard voice.

Dressed in a loose wrapping gown, she draped a shawl over her shoulders to make herself respectable. Although she had no desire to open the door, she nevertheless obeyed Giorgio's order.

He held a candlestick aloft and peered past her into the room. "I thought I heard voices."

She shook her head. "I was talking to Copper. He wakes me up in the middle of the night sometimes. He's a lively little creature."

Giorgio threw a cursory glance at the kitten rolled into a ball in her embroidery basket. He had slept through Carey's visit. Francesca wished Giorgio would leave.

"Why is the window open?" he asked suspiciously.

"The night has been awfully hot. I needed to air out my chambers." Her voice held an edge of anger. "Why all these questions, Giorgio?"

"I worry about you. All sorts of ruffians roam the streets at night, and burglars climb walls to seek entrance to a house." He gave her his widest smile and patted her shoulder. Francesca shivered with sudden revulsion. She knew she ought to be grateful for his protectiveness, but she resented his intrusion. His bedroom was right below hers. Even though the bed didn't creak, what had he heard?

"I'd like to go back to sleep now if you don't mind," she said nervously. What would Giorgio do if he found out she had admitted Carey into his house? The Italian expected propriety; his values were solid and bourgeois—and he had offered her marriage. He would be livid and he'd throw her out.

He bowed at the door. "I'm here to shield you, if need be." His gaze strayed to the swell of her breasts under the shawl, and his fist clenched around the door handle. His smile was wolflike as he closed the door. "Good night, my love."

My love. Uneasiness crept through Francesca, and her skin became cold. The night was still warm, and the wind balmy as she leaned out the window to scan the street below. The only sounds were those of the revelry coming from the inn across the street. She shut the window, fastened the latch carefully, and pulled the curtains. She took off the diamond ring and hid it deep in a drawer. She would wear it if she decided to accept Carey's offer.

Returning to her bed, she curled up under the thin blanket, but sleep eluded her. She was torn between elation and worry. Carey's love had made her whole, but his eagerness tormented her, as did Giorgio's.

She was being hounded by two men, and she abhorred the idea.

The next morning Francesca's head was heavy and her eyes burning from lack of sleep. She dressed, her limbs sluggish with fatigue. Remembering Carey's scathing comment about her brown serge dress, she chose a bright-blue muslin that parted over a cream-colored underdress. The neckline was covered with a white linen neckerchief. It was her best Sunday gown, which Estrella had kindly given her.

As she pinned up her hair, the bells pealed at St. Martin's Church nearby. An infant cried and a dog barked. Copper was breakfasting on some meat scraps left over from last night's dinner.

As she made tea from boiling water in the black pot on the hob, Francesca thought about Carey. A tender smile curving her lips, she fried a slice of bread in a skillet that stood on a trivet in the fire. She already missed him. After their argument last night, would he expect her to say yes without reservation? She sighed in a burst of anguish. What if she couldn't give him an affirmative answer?

After a strained luncheon with the D'Angelos, during which Giorgio stared at her suspiciously, Estrella saïd, "Oh, I almost forgot. A note was sent over from the Crimson Rooms." She retrieved it from the corner cabinet and handed Francesca the envelope. "No distressing news, I pray."

Francesca instantly recognized her mother's stationery. She tore open the envelope and read the few lines that Perkins, Lady Childress's abigail, had penned.

"My mother wishes to see me," Francesca explained hesitantly. "I'd better visit her this afternoon."

Wondering apprehensively what her mother wanted, she left the room to prepare for the visit.

It was with a heavy heart that she entered the town house in Leicester Fields. Robbins, the butler, informed her that Lady Childress was much better, but she was in low spirits.

"She has finally realized she cannot refuse to see me forever," Francesca said to the old butler, whose round face was creased in concern. "I will go up to her."

Robbins wrung his hands. His burgundy velvet livery was rumpled and his wig untidy, as if the air of decay that hung over the house had infected the staff. Nothing had changed since her last visit. The silver salver used to hold invitations in the hallway was still empty, and the vases were conspicuously empty of flowers.

Francesca's stomach tightened into a searing knot of anxiety. She knocked on her mother's bedroom door. Perkins opened it a crack. When she saw who it was, she opened it wide.

"I hear that Lady Childress is much better. I'm sure she'll be delighted to see me," Francesca said in carrying tones. Perkins sniffed as Francesca stepped into the dimly lit bedchamber. Her mother was sitting by the window in an invalid chair with a high back and wheels. The curtains were drawn, hiding the lovely day outside. On an impulse, Francesca went over and parted them, letting sunlight flood the room. "There, that's much better. Sunshine and fresh air are the best restoratives," she said.

The older woman was shrouded in a blanket and wearing a plaid shawl across her thin shoulders. She warded off the sharp daylight with her arm. "Perkins! Pull the curtains this instant," came the querulous order.

Francesca sighed and sat down on the chair opposite her mother. It wouldn't do to push her too hard on this important first meeting since the tragedy. The room was just as she remembered it—done in gold and cream, with a white carpet displaying an intricate pattern of leaves and birds. The bed hangings were white and silver brocade, and the polished surfaces of tables and chests were covered with miniatures, tiny vases, statuettes, and bowls filled with either cut flowers or bonbons. However, an air of decay permeated the atmosphere even here.

"Staring, are you? Wondering what you can get for the lot when I'm gone?" Lady Susanna Childress's voice was bitter.

The knot in Francesca's stomach tightened. "If you recall, I haven't been here for months. I notice that nothing has changed."

The older woman shrugged under her plaid shawl. "I'm surprised to find you free—even alive. I take it they haven't found proof that you murdered Kane? What propelled you to do the filthy deed? It was the greatest shock of my life. Brought on this stroke, y'know."

Francesca fought the tears burning behind her eyelids. "I didn't do it." Yet guilt washed through her. Just being a bystander to Leonard's death made her feel partly to blame for her mother's current decline. The shock had brought on the stroke.

Sorrow filled Francesca as she stared at the older woman. There was not much similarity between them, except for their height. Sometimes Francesca wondered if this heartless woman was really her parent. Lady Childress had never loved her as she had loved Teddy, Francesca's younger brother. It saddened Francesca that her mother indirectly blamed her for her brother's death—as she had since the moment of Teddy's carriage accident.

Lady Childress's dark hair was heavily laced with silver strands, and her blue eyes and pale, finely wrinkled skin were unlike Francesca's flashing dark eyes and rich, creamy complexion. The patrician curve of their noses did bear a resemblance, as did the proud tilt of their heads. Because of the stroke, half of Lady Childress's face sagged slightly, and it pained Francesca to see the change. Old age was claiming her mother, and it gave her a premonition of finality.

"You have yet to prove your innocence, Francesca. I warned you that Kane would destroy you. I did everything in my power to prevent your marriage to him, but off you went! Like an anointed knight, you had to charge off and sacrifice everything to your sire. Childress was a fool, and you might have understood that your sacrifice would not stop his gambling. I knew your marriage to Kane would come to a bad end," she concluded. Her eyes bore into Francesca, belying the frailness of her shrunken body. "You never had any sense."

Francesca fought her tears valiantly. "I don't care what you thought of Leonard Kane. He's dead. However, I do care that you believe I'm guilty of murder. How can you—?" She fumbled for her handkerchief in her cloak pocket.

Lady Childress sniffed, looking everywhere but at her daughter. "If you had shown any sense, you wouldn't have sent your brother to his death in that coach."

Francesca refused to answer her taunt.

The book Lady Childress had been holding in her hands slipped to the floor. "Perkins! Leave us alone," she ordered the maid standing stiffly behind her chair. When the maid had closed the door, Lady Childress said, "In your predicament, Francesca, you won't find another husband. How will you survive?"

Her words stung Francesca. She lifted her head high. "As a matter of fact, I have already received two proposals."

The older woman's eyes widened, but she quickly

masked her surprise with an air of contempt. "Who would have you after hearing about your sordid past?"

"They know everything about my past." Her heart fluttered as she mentioned Carey's name. "He's the one I love."

Lady Childress's lips worked. "McLendon?" she spat. "He's a jackanapes—a fop and a gambler." Her eyes shot icy fire. "I should have known. You would attract his type, of course."

"He loves me."

"Pshaw! He says so, perhaps. He must be between wealthy mistresses. Who's the other man?" When she was angry, her words slurred together.

"He's Italian, a jeweler who set up business in Haymarket. I work there, designing brooches, rings, and pendants."

The air seemed to have left Francesca's mother's lungs. Her chin trembled. "Not *trade*, again! Kane was trade, and now you have found another one, and a foreigner to boot."

"You need not fear. I have no desire to marry Giorgio D'Angelo. His sister is a good friend. She has been nothing but kind to me."

Lady Childress thought for a moment. "If he's well-to-do—and a jeweler would be—he would chose a respectable young woman to wed, not a murder suspect like you."

Francesca could not withstand her tears at such hateful words. The last few weeks had strained her almost past endurance, and in these familiar surroundings the dam she had built against her bad memories burst at last. Hiccupping into her handkerchief, she struggled to control her tears. Her mother would never console her; she would only give her a scornful pat on the head and send her away. That had been Lady Childress's way of handling Francesca's sorrow in the past. If she had hoped for advice about her current predicament, Francesca knew she'd come in vain.

Yet the older woman was remarkably quiet. Francesca cursed herself for losing her composure. The doctor had said that excitement was bad for the convalescent lady.

Francesca blew her nose. She couldn't make herself raise her eyes to her mother's face. Silence hung heavy in the room, which smelled of camphor and violets. The scent was so familiar that it was almost part of herself. She drew a deep, shuddering breath. However harsh the old woman was, Francesca still loved her.

"I shouldn't have burdened you with my problems," she said, her voice hoarse with tears.

Lady Childress sighed, and some of the tension evaporated. "I cannot say I approve, but you're obviously making do with what you have. In due time, you'll have a better existence. You're stronger than I thought."

Francesca's gaze went to her mother's face. She saw sadness mixed with fatigue. "Yes?" She furtively wiped her eyes with the back of her hand.

"Perhaps it was my fault—and your father's—that you gave yourself to Kane." The old voice trembled slightly, as if Lady Childress was under exceptional emotional strain. "We should have solved our financial problems without Kane's money, and protected you. You were always an innocent and gullible child."

"Not any longer." Francesca straightened her back, relief slowly filling her, along with a golden hope that her mother didn't really despise her. Not deep inside, whatever she showed on the surface.

"We were all young once. I made mistakes, though not as serious as yours, of course. I knew to stay in my place in society. Position is everything." Two red spots burned in Lady Childress's cheeks and her gaze flitted around the room. ''I don't regret what I did then. And now I'm too old to care. I'm going to die soon, y'know.'' She sighed, her hands trembling. ''The strength is slowly seeping from my body, from my very bones. I'm weary.''

Francesca slid to the floor next to her mother's chair. ''That's nonsense! When my reputation is clear, I will take you to one of the watering places, Tunbridge Wells perhaps, or the seaside.'' She gently touched the dry old hand. It was so cold and lifeless. ''You know how much you used to like the resorts.''

''Those were the days when my blood flowed hot in my veins. Now water flows through my body.''

Francesca wished that her mother would touch her, but the old lady sat rigid in her chair, with a faraway look in her eyes.

Francesca was thinking of her love for Carey McLendon. ''Did you love Father?'' she asked.

Lady Childress started, her eyes misting over. The bony fingers fiddled with the fringe of the blanket. ''What an extraordinary question! Of course I loved your father. Childress was the finest, the gentlest man in the world.''

Which was true, Francesca thought. She wondered why the mention of Lord Childress seemed to disturb her mother.

Suddenly the older woman gripped Francesca's arm. ''You must not marry a . . . a man illegitimately born, like Carey McLendon. Your name will be ruined forever.'' Her voice rose, and her breathing grew jagged. ''If you have to marry, then choose the Italian. At least he has a name!''

''But Mother—''

Lady Childress's eyes turned icy once more. ''Are you going to argue again? Always stubborn, even when you were a little girl. Nothing pleased you then, and I see you haven't changed since losing your first husband."

Francesca listened in amazement as her mother's voice grew harsher with rising anger. Why was she suddenly furious? "I don't love Giorgio," she whispered.

"Bah, love! You need a man who can provide for you, and the Italian seems to have enough for the both of you. When he tires of your body, a few months after the ceremony, you will be well set up with your own servants and the control of the household accounts. Love is but a fleeting emotion."

Francesca listened in silence. She had never heard her mother speak in such a way.

Lady Childress's voice softened. "Take my advice on this. I've lived a long life—not as long as one might hope, but long enough to know the way of the world."

"I must find my own way. That's what I told Carey. I don't want to be thrown onto the street if the man I marry tires of me. I must secure my own future."

"Kane didn't abandon you."

Francesca didn't know how much to tell her mother of Leonard's violent temper, his absolute control over her life. "No, he died. Yet the circumstances left me on the street, and his family turned their backs on me." As you did, too, she thought.

"I can only pray that no one saw you enter this house today," Lady Childress said with her usual asperity. "I care what people think about me, even if you don't."

Francesca flinched as if her mother had slapped her. She rose slowly. "I assure you, if anyone did, they wouldn't recognize me in these humble clothes." She touched her simple blue gown.

As if seeing her for the first time, Lady Childress

frowned. "You're right—you look like one of my maids." She sighed heavily. "To think that you've fallen this low."

Francesca found that the moment of compassion and near-understanding with her mother had passed. "I'm healthy, and I'm not starving." She bent to kiss the wrinkled brow. Her mother smelled of violets, as she always had. "May I come again?"

"If you don't marry McLendon, you may visit."

Dread filled Francesca. She might not see her mother again if she decided to accept Carey's offer. "You drive a hard bargain."

Lady Childress hammered the armrest of her chair with her bone-white fists. "I've had enough heartache to last me a lifetime! Don't heap more disappointment on my head."

Francesca's gaze lowered. "I won't." *I love you,* she added silently, turning toward the door. "Goodbye."

Lady Childress muttered something unintelligible as Francesca slowly closed the door behind her. She got a last look at her mother as a ray of sunlight found its way through the curtains and touched the bent old body. Francesca could not resent this broken person who once had been strong and quite invincible. What heartache had her mother experienced? Francesca's breath caught at the realization of how little she knew her mother. She had spent her childhood with a stranger.

She passed the rest of the afternoon walking in Green Park and returned to Haymarket only as darkness was falling. Cauliflower Arnold was waiting for her as she reached the shop. He looked tired, his shoulders slumped. "Where 'ave ye been, Miss Francie? I've been waitin' 'ere an age."

Francesca noticed a white bundle of fur at his feet. "Who's your companion?" she asked, and bent to pat the furry head of a young mongrel.

" 'E's almost full-grown. Won't be a spot o' bother fer ye. 'Sides, 'e be good company fer Copper.''

Francesca's eyes widened. "You're bringing *me* the dog?"

He shrugged. "I did last night, but Mr. M. told me not t' barge in on ye. 'Twas late.'' He scratched his massive head. "Yet 'e did. Then after 'e left I 'ad to stay outside all night watchin' yer window. I had th' night off. Then th' Watch tole me t'leave th' area. Fairly shook 'is pole at me an' rattled 'is lantern, 'e did.'' He chuckled. "Not that I was frightened, mind ye.''

"You watched my window?''

"Mr. M. paid me t' keep an eye on ye. 'E doesn't like th' Italian bloke.''

"That's obvious,'' Francesca said with some asperity, although Carey's thoughtfulness warmed her heart. "You waited for me all day here?''

"Naw, I jest arrived to give ye th' dog. Naught but a li'l gift.'' He awkwardly handed Francesca the string that was tied around the dog's neck.

She looked down at the dirty white bundle and lost her heart as the dog tilted his head to one side and wagged his quill-like tail.

"I niver found out what 'e is—a mixture o' fine noble breeds, no doubt. I named 'im Chance.''

The mongrel whined and wagged his tail hopefully. Francesca bent to rub his ears. "Chance?''

"Aye, I was playin' a bit o' dice with me brother wot's visitin' Lunnon. I wondered wot's the number t' 'ope for, an' th' mutt woofed three times.'' Arnold laughed. " 'Three!' I said, and by golly, he was right. Three came up and I fairly fleeced me brother in th' end.''

Francesca wiggled the string. "If he brings you luck, then you ought to keep him.''

"Can't say I can . . . Miss Rose told me t' get rid of 'im.''

"Very well," Francesca said with a sigh. "Chance can keep Copper company—for now."

"Thankee. I knew ye would take a broad view on th' dog. Chance's ever so good."

The mutt was still wagging his tail. "There's one other thing," Arnold said. He glanced cautiously at Francesca and fingered the brim of his hat. "I don't know if I should tell tales."

"What is it?" A premonition of bad news spread through Francesca.

"Th' Italian challenged Mr. M. this mornin' t' a card game at th' Crimson Rooms tonight. Thought ye'd want t' know."

Francesca's eyes widened. "A card game? Why?"

"They'll be playin' over you. I'm certain th' Italian's tryin' t' force Mr. M. t' give ye up. 'E was a-spittin' curses at Mr. M. in Bond Street."

Francesca stared in outrage. "Gambling over me? Why, the utter nerve!"

Cauliflower Arnold nodded, looking uncomfortable. "Th' way o' th' world. But mind ye—Mr. M. didn't want t' be involved, but Mr. D'Angelo said 'twas that or a duel."

"I must stop this madness," she said grimly, and rushed inside. Chance bounded after her, barking gaily.

Chapter 21

⁂

Francesca paced her room, oblivious to the angry hissing with which Copper greeted Chance.

"Oh, hush!" she finally scolded, losing her last shred of patience. "Chance will be part of our home. You don't own our rooms, Copper." Nor do I, she thought. She had not much she could call her own.

Copper settled down at last, but Francesca could find no solution to her agonizing thoughts. Had she been wrong to turn Carey away last night? And now this latest disaster! A card game where she was at stake. Should she throw caution to the winds and give Carey the answer he most longed to hear, before he went to meet Giorgio? Should she let fear rule her life? No man could be as vile as Leonard Kane had been, especially not Carey. There were too many conflicting thoughts in her mind. In a fit of despair, she clutched her head and groaned.

Weighing the possibility of living the rest of her life alone, against the prospect of having Carey's love, Francesca realized that her days would be barren and cold without him.

"I have to stop this," she said aloud. "Shall I go to him?"

Chance, who was curled up before the fireplace, lifted his head and thumped his tail on the floor. He seemed to be saying yes as his head bobbed once.

She gave an exasperated laugh, remembering how Chance had gotten his name. Perhaps he had a sixth sense, after all, as Arnold had implied. She would take Chance's advice and visit Carey.

She threw a cloak over her shoulders, heedless of her disheveled appearance. A new urgency claimed her. What if it was already too late? Carey's patience had been worn to a breaking point.

Francesca ran downstairs in the dark. There was no sign of Estrella or Giorgio. He had not been home, although the hour was past dinnertime. Was he already at the Crimson Rooms waiting to challenge Carey? She scanned the street for an empty sedan chair, but there was none in sight. Without thinking twice about the dangers lurking in the dark alleyways, Francesca braved the narrow back streets that would bring her to the edge of St. James's. She ran until she reached Jermyn Street, then turned up Piccadilly, which was more brightly lit. It had begun to rain heavily. Tendrils of wet hair lay plastered to her forehead. Soon she would be in his arms. Don't let me be too late, she prayed.

Carey dragged off his sodden clothes and Bigelow frowned at the heap on the floor. " 'Tisn't right ruinin' such a handsome coat," he said with a sniff. "Such sorry waste."

"Damn the coat! 'Tis nothing compared to what I might lose tonight."

Bigelow's bushy eyebrows shot up, and his bulbous nose quivered in disdain. "Gambling again, sir?"

Carey's furious gaze could have crumbled a rock. "I had no choice but to accept the challenge. I'll be engaged in the most important gamble of my life."

"Ye'll be sick with inflammation of the lungs," Bigelow said matter-of-factly, and picked up the

clothes, shaking them out with a disapproving tut-
tut.

Carey pulled on a pair of dry breeches and dried
his chest with a towel, which he then hung around
his neck. Barefoot, he crossed the room and looked
at the dreary drizzle outside. A fog was forming over
the city, not one of the heavy, evil-smelling fogs of
autumn, but a light milky mist.

He dressed hurriedly, then fastened a rapier to his
side and threw on a heavy cloak. Then he walked to
the door and called out, "Don't wait up for me, Bigelow. The game might take all night."

Darkness closed around him until he turned the
corner of Piccadilly.

The sedan-chair stand was lit by a line of torches.
He stepped inside a chair and slammed the door after ordering the carriers to take him to Covent Garden.

Francesca looked at the house numbers and found
the one where Carey lived. She banged on the door,
and a gnarled man opened the door a slit. "Is Mr.
McLendon in?" she asked. "Tell him Francesca Kane
is calling."

"Ah! Miss Francesca. Mr. McLendon just left. 'E
'as an urgent meetin' at th' Crimson Rooms, I believe." He peered out into the darkness. "Do ye
want me t' escort ye back 'ome?" Suddenly he found
himself addressing the empty landing. Shaking his
head, he closed the door. "In such a 'urry she didn't
even 'ave time t' say good-bye."

The Crimson Rooms were hot and stuffy with ci-
gar smoke. Carey greased Cauliflower Arnold's palm
at the door. "Is the Italian here?"

Arnold shook his head. "Not yet." He glared at
Carey. "This kind o' gamblin' is wrong, Mr. M. I
told Miss Francie what ye're aimin' t' do."

"You shouldn't have! I'm doing this to save her from further harassment by the Italian." Carey swore under his breath and hastened through the dimly lit hallway. The salons were filled with gamblers, gentlemen and ladies alike. The crush was unbearable, and he didn't recognize anyone in the dim, smoky rooms, no one except Letty Rose. She waved at him, and he lifted his hand in response. He made his way to the spot beside the hazard table where he'd seen her, but when he arrived he had lost her in the crowd.

"By thunder!" he cursed under his breath. "Seems that everyone's eluding me tonight."

He finally caught up with Letty Rose in the foyer. "The Italian just arrived," she said, pointing toward the door. "He's a good customer. The way he spends his money, he must be doing a roaring business at his shop."

Carey gave Letty Rose a penetrating stare. "What do you know about him?"

Her gaze slid away, and her lips pouted rebelliously. "Not much, although he spends some nights in my bed." She placed her hands on her hips. "I know he's angry with you for dogging Mrs. Kane." She paused, letting the words sink in. "In fact, I've been instructed to arrange the game tonight."

"What if he loses?"

"He never loses."

Carey stared across the room at the Italian. The challenge was ridiculous. But if he won, he could force D'Angelo to relinquish his hold on Francesca.

No! That wouldn't work. No matter what happened tonight, she would make her own choice, and she liked her work in the goldsmith shop. He couldn't forbid her to work there. He was doomed to failure either way. In a quandary, he wished he had considered his options more carefully.

One solution was to ask D'Angelo to stake a king's

ransom . . . If he won a large bet tonight—and included the monetary gift his Jacobite friends had given him—he might have enough funds to buy an estate in the country, plus a healthy stock of horse-flesh. If D'Angelo's business was ruined, he would have to leave town. But then, Francesca would be without work—unless the Italian persuaded her to come with him.

"Are you ready?" Letty's shrill voice cut through his anxious thoughts

"Yes, bring him here."

"Perhaps my private rooms would be better."

Carey shook his head. "No, we need witnesses, many witnesses. I don't trust D'Angelo any more than I would a common pickpocket."

Letty Rose laughed. "Wait here."

Giorgio D'Angelo viewed him scornfully as he crossed the hallway, and Carey returned his stare measure for measure.

"McLendon! I knew you wouldn't say no to a challenge, since you are a gambler at heart." He eyed Carey's elegant clothes. "And a duel can be so unpleasant. I have no taste for fighting. I like more refined ways of combat."

Carey raised his eyebrows in contempt. "What card game do you prefer?"

D'Angelo laughed. "Hazard is my game."

Carey narrowed his eyes. "Whose dice?"

"The house's, of course," D'Angelo said with a smirk and a light shrug.

"Very well, hazard it is." Carey's hands were strangely clammy, as if his life hung in the balance with this wager. And perhaps it did; he felt as if he were betting against the devil. Shaken by the sudden image of evil, he strode into the main salon where the hazard table was located. He waved at one of the waiters to bring forth a new set of dice and a new leather cup. He wouldn't give D'Angelo a chance to tamper with the gambling apparatus.

The Italian laughed disdainfully, and the two men captured everyone's attention in the room. The talk that had hummed in the air slowly quieted, and the gamblers closed in around Carey and D'Angelo.

Carey recoiled at the grating sound of his adversary's laugh and vowed silently that he would win. He had to.

"There will be no betting against the house," Letty Rose called out after joining them at the table. "These gentlemen will play against each other."

A ripple of excitement ran through the room, and whispers hissed from ear to ear. Who were the gentlemen? How much was really at stake?

Carey straightened his aching back and followed the movement of the leather cup in Letty Rose's hand. "Shall we toss a coin to see who'll start?" she asked.

Carey nodded tersely and D'Angelo smirked again. Carey wished Francesca was there to see the Italian now, in his true character. He sighed heavily. Urgency coursed through him. Some motive other than compassion for Francesca was hidden behind D'Angelo's offer to employ her in his shop, Carey was sure of it.

Letty Rose flipped a guinea, and the Italian laughed as he won the toss. He took the leather cup and shook it vigorously. "We start out low—one thousand pounds. Are you up to it, McLendon?"

McLendon tightened his jaw at the outrageous bid. "Of course," he said, and scribbled the amount and his name on a piece of paper.

D'Angelo rolled the dice onto the green baize and the onlookers pressed forward to see the pips.

"Five. He has a main point." Letty Rose called out. She scooped up the dice with the cup and gave them to D'Angelo. "Roll for the chance point."

Now the Italian had as many rolls as he needed to get another five, unless a twelve, two, or three appeared first. Then he would lose. He rolled the dice, his black eyes mocking Carey. The dice tossed wildly across the table and came to a standstill below Letty Rose's sharp eyes.

"Four."

The next roll he had a four again, and the next an eleven.

A light sheen of perspiration covered Carey's brow. He refused to think about the possibility of losing. The only money he had was what Lord Mountjoy had given him, and he had no desire to touch it, but if he lost he would have to pay. If he won the thousand pounds, he would have something to stake.

D'Angelo's hands moved very fast, and it occurred to Carey that the Italian was an expert at the game—and more. The suspicion of false play he had had the first time he watched the man win at this very same table came back with renewed force. But the dice were not D'Angelo's . . . The dice belonged to Letty Rose and she played fair.

"Three!"

Carey was pulled out of his reverie. Dazed, he glanced at Letty Rose. D'Angelo had lost the first round.

The Italian shoved his note across the table with a twisted smile. "Is Lady Fortune protecting you tonight, McLendon?"

Carey said nothing. This was some trick. D'Angelo would let him win some, then lose everything. He didn't touch the note, but scooped the dice from the table. Letty Rose's eyes looked larger than normal. Yes, she was frightened, he noticed. Her cheeks were red, and her brow was moister than his own. He tossed the dice casually in his hand, then weighed one carefully between thumb and forefinger. It seemed heavier on one side, as the pips of two always fell face-down. The ivory was smooth as silk against his palm. He decided that he had nothing to lose but the thousand pounds and the possibility of ridicule if he was wrong.

"The dice are loaded," he said.

A hiss of outrage went through the spectators, and the fog of smoke seemed to swallow his adversary. D'Angelo will dissolve like the evil spirit he is, Carey thought with sudden amusement.

"What do you mean, loaded?" Letty Rose shrieked.

"They are weighed down on one side." Carey tossed the dice on the table.

"You won, McLendon! How can you invent such a daft accusation?" Letty Rose was wringing her hands, close to hysteria.

Carey grew more convinced that he was right. "Does anyone here wear a weapon heavy enough to crack the dice?" he called out.

"This is an outrage!" D'Angelo cried. "He's lost his mind."

Murmurs flew around the room. No one stepped forward. Holding one of the dice in his hand, Carey strode to the door leading to the foyer. "Arnold! Please bring me a chisel and a hammer," he ordered.

The doorman scratched his head but obeyed, closing the front door. Carey waited impatiently, praying he was right. The murmurs were turning hostile.

Arnold returned, carrying the tools. He followed Carey to the table.

"Break this die, Arnold." Carey held his breath as the giant braced the chisel against the ivory and gave it a whack. The ivory split. Carey pounced on it before anyone else could. He found that the pips on one side had been drilled deeper, and slivers of lead applied and covered with paint.

"It seems Letty Rose uses loaded dice in her salons," Carey drawled.

"That's not true," Letty Rose wailed. "The Italian must have brought them inside." To be heard over the roar, she shouted, "I'll have all the dice checked. Arnold! Do your duty with your hammer."

The hum slowly died down as a new box of dice was brought in. Letty Rose stood very close to Carey, as he weighed the broken ivory of the loaded dice in his hand. "You knew it had been tampered with, didn't you?" He whispered.

At her startled glance, he knew he had hit on the truth. "Why did you do it? What does D'Angelo threaten you with?" He placed a steadying arm around her shoulders as she grew paler. She threw a fearful glance at D'Angelo, and Carey felt her stiffen. Then she trembled suddenly, as if she were about to fall into a faint.

"Nothing . . . everything I do displeases him," she whispered. "He's an evil man. Evil." Carey could barely make out the words. Something was terribly wrong, and when he looked at the Italian through the smoke, he encountered the coldest, cruelest gaze he had ever seen. He sucked in his breath in anger and amazement. Francesca worked for this man; she might be in danger even now, because D'Angelo realized that his game had been discovered. She must be told about his cheating.

Short of killing the Italian, Carey knew he had to find a way to destroy him for Francesca's sake. He released Letty Rose and stepped up to the Italian. He would have to ruin D'Angelo, force him to leave London.

"Although you should be barred from here, I suggest a hand of the simplest card game to determine the future of Mrs. Kane. We choose one card each, and the first to get to the card of his choice as they are revealed from the top of the deck wins. All or nothing on one card.''

The onlookers' amazement was palpable in the room.

''I don't want to play more than one game with you,'' Carey continued inexorably. ''As I said, all or nothing.''

D'Angelo's eyes smoldered with barely suppressed fury. ''*I* was the one who challenged *you*.''

''Have you turned fainthearted?'' Carey's voice carried across the room, and the spectators laughed.

Two red spots flared on D'Angelo's cheeks. ''Very well. If I win, you're never to see Mrs. Kane again. Is that understood?'' He lowered his voice so that only Carey could hear. ''If you don't obey, I will kill you.''

Contempt shot through Carey. He sensed that the Italian meant every word. He nodded curtly, although he had no intention of keeping the promise if he lost. ''And I want your business in return, including your inventory.''

D'Angelo started, his lower jaw falling slightly. ''My business? Whatever for? You don't know the first thing about jewelry.''

'' 'Tis never too late to learn, is it? Besides, you have an accomplished journeyman who can produce anything in gold.''

D'Angelo narrowed his gaze. ''That's a most ridiculous demand. You would fail in your first year. Why my business?''

Carey shrugged with pretended indifference. ''I'll ruin your reputation, force you out of London.''

''I'll start another business.''

''And I'll spread the rumor among my noble friends that you cheat at dice. No one would patronize your business after that.'' Carey did not avert his gaze as the Italian's glance glimmered with a deadly threat.

"If you lose, you'll have to convince Mrs. Kane that you hate her and never want to see her again," D'Angelo snapped.

Carey's lips curved sardonically. "A fresh pack of cards, eh?" He motioned to Letty Rose, who seemed reluctant to join them. She threw a fearful glance at D'Angelo.

A few minutes later the two men were sitting in a smaller salon at a table for two. Letty Rose had brought an unused pack of cards of French design. The other gamblers had grouped around them, tense anticipation making everyone breathless.

Carey asked sharply, "What card do you choose?" He spread out cards, face upward, on the green baize.

"I think the king of diamonds is a suitable choice, don't you?" D'Angelo's voice was icy.

"I choose the dark king of spades," Carey said.

"But you'll never be a king." D'Angelo sneered, and called for one of the footmen to bring him a snifter of brandy.

One of the onlookers shuffled the cards and another cut the deck. Carey's heartbeat quickened as the stack lay in the exact center of the table.

Another spectator flipped a coin. "Mr. D'Angelo starts."

D'Angelo's eyes were hooded as he lifted the first card. The five of spades.

A sigh of relief quivered through Carey. His fingers were stiff as he flicked over the next card. Ace of hearts.

Whispers darted from ear to ear, and a peculiar restlessness possessed the crowd.

"I will win this, of course," D'Angelo said, studying Carey's face over the rim of the snifter. He turned a card. A hiss went through the room as the first court card came up. It was the knave of clubs.

Carey's heartbeat pounded in his ears, and he

wiped his palms on his breeches. This was the chance of a lifetime. If he won, Francesca would be free. He would give her the jewelry shop. Nine of clubs. Disappointed, he frowned at the humble card.

D'Angelo interrupted his thoughts. "You will not be able to use my shop—if you win it. My name and mark are registered in the assay office in the Goldsmiths' Hall. You're not qualified to have your mark registered, so you could sell nothing under your own name. The shop would only do outwork; it would have no distinction."

"Who says *I* would run the shop? I can always sell it and use the profits to fulfill my own goals. Turn the card."

D'Angelo leaned closer, his face red with anger. He was about to say something, but Carey pointed at the pack. "Well?"

D'Angelo flipped over a card, and stared at it. Two of spades.

"Lady Fortune is with me tonight," Carey growled between strangely stiff lips. He could barely lift his hand to the deck. The whole room took on a quality of unreality, and the air seemed to be steadily thickening. He looked up and noticed his friend Charles Mortimer for the first time. Standing at the edge of the crowd, Mortimer nodded at him. With renewed vigor, Carey gripped the card and turned it. The silence was deafening. A king.

"But 'tis the king of hearts," someone chirped, and Carey fell back against his chair.

D'Angelo's face was pale except for the red spots of agitation on his cheeks. "You must make Mrs. Kane hate you, so that she accepts my proposal voluntarily," he whispered hoarsely. "I wouldn't necessarily want to use force against her."

"Turn the next card!" Was that stony voice really his, Carey wondered, shaking inside.

D'Angelo's brow was now gleaming with perspiration, and he tipped over the next card. Carey barely dared to look. It was the six of hearts.

Carey and Lord Mortimer exchanged glances. There was some commotion by the door, but Carey returned his attention to his adversary.

"Your turn, McLendon."

Carey reached for the next card. This could easily be it. Anxious to get it over with, he flipped the card over.

A flutter of excitement went through the crowd. Another king—the king of clubs. Carey trembled so much he could barely keep upright in his seat.

D'Angelo moved his hand to the pack, his eyes bulging with strain. The card grated against the others.

"Another king!" called out a gambler leaning over D'Angelo's shoulder.

Carey couldn't concentrate on the court figure on the table. It seemed to move about on the table. Smoke wreathed over it, stinging his nose as he peered closer.

"The king of spades," someone shouted as he saw the upheld sword in the king's hand. Carey glanced at D'Angelo, holding the other man's eyes for the longest moment.

Something dark and incredibly ominous flickered through D'Angelo's eyes. "You have won."

Carey was weak with relief. He looked up and thought that he was dreaming, for there stood Francesca. Her hair was in a wild tangle. Her clothes were disheveled and her face was streaked with tears.

She took one step toward him, raised her hand, and gave him a stinging slap across his cheek. "How could you! How low can you sink, avenging your hurt pride gambling just because I didn't accept your proposal!"

Utterly surprised, Carey pushed his chair back.

He reached for her, but she stepped away. Her voice was harsh and low. "Arnold told me about the game here tonight. You had to ruin my livelihood, didn't you? If you think you can force me to marry you by taking away the shop that gives me work, you're completely mistaken." Her eyes blazed. "The business is all the D'Angelos have! And you never once thought of Estrella. What will become of her?"

"But I didn't—" Carey began, holding up his hands to stop her flow of words.

"How could you agree to this game! I never want to see your villainous face again," she spat, and swung away. Holding her head down, Francesca rushed from the room. When she had slammed the front door, it was so quiet he could hear his own breath.

"Well! It seems that I didn't lose, after all," D'Angelo drawled, flicking the king of spades contemptuously.

Why didn't she berate the Italian for gambling away his business? Carey thought, his elation completely evaporated. "You will honor your bet. I'm now the owner of your shop," he said between gritted teeth.

D'Angelo shrugged with studied indifference. "Make the best of it." He stood up and sauntered to the door. "I will have the papers drawn up."

Carey sank down on the chair and reached for the brandy bottle beside D'Angelo's empty glass. As he took a deep swallow, the crowd moved to seek other entertainment in adjoining salons.

"High stakes, eh?" Lord Mortimer's voice said close to his ear. "You had the devil's own luck, y'know."

Carey looked in amazement at the next card Lord Mortimer had flipped over—the king of diamonds. "I say!" He glanced into his friend's thin face. "I'm glad you haven't abandoned me." He held out the bottle to Lord Mortimer.

"Your beloved has, though."

Carey swore under his breath. "She's blind! I'll find a way to explain everything to her."

Lord Mortimer lifted his eyebrows quizzically. "She doesn't seem to want any explanations. She ordered you to hell, loudly and succinctly."

"Ah, Morty, why is love such torture?" Carey rose and placed his arm around the earl's shoulders. "Don't ever fall in love." They wandered off toward the faro table, and Carey went on, "I'll have to warn Francesca about the Italian, even if she refuses to see me."

"Why?" Lord Mortimer asked.

"The challenge was about Francesca. He knows she doesn't love him, but he's willing to do anything to wed her. He proposed to Francesca, and I cannot understand why. I don't think he loves her." He sighed. "There's another reason, and I intend to find out what it is. D'Angelo is a dangerous man. I must go after Francesca and talk to her, make her understand why D'Angelo challenged me."

"A good idea." Lord Mortimer replied, and glanced with longing at the faro table. He decided to stay at the Crimson Rooms, and Carey left alone. The distance to Haymarket was three miles, and there was no sedan chair in sight. He prayed that Francesca had found one and wasn't walking without company. He touched the hilt of his rapier and hoped he wouldn't have to use it.

The night was filled with voices and hoofbeats. He met a watchman with his chain and lantern, and a group of young blades weaving back and forth in drunkenness. He furrowed his brow when he recognized Lucas Halden and his ubiquitous red-haired companion. Carey stepped out of the way for the men, but Halden recognized him.

"Look, 'tis that blasted McLendon," he called out, slurring his words. "Shall we give him a go? This time he won't get away."

Carey swore and whipped out his rapier. "As usual you play underhandedly, Halden. Are you too much of a coward to meet me at dawn—man to man?"

Halden snarled an oath and pulled out his sword, as did his cronies, and they circled Carey. With a series of fast lunges he managed to break out, freeing his back. To his advantage, the other men were unsteady on their legs.

"We should end this quarrel once and for all," Carey said to Halden, who was steadily advancing, delivering thrusts that Carey easily deflected. "I have no desire to keep this feud alive, and I don't know why you bear a grudge against me."

"You've accused me of cheating at cards and molesting females." Halden increased his speed, but his jabs were clumsy. "That's more insult than a gentleman should have to accept."

Carey clenched his teeth and concentrated on the fight. The other men were advancing and he had difficulty staving off every sword within parring range. Perspiration began to roll down his face, and his arm started to weaken with fatigue. With a rapid feint, he managed to get under Halden's guard and slash open his coat. Like a roaring bull, the wounded man charged forward.

Carey sidestepped and Halden hurtled by, propelled by the force of his own attack. He lost his balance and toppled in the filth on the cobblestones.

Swearing, he rose to his knees and began jabbing at Carey's legs.

In a mad dance, Carey fought to keep his attackers at bay. He nicked one in the shoulder, another in the elbow. A pinprick of pain stabbed at the back of his knee, and he whirled around, ready to impale

the crouching Halden. He came eye to eye with another enemy, this one unarmed.

"I didn't expect help from you, Halden," Giorgio
D'Angelo said, and pushed Carey toward the other
men.

Halden struggled to his feet. "D'Angelo? What
are you doing here?"

"I was following McLendon, hoping for an incident like this. 'Tis too good to be true."

Carey struggled against the swords that hemmed
him into an ever-tightening circle. "Damn you to
hell," he spat and delivered a thrust into the red-
haired man's thigh.

"Shall we finish him off?" Halden said.

Carey heard him through a red fog of pain and
exhaustion. With a desperate pass of his rapier, he
tried to pierce his tormentor, without luck.

"No . . . we may need him alive a little longer,"
D'Angelo said thoughtfully. "He could be a powerful weapon in my plans." He delved into his
pocket and pulled out a heavy money pouch. Jin-
gling it, he said, "If you deliver McLendon to my
house, trussed up and subdued, this will be yours."

Halden viewed the pouch eagerly. "I suppose that
is not too much to ask." He rubbed his chin
thoughtfully. "However, I had hoped to put an end
to him. He's been a thorn in my side."

D'Angelo shrugged. "You can have him later—
when I'm done with him."

Halden laughed cruelly. "Will there be anything
left of him?"

D'Angelo chuckled. "I don't aim to kill him. I
promise you that pleasure."

Halden nodded and took a step forward. Lifting a
rock from the ground, he shouted to his cronies to
stop fighting.

Carey reeled across the cobblestones, barely seeing his tormentors as blood from a cut above his

eyebrow ran into his eyes. Thinking he was standing by a wall, he flung out his arm for support, but all he touched was air.

Dimly, he noticed Halden advancing steadily, two heads seeming to grow out of his collar. Then a sharp pain sliced through his skull, and merciful blackness swallowed him.

Chapter 22

～～⁓⌒◯◯⌒⁓～～

Francesca bent over the design on the table in front of her. She was sitting in the deserted workshop, the glowing embers in the charcoal hearths still sending out a comfortable warmth. The only light in the room came from the dripping candle on her worktable. The night was silent and cool, and a drizzle dampened the air outside. Chance, the mutt, was lying on the flagstones below the hearth, his head resting on his front paws.

Tears flowed freely down Francesca's cheeks. She was working on a brooch in the design of a peacock with spread tailfeathers. "This is useless now," she whispered. "All my dreams have been shattered with one turn of a card. How could Giorgio gamble everything away?" She was sure that Carey would sell the shop, and she would be forced to move again. But where? Was this his revenge for turning down his proposal? He couldn't be that vindictive—or could he? Had she been foolish to trust him?

The door creaked open and Estrella stepped inside. "I was worried about you. 'Tis late; when you weren't in your rooms, I imagined terrible things." She looked at Chance, who barked in a desultory fashion and returned to his nap.

"I . . . I took a walk. Sometimes I feel closed in."

Estrella sat on one of the three-legged stools next

to the long workbench. "You're upset over Giorgio's proposal? He can be so very blunt sometimes."

Francesca nodded, unwilling to divulge what she had witnessed in the Crimson Rooms. Estrella would be shocked when she found out that her brother had gambled away their home and livelihood. Giorgio would have to break the awful news himself.

"You seem so sad," Estrella continued, plucking nervously at her black skirt. Her hair was swept up in a frivolous style, her masses of curls adorned with velvet roses. Estrella's excitability was more evident tonight than usual. Did she sense what had happened? Francesca wondered. The Italian woman seemed to know something she didn't.

"Do you love Carey McLendon very much?" Estrella asked.

Francesca nodded miserably. "But he has shown me that he doesn't mind staking everything on a card. He's a wastrel, yet I cannot change my foolish heart." She sighed. "However, I'm strong enough to withstand my yearning."

"It might be for the best."

The two women exchanged probing glances, and Francesca grew uncomfortable. She sensed that Estrella was hiding something. "Are you speaking from experience?" she whispered.

Estrella hesitated for a moment, then shrugged. "No . . . I have never loved a man."

A hint of unspoken secrets veiled Estrella's voice and her gaze shifted uneasily. As anguish gripped her, Francesca fidgeted in her chair. "You seem sad and lonely. If you don't want to confide—"

Estrella patted Francesca's arm. "You have become my friend, and I'm sorry that Giorgio can't control his infatuation for you." Her lips trembled. "He will eventually push you away with his ardor. Yet I wish you two—"

"Why would you like your brother to marry me, when you know I don't love him?"

"Love isn't everything," Estrella said with a contemptuous toss of her head. "Position, comfort, enough money to buy what you want—"

Francesca's gasp quieted her. "You sound so callous, Estrella. I've never heard you speak like this before."

"You have been too occupied with thoughts of your lover—and your past." Something cold glittered in Estrella's eyes, then she lowered her eyelashes.

"Giorgio told you about Leonard Kane?" Suddenly restless, Francesca rose. "Shall we go inside? 'Tis growing late."

Estrella placed a detaining hand on Francesca's arm. "Don't worry. If I for one moment thought you were a murderess, I would never have let you inside my house." She stood up. "I know better."

With growing uneasiness, Francesca followed her. She clutched her sketches to her as if they could give her comfort. Her life had taken on an unreal quality. They said good night outside Estrella's bedroom door, but as Francesca went to her own rooms, she noticed that Estrella wasn't going into her chamber.

Francesca closed her door and fumbled for the key in the dark. It wasn't there. She lit a candle and stared at the lock. The key was gone. As she searched the floor, thinking it had fallen out, she heard a scraping sound on the landing. Then a key turned in her door from the outside.

Frantic, she set down the candle and tried the handle. It wouldn't move.

"Help! Let me out!" she cried, and banged on the wood until her knuckles were raw. The person who had made her rooms into a prison was gone, and Francesca shivered with apprehension. What was happening? Had everyone she liked and trusted turned against her?

Unable to sleep, she sat up most of the night. A blanket wrapped around her, she cradled Copper in her lap. Thoughts whirled furiously through her head, but she could find no answers to her questions.

Long after midnight Francesca heard the door being unlocked. She ran to fling it open, but no one was standing outside. Apprehensive, she walked downstairs and stepped into the D'Angelos' parlor. Chance followed her and slid into the room first.

Although prepared for something awful to happen, she nevertheless flinched when she saw Giorgio sitting in the armchair before the fireplace, a wineglass in his hand. "What—?" she whispered. "Why did Estrella lock me in my room?"

"Come in," he ordered. "And shut the door."

Too startled to do anything but obey, she closed it behind her. "I didn't know you had returned home."

With a vicious kick, he sent the footstool before him flying across the hearth rug. "Sit down."

Francesca lifted her chin a fraction and remained standing just inside the door. He glared at her, but he did not demand her obedience.

"You witnessed my humiliation tonight, Francesca."

She nodded, and anger flared within her. "What in the world induced you to gamble away everything you own? What about your responsibility to Estrella and the people who work for you?"

He rose and stretched to his full height. He wore a threatening expression as he advanced slowly toward her. She was aware of every ominous footfall on the wooden planks. Chance bounded toward Francesca, as if sensing that he had to protect her, but Giorgio kicked the dog aside, and he ran squealing with pain under the dining-room table.

"How dare you!" Francesca cried, moving toward Chance, but Giorgio halted her with a quick jerk of her arm. She suppressed her pain, sensing that she would have to be careful lest he resort to more violence.

"Francesca, the moment of truth has approached at last. To humor Estrella, I've decided to return to Italy. The arrangement will also suit my future business ventures." He sighed. "It was unfortunate that I lost my shop, but I will start anew in Italy."

Francesca stared at him, her eyes wide in horror and her mind spinning. "I don't understand. You just established your business here, and you are, or rather *were*, on the brink of great success." She retreated a step as she saw the angry—or was it evil—light in his eyes. "Why Italy?" she went on. The solid wood door pressed against her back.

"I can't very well open another shop here after tonight's scandal. 'Twill be all over London by tomorrow. Customers will shun us." He raked a hand across his stubbled chin and stared at her from under hooded eyelids. He smelled of sour wine.

Francesca sensed the devious course of his mind, and she shivered. She groped for the handle behind her and jumped as he reached out to grip her shoulder.

"Will you marry me anyway?"

She gasped in surprise, and he went on, his gaze searching her face, "Don't dare to say no."

Francesca struggled for a reply. Her mouth was parched, and her legs trembled. "I . . . no, I cannot marry you. Really, I don't love you, and after tonight—" She spoke with great effort. "—I don't trust you. Estrella—or you—locked me in my room." She could never consider marriage with this man, who frightened her more with each passing day.

His face twisted, suffused with anger. "I cannot understand how you dare to turn me down. You have nothing, Francesca! Even less than you had before you came here. Has it occurred to you that I could throw you out on the street if I cared to? Or treat you like a slave?"

Francesca paled. "You're forgetting yourself. It must be your heavy loss that's befuddling your mind."

He squeezed her shoulders so hard that she whimpered in pain. "You will marry me, and that's final."

Her breath rasped harshly as she gathered her courage. "No!" she cried.

He laughed and pulled her hard against him. She flung out her arm and hit a decanter on a table. It bounced off his shoe and rolled across the floor, spilling the liquid. "Damn!" he swore, his teeth baring. "You will see. Soon enough you must accept my offer, and be grateful that someone will have you—after I tell you the truth about yourself."

She gasped, her eyes dilating with shock. "Wh—what are you talking about?"

He dragged her across the room and pushed her into the chair by the hearth. Fear crawled through her, and her limbs turned ice-cold.

"Do you want your mother to die from shame?" he asked in a deceptively soft voice. When Francesca didn't immediately respond, he leaned over her and repeated the question. This time his voice was rough with barely controlled anger.

"No, but there's no reason—"

"Then listen carefully." He pulled away and went to stand in front of the empty fireplace. "Your father was Lord Childress, of Leicester Fields?"

"Of course! What a strange question." Her neck felt stiff with tension.

He laughed suddenly. "That's what you think.

No, Francesca, Lord Childress was not your father. His younger brother, the Honorable Edwin Farnley, was your father. Lord Childress was your uncle.''

Francesca clutched the armrests of her chair so hard that one of her nails broke. ''My uncle? That's impossible!''

He rolled back and forth on the balls of his feet and folded his arms across his chest. ''Not at all. Your mother had an affair with Edwin Farnley, right under her husband's nose, no less.''

''You'd say anything to make me surrender,'' Francesca snapped, springing out of the chair. He pushed her back down and took an old leather-bound book from the side table. Opening it to a page that he had marked with a black ribbon, he shoved it under her nose.

''Read this. It is Edwin Farnley's diary.''

Francesca's hands trembled as she held the book. It was an old journal, the page covered with a precise script that was easy to decipher. The date at the top was August 14, 1722. Her birthday! She felt suddenly light-headed.

This morning my daughter was born. It's the saddest of days, since I won't be able to call her my own. Francesca her name will be, the Italian version of Frances which was my beloved mother's name. My Susanna . . . oh, my darling Susanna, how will I find the strength to be parted from you? The Italy I love will be desolate without you and our infant daughter. How could you marry Childress when you loved me? Was it the title and the money? It must have been since you couldn't wait for me to return to England for you. I despair that wealth and social position mean more to you than our love, even though you bore our child.

"Oh, no . . ." Francesca stared at the words which blurred before her eyes. "You've invented this to torment me."

Giorgio laughed, a cold, contemptuous sound. Francesca tilted her head back to study him. This was not the Giorgio D'Angelo who she had first met in Covent Garden. This was a demon, and she was the victim of his torture.

"You are Edwin Farnley's bastard daughter," he hissed, and she sensed that it was true. "Your mother must have been carrying you when she decided to marry Childress. Rather than live in disgrace, she wanted a name for herself and for you—a titled name. And then they visited Farnley in Italy at the time you were born." He snorted. "Callous woman, your mother. She has carried this secret for a long time, and 'tis bound to be a heavy burden after all these years."

Francesca snapped the book shut. "What do you want from me?"

"Ah! At last you understand. I have waited patiently for this day, although I had hoped my charm would persuade you to come to me willingly." He tapped his toe on the floor and gave her a glance full of greed. "You will marry me. If you still refuse, I will—"

Francesca flinched, feeling the trap closing around her. "And what if I say no?"

He shrugged. "If you are that foolish, I'll have McLendon killed. He is even now lying in our cellar, wounded, and most likely bleeding to death."

"Killed? Cellar?" Her lips were stiff, and her hands clammy with fear. She catapulted out of the chair. "You are a beast! Does Estrella know about this?"

His lips curled sarcastically. "Estrella is a weak fool. She knows I'm planning to wed you, and she won't stand in our way. She's even now guarding your lover." He came closer and leaned over her. His eyes glittered with a strange light. "You will marry me now, won't you?"

Francesca looked to the floor to avoid his gaze. Dread weighed her down. This was worse than any nightmare. She knew now that Giorgio was capable of executing his threats. "Why do you want to marry me when you know I abhor you?" Confusion and anger swirled in Francesca's mind. She needed time to think, to plan her escape. Why had her mother kept her illegitimate birth a secret? The answer was clear. Her mother could not have borne the scandal. Besides, according to Edwin Farnley's journal entry, she must have cared only for the title of baroness, and the Childress money.

"Why do you want to wed me?" she insisted.

"Ah! That is a secret for now. You'll find out as soon as we reach Italy."

"He was a black sheep," she whispered, recalling the story of her Uncle Farnley.

Giorgio chuckled. "Yes, Farnley certainly was the black sheep of the family. Having a weak chest, he spent most of his life in the warm climate of Italy. That's how I came to know him. A lonely, but clever, fellow." He pinched her arms ruthlessly. "Well? Your answer!"

She lifted anguished eyes to his face, hating him with unrelenting passion. She would have to do this to save Carey if he was indeed incarcerated in the cellar. Gasping, she thought she would faint from fear. Carey . . . Carey. "Yes, I will marry you."

He released her, his radiant smile—his weapon— wreathing his face. To her it now looked like a wolf's grin. "I knew you would see the importance of keeping the scandal at bay." He slapped her chin lightly and she cringed. "You wouldn't want Mc-Lendon to know that you're a bastard, would you?

He adores you and your noble birth, a state *he* can never achieve.''

The dreadful truth about her illegitimate birth began to seep into her consciousness. Giorgio must be wrong! ''You're very cruel. What do you gain from this? I assure you, you won't find happiness with me. Your life will be dull and empty without affection.''

His eyes clouded over. ''I don't care for romantic nonsense. However, I have coveted our physical union ever since I first saw you. You have everything a true lady should have—beauty, dignity, compassion—I madly desire you. But that's beside the point. Lovemaking can wait. We'll return to Italy for the ceremony.''

Sick with worry over Carey, she whispered, ''I have no desire to go to Italy.''

''What do you have here to hold you back? Do you want to be reminded of your failures in England? Your husband was killed, perhaps even by you. I have no guarantee that you're innocent of his murder.''

Francesca shivered as if the room was ice-cold. ''I don't understand you at all. You're willing to marry a possible murderess?'' She wished she could say that she had killed Leonard, so that Giorgio would turn away from her.

He laughed. ''I don't care about your past. I have the power to crush you, so don't anger me.''

Francesca shuddered at the coldness of his voice. She couldn't stand to listen to him—his words seemed to vilify everything decent in the world. Yet she had no choice but to accept Giorgio, if she wanted to protect Carey.

''Very well, you have won. But you must promise to free Carey.'' She sighed, her shoulders slumping. She knew she couldn't make Giorgio do anything. The thought of Carey suffering in the dark cellar made her want to kill the Italian. Somehow she would have to save her beloved. "I wish you would tell me the whole story of Uncle Farnley," she said, to gain more time to think.

"It's all there in the diary. You know how to read, don't you?"

Francesca reached listlessly for the journal, but he grabbed it away before she could touch it. "You shall read it later. Now I want you to pack. I'll have to turn over the premises to McLendon tomorrow—or to his heirs, whoever they are." Almost as an afterthought he said angrily, "I would never do it, except that there were too many witnesses at that disastrous card game."

He pushed Francesca from the room and up the stairs. He shoved her inside her parlor, then locked the door behind her. "Pack your bags, Francesca."

There was nothing she could do except fume in silence. Was Carey really lying wounded in the damp, dungeon-like basement, or was Giorgio lying to make her do his bidding? She bit her lips until she tasted blood, and her eyes ached with unshed tears.

As if in a trance, she packed her meager wardrobe, wondering what would happen to Copper and Chance. Surely Giorgio wouldn't allow her to take them with her. Hollow with misery, she curled up on her bed without undressing. Unable to bear the thought of the future, she wished she could fall into oblivion, but sleep would not claim her. The words *illegitimate* and *bastard* danced wildly in her head, bringing a new depth of humiliation. What she had believed to be her legacy—her life—had been nothing but a lie. Not only did she feel betrayed, but she was now further alienated from the world she had known.

Copper slept rolled up beside her all night, as if sensing her agitation. Chance was curled into a ball on the rag rug beside her bed. But their loyal companionship could not soothe the anguish inside her heart. How could she have misjudged Giorgio so completely? Carey had been right all along to distrust him.

"Mother, I'm still gullible," she whispered into the night. " 'Twill never change. I was taken in by the Italian's flashing smile."

The next morning, she was so tired she could barely keep her eyes open. She looked at her image in the mirror, noticing her swollen red-rimmed eyelids and deathly pale cheeks. She barely found the strength to drag a brush through her tangled hair. She felt as if her entire body was heavy with tears, but she couldn't cry.

A few minutes later, the key turned in the lock, but no one entered. Francesca opened the door, but hesitated before going downstairs. As she glanced out the window, hardly noticing the bleak rainy day, Estrella came in, her skirts swishing. She was a different woman. Gone was her habitual air of frenzy.

"I hear that congratulations are in order," she chirped. " 'Tis the happiest day since I came to England."

Francesca watched Estrella's expression suspiciously. Had she known the secret of the diary all along?

The Italian woman crossed the room and pressed Francesca's cold hands. "Giorgio told me we're returning to Italy. I'm excited beyond belief, and I'm so glad you changed your mind about marrying him." She sighed, her eyes shining. "He'll make you happy."

"Don't you dare pretend with me!" Francesca said hoarsely, snatching her hands away. "Did he tell you why I accepted his proposal?"

Estrella's eyes widened with mock innocence. "He said you changed your mind."

Francesca's spirits fell even lower. Estrella would never be her ally. "You're a heartless liar."

Estrella wrung her hands excitedly, as if she hadn't heard the accusation. "You will love Italy. Your wedding ceremony will be so romantic."

Francesca could not speak. She clutched her hands in the folds of her skirt and swallowed hard. She would have to find a way to escape.

"Have you finished packing?" Estrella glanced into the bedroom, noticing the bandboxes. "I cannot wait to leave this gloomy city."

Francesca wondered how much Estrella knew about Giorgio's loss at the card table. "Aren't you surprised that your brother gambled everything away?"

Estrella's lips curved cynically. "You see, I know my brother. He'll be as successful in Italy as he was here. Yes, even more prosperous."

Francesca shuddered. She was becoming more and more trapped in the D'Angelos' web, and could see no way to extricate herself, or penetrate the wall of secrets that shielded the Italians.

"Well, let's go down, shall we?" Estrella turned toward the door with a supercilious smile.

Francesca was seized with fury at her mocking deception. She lifted the ornate vase that Estrella had placed in her room when she moved in, and with as much power as she could muster, threw it at the other woman. The vase hit Estrella's head with a thud and she crumpled to the floor without a sound.

Afraid that she had killed the woman, Francesca ran downstairs. The parlor was empty, but she could hear voices coming from the back stairs, and heavy footfalls on the front stairs. There was no escape. She recognized Giorgio's muffled voice at the rear door.

Without hesitating, she lifted the heavy iron poker

by the fireplace and hid behind the draperies that divided the parlor from the dining room.

Her arms trembled as she held the poker aloft. A few seconds later, Giorgio stepped into the room. Francesca peered at him from the edge of the curtain. He looked hard and tense, and he carried a flintlock pistol in his hand. She held her breath as he drew level with her. Stifling her fear, she brought down the poker. It glanced against his head and cracked into his shoulder.

"Damnation!" he swore, gripping his arm.

Francesca dashed toward the door, but as she tore it open, she fell into the arms of Lucas Halden.

"What's happening here?" he asked, restraining Francesca.

Giorgio lurched to her side and grasped her arms. Dragging her inside, he shook her until her teeth rattled. "You shall pay for this! Where's my sister?"

Francesca refused to look at him, and his grip was so hard that she could only moan. "Go find Miss D'Angelo," Giorgio ordered Halden. Then he pushed Francesca through the door and down the steep stairs, all the way down to the basement, which smelled of ale and mold. Torches flared fitfully in brackets along the narrow passage and Francesca could barely breathe for all the smoke.

"Where—?" she wheezed.

Without a word, he pushed her brutally through a door, and she fell to her knees on the grimy, damp floor. There, on a pile of straw, lay Carey. He was unconscious, and when she tried to wake him, Giorgio laughed contemptuously. Dried blood caked Carey's forehead, and his skin was icy and moist. A purple bruise was spreading at the hairline of his right temple. She touched his beloved face and pulled off her neckerchief to dab at the cold sweat on his forehead. Her heart aching with tenderness, she smoothed back his hair.

"I'll let him live if you tell him you're going to wed me," Giorgio snarled. Without waiting for an answer, he fetched a pitcher of water from a corner, pushing Francesca aside, and upended the vessel over Carey's still face.

"No!" Francesca cried.

Giorgio hid partially behind the open door, and Francesca saw that he was holding the pistol pointed at Carey's head. "Tell him," he grated. "Now!"

Carey sputtered as water filled his nostrils. He struggled to sit up, groaning with pain. Clutching his head, he became suddenly aware of Francesca's presence. Dazed with pain, he reached for her with outstretched arms.

She held back, watching the barrel of Giorgio's pistol from the corner of eye. Crying inside, she knew she had to protect Carey at all costs. If she made him believe that she didn't love him any longer, Giorgio might let him live.

"Where am I?" Carey asked wearily, dropping his arms.

Francesca could barely speak from terror and longing. "At Haymarket, in the cellar."

He tried to gain his feet, but his head ached too much. "I remember fighting with Lucas Halden . . . then D'Angelo arrived and all went black."

Francesca wrung her hands. She wanted to smooth the tension from his face and bathe his wounds. His clothes were filthy and ripped in several places. But if she wanted to save his life . . .

"I'm going to marry Mr. D'Angelo, Carey. I've decided to return to Italy with them today." She paused. "This is our good-bye."

Carey's eyes widened in shock. "Only because I won his shop in a card game? He challenged me, by God! He's jealous—he wants you for himself." Carey longed to shake her. "Don't you understand?"

Francesca lowered her eyes. "I'm not going to argue with you. I abhor what you did, and I will never forgive you. I'm leaving today.'' She clasped her hands together so hard that she thought her bones would break.

He grasped her shoulders and tried to pull her close. ''You can't do that, Francesca. You said you loved me.''

Francesca took a deep, uneven breath and closed her eyes. She hated herself as she said the next words. ''Not anymore.'' Her voice faltered. ''What we had was nothing but a fleeting fancy.''

He shook his head in disbelief. ''Have you gone mad?''

''No.'' She struggled to her feet. ''There's nothing more to say.''

''I'm lying here by his orders, don't you see? He had me brought here after Halden assaulted me.''

Francesca hesitated, glancing toward the door. Giorgio's eyes glittered with an evil light, and she knew she had no choice but to continue lying.

''Giorgio would never do this. Halden must have put you here.'' She hurried away as his cry of anger bounced off the walls.

''Fool!'' he shouted after her. ''Open your eyes!''

The door clanged shut on the damp prison, and Giorgio joined Francesca at the top of the stairs.

''You did splendidly,'' he purred, leading her by the arm back inside. ''I'll lock you in your room until we're ready to travel.''

''You promised not to kill him,'' she pleaded. ''So why do you leave him down there to die? He will die unless he gets care.''

Giorgio laughed. ''Your concern for McLendon is over. Forever.'' As she moaned in outrage, he pushed her into her room and bolted the door. Estrella was no longer stretched out on the floor.

Trembling and desolate, Francesca gathered Copper into her arms. Chance was whining, sensing the tension in the house. What would happen to her beloved Carey, and what would happen to her pets? She pressed her nose against Copper's head and wept.

Chapter 23

She had abandoned him. She had abandoned him. The word *abandon* ripped through Carey's brain over and over. The knowledge brought him to a sharp edge that he thought would cut him into fragments of pain. She hadn't even given him a chance to hold her, to argue against her decision. She had been so cold, so changed, that she hadn't even touched him.

Carey was unaware of the pounding in his head and the icy damp stillness of the cellar. But he grew alert at the sound of the door creaking open.

In the flickering light of the torches, he recognized Lucas Halden. "What are you doing here?" he croaked.

"I promised the Italian I would finish you off. He and the women left five minutes ago." He was holding a lethal-looking dagger in his hand. "You're not so arrogant now, McLendon, and your foppish clothes are positively foul."

Carey moved as far back as the ropes around his ankles would permit. "Don't touch me, or I'll strangle you with my bare hands, Halden." When the other man didn't stop advancing, he continued, "This is ridiculous. You're obsessed with getting revenge. You beat me in King Street. Isn't that enough?"

"Turning cowardly now, McLendon?" Halden moved slowly forward, his dagger raised.

"You're the coward who attacks a bound and wounded man," Carey spat. So this would be the end, he thought. I will die in a dirty cellar, not honorably on a dueling field. "Let us at least fight like men," he pleaded.

"You shall fight no more." Halden raised the dagger over his head, and Carey closed his eyes, waiting for the searing pain that would end his life. He instinctively rolled aside, but his limbs were so stiff with cold that he failed to move further.

Holding his breath, he braced himself for the end.

Then a shot blasted through the cramped quarters, deafening him. He clamped his hands over his ears as Halden staggered forward two steps and fell into the filthy straw.

Carey stared at the door, hoping wildly that Francesca had returned. Instead, Charles Mortimer stepped inside.

"Thank God!" Carey groaned. "I can always count on you, old fellow."

After giving Halden, who had fainted from his thigh wound, a vitriolic glance, Mortimer fell to his knees and began attacking the rope at Carey's feet with Halden's knife. "I went to see you this morning, and Bigelow told me you'd been gone all night. He was very concerned, and when I later confronted Letty Rose, she admitted that you left right after we parted at the Crimson Rooms." He managed to cut through the thick rope, and Carey massaged his ankles. "I came by here to find out if Francesca had seen you." He helped Carey to stand. "The nest is empty except for a few pieces of furniture, Francesca's pets, and some sheaves of sealed papers on the dining room table."

"The shop papers. These premises are now mine." Carey could find no happiness in the fact.

"D'Angelo has taken Francesca to Italy to marry her." He rotated his shoulders until some feeling returned.

"Italy? But she loves you, Carey."

"She told me she's changed her mind," Carey spat contemptuously.

"Nonsense! She doesn't appear to be flighty. Somebody must be blackmailing her. Don't you see?"

Carey studied his friend closely. "I don't know. She sounded sincere enough. She wouldn't even touch me."

Mortimer flicked Carey's battered coat with the tip of the knife. "I'm not surprised. A pig is cleaner."

Halden moaned and turned over. Lord Mortimer bound his feet with the rope that had shackled Carey.

"You can't leave me here," the man cried, eyeing his bleeding leg. "I'll die."

"That would serve you right, Halden," Mortimer said, "but I'll send Cauliflower Arnold here to put some sense into your thick head—before he hands you over to the nearest magistrate." He turned to Carey. "Arnold must also look after Francesca's animals."

"Yes. Let's get out of here." Carey didn't even deign to look at Halden as he stumbled from the foul cellar.

The cobblestone yard was filled with fog. "I'll find some horses at the livery stables. We must ride after the Italians," Lord Mortimer said and ran down the street. "There's no time to lose."

Although his head was pounding viciously, Carey recognized Justus Preston, who was standing bewildered just inside the door to the workshop. After limping over the cobblestones, he explained everything to Preston and the apprentices. He promised them extra pay if they stayed on at the shop until he returned with Miss Francesca, and Preston vowed to look after things. Carey dashed off a note to Arnold and asked one of the apprentices to deliver it to the Crimson Rooms. Arnold would convince Halden to change his ways, Carey thought grimly.

Preston offered Carey his humble, although clean, jacket and three-cornered hat. By the time Lord Mortimer returned, Carey was ready to ride after the Italians.

"They have almost an hour's lead," Carey said and swung into the saddle.

"Where did they go? Southampton?"

"Yes, I'm sure they must be heading for a merchant ship to Italy." Carey pressed his hat lower over his eyes as the horse tore past wagons and carriages on the narrow streets. "We'll have to ride like the wind to reach the docks in time to stop them."

They left London in silence, heading southwest toward the coast. Riding at full speed, they might just overtake the Italians in their slower carriage.

They soon realized that the change of horses they hired in Guildford were not up to the exertion, and they ended up going ten miles out of their way to the nearest livery stable. Then Carey's next horse lost a shoe. "We're not meant to get there in time," he complained, cursing under his breath.

"Don't fret, old fellow," Lord Mortimer said, his lips pinched into a severe line. "We'll catch up with them sooner or later."

Yet his prediction seemed doomed to fail. As their horses stormed through Southampton toward the docks, they prayed they would be in time. At the last livery stables they had been told the ship was to depart at seven o'clock that night.

Just as their horses galloped into the harbor, the passengers cheered on deck as the three-masted frigate pulled out of the bay.

Carey threw his hat on the ground in anger.

"Damn!" He scanned the crowds waving along the railings, but Francesca was nowhere in sight.

"Bad luck, hey?" Lord Mortimer clamped a hand on Carey's shoulder.

They stared in frustration as the sails were unfurled, bearing the frigate further away from the wharf.

"Perhaps they missed the ship as well," Lord Mortimer said.

They exchanged glances, Carey's eyes lighting with hope. He scanned the docks filled with people and cargo, but he recognized no one. His hope trickled away.

"We'll have to take the next ship out," Lord Mortimer said.

"Yes, I'll be damned if I'll let her marry that scoundrel."

"My sentiments exactly," Lord Mortimer said, and slid off his horse to find out when the next ship to Italy was expected to leave.

They found out that no ship would sail until the following week. Dispirited, they decided to eat while calculating what to do next. They rode to a tavern a mile north of the harbor, at the edge of town.

"Why did this have to happen? I warned Francesca about the Italian," Carey said, after ordering a tankard of ale. "She wouldn't listen." He sat down at a table and pushed his hat toward the back of his head. The serving wench glanced at him suspiciously, and Mortimer whispered that he ought to wash the blood off his face, since he looked like a veritable buccaneer. When she returned Carey asked the girl where he could wash, and she offered him a room and a pitcher of hot water.

"I feel slightly better now," he announced after refreshing himself. "The wench even brought a comb and a razor, and a patch for the wound." He indicated the white square that covered his eyebrow.

Lord Mortimer nodded and pointed at Carey's plate, which was heaped with ham and eggs. "Eat. That will make you feel like a prince."

"I doubt it," Carey grumbled, but he obeyed nevertheless, suddenly realizing that he was starving.

"Where yer goin'?" the servant asked them as she refilled their tankards. She peered at them from under her floppy mobcap. "Seems that ye're in a blinkin' 'urry."

"We were going to Italy, but the ship has already left," Lord Mortimer explained. "We had the devil's own luck." He drank deeply from the tankard and winked at the girl.

"Ye're not th' only ones then. A coach stopped 'ere no more than fifteen minutes afore ye did. An Italian toff 'e was if I bain't mistaken, seein' as 'twas an Italian ship leavin' th' 'arbor today."

Mortimer and Carey exchanged incredulous glances. "Could it be?" Carey murmured.

"Tell me," Mortimer said, "did the man travel alone?"

The wench hid her hands behind her white apron and shook her head with an important air. "Nay, 'e wasn't alone. Traveled wi' two ladies, both dark-'aired. Outright lovely they were," she said with longing in her voice, touching her own copper curls beneath the cap.

"It's them," Carey said, rising from his seat. "In what direction did they go?"

"Toward Portsmouth, I reckon. The eastern road goes t' Portsmouth and Chichester. They turned in that direction."

Mortimer paid for their meals and gave the girl a shilling for her information. "This time we'll overtake them," he said with relish. "There's nothing as invigorating as a mad dash through the verdant countryside.''

Carey dug his heels into the flanks of his mount and rolled his eyes heavenward. His head pounded as if someone was repeatedly beating it with a hammer. ''It takes someone like you to find exhilaration in a chase of life and death.''

Chapter 24

Francesca stared with loathing at her traveling companions—her gaolers. Giorgio had bound her feet, and refused to let her out when the coach stopped. Her physical needs of hunger and thirst went ignored, although Giorgio and Estrella dined at an inn along the Portsmouth road.

Besides her worries for Carey, her head was filled with questions. Had he died from his injuries, or was he still alive? Anger made her confront the brother and sister fearlessly. "Why are we going to Portsmouth?"

Giorgio smiled and answered with an air of contempt. "How curious you are, my dear. Since we cannot find another Italy-bound ship until next week, I've decided to visit my associate, Mr. Clarence Ingram, outside Beachy Head in Sussex. He won't mind having us as guests for a few days. Besides, I have to make a financial settlement with him." He rubbed his chin thoughtfully. "We might even get married here in England. Why wait? I'll ask Ingram to help me procure a special license, and find a priest to wed us in Sussex."

Ingram! Francesca's eyes flew wide at the name. She was on the verge of explaining that she'd been locked in Mr. Ingram's cellar, but she snapped her mouth shut as realization dawned—Ingram was the old man who had hired the highwaymen to hold up the carriage, and Giorgio knew Ingram . . . It couldn't be a coincidence. Giorgio must have been involved with Leonard's death.

Francesca burned to confront the Italian with her suspicions, but if she kept quiet, she might find a way to use the knowledge against Giorgio. How, she didn't yet know.

As the notion of Giorgio's guilt took root in her mind, Francesca's thoughts traveled in ever-wider circles. If he was responsible for Leonard's death, he must have known about her before they had met in London. Had he been the man who had bludgeoned her that day in the sand dunes? Had he planned to kill her when Carey happened to ride by? But why? And why was he even now planning to wed her?

Squirming uncomfortably on the seat, Francesca looked everywhere but at the Italians.

"What's wrong with you?" Giorgio chided her. "Uneasy at the thought of marrying me?"

"Yes, I am," she replied frankly. "I don't know why you'd want to have a loveless marriage. It certainly won't make life easier for any of us."

Giorgio shrugged. "You don't know all my reasons, but you soon will." He delved into his portmanteau and pulled out Edwin Farnley's diary. Tossing it in her lap, he said. "Read. There's plenty of time before we reach Beachy Head."

Filled with apprehension, Francesca held the old book. If the facts in the diary were true, she had been born on the wrong side of the blanket, just like Carey McLendon. The man she had believed to be her father had been her uncle. She had loved Lord Childress like a father. In the truest sense, he had been her papa.

Hot tears pressed behind her eyelids. Her entire life had been a lie. Her mother had known the truth, yet never told her. Digging her nails into the palms of her hands, Francesca managed to control her emotions. It wouldn't do to have her enemies know her distress. She couldn't bear to see them gloat. She threw a contemptuous glance at Estrella, the woman she had considered her friend.

"How could you be so false?" she asked hoarsely. "You seemed an honest person."

Estrella shrugged. "I still am, but my first responsibility is to my brother. I don't question his judgment—not in this case. He'll make you happy when no one else will." She patted Francesca's arm with false friendliness. "Just remember that you're considered a murderess in the eyes of the world. Giorgio will give you back your respectability. No one in Italy will know your background." Estrella smiled. "As for me, I didn't like being knocked down with a vase, but I won't let it ruin our friendship."

Francesca gasped and pulled as far away from the other woman as she could. Estrella's reasoning made her feel nauseated. The D'Angelos had no notion of right or wrong; they were happy to take whatever they wanted, even if it involved murder. Francesca shivered at the thought, wondering how long they would let her live. Until after the ceremony?

"I'm no friend of yours," she said. " 'Tis still a mystery to me what you'll gain from marrying me, Giorgio," she added, addressing Estrella's brother.

He pointed once more at the diary. "You must read it. Then you'll understand that I have no choice but to marry you."

Francesca glanced at the journal with loathing. "You're capable of killing to get what you want."

His eyebrows shot up. "Killing?"

Had he sensed that she meant Leonard? "I mean . . . you left Carey McLendon to die in your cellar. That's cold-blooded murder."

Giorgio leaned forward, his eyes mere slits of anger. "Be silent and read the diary, or else I might have to hurt you."

Francesca flinched as he raised his hand menacingly, but she met his gaze without hesitation. She'd do her utmost to pretend that his threats could not touch her. Nevertheless, she sat in her corner and opened the old tome, then started reading from the beginning.

Side by side, Carey and Lord Mortimer rode as fast as they could through the countryside. "Do you think they headed into Portsmouth? That's a fairly large town. Would be hard to find them there, old fellow," Mortimer said.

"We'd better halt at every inn along the way to ask if they've stopped." Carey felt breathless with worry. "Why would they want to visit Portsmouth? The dock master told me that no other ships along the south coast were leaving for Italy."

"We'll discover the reason soon enough, I imagine."

Carey yearned to spur on his hired horse, although he knew the bony nag could not gallop any faster. His anxiety over Francesca urged him forward. He was oblivious to the beauty around him, the gentle green slopes divided by hedgerows where birds chattered. The golden sun warmed his back, but all he could think of was the Italians' coach. Would he come upon it at the next bend in the road?

As afternoon darkened into twilight, they arrived at the outskirts of Portsmouth. Almost before the horses could stop, Carey was out of the saddle and asking the ostlers about the Italians, but the answers he got were invariably negative.

At a livery stable they changed horses. This time, the only mounts left to choose from were an ancient gray and a horse with an odd kick in its gallop.

"Where to now, old fellow?" Lord Mortimer asked, wiping his brow. "I'm hot and thirsty."

Carey nodded. "So am I. Did they mayhap stop at the next inn closer to the city?"

Since Mortimer could not answer that question, he shrugged and turned his mount in the direction of the center of Portsmouth. "The only way to know is to find out," he said cryptically.

Carey flicked his reins. "We'll eat at the next inn, even if there's no sign of Francesca."

It was quite dark by the time they reached the next inn, the House and Turtle. Weary, they ordered large pewter tankards of ale. The thin, bespectacled landlord had not seen the Italians. "They didn't stop here for dinner," he added.

"Where's the next tavern?" Carey asked with a deep frown.

"That'll be the Seafarer, three streets south of here. Almost by the harbor."

Carey and Mortimer exchanged exasperated glances. The landlord left after recommending a dinner of his wife's shepherd's pie.

"I have a terrible feeling they didn't come this way," Carey said, rubbing his aching temples. "But where did they go? We've lost precious time."

"Just remember that they don't suspect we're on their heels. They are not in a hurry now, like they were to reach Southampton." Lord Mortimer took a swig of ale. "We'll catch them tomorrow."

Carey slumped back against the timbered wall and stared into the huge empty cavern of the fireplace to his right. "We might as well sleep here. No use searching all night."

Mortimer nodded. "I'm sure they are resting at an inn as well."

"And tomorrow we'll find some faster horses," Carey said with a wry grin. "The gray mare I have will give me a permanent back injury if I ride her any longer."

After eating a hearty dinner, they decided to go to bed early and continue their search at dawn. Carey refused to dwell on Francesca, but however much he struggled, her lovely face swam before him. She had told him calmly and succinctly that she was going to marry D'Angelo. Was he a fool to pursue her? Would she laugh at him when he came face to face with her? Tossing on the horsehair mattress, he realized that he just had to know whether she really wanted to marry the Italian or not. He had to ask her one more time if she still loved him. If she didn't, well, then he'd been an utter fool to believe in her previous declarations. Her dark eyes had been so sincere . . . On that thought, Carey finally fell asleep.

The following morning they rode out of Portsmouth after spending two hours searching the other inns in town—without luck.

"They'll be at the opposite end of the world before we find them," Carey said angrily, putting his heels into the flanks of his mare. Not only had they not found the Italians, but there were no other livery horses to be had.

Carey would have to suffer the gray's bone-jarring jog until they could locate new mounts. Their slow progress tried his nerves. At this pace they would never catch up with the coach. His hands tightened around the reins. He'd ride until he found Francesca, even if it took all day and night. They had to be somewhere along the road.

That morning Francesca finished reading the diary and closed it with a deep sigh. There was no doubt about it; Edwin Farnley had been her father. He had once loved her mother, but had she loved him? Lady Susanna Childress was a bitter woman. Would she have been different if she'd lived with Edwin Farnley? So many questions, and Farnley wasn't alive to answer them.

Francesca threw a cautious glance at the Italians. They were taciturn this morning, barely paying any attention to her after they had climbed into the coach.

Giorgio had warned her to keep silent at the inn, or he would kill her. Knowing that he was capable of violence, she had obeyed, however much she longed to draw attention to her dilemma. Giorgio had bound her wrists to a bedpost, and she had slept in fits and starts while her stomach growled with hunger and her mind struggled with worry.

"How did you know Edwin Farnley?" she asked. "He was no relation of yours, was he?"

Giorgio and Estrella exchanged veiled glances, and Francesca wondered what went through their minds.

"No . . ." Giorgio stared at her vacantly. "But Farnley was my friend. He gave me work in his shop when I was a boy."

Estrella gave her a supercilious smile. "You see, we weren't born in the country like we told you. We lived in Rome all our lives."

"So everything you explained in London about your past is false?" Francesca shrank into the corner, the wooden trim on the wall gnawing into her shoulders.

"Yes—in a way—but it's true that we're from a large family. Our father was so poor he couldn't put food on the table for us every day," Estrella said, looking away.

"Then your father found me," Giorgio continued. "I once saved him from being trampled by a horse. He was grateful and offered me work." Giorgio sighed as if filled with longing. "I worked for him all my life, actually *slaved* for him. He was a rich jeweler, while I was a man who had the talents to enrich his coffers." Giorgio's face reddened with anger. "He taught me everything he knew about the jewelry business, and when he recognized my talent, he made full use of it. One would have thought he might have given me something in return when he died."

"He did," Estrella said. "Don't forget the stipend."

Giorgio snorted. "A pittance! I was worth much more, but he treated me like a lowly servant. It was as if he never wanted to let me forget that he'd pulled me from the gutter, when in fact he should have treated me like a son. I was literally his right-hand man. My designs enriched his coffers."

Francesca listened in surprise. There was nothing about Giorgio that suggested his birth had been lowly. But the icy gleam in his eyes reminded her of his ruthlessness.

"Farnley didn't even know you, Francesca!" he spat. "What have you done to deserve his money? I gave him the best years of my life. I was more loyal than a son, but he left me only enough funds to establish my own business." His hands gripped the top of his walking cane fiercely. "Farnley was a mean and despotic man. The only person he ever cared about was your mother—and then you."

"Are you harassing me to exert revenge against him?" Francesca asked, her voice barely audible.

"The fact of the matter is that you're a very affluent woman," Estrella said. "And now you will share your wealth with us. Farnley was as rich as Croesus when he died."

Francesca felt faint. "Wealthy?"

Lord Mortimer wiped his forehead with a handkerchief. "Deuced hot, isn't it? I wager we'll have a thunderstorm before nightfall." He was limping along the dusty lane, holding his horse's slack rein.

"How's your ankle?" Carey asked as he walked beside his friend. "How much longer can you go on?" He gave Lord Mortimer's horse a contemptuous glance. "Serves us right for not waiting for decent nags. Just when I think things can get no worse, your horse rears at a swooping bird, and then goes lame. A bird!" His voice was hoarse with disgust. "Someone must have cursed us to give us such rotten mounts."

Lord Mortimer laughed and halted. He tore off his coat and hung it over the pommel. "Can't say we were blessed." He unbuttoned his waistcoat. "A glass of ale would be a godsend."

Carey slapped his shoulder. "You shall have one at the next tavern, one with ample froth." He sighed. "Without your company, this would have been a lowering race indeed."

Lord Mortimer gritted his teeth. "We'll catch them yet."

"But there isn't a trace! Where could they have gone?" Carey shielded his eyes from the sunlight and stared along the winding road. "No one recalls seeing them."

"I'll bet they drove straight to Chichester. There are bound to be good livery stables there."

"But *where* are they going? I'm more puzzled by the minute." As Mortimer mumbled that he had no idea, Carey creased his forehead in thought.

After walking another fifteen minutes, they arrived at an unprepossessing roadside inn, a so-called hedge tavern. Groaning, Mortimer flung himself onto a bench under a spreading oak.

"I'll find you that ale, old friend," Carey said, fastening the reins of their horses to a post.

He returned a few minutes later carrying two tankards. The shade was cool, but the wind blew clouds of dust along the ground and under the trees. When their thirst was slaked, a fat matron dressed in a gray homespun gown and a voluminous apron emerged from the tavern.

"Do ye want food as well? Can't say I 'ave anything but cold roast goose, boiled tongue in jelly, and bread."

Mortimer eased himself upright and smiled. "Sounds heavenly."

"Have you seen a coach with an Italian couple and a young woman this morning?" Carey asked after wiping the ale foam from his mouth.

"Italian? 'Ave no idea, but a coach stopped 'ere for a few minutes, and a dark gent with a flashing smile bought some bread." The woman nodded. "Very natty cove 'e was, but Italian? I don't know."

"He doesn't have an accent."

The woman shrugged and picked up a broom that was leaning against the wall. "Could 'ave been 'im then."

Carey described Giorgio's every feature as best he could, and the woman nodded in recognition, but said she hadn't seen anyone who looked like Francesca or Estrella.

Frowning, Carey pondered her words. "Can you tell me in which direction the coach went?" he asked.

With a sweep of her broom, she pointed east, toward Chichester.

"Seems that we're on the right road, anyhow," Lord Mortimer said with satisfaction and drank more ale. He smiled at Carey. "They won't get away from us now."

"How long ago did they drive by?" Carey continued, as the matron swept the path to the door.

"I'd say 'bout two 'ours ago."

Carey set down his tankard with a crash. "Do you know where we could find two fast horses? Neither my friend nor his horse can walk any longer."

She gave them directions to an inn closer to

Chichester. "They might 'ave changed 'orses there as well. Th' toff said they were traveling far."

Far? Carey pondered those words as he rode off to get the horses for Lord Mortimer and himself. How far, and to where?

Francesca slept in a corner of the coach. At Chichester they had found a fast team that was bringing them ever closer to their destination—Mr. Ingram's house outside Beachy Head in Sussex.

How would she find a way to escape her tormentors? All they wanted was her money—an inheritance she hadn't even known she possessed.

"We'll be there tonight," Giorgio said, breaking into her thoughts.

Francesca sat up, noticing that great clouds had covered the afternoon sun. A distant rumble echoed. Anger and dislike coursed through her as she regarded the man on the seat across from her. Estrella was sleeping in her own corner.

"Why did you seek me out here in England?" Francesca asked. "You could have asked Farnley for funds and started your own business in Rome."

Giorgio bared his teeth in a wolfish grin. "Marriage to you will bring me so much more." He toyed with the ebony knob of his walking cane. "You see, your father made a mistake when he told me what was in the will. His last order on his deathbed was that I come here and inform you of his will, and bring you back to Italy. The legal advisors would explain everything to you there."

"Why didn't they send me a letter?" she asked in bewilderment.

He shrugged. "Since I was going to fetch you personally, I convinced them it was a waste of time to contact you." His laugh made her shiver with fear. "They trusted me, you see, your father's *slave* for so many years."

Darkness shrouded the trees outside the coach, and a crash of thunder shook the air. Francesca flinched and moved further away from the window. "The only problem in your scheme was that I was already married," she said, her voice breathless with fear.

His face split into that bright smile that she had come to loathe, and she knew for certain then what she had begun to suspect—that Giorgio D'Angelo had instigated Leonard's death.

Carey brought back two fresh horses to the hedge tavern where Lord Mortimer had downed quite a few tankards of ale with his dinner. Great raindrops were already splashing the road, and the darkened skies promised a fierce storm.

"We're going to be drowned like rats," Carey said, staring at the roiling lead-gray clouds.

"We can't let that stop us," Mortimer said, and limped to his new mount. "I've ordered victuals for you, old fellow. You can eat while we're underway."

Carey nodded, ignoring his growling stomach. Pressing his hat low over his eyes, and sweeping his cloak closer around his neck, he guided the horse onto the road toward Chichester. "They were seen at the livery stables," he shouted to Mortimer over the storm.

"I wonder where they were heading."

Thunder cracked overhead. "The Italian told the ostler they were going into Sussex."

Mortimer pulled his hat lower as the rain poured down more heavily. "Sussex? Why in the world—?"

Carey smiled grimly. "I don't know why they'd go there, but I think their destination is an estate outside Beachy Head, just west of Eastbourne."

"*Eastbourne?*" Mortimer said, aghast. "We've no time to lose if we're to catch up with them. 'Twill be a miserable night . . ." His voice died away as he pushed his heels into his horse and took off like the wind. Tree branches tossed dangerously in the gale, but Lord Mortimer laughed.

"Trust you to enjoy a little adventure," Carey called after his friend, as he charged down the road in his wake.

Chapter 25

Francesca stared with suspicion at the elderly female servant who opened Mr. Ingram's door. Would she try to close the door in their faces, just as she had done the first time Francesca came to visit?

"Mr. D'Angelo," she crowed, and opened the door wide. "Come in, come in. 'Tis rainin' terribly."

Giorgio pushed Francesca inside. She stumbled and almost fell, since her hands were bound. The servant stared at her and flinched in recognition.

"You! What's she doin' 'ere?"

Giorgio stared suspiciously at Francesca, then at the servant. "Do you know her?" he barked at the old woman.

"Yes! Bless me, but she was 'ere once t' speak with Mr. Ingram."

Giorgio gripped the woman's scrawny arms and shook her. "Why didn't you write to me? She could have ruined everything!"

The servant shrank back. "Mr. Ingram thought it best not t' return 'ere for a while. We just came back from th' Isle o' Wight.'Adn't time to send word t' you."

Muttering under his breath, Giorgio finally let the woman go. He shot a furious glance at Francesca, then stalked to a door on the opposite side of the hallway and pushed it open.

"Edith? Is that you?" a querulous male voice called from within.

"No, 'tis I, D'Angelo. I've come to settle our business once and for all. I also thought you might help me resolve a delicate matter." He returned and gripped Francesca's arm. After snatching off her damp cloak, he shoved her through the door to a library, bathed in dim candlelight.

An old man, presumably, Mr. Ingram stared hard at her. So, she thought, this was the man Carey had searched for so desperately.

"What matter?" Mr. Ingram said, as he scrutinized Francesca.

"A special license. I'll marry Mrs. Kane here in your home if you don't mind, Clarence."

Clarence Ingram continued to look at Francesca. "You're as lovely as I recall," he said in a brittle voice. "I was sure you were dead in the sand dunes."

"Right now I almost wish I were," Francesca whispered. He was wearing a brown coat adorned with brass buttons and a thin braid of gold thread. A steel-gray scratch wig covered the wisps of white hair jutting above his ears. The skin on his face was pasty and paper-thin, the nose sharp and the lips thick. His ice-blue eyes were embedded in wrinkles. It was quite an ordinary face, Francesca thought, just as Carey had described.

"You really wanted me dead?" Francesca asked with stiff lips. Her limbs felt icy with fear.

He cackled and pulled out chairs for everyone. "No . . . I'm not a murderer."

"You are," she whispered, her gaze riveted to the man who had sent those lead balls whizzing past her head after she and Cauliflower Arnold had managed to escape from the cellar.

"If you're talking about the shots I took at you, they were intended only to frighten you away. Until today, I had no desire to speak with you." He indicated a chair for her, then patted Giorgio's arm. "But now that *he* has brought you here, things are different."

"Different?" Francesca asked, refusing to sit down.

Mr. Ingram bowed to Estrella and led her to an overstuffed armchair, then sat down beside her. Giorgio, who had been watching Francesca through half-closed eyelids, turned his gaze to the old man.

"I don't understand," Francesca said.

Ingram peered at Giorgio. " 'Tis obvious you haven't explained. I'm sure we can all deal fairly together."

"Do you know me, sir?" Francesca asked. "I certainly haven't met you before."

Mr. Ingram muttered something and gave her a sidelong glance. "Who could forget your face, miss? You look just like Farnley did in his youth."

A sudden stab of regret pinched her heart as she realized she would never be able to meet her father. Evidently this man could put the puzzle pieces together. "I didn't know Farnley."

Mr. Ingram flinched. "You should be glad you didn't know him, Mrs. Kane. He was a ruthless man." Spittle flew from between his yellowed teeth and his eyes smoldered with anger. "A first-class viper, Farnley was."

Francesca's voice shrunk to a whisper. "Why are you so angry? What did Edwin Farnley do to you?"

Mr. Ingram leaned forward threateningly, his face red with fury, his wrath almost palpable. Then he sighed heavily, resting both knobby hands on the top of his stomach. He peered at Francesca, his eyes at once shrewd and calculating. "You really want to know all about your father? 'Tisn't by any means a nice story.''

His question sent a tremble of fear down Francesca's back. She wasn't sure she wanted to hear the tale, but she nodded uncertainly.

"Very well." Mr. Ingram's eyes took on a faraway look. "Even though he came from an aristocratic family, Farnley and I were poor, y'know, poor as church mice. The Childress money went with the title. I met Farnley at school—we went to Oxford together for one year. After that, our education ended—mine did, anyway." His voice rose slightly. "Your father was fortunate at cards. Had the devil's own luck."

"He gambled?" Francesca asked in surprise. "He didn't mention it in his journal."

"Never mind! He gambled. Won fifteen thousand pounds one night."

Francesca gasped.

" 'Twas a fortune, Mrs. Kane. We opened a shop on Long Acre. Sold old furniture, porcelain, and jewels. Sort of an auction chamber, if you must know. We bought up estates."

"Cheated the sellers, most likely," Giorgio said under his breath.

"Farnley made gold from everything he touched. A regular Midas he was," continued Mr. Ingram, seeming not to hear Giorgio's comment. "When he decided to specialize in jewelry, which was the most profitable business, I agreed."

"How long did you work together?" Francesca asked.

"Forty years. Farnley was a wild young buck. Got himself involved with your mother, Lady Susanna. He did it only to spite his older brother, who later inherited the Childress barony. More envious than the devil was Farnley. Still, I think he once had a soft spot for your mother."

Silence reigned for an interminable moment, as the old man became lost in memories.

"What are you trying to tell me, Mr. Ingram?" Francesca finally asked.

He gave a dry laugh. "Farnley grew tired of his life here. He took our entire inventory of gems, and disappeared to the Continent. If you must know, he left me to maintain a London office for the business which was flourishing abroad. But the London office was the least lucrative, and Farnley knew it. He wanted to keep me on a tight rein, y'know, and I had no choice but to continue working with him, since I had invested all my meager savings into the business." Ingram rose and advanced threateningly toward Francesca. "Not only did he cheat me out of my part of the wealth, but he willed everything to you, who truly has no right to the fortune I have worked all my life to amass." He pointed at Giorgio. "We are the rightful heirs, and no slip of a woman will take that from us."

Ingram leaned over her, his eyes bright with anger, and Francesca backed away. Every person in this room was her enemy, although she had done nothing to harm them. She clutched the back of a chair to keep from losing her composure. They mustn't know how frightened she was.

"I'm sure we can discuss a . . . settlement," she whispered. "I never dreamed of inheriting two hundred thousand pounds."

"Settlement? Bah!" the old man spat. "My whole life went to serving that *snake* who was your father. He would have cheated the devil himself if he'd had a chance."

Francesca's hands trembled so much that she could barely hold on to the chair. "What do you propose?"

Giorgio cleared his throat and moved toward her. "We will marry. Then, as soon as I control the fortune, half of it will go to Mr. Ingram. After all, he's entitled to an equal share of the riches."

"It would be easier just to kill her," Estrella said.

Francesca gasped and swayed as unconsciousness threatened to overcome her. Mr. Ingram shrugged and raised her face with a finger under her chin. "Why waste such beauty? She will make a good wife, especially since she's quite knowledgeable about the jewelry business. Besides, without direct heirs to the fortune, the legal battles would go on forever."

"I don't want to marry . . ." Was that feeble voice really hers? Francesca wondered, aghast. "I don't deserve this treatment." All she could think was that these people had killed Leonard Kane. She might have been killed too if Carey hadn't happened to ride by on the Eastbourne road that day. Where was he now? Was he dead as well? The thought was too terrible to consider. She held on to the chair until her legs seemed about to buckle under her.

"When I saw you, Francesca, I thought marriage would be the ideal solution," Giorgio said. "After all, murder is so—untidy."

Francesca braced herself against the chair. "What did you do to Leonard's and the coachman's bodies?"

Silence hung heavy in the room as the three conspirators exchanged knowing glances. Francesca wanted to scream out her fear and anger, but her lips seemed to be sealed together.

"Alas, the carriage was engulfed in flames," Ingram whispered softly. "Right here in the garden."

Francesca finally lost her grip on the chair and slid to the floor in a dead faint.

When she awakened it was the middle of the night. She must have slept for a few hours. By the light of two candles she saw that she was lying on a bed in a sparsely furnished bedroom where dust covered every surface. She heard voices outside her door. Hoping that someone was out there who might help her, she struggled up off the bed. Curiously light-headed, she pressed her ear to the door. She recognized the voices of the two Italians, lowered to whispers.

" 'Tis impossible to get the special license by tonight," Estrella said.

"I'll marry her anyway. Who will know the difference? Ingram says he can bribe a justice of the peace from Eastbourne to wed us." Giorgio sounded so sure of himself that Francesca clenched her teeth in anger.

"I will see to it," he went on. "Promise not to leave her alone for one second. We cannot let her escape before the ceremony."

"What about Ingram?" Estrella whispered. "He's an old nuisance."

"He will soon join Leonard Kane in his grave. I'd much rather share my fortune with you than with that old idiot."

"We needed his help—"

"Hush! Not anymore, Estrella. Don't be weak-hearted now."

Estrella said something that Francesca couldn't discern. She heard Giorgio walk down the stairs, and Francesca hurried back to bed. Burrowed under the covers, she was aware when Estrella opened the door and stood watching. Icy fear trickled through her. Somehow, she had to find a way to escape from this nightmare.

Chapter 26

Carey and Lord Mortimer crept up to the mansion. They had left their horses half a mile down the road so as not to alert anyone to their presence. They waited in the darkness for some clue that the Italians were actually present in the house.

The wind whipped through the trees, chasing clouds across the sky. It had stopped raining, and the ground smelled of wet soil and grass.

"Look," Carey whispered as he crouched behind a hawthorn bush. "Someone is coming out."

Candles, held aloft by an old woman, flickered in the doorway, illuminating a male figure dressed in a voluminous cloak and a tricorne. The man turned his head momentarily, the candlelight falling directly on his face.

"By thunder! 'Tis the old man I saw at the accident—it's Ingram!" Carey said. "The old sod has returned, then, and there's a carriage at the back of the house. I could swear it belongs to the Italians."

Five minutes later the coach left the house, passing within a few yards of Carey and Mortimer.

"Ingram's in that coach. I wonder what business he has in the middle of the night," Mortimer said thoughtfully, shaking the raindrops from the brim of his hat. "That's the D'Angelos' coach though."

Carey's teeth gleamed white as he smiled. "You're

right—which must mean that Francesca is in the house."

"I hope you're right, but remember—we're only two against who knows how many enemies inside."

"Yes . . . we must be careful. Let's sneak up to the windows. There's light in the front parlor."

Together they moved across the yard, darting from one tree to another. The wind muffled any noises they made, and the waving tree limbs and bushes shielded their movements.

"Let's wait a while longer. Perhaps everyone's asleep at this hour, but we don't know. Someone might be standing guard," Carey said as they stood below the parlor windows. "No one's inside that room. If Francesca is here, she's most likely upstairs in one of the bedrooms."

They waited for several long minutes. When there was no movement anywhere, they decided to enter the house. Yet, as they went over their plan, the rattle of wheels could be heard in the distance.

"The coach is coming back," Mortimer whispered. "What's happening here? Something strange, I wager."

They waited in grim silence as the carriage pulled up to the steps and two old men alighted.

" 'Tis Ingram and some other chap," Carey whispered. He studied his turnip watch by the light from the window. "Two o'clock. Highly irregular goings-on, don't you agree, Morty?"

Lord Mortimer muttered something unintelligible. "More people are awake," he said. "Look! There's D'Angelo himself."

Carey stiffened, and fingered the rapier at his side. "This time he won't get away," he growled. He was about to step forward into the light.

"Wait!" Lord Mortimer gripped his arm. "Something is afoot in the parlor."

The old servant woman was lighting more candles. Minutes later, Francesca appeared in the doorway, flanked by the two D'Angelos. Her hands were tied at the wrists. Carey swore under his breath.

"The man who Ingram fetched is a justice of the peace. He's going to marry Francesca and the Italian," Lord Mortimer said as they watched Giorgio pull Francesca in front of the old man who was wearing a red cloak. "Blast it all! Have they no decency?"

Carey pulled out his rapier and the steel sang against the metal of the scabbard. "I know we're uninvited guests, but at least the bride will be happy to see us." With a leap he was over the hedge and running up the front steps. He kicked the front door open and ran inside, followed closely by Lord Mortimer. As Carey flung the parlor door wide, Mortimer stayed hidden in the shadows of the hallway. Carey stormed into the room, and all eyes turned toward him.

Giorgio D'Angelo looked as if he hadn't slept for many days. Dark stubble covered his jaw, and his hair hung in limp strands around his face, giving him a demonic air. His features creased with contempt when he saw Carey, and he whipped a pistol from his waistband. His hand was steady as he aimed the pistol at Francesca's heart.

A sharp pain seared her chest, as if the bullet had already penetrated her. Her legs trembled, and her breath came in agonized gasps. "Carey!" she cried out. "Be careful."

"I'm not surprised to see you here, D'Angelo." Carey stepped closer, his rapier held high.

Francesca waited breathlessly for the shattering crack of the pistol to fill the room, for real pain to rip through her chest, but nothing happened. Carey, stiff with tension, didn't take his eyes off Giorgio.

"Let her go! This time we'll fight honorably, if

you even know what the word means,'' Carey said. He motioned for the others to move away, but they stood as if rooted to the floor.

"I hoped you would die in the cellar, McLendon. It would have been easier. But you—or Francesca—will die from a pistol wound tonight. Who—?''

Lord Mortimer cut off D'Angelo's taunts by jumping through the door and hurling his rapier at Giorgio. It hit the slim barrel, and the pistol went off, the bullet drilling a furrow in the parquet floor. Splinters spattered the room. Before Giorgio could recover from the surprise attack, Lord Mortimer threw himself against the Italian. They both fell over an old moth-eaten wing chair, which broke under their combined weight.

Mr. Ingram drew back, his hands trembling visibly. "Stop this madness! Stop it!'' he cried. When his words had no effect, he stumbled blindly from the room. " 'Tis too late to change the past. 'Tis too late to change the past,'' he kept saying over and over again. He clutched his ears, as if deafening screams were assaulting his mind.

Carey gripped Lord Mortimer's arm and hauled him to his feet. The Italian shook his dazed head.

"Don't finish him off, Morty. I'll do it,'' Carey said. He hauled his friend's rapier from the floor and tossed it toward Giorgio. "We'll fight like gentlemen, this time to the end.''

"Enough bloodshed!'' Francesca cried, but Carey refused to look at her. She dared not approach him as he was getting ready to fence. He tore off his coat and waistcoat.

Lord Mortimer caught her hands and pulled her toward the door, but she resisted his gentle tugging. "No . . . I have to stop this.''

"No!'' Lord Mortimer's voice was as sharp as a pistol crack in her ear, and she stared at him in puzzlement.

" 'Tis the only honorable thing McLendon can do. D'Angelo has made your life miserable," he said.

The Italian was laughing hysterically as he whipped off his coat and lifted the rapier. He flexed his arm and slashed the air twice to test the feel of the weapon. "I never thought you were this stupid, McLendon. I've trained with the masters in Rome."

"I understand now that you killed Francesca's husband. I should have solved the riddle earlier, but I thought no one could be as evil as you've been."

D'Angelo lunged, and the swords rang out as they clashed. "I did her a favor. She was well rid of Kane. She knows I would have been a caring and attentive husband, and an able caretaker of her inheritance."

"Liar!" Carey spat, and delivered a riposte that slashed Giorgio's shirt and sliced his upper arm. The Italian swore, baring his teeth.

"You planned to kill Francesca too, and she would have been dead if I hadn't arrived on the murder scene in Seaford." Carey drew his arm back to deliver a jab.

Giorgio laughed and parried another lightning-fast thrust. "You have no idea what you're talking about, McLendon . . ." His breathing was growing labored. "What I cannot have, she shall not have. That's justice." He staggered back. "She always resisted me."

Lord Mortimer laughed as he held a protective arm around Francesca. "I don't blame her. Mrs. Kane's a lady of taste."

"He was trying to force me into matrimony to get my inheritance," Francesca said, weeping.

"Inheritance?" Carey said, surprised. "What are you talking about?"

Giorgio, who seemed to gain strength from his rising anger, sprinted at Carey. The blade whistled through the air, almost piercing Carey's chest before he sidestepped at the last moment.

With a series of thrusts, Carey pushed the Italian into a corner of the room, but Giorgio jumped over a chair and swung toward the middle of the floor, staunchly defending himself.

"Sometime during your career you strayed from the path of honesty, D'Angelo." Carey pivoted and pierced D'Angelo's shoulder. "That's for the terror you put Francesca through."

Bright red stained the Italian's shirt. He groaned and staggered back, his hand slackening. Carey bore down on him, slicing his rapier sideways. A streak of red crossed Giorgio's chest from heart to armpit. "And that's for battering my head." He gouged the left arm. "That's for leaving me trussed up and bleeding in the cellar."

A wail rose from the doorway. Carey was momentarily distracted, and Giorgio made a desperate lunge. He stabbed Carey's upper arm, and the Scotsman staggered back with the impact of the thrust.

Giorgio whipped his arm back and made another attack, which Carey barely managed to deflect.

Francesca eyed the black-clad woman in the doorway. "Estrella, stay back!"

Estrella gave her a strange look, as if she had no idea who was speaking to her, and raised a pistol in her hands. She aimed it at the struggling men, and Francesca froze in fear.

Lord Mortimer watched Estrella lift the pistol. Shielded by a tall cabinet, he inched toward her.

Francesca took one step toward the Italian woman, but Mortimer shook his head at her. Anxious to deflect the pistol's aim from Carey, Francesca nevertheless obeyed Lord Mortimer. In shock, she stared at the fencing men.

Giorgio and Carey fought until perspiration streamed down their faces and their hair was glued to their foreheads. The bloodstains grew on their shirts, drops spattering the floor. Carey had more stamina, and his stubborn attacks were tiring the Italian.

"Confess you killed Leonard Kane, D'Angelo," Carey demanded between tortured breaths.

Giorgio screamed in fury, his rapier going in wide, desperate circles. "I would have made her happy. Farnley was obsessed with the thought of her—his secret daughter in England."

Carey's steps faltered momentarily. "Daughter?" He threw a bewildered glance at Francesca, and she nodded.

Estrella had moved slowly toward the center of the room, her hands shaking around the pistol. A shadow grew behind her as Lord Mortimer got closer. Francesca watched, numb with fear. Suddenly he whipped his arms around Estrella and jerked down her arms. But at that exact moment she squeezed the trigger.

"*No!*" Francesca screamed as the shot thundered through the house. Her eyes widened in horror as she watched Giorgio crumple to the floor, the life seeping from his body. Blood, pumping from a crater in his chest, drenched his shirt with crimson.

Sobbing uncontrollably, Estrella collapsed beside him, pulling his gray face into her lap.

Carey tossed his rapier across the room in disgust and moved stiffly to the nearest sofa. Blood streaked his sleeve, but he seemed oblivious to the pain.

Clarence Ingram staggered back into the room, muttering to himself, and sank down on a chair.

Francesca ran across the room and threw her arms around Carey where he was slumped, utterly exhausted. He smiled at her and cradled her close with his unhurt arm. "Your cohort is dead, Mr. Ingram" he said. "You'd better explain everything."

Lord Mortimer pointed a sword at the old man, to prevent him from bolting. The justice of the peace entered from the hallway, where he'd fled earlier. "I've sent Bertie for the magistrate in Seaford," he said. "Tonight we'll finally learn all there is to know about the Kane murder."

"Start from the beginning, Mr. Ingram," said Squire Dow, the Seaford magistrate. He was a heavy-jowled fellow dressed in burgundy satin and an untidy wig. His cocked hat was balanced on one knee as he sat in the best chair of the house.

Mr. Ingram hung his head, then peered at Francesca from under half-closed eyelids. "Perhaps you'd better tell them what Giorgio told you first."

"And let you weave a suitable story around it? Never, Mr. Ingram. You tell your version first."

They were sitting around the table in the dusty dining room. Late morning sunshine mellowed the stark furniture. Carey was quiet and pale as Francesca bound his wound with strips of old sheeting that the servant had brought to her. Lord Mortimer was staring out the window and Estrella, crying hysterically, was sitting by the door which was guarded by one of the magistrate's men. Giorgio's body had been carried outside. "I didn't mean to shoot him," she sobbed repeatedly.

"I know now 'twas a mistake to hold a grudge against Farnley. It poisoned my life," Ingram went on. "When D'Angelo approached me with his plan, I agreed to aid him."

"What was the plan?" Squire Dow went on.

Ingram shot an angry look at Francesca. "Edwin Farnley left his daughter to be raised by Lady Childress, then he willed her his entire fortune—the fortune that Giorgio D'Angelo and I worked so hard to help him amass. It's all described in Farnley's private journal, which is now in Mrs. Kane's possession. Farnley gave us a mere pittance in his will."

Carey stared from Francesca to the old man. "Now explain to me what right—?"

Squire Dow raised his hand to quiet Carey. "Please continue, Mr. Ingram. How did you go about murdering Kane and his coachman?"

Ingram sighed heavily. "D'Angelo and I decided to get our share of the fortune by murdering the Kanes. I hired a gang of highwaymen to hold up the Kane carriage on a secluded strip of the Eastbourne road. The murders would look like the aftermath of a robbery, but D'Angelo said he wanted to finish off the Kanes himself." He gave Francesca a long, veiled glance. "He and Miss D'Angelo rode up and fired several pistol shots, which killed Mr. Kane and the coachman. Then he pulled you out of the carriage and bludgeoned you. The highwaymen were paid well, and swore never to speak of the event. Of course they never knew the identity of the Italians."

Sitting down at the table, Francesca stared in horror at her former friend. Estrella's face was tear-stained and contorted; she was lost in grief.

"I wish I had killed you that day," she said hoarsely, gazing at Francesca. "But Giorgio said no when he saw how beautiful you were. I've always put my brother's desires before my own, so you lived." She blew her nose loudly. "He was obsessed with the Farnley fortune, and would do anything to get it. When he found out that you lived in London, he decided to settle down there and marry you." She burst into tears again. "He was bewitched by your beauty. In London, he hired a group of ruffians to frighten you so that his gallant rescue would impress you."

Francesca recalled Giorgio's merciless beating of the man in the gutter that evening in Covent Garden.

"And he tried to kill me several times," Carey added.

Paying no heed to him, Estrella went on. "When I learned to know you better, Francesca, I suffered terrible anguish. You were always kind to me, and I had the death of your husband on my conscience." All color had drained from Estrella's face, and she sagged against the back of her chair, gasping for breath. "I shot him because I dared not cross Giorgio."

"So what Mr. Ingram said is true?" Squire Dow asked.

"Yes . . . yes, my brother planned the murders, and he shot the coachman. He also made several attacks on Mr. McLendon's life, since he was an obstacle to Francesca's heart."

Carey gripped Francesca's hand and squeezed it hard. His hand trembled, and Francesca looked at him. It was as if a great burden had been lifted from his shoulders. Peace smoothed the furrows of his brow, and he smiled in triumph.

"I knew we would learn the truth one day," he whispered. "I always thought Lucas Halden was behind the attacks. He was behind some, but it was D'Angelo who hired someone to shoot me in the park. He also hired the false Hitchins to kill me in Seaford." He added, "Tell me, Estrella, did you leave a silk mask behind you at Seaford?"

Estrella nodded. "Giorgio tore his off and tossed it away. I clearly remember that."

"Mr. Ingram," said Squire Dow, "you'll be tried for conspiracy to murder and concealment of evidence. You might hang for that." He turned to Estrella. "I can't give you much hope, Miss D'Angelo. You just confessed to killing a man."

Estrella's face seemed to crumple further. "I'm responsible for Kane's death." Tears streamed down her face, and she hiccupped. "I don't want to live without my brother. I welcome the death sentence."

She glanced viciously at Mr. Ingram. "I hope you will hang beside me."

"One more thing," the magistrate continued. "What happened to the bodies and the carriage?"

"The bodies are buried in the garden here," Mr. Ingram said, as if in a trance. "We burned the carriage. I'll show you the exact spot."

"Very well." Magistrate Dow rose and nodded to the man at the door. Estrella held out her hands for the manacles that dangled from his fingers. With sagging shoulders, Mr. Ingram let the magistrate lead him toward the waiting carriage outside. At the front door, the old man turned and stared for a long moment at Francesca.

The magistrate's man led him outside as Francesca watched, her heart filled with revulsion.

"I'll make sure there isn't any blame attached to your name, Mrs. Kane," the magistrate said. "However, you'll be called as a witness at the trial, and I must ask you to send your father's diary as evidence. I'm sorry for suspecting you in the first place. The newspapers will get wind of this, and then you'll be publicly exonerated."

"Thank you." Francesca pressed her face against Carey's shoulder as tears burned her throat. Everything that had happened during the summer flashed through her mind.

The door closed behind Squire Dow and Lord Mortimer drew an audible sigh of relief. "This calls for a toast, don't you think?" He bent and looked into the shelves of the sideboard for a bottle of wine. "You'll be free to take up your former position in society, Francesca."

"Not after I worked in a gambling salon," she said, pulling gently away from Carey's embrace. "Although I'm not guilty of murder, I'm still notorious."

"You have to explain everything to us," Carey said and pulled her down beside him.

Francesca described the events that had occurred since the night of the fateful card game when Carey won the jewelry shop. "I have Farnley's diary in my room upstairs, but I didn't tell the magistrate that since I want you to read it first. However, 'tis clear that I'm Farnley's illegitimate daughter. Evidently he died a very rich man, and he left his fortune to me. Giorgio began pursuing me for the inheritance."

"We ought to confront your mother with Farnley's journal, don't you think?" Carey asked.

"Yes . . . I'd like to hear her version of the story."

Lord Mortimer chuckled. "It's strange how fortunes change. From being a murder suspect and a gambling-salon hostess, you have become a free and fabulously wealthy woman."

Francesca smiled wryly. "I assure you, not in my wildest dreams—"

"She won't have anything to do with me now," Carey said ruefully.

Mortimer threw back his head and laughed. "I hope she doesn't. I wouldn't mind having a try at her fortune myself." His eyes twinkled. "Then again, courtship is tedious business."

Laughing, they left Ingram's house after Francesca had collected her belongings. In the coach they hired in Beachy Head, Carey read most of the journal, as Francesca slept with her head on his shoulder, her hand holding his tightly even in sleep.

Later that day they arrived in London. After leaving Lord Mortimer on his own doorstep in Jermyn Street, Carey brought Francesca to his own lodgings. Bigelow greeted them with delight, and Francesca was pleased to find Copper and Chance there.

"Cauliflower Arnold brought 'em 'ere this

mornin'. 'E left 'is employment at the Crimson
Rooms and 'ad to go away for a few days. Said 'e
was takin' a rest, an' then 'e would ask ye for work,
Mr. McLendon.''

"Good! I could use a strong man in the country."
Carey dismissed Bigelow from his duties for a few
hours. "I have many things to discuss with Miss
Francesca," he said.

Bigelow nodded, his face creased in a wide smile.
"I'll go to the market, and then 'ave a pint at th'
ale'ouse.''

The night was balmy, as dark as black velvet and
studded with stars. A man shouted in the street,
and carriage wheels rattled over the cobblestones.

Carey touched Francesca's hand, sliding his index
finger over the tender skin of her forearm. "You're
shining tonight," he whispered. His hand wandered higher to touch the curve of her breast. "Your
skin is luminous and your hair has caught the glimmer of the stars.''

Hot tendrils of pleasure curled through her. His
eyes were veiled with warmth and longing, and a
new peace settled over them, as if he sensed her full
acceptance of him.

"I realize that life is much too short to waste it
having doubts. I would like to become your wife, if
the offer still stands," Francesca whispered, a tear
glittering in the corner of her eye.

He caressed her cheek as if she were made of the
most delicate china. "You're not afraid that I will
stifle your freedom?''

She smiled. "If you do, then I will just tell you to
stop.''

He laughed. "That's an excellent idea. You know
that I will always listen to you, because I like to . . .
argue the points of your reasoning." He pulled her
into his arms, burying his face in her hair.

"Rogue," she admonished, filled with contentment. Her blood quickened as the palm of his hand traced the contours of her spine through the thin silk of her sea-green gown. Her breath shortened as he touched the padded stomacher of her bodice to caress her breasts.

"Oh, my darling . . ." he whispered. He looked into her eyes, then said, "You must rest, Francesca. You're exhausted. We have all the time in the world to get reacquainted. I want to finish reading the diary before going to bed."

Francesca nodded and walked into his bedroom. His touch had conjured up so many sensations in her body, leaving her full of yearning. Her skin was hot all over, and her breasts felt heavy, the peaks throbbing with unfulfilled desire.

After undressing, she stretched out on the bed, clad only in a thin shift. The sheets smelled of Carey, and she buried her nose in the pillow. The soft night air caressed her through the open window. A persistent throbbing in her blood reminded her how easily Carey aroused her passion, and how much time had passed since she had intimately tasted his love.

Francesca could not sleep. Tossing from one side of the bed to the other, she thought of Carey, who had yet to join her. Moonlight slanted through the window, bathing everything in the room in a silver sheen. Staring at the ceiling, Francesca knew she would not sleep unless she could find release in his arms.

Anticipation coiled through her, starting at her toes and curling slowly upward. It bubbled like champagne in her stomach. She would give Carey a pleasant surprise when he arrived.

Half an hour later, Carey undressed quietly and slid into bed beside her. He settled himself gingerly, careful not to disturb her rest. Suddenly, soft pliant skin and round curves slid against his back. Laugh-

ing, he turned and captured the warm, yielding body
in his arms. The sweep of her silky hair over his
chest and stomach brought desire to life everywhere
in his body.

"Francesca . . ." he whispered, wholly intoxicated by her scent and the exquisite touch of her
fingertips along his thigh.

"Carey," she sighed. She covered him completely
with her body, her generous curves driving him to
distraction.

The feel of his hard muscles and soft skin made
her ache with longing to be one with him. She slid
gently over his chest, undulating her hips until the
hot proof of his ardor pressed against the moist place
between her thighs. Her breath grew ragged, and
under her hand, his heart beat violently. The hair
on his chest tickled the roseate crests of her breasts
until they tightened and throbbed.

With a powerful lift, he tossed her onto her back.
His teeth gleamed in the weak moonlight filtering
through the curtains. "I like you . . . bold like this,
Francesca." His hair tickled her neck as he bent to
take a nipple in his mouth. Sucking hard, he brought
her quickly into a state of breathless anticipation. He
repeated his attentions to the other breast until a
moan of pleasure slipped from her lips.

She covered his neck with fervent kisses, seeking
to touch every part of him. The hard biceps bulged
under her hands, and his chest heaved in rapid
breathing, bringing his hard stomach in contact with
hers. The tantalizing feel of his skin made every fiber of her being strain toward him.

"Do you want me?" he murmured. He moaned
as her hand closed around his throbbing shaft.

His breath came in hot gusts against her neck as
she replied, "Yes—yes, please, Carey."

He traced a slow pattern between her thighs, and

she folded her arms around his chest and held him hard against her, as if she would never let him go.

"I adore you," she whispered. She entwined her legs slowly with his and brought him toward her. The velvet tip of him touched her, and penetrated, deeply, deeply, until he was completely within her.

Tension vibrated in her, heightening as he lay still, staring at her face. Bracing himself above her on his elbows, he brushed her hair back. All she was aware of was the hard length of him within her. His heartbeat became hers as he ever so slowly pulled out, then drove into her with a force that left her gasping and pleading for more.

"I adore you, too," he said hoarsely. "Within your warmth is where I always yearn to be." He moved faster now, yet still savoring the sensations of every thrust. His loving brought her to a quivering plateau of molten pleasure, and finally she dissolved into wave after wave of shuddering release.

"Darling . . ." he cried out as he wrapped himself around her and drove into her with trembling, seething force. He almost crushed her in his violent release, but it didn't matter; she felt no hurt, only oneness with his hard body, and shivering joy. Her body was softened by the heavenly bliss coursing through her, and she was sated from head to toe.

Glowing with contentment, they rested in each other's arms. Now Francesca could sleep at last.

The next morning, relaxed and filled with happiness, they played with the kitten. Bigelow served them breakfast, then left them alone on the pretext of walking the dog.

Francesca sank down on a footstool beside Carey's chair and leaned her chin on her knees. "I understand now why Mother always acted so strangely toward me. I sensed a distance in her, a secret. Perhaps it was guilt. Sometimes I caught her staring at me as if she was seeing a ghost."

"You could confront her with the truth, and hear her version of the story." Carey caressed her hair gently. "That's your right, you know."

Francesca's lips trembled. "I've always been in awe of my mother. She's a forceful, cold woman. But the illness has weakened her. She might even die soon."

"Then it's all the more important that you resolve the differences between you."

Francesca gripped his hand. "Has it occurred to you that you and I are both of illegitimate birth?"

He smiled. "Yes . . . but that doesn't change anything, does it? No one needs to know the truth about your birth, and I've lived so long with my 'brand' that it's become a part of me." He squeezed her fingers. "Can you accept it?"

Francesca nodded slowly. "In time, I'll get used to the idea." She leaned her cheek against his hand. "At least I know how you feel. An illegitimate child doesn't belong anywhere."

"Yes—but an illegitimate child is no less worthy as a person, although thoughtless people might scoff at such a statement. Once you accept your own worth, nothing can really harm you."

"All I wanted was respectability and freedom. I saw in Giorgio a way to achieve both."

"He did honest business in Haymarket. Your designs are valued in London; in fact, you could return there and continue your work. Before long you'll be a famous designer. Do you want to continue your profession?"

"I love my design work."

She heard his slow exhalation of breath. Had he been worried about her answer? "I promise not to . . . er, devour you whole, my dearest. The jewelry shop is yours to manage as you wish. We shall start anew, learning all sides of each other's characters. I respect you and your work."

"Yes," she whispered, barely able to speak as emotion filled her. She rose from the footstool. "If you've finished reading the journal, you know that I was conceived in love. For some lovers a lifetime together is impossible, as it was for Edwin Farnley and my mother."

"We won't let that happen to us," he said with earnest intensity.

"No . . ." Francesca said happily, and planted a kiss on his lips. She sensed the fire within him as he held out his arms toward her. Without a word, she stepped into his embrace. They stood so tightly together that they could hear each other's heartbeat.

An hour later, they stood in the hallway of the town house at Leicester Fields. The rooms were hushed, and Francesca sensed an odd tension—or was it only within herself?

"Come up, Mrs. Kane," said Perkins. "However, I warn you, your mother is very weak."

Fear clutched Francesca's heart. "How weak?" She ran up the stairs, followed closely by Carey.

Perkins could not hide the tremble in her chin. "I'm afraid she isn't long for this world."

Francesca gasped, pressing her hand to her heart. She entered the dim room. Carey waited outside.

The curtains were partly closed, and the four-poster bed with its white-and-silver hangings was in shadows. Francesca saw her mother's slight form under the cream-colored quilt.

She dropped to her knees and listened to the laborious sound of her mother's breathing. The face was sunken and pale, blue circles accentuating her hollowed eyes. Francesca sensed the specter of death hovering in the room like an old dusty crone—waiting, waiting, always patient.

"Mother?" she whispered. "It's me."

Lady Childress's hands fluttered on the coverlet

and her eyes opened. Slowly she turned her head toward Francesca.

Francesca found herself holding her breath. What would she read in her mother's eyes?

Confusion filled Lady Childress's face. She appeared to be so far away. "Francesca? Is that you?" The voice wasn't more than a breath. "I thought I had lost you. There's so much that has to be said." Her eyes filled with tears. "I've wronged you, I know that." She gestured at Francesca. "Come closer." The thin voice trailed off.

Francesca leaned forward, bracing her elbows on the mattress. "Tell me about Italy."

"Italy?" Lady Childress's voice intensified. "I was there once. Lovely country . . . and such warm people." Lady Childress seemed to be floating freely in her old memories. "I once loved a man who lived there, a handsome young man who loved me too."

"I know."

Lady Childress clutched Francesca's hand. The thin fingers had about as much strength as tiny bird claws. "Is he still alive then?"

Francesca shook her head. "No, he's dead. He wrote in his diary that he loved you, Mother." She held up the leather-bound journal.

A smile slid over her hollow features. Lady Childress caressed the book with trembling fingers. "I knew he loved me, and I was a fool not to stay with him. But I feared the scandal. After all, I was married to Childress."

Francesca could not speak. Tears threatened at the back of her eyes. "Edwin became a very rich man," she said, watching the frail blue-veined hand touch Farnley's tightly written pages.

A silence fell, and Lady Childress gazed at Francesca. As the younger woman raised her eyes, she saw the tenderness in her mother's eyes. Her heart leaped with joy. Such moments had been all too rare between them.

"You are so like him, y'know. Same fiery coloring. But he had a nasty temper, which you don't."

"You should have told me the truth about my birth," Francesca finally dared to say. The old secret was out at last, bringing with it a gust of clear, peaceful air.

A tear slid down the old papery cheek, and the gaze wavered. "Yes . . . that was my greatest sin. Every time I looked at you, I felt guilty." Her voice quavered, and the fingers clutched the coverlet feebly. "Can you ever forgive me? And I know you had no part in Teddy's death, even though I blamed you in my sorrow."

Francesca brushed a hand across her brimming eyes. Emotion threatened to choke her. "Have you forgiven yourself, Mother?"

Lady Childress nodded slowly. "I did love Farnley. You were born out of love, and I don't think love's a sin."

"I wonder if Carey's parents loved each other," she mused aloud.

"What?" The old woman strained to look at her in the gloom. "Who's Carey?"

"The man I love. He's here with me. Do you care to see him?"

Lady Childress squeezed her hand with sudden eagerness. "Yes."

Francesca rose and went to the door. Carey's face was set in grim lines as she beckoned him inside. "She wants to see me?" he asked incredulously.

"Why wouldn't she? I told her you're the man I love."

His face softened slightly, and Francesca's heart beat faster. She prayed that her mother would accept Carey for what he was, a caring, sensitive man, capable of abiding love.

"Come closer, young man," Lady Childress said as Carey hesitated at the foot of the bed. He clasped his hands behind his back and took another step.

Francesca sat on the edge of the mattress and held her mother's hand. "This is Carey McLendon."

"McLendon?" Lady Childress tossed her head on the pillow. "You'll be the subject of gossip, Francesca. Mr. McLendon is a fop and a gamester. You, of all people, should know he has no name to call his own."

"My father's name is good enough for me," Carey said quietly. "He's McLendon of Aviemore."

Francesca leaned over her mother and smoothed back the dry wisps of hair from her brow. "McLendon is a name good enough for me, too, Mother. The mystery of Kane's death has been solved, thanks to Mr. McLendon. He stood beside me throughout the entire ordeal."

Lady Childress stared at Carey as if seeing him for the first time. "You helped my daughter to clear her name?"

Carey sank to his knees and took one of the trembling hands in his. "I would go to the ends of the earth for your daughter, Lady Childress."

Warmth flooded Francesca at his words. "Mother, without his help, I would have been trapped in a marriage to Giorgio D'Angelo. Giorgio killed Leonard Kane to get his hands on Edwin Farnley's inheritance. He might have killed me too that same day if Carey hadn't arrived before he could do it."

Lady Childress closed her eyes, gathering her strength.

"I'm afraid this might be too much for her," Francesca whispered to Carey. They waited, holding those old hands as if trying to give energy to the withered body under the covers.

"The only thing that truly counts is love," Lady Childress murmured. "Without love you have nothing." Her pale lips parted in a smile as she looked at Francesca. "There's hope for you yet, my girl. I never was a good example, but I hope you're more giving than I ever was."

"Francesca has the kindest soul," Carey affirmed.

"Do you love this rapscallion?" the baroness went on.

Francesca nodded, her cheeks heating with embarrassment. "Yes, I love him very much." She dared not look at Carey, but she sensed the elation surging in him.

"Can you provide for my daughter in the manner to which she's accustomed?" Lady Childress asked Carey.

"Yes." No hesitation tinged his voice.

The baroness struggled with her hands, joining Francesca's fingers to Carey's warm clasp. "You have my blessing. Don't waste your lives—build a happy life together."

Tears of joy streamed down Francesca's face as she kissed her mother's cheeks. "Thank you," she whispered. "I love you."

Lady Childress touched Francesca's hair tenderly. "I wish I had dared to say those words more often to you, my girl." She closed her eyes. Her face was illuminated with an inner light of peace. "I love you, too."

Carey ushered Francesca out of the bedroom. The corridor was hushed.

"I heard you confess how you feel with my own ears," Carey said, gathering her into his arms. His eyes were smoky and moist, and Francesca realized the wetness was tears.

"Will you marry me?" she asked breathlessly. "I don't care who you are, where you came from, or where you're going. But I know I want to spend the rest of my life with you."

"Go down on one knee and ask again," Carey said, mischief lighting his face.

Laughing, Francesca began to slide down, but he caught her and pinned her hard against him. "I accept your proposal humbly." He paused. "I hope you'll wear my diamond ring from now on."

Francesca nodded and traced his lips with a fingertip. "Yes, with pleasure. In fact, I have it right here where I've been carrying it." She pulled a thin gold chain from her pocket and showed him the glittering ring.

He slipped it onto her finger, and she blushed with pleasure. "You're always so caring—it's one of your most endearing traits," she said.

A light danced in his eyes. "Only one of thousands."

"Exactly." Francesca lifted her lips to receive his kiss.

Epilogue

Two months later . . .

"**Y**ou can open your eyes now, Francesca."
Carey released the blindfold and stood behind her, holding her shoulders in a firm grip as she stared at the idyllic scene in front of her.

"You really bought the house outside Burgess Hill?" she asked incredulously.

"I told you, anything is possible if you offer enough money."

Francesca stared in wonder at the brick house nestled in the well-ordered garden. Tall lime trees stood sentinel on either side of the gates, and the gravel path was newly raked.

"Since I'm married to a genius jewelry designer, I thought I'd better find the perfect 'setting.' "

Laughing, she curled her arms around his neck. "You really are serious about becoming a country squire with manure on your boots."

He shrugged, tracing the contours of her face. "I always told you that, didn't I? Gambling is over, and so are my soldiering days. I will settle down, grow a paunch, and raise five . . . no! . . . *ten* children while my wife supports me with her goldsmith's designs and her vast Italian inheritance." He laughed. "Your journeyman, Mr. Preston, said I had no flair for the goldsmith craft, but that I might be the right person to grow green things. I'll try my hand at farming.''

''With a stubborn jaw like yours, I'm convinced you can do anything, Mr. McLendon.''

And she sealed her affirmation with a long, lingering kiss.

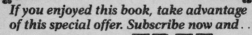